P9-CEB-040

PLAIN JANE

Books by Fern Michaels

Books by Fern Michaels (Continued)

Hokus Pokus
Hide and Seek
Free Fall
Lethal Justice
Sweet Revenge
The Jury
Vendetta
Payback
Weekend Warriors

The Men of the Sisterhood Novels:

Hot Shot
Truth or Dare
High Stakes
Fast and Loose
Double Down

The Godmothers Series:

Far and Away
Classified
Breaking News
Deadline
Late Edition
Exclusive
The Scoop

E-Book Exclusives:

Desperate Measures
Seasons of Her Life
To Have and To Hold
Serendipity
Captive Innocence
Captive Embraces

Captive Passions
Captive Secrets
Captive Splendors
Cinders to Satin
For All Their Lives
Texas Heat
Texas Rich
Texas Fury
Texas Sunrise

Anthologies:

Home Sweet Home
A Snowy Little Christmas
Coming Home for Christmas
A Season to Celebrate
Mistletoe Magic
Winter Wishes
The Most Wonderful Time
When the Snow Falls
Secret Santa
A Winter Wonderland
I'll Be Home for Christmas
Making Spirits Bright
Holiday Magic
Snow Angels
Silver Bells
Comfort and Joy
Sugar and Spice
Let it Snow
A Gift of Joy
Five Golden Rings
Deck the Halls
Jingle All the Way

FERN MICHAELS

PLAIN JANE

KENSINGTON
PUBLISHING CORP.

www.kensingtonbooks.com

KENSINGTON BOOKS are published by

Kensington Publishing Corp.
119 West 40th Street
New York, NY 10018

Copyright © 2001 by First Draft, Inc.
Fern Michaels is a registered trademark of First Draft, Inc.

This book is a work of fiction. Names, characters, businesses, organiza-
tions, places, events, and incidents either are the product of the author's
imagination or are used fictitiously. Any resemblance to actual persons, living or dead, events, or locales is entirely coincidental.

To the extent that the image or images on the cover of this book depict a
person or persons, such person or persons are merely models, and are not
intended to portray any character or characters featured in the book.

All rights reserved. No part of this book may be reproduced in any form or
by any means without the prior written consent of the Publisher, excepting
brief quotes used in reviews.

All Kensington titles, imprints, and distributed lines are available at special
quantity discounts for bulk purchases for sales promotion, premiums,
fund-raising, educational, or institutional use.

Special book excerpts or customized printings can also be created to fit
specific needs. For details, write or phone the office of the Kensington
Sales Manager: Attn.: Sales Department. Kensington Publishing Corp.,
119 West 40th Street, New York, NY 10018. Phone: 1-800-221-2647.

The K logo is a trademark of Kensington Publishing Corp.

First Kensington Hardcover Edition: March 2001

ISBN-13: 978-1-4201-2311-1 (ebook)
ISBN-10: 1-4201-2311-4 (ebook)

ISBN-13: 978-1-4967-3446-4
ISBN-10: 1-4967-3446-7
First Kensington Trade Paperback Edition: March 2021

10 9 8 7 6 5 4 3 2

Printed in the United States of America

*For Melba Johnson, Beth, Ron, and Eric Goins.
Lindsey and Misty, too.*

Dear Reader,

My reader mail has been telling me for years that you like it when I include a dog in my writings. That's so easy for me to do because I am an animal lover and have five dogs of my own.

Before I started writing this book, I saw something on the early-morning news that broke my heart and brought me to tears. It was the funeral of a K-9 Police Dog here in the state where I live. He was killed in the line of duty. Had he been wearing a bulletproof vest like his partner (a human police officer), he might have survived. However, tight budgets don't allow for such things. Because I never wanted to see a funeral like that again, I donated twenty-two bulletproof vests to our K-9s here in my state. During that time I learned so much about these remarkable animals. They are extremely intelligent almost to the extent of being human in their understanding. They are dedicated, loving, and so very beautiful. It also made me start to wonder what happens to these dogs when they retire at the age of seven years.

In this book you are about to read, there is such a dog, and I named him Flash. He was put up for adoption at retirement. He is a composite of all the dogs I had the pleasure of meeting. Because of his superior intelligence, he knows how to buckle up in a car, knows how to open and close doors, knows what to do when there is an "officer down" call. He can kill if ordered to do so or he can merely hold his quarry at bay. He will shake your hand, give you a smooch, tussle with you on the floor, and guard his family with his life. He truly is man's best friend. In this particular case, woman's best friend. I hope you enjoy Officer Flash, Shield #23, as much as I enjoyed creating him.

Fern Michaels

Prologue

༄

Louisiana State University
Baton Rouge, Louisiana, 1988

Jane Lewis closed her book and heaved a huge sigh. If she didn't know the material now, she would never know it. She rubbed at her aching eyes with the palm of her hand, confident that she would ace her last final in the morning. She looked down at her watch and sighed again. She'd spent the entire day and evening in the library without eating. She realized suddenly that she was hungry, starving actually. Another sigh escaped her lips when she thought about the weight she'd put on since coming here to LSU. Forty pounds to be exact. She was going to work out and take off the entire forty plus ten more this summer if it was the last thing she did. It probably would be, since she was so out of shape.

Jane turned when she felt a hand on her shoulder. "Is your name Jane and are you in Acadian Hall?"

"Yes, I'm Jane Lewis. I've seen you from time to time, but we were never introduced," Jane said, standing up to offer her hand.

"Connie Bryan. I'm on four. You're five, I think. I was wondering if you would mind if I walked with you if you're going back to the dorm. It's late, and I hate walking alone. I hate to admit it, but I'm a real *scaredy* cat."

"Sure," Jane said, gathering up her books. Connie Bryan was everything she ever wanted to be but could never be— petite, blond, 105 pounds, and so popular she'd been voted Homecoming Queen. She dated the star quarterback and rumor had it they were getting married in June.

"You ready for graduation, Jane? I have two finals tomorrow, and that's it. How about you?" Connie asked, falling into step beside Jane.

Jane blinked at the girl's obvious friendliness. "My last final is at eight. I feel pretty good about it. Is it true you're getting married after graduation?"

"Yes. My mama is planning the wedding as we speak. She told me she was addressing the invitations tonight. The last fitting on my gown is Saturday. I can't wait. All I want to do is get married and have a whole houseful of children. Todd does, too. I'm going to teach for a year or two before we start our family. How about you, Jane?"

"I'm going on to medical school. Tulane. I'm anxious about that. I don't think I'm marriage material, at least not yet. I want a career."

"Commendable. Four years of college is enough for me. Do you have a specialty in mind?"

"Pediatric medicine. I might switch up and just do general medicine. I'm not sure. Do you mind if I ask you a question?"

Connie laughed. "It's really dark out here, isn't it? Gives me the creeps. I'm so glad you're walking with me. What's the question?"

Jane looked around. Normally the campus was a beehive of activity even this late in the evening. Tonight, though, with finals pretty much over, a lot of the students had already left, hence the quietness at this late hour. "A couple of the lights are out. I noticed it last night. My question is, how did it feel to be chosen Homecoming Queen?"

"It was the second most exciting moment of my life. The first was meeting Todd and knowing I'd met my soul mate. Are you seeing anyone special?"

Jane laughed. She wished she could think of something smart and witty to say to the pretty girl walking along with her. "No, I'm not seeing anyone special or otherwise."

"You just haven't found the right guy yet, Jane. But you will in time. The moment you look into someone's eyes and know that person is your destiny, it's like no other feeling in the world. Todd and I are going to have such a wonderful life. We have our house all picked out, the furniture, even the kitchen dishes and place mats. We want four children and neither one of us cares if they are boys or girls as long as they're healthy. We even picked out names. I'm going to bake and decorate for the holidays. We're going to have Christmas trees in every room in the house. Todd and I both just love Christmas. We met right before Christmas break our first year here at LSU. I can't wait. I think about it all day, and I dream about it every single night. God has certainly blessed me."

"You're very lucky, Connie. I wish you all the happiness in the world," Jane said sincerely.

They came out of the darkness like stalking wolves. It was hard to distinguish how many there were until they started to talk. Five—and one hovering outside the immediate group— Jane thought, as the fine hairs on the back of her neck stood on end. Odd man out. Then she started to shake, or was it Connie who had suddenly grabbed her arm in a viselike grip?

"Well, lookee here, boys. We snagged us a real little beauty. *The* school beauty, to be exact."

"What . . . What do you want? Leave us alone," Connie managed to squeak before a hand was clamped over her mouth, and she was pulled away from the safety of Jane's plump arm.

"Come on, you guys, cut it out. This isn't funny," Jane gasped before a hand was clamped over her own mouth.

"It's not supposed to be funny, so shut up. One more peep out of you, and you'll get a chop to the neck. We have plans for Little Miss Homecoming Queen, don't we, guys?"

Jane struggled to free herself, but the arms holding her were muscular and hard. In that moment she knew escape was not an option. She watched in horror as three dark forms dragged Connie off the path and into dense shrubbery.

"You can't do this," Jane whimpered behind the smelly hand, knowing she was going to be next.

"I thought I told you to shut up. We aren't interested in a fat tub of lard like you."

Jane kicked backward, hoping her Nike would meet flesh. It didn't. She felt a hard jab to her stomach and then one to her chest. She went limp with the pain. She sensed rather than saw the boy on the sidelines leaving. With the side of her face to the ground, she could hear running feet. Maybe he wasn't one of *them*. Maybe he was going for help.

It seemed like an eternity, but it was only minutes before the boys traded places. A moment later she was free, kneeling on the ground, crying with pain, knowing what was happening to Connie Bryan. She had to do something besides moan and whimper. She struggled to her knees, anger rivering through her. The moment she was on her feet, she screamed at the top of her lungs, the sound carrying in the quiet evening. She felt her head snap backward as a knee jabbed into the small of her back. She bit down on the hand covering her mouth and knew she drew blood; she'd bitten the boy to the very bone. She spit the blood from her mouth.

"What the hell . . ."

"This goddamn beached whale needs a lesson. Which one of you wants Miss Piggy?" an oily voice offered. "No takers?"

Jane heard them leave, laughing and slapping each other on the back. She crawled over to the shrubbery, to where they had taken Connie. She gathered the girl into her arms. Her head rolled listlessly. "Connie, I have to leave you here for a few minutes while I get help. I can keep screaming, but it probably won't do any good. I'll be right back."

"No!" the shaking girl whispered. "Don't tell anyone. Help me. I can walk. I just need to lean on you."

"Let me get the campus police. They'll call the regular police. You need to go to a hospital or the crisis center."

"No! Did they . . . ?"

"No. They didn't want any part of me. They said I was too fat. I tried to get loose to help you, but they held me down. Are you sure you can walk?"

"I can walk. When we get close to the dorm, will you go inside and bring out a coat or something? Can I stay in your room, Jane? My roommate is still here."

"Of course you can stay with me. You need to see a doctor, Connie. You have to report this. Are you listening to me?"

"We'll talk about this later. Just get me inside and into the shower. Please, Jane."

"You . . . you can't wash away the evidence, Connie. Listen, I know where the crisis center is. I can take you there right now. Please."

"No. Not now. Be my friend and help me, please."

"There's Acadian. Stay in the shadows, and I'll run in and get my raincoat. Are you sure you're all right?"

"No, I'm not all right. Will you hurry, please."

Jane lumbered off, her thoughts so chaotic she thought she was going to pass out. Pretty, petite Connie, gang-raped. *Tub of lard. Beached whale.*

Inside the dorm, Jane stepped into the elevator and rode it to her floor. She rummaged for her raincoat, her hairbrush, and the empty bottle of Robitussin that she kept brandy in for the severe cramps she experienced every month. She galloped back down the hall, not bothering to lock her door. The elevator was in use, so she used the stairs. Students coming into the building stared at her, some of them shouting greetings while others mumbled and muttered about finals the following day. Jane ignored them all as she raced to the spot where she'd left Connie.

"Drink this, it's brandy. Take two long, hard pulls. Let me brush your hair. Now, slip into this coat and belt it so your torn clothing doesn't show. When you feel steady enough to walk, I want you to lean on me. There's some activity on the first floor. You can pretend you had too much to drink."

"I don't drink, Jane."

"Okay, we'll say you just feel sick. I don't like this. You need to see a doctor. Please, change your mind and let me call the authorities."

"No, Jane, not now. Let's just get out of here, okay?"

"All right, all right, but this is against everything I believe in. We can't let those guys get away with this."

"We don't even know what they look like. I can tell you what they smelled like, but not what they looked like. One of them made me swallow his . . . you know. I threw up all over him."

Jane wanted to cry. Her hold on Connie tightened. "There's the dorm. I only see a few people. Can you make it?"

"Yes."

"Then let's go. Someone turned the lights down. It must be after midnight. Good. The elevator is open. Just hold on to my arm."

The minute Jane locked the door to her room, Connie slipped to the floor and curled into the fetal position. Hard sobs wracked her body. Jane dropped to the floor and stared at the young girl helplessly. "You can't let them get away with this, Connie. You just can't."

"You know how that works, Jane. They were all jocks. They'll lie the way they always do. Campus rape is a fact of life. I can't identify them, that's the bottom line. I'm done crying now. Help me into the shower. Promise me you'll stand guard, okay?"

"I promise. Connie, you can't wash away what happened."

"I can try. Do you think for one minute Todd would want to marry me once he found this out? He wouldn't. No man would. This is between us, Jane. If you tell, I'll deny it. I want you to understand that."

"Then Todd isn't the person you think he is. You didn't invite that violation. You're a victim, dammit. If you do nothing, they get away with it. They'll do it to someone else."

"Then it's their problem. I'll deal with my problem in my own way. I have two finals tomorrow, and then I'm driving home. All I have to do is throw my suitcases in my car. I took the rest of my stuff home two weeks ago. I need a few hours' sleep. Please don't look at me like that, Jane. Please. All I want right now is for you to be my friend and help me. Are you sure it's okay for me to sleep here tonight?"

"I don't have any extra sheets, just the ones on my bed. Like you, I took the rest of my stuff home a few weeks ago. I do have an extra blanket, and you can use my raincoat for a cover unless you want me to go down to your room for your things. My stuff is going to be much too big for you."

"Do you have an extra pair of pajamas? I'll worry about the rest of my stuff in the morning."

"I wish you'd let me do something, Connie. I don't feel right about this."

"I'm doing what I have to do. Can we go to the bathroom now? Throw my clothes away, even my shoes."

Jane opened a drawer and pulled out a brown-paper grocery bag. "I'll take care of it."

"I wish I'd taken the time to know you before all this happened, Jane. It's so strange. I trust you the way I trust Todd."

"Obviously you don't trust him enough or you'd get help. This whole ugly scene could make your relationship stronger."

"If you believe that for even one minute, I have a couple of bridges I can sell you. Make sure you don't let anyone in the bathroom."

"I promise. I'll send everyone down to the next floor. Here's some soap, a towel, and a washcloth. I'll carry the pajamas."

A half hour later, Jane opened the bathroom door. Steam spiraled upward and then sailed out the open door. "Connie, you've been in there long enough. You need to come out now."

"I don't feel clean yet. Just a while longer."

Jane walked over to the shower and turned off the water. "All the showering in the world isn't going to make you feel clean unless you do something about it. You're going to need to talk to a counselor when you go home. Will you do that?"

"I don't know. Probably not. It's a small town. People talk. How long do you think it will take for the bruises on my thighs and upper arms to go away?"

"A week, maybe two. Slacks and long sleeves will take care of that. The bruises and the gouges are the least of your problems. I have a camera. Do you want me to take pictures of your bruises? The police do that all the time in rape cases. Just in case you change your mind and want to report the incident later on?"

"No. I'm not going to change my mind. What I would like is some more of that brandy so I can go to sleep. Did you lock the door?"

"It's locked. Sleep in my bed, Connie. Don't argue, just do it."

"How can I ever repay you for all your kindness to me this evening? Will you sit with me till I fall asleep?"

"I'm sorry I couldn't do more. I'll sit right here."

"Do you know what one of those bastards said to me

while he was raping me?" Connie said sleepily. "He said, 'silence is golden.'"

Jane's shoulders drooped. The minute she heard Connie's breathing even out, she started to shake. Like Connie, she wanted to curl into the fetal position and suck her thumb. She couldn't do that, though. She had to stay alert and watch over her new roommate in case she woke during the night.

What she could do was roll up the arms and sleeves of Connie's pajamas and take pictures of her cuts and bruises. Just in case.

She slipped the Polaroids into the paper grocery bag without looking at them.

Then Jane Lewis did something she hadn't done in a very long time.

She prayed.

"This is it, kiddo, your big day!" Trixie McGuire, Jane's godmother, said happily. "How does it feel to be graduating fifth in your class?"

"It feels great. Trix, do you mind if I leave you for a few minutes. I have to find someone before all hell breaks loose."

"Go ahead, honey. Fred and I will go to our seats and wait. Take all the time you need."

Jane fought her way through happy, laughing students and their equally happy parents until she spotted someone she recognized who might know where Connie Bryan or Todd Prentice were. She nudged a perky redhead, and asked, "Have you seen Connie Bryan or Todd Prentice?"

The perky redhead stared at Jane for a long minute. "Didn't you hear?"

Jane looked up at the fluffy white clouds and the patches of deep blue sky overhead. Her instincts told her that whatever the redhead was going to tell her, she wasn't going to like it.

"Hear what?" she whispered fearfully.

"Connie killed herself two days ago. Todd didn't come to graduation. He's having a real hard time of it. Were you friends with Connie?"

"Yes. Yes, I was," Jane stammered as she made her way through the crowd, tears streaming down her cheeks. She thought about the brown bag with Connie's clothes, shoes, and pictures that she'd taken home with her and were now in Trixie's garage. Just in case. Next week she'd come back and file a report with the authorities. If it stirred up a can of worms with Connie's family and Todd, then so be it. They deserved to know the why of her death. No death should be in vain. She wiped at her tears with the sleeve of the long, flowing gown as she took her place near the end of the graduation line.

1

Rayne, Louisiana, 2000

Shivers of excitement raced down her spine as she watched him walk across the crowded restaurant toward her table. He was right on time, but then she knew he would be. Like herself, he was a professional with a full schedule of patients, so he knew the importance of being prompt.

Tall, dark, and classically handsome, Dr. Michael Sorenson was a hunk in every sense of the word. He was also a man who was comfortable in his own skin, a not-too-often-seen trait that made her heart flutter—the same way it had the first time she'd seen him all those years ago when he and his family moved to Rayne.

Dr. Jane Lewis felt her eyes squint behind her wire-rimmed granny glasses as she tried to imagine how her godmother, Trixie McGuire, would describe the good doctor. Knowing Trixie, she would say something embarrassing like "he's probably hung like a Moscow mule." In spite of being seventy-four, Trixie loved to stare at men's belt buckles. And when it came right down to it, Jane did, too.

Suddenly, he was standing in front of her. "Jane, it's good to see you again. It must be . . ."

"It's been a long time," Jane said, motioning for him to sit down opposite her. *Muscular. Works out regularly. Great tailor. Really fits that suit.* He was so put-together she felt like a dowdy spinster in comparison. She watched, fascinated, as he reached for his water glass. *Fabulous hands. Big, strong hands.* Trixie would probably say, "all the better to explore a body with." Jane felt herself blushing. "So, how's it going, Mike?" *Brilliant, absolutely brilliant dialogue here.*

"Couldn't be better. The practice is thriving. I even took on an associate so I could get away and play tennis once in a while. And I finally got around to buying a house last spring. Believe it or not I mow my own lawn and even cook a meal from time to time. Oh, and, I almost forgot, I adopted a stray cat. She's an inside cat now and a great companion. I call her Noodle. How about you, Jane? By the way, congratulations on your radio show. What a coup! I'm jealous."

So he knew about her show. Good. She hated blowing her own horn. "Thanks," she said modestly. What should she tell him about herself? She mentally ticked off the things he'd told her and compared them to her own life. Her practice was thriving, too, but even if she had an associate, she wouldn't play tennis. She was lucky to get to the gym once a month. Like him, she owned her own home but instead of grass, she had glorious, foot-high weeds. As for cooking— she could make a gourmet meal from freezer bags, cans, and boxes with the best of them. And if it could be microwaved— all the better. "I have a nice little house in Rayne. It's on the town's historical register. It has a ghost. And a dog ghost," she blurted, then wondered what had possessed her to tell him that. She was nervous. Befuddled actually. Was it because he was so good-looking, or did his smooth confidence intimidate her? Even in high school, he'd been confident and good-looking, she reminded herself. *And back then he wouldn't have given you the time of day.*

Mike leaned across the table. "Ghosts? Are you putting

me on? Tell me about them. I've always been interested in the paranormal."

Jane squirmed in her chair. *Open mouth, insert foot,* she thought. "Well, it's just a rumor actually. The story goes that a young man fell in a well on the property, and his dog just sat and pined away for him until he died of starvation. To tell you the truth I haven't seen them, although there are times when Olive gets *spooked.*"

"Olive? Your daughter?"

"No," she chuckled. "My dog."

"I'd like to try to get a look at your ghosts, that is unless your significant other would object."

"No, I don't think Olive would mind," she said, laughing lightly. "I live in the old Laroux house at the end of town. It used to be a rice plantation. You know the one, don't you?"

"That's where you live! My God, I tried to buy that house before I went into practice in Lafayette, but it was part of an estate and not for sale. It was pretty run-down as I recall, but I would have been willing to invest a few bucks in it had I been lucky enough to get it."

"Believe me, it took more than a few bucks to get it so it was even habitable. It reminds me of that movie. You know, *The Money Pit.*" She felt her hat slip and settled it back on her head.

"For some reason I thought you'd head for N'awlins or points north after high school. I never thought you'd stay in Rayne."

He'd thought about her. "Why would you think that?" She looked up to see the hovering waiter. "We better order." As Mike perused the menu, Jane gazed around at the restaurant. Tassels had been Mike's choice, she'd just made the reservation. Obviously, her colleague liked fine things. The menu was pricey, the decor beautiful, the waiters discreet, and the tablecloths and napkins were a blend of linen and cotton. Everything the eye could see was burnished and polished. She didn't see anyone she knew, but then who in Rayne would bother to travel twelve miles to Lafayette for lunch?

"I'll have the Cajun crab pie, French dressing, and a glass of house wine," Jane said.

"Ditto," Mike said, then waited until the waiter left before continuing their conversation. "How about I come by tonight? Today's my short day."

"Tonight?" She really hadn't thought he was serious. "I— Well—Today's my long day, so I won't get home much before seven. If that's not too late, then it's okay with me." Her heart skipped a beat at the thought of him coming to her house. She tried to ignore the feeling.

"I'll pick up some Chinese. Do you have beer?"

"Of course I have beer. Doesn't everyone?" Jane quipped.

"Ya never know. Now, tell me what this is all about. I like a free lunch as much as the next guy, but what do I have to do to earn it?"

He certainly didn't beat around the bush. Jane leaned back into her chair. "I have this patient I can't seem to get a handle on. There's something . . ." She shook her head. "I have this awful feeling the guy is setting me up for something. I learned early on in my career to pay attention to my gut feelings. I suppose the case is a classic textbook one. At least on the surface."

"What's his problem? Is he a psycho?"

"I don't know. I should know, but I don't. He's saying all the right things. I'm saying all the right things. It's not going anywhere," she said, putting her hands on the table. "I've seen him three times so far, and I'm still at square one. I suspect one of his problems is that he's very controlling." She took a sip of her wine. "Frankly, I think he might do better with a male psychiatrist. I was wondering if you would consider sitting in on one of his sessions. Maybe you can get a feel for what he's all about. That is, of course, if he's agreeable."

"Sure. Just let me know when and where. What's his main problem aside from all the standard stuff?"

"He *said* his wife was raped and that he's having a hard time dealing with it. He's lost his sex drive, claims he can't bring himself to touch her. He's even having trouble being civil to her. I understand that he is angry, but his anger is directed at his wife for refusing to go to the police. I have this feeling that he's lying. I think he didn't want her to report it. He said she quit her job and hides out in the house all day."

"Children? Other family? Pets?"

"Not that he's mentioned, but I don't know whether or not to believe him. He has this smirk on his face all the time. Last week I wanted to pop him." She laughed to cover her frustration, then leaned forward. "He listens to my radio show. The other day he rattled off some of the problems people had called in with and told me he didn't agree with my advice. Said I was too flip, too giddy. That was the word he used: *giddy.* I am not giddy," she said between her teeth. "I do try to be upbeat, but I'd hardly call that being giddy. If I have even the faintest inkling a caller has a really serious problem, I always suggest they get help. Sometimes I have them stay on the line and talk to them after the show."

"You don't have to defend yourself to me, Jane. I know your reputation, and I've heard your show. You said you thought he was setting you up for something. Can you be more specific?"

She took a deep breath then let it out. "I wish I could but it's really just a *feeling,* Mike." She thought a moment. "Last week, during his session, it occurred to me that everything he was saying was . . . rehearsed. Almost like he's reading from a script. He's got some kind of mental list, and he gets upset when my questions take him away from what he thinks I should be asking. When I tested my theory, he got hostile with me and told me to stick to the subject." She sat back, crossed her arms.

"What's he say when you ask him about his wife?" Mike queried. His facial expression told Jane he was concerned.

"Not much . . . You know, I have to wonder if he isn't lying to me, if he really even has a wife. I've called his house, and no one ever answers the phone. If his wife quit her job and is 'hiding out' at home, where is she and why doesn't she answer the phone? When I asked him if she'd ever had counseling, he got in my face and said *he* was my patient, *not* his wife, and that he would take care of her. I—" She started to tell him that she'd gone to his house but decided against it at the last second.

"Maybe he's the one who raped her when she said no and he said yes. You get them from time to time, the pigheaded, know-it-all macho types who think they own the women they married. Or maybe she's the one who shut down, and he can't handle it. Do you get the impression he could be physical?"

"Absolutely."

"I mean no disrespect here, Jane, but maybe he thought he could bamboozle you easier than a male shrink. The bottom line is, if the guy scares you, cut him loose. There's no law that says you have to keep him on as a patient. Refer him to someone else."

"He doesn't scare me exactly, but he does make my skin crawl. As for cutting him loose, I wouldn't have a single qualm except—what if there is a wife and she really has been raped and goes into a deep depression and . . . and . . . does something to herself? How do you think I'd feel if that happened?"

"Like shit, of course, but you know as well as I do there's

a lot of 'what ifs' in our business. You also know that psychiatry is not an exact science. And you're not nine-one-one."

Even though he was right, it wasn't what she wanted to hear. "Did you ever lose a patient, Mike?"

"No."

"Neither have I, and I don't want to lose one now. Why can't we just call 'the wife' my invisible patient?"

"You can say and do whatever you want, Jane."

Now he was patronizing her. "What would you do?"

"After what you've told me—I'd cut him loose. You're spending too much time and energy on this guy, and you have other patients to think about—patients who are being honest with you and who really need your help."

Again, he was right, Jane realized as she thought about the sleepless nights she'd spent since first meeting Brian Ramsey. Only once before had sleeping been a problem, right after learning about Connie's suicide. . . .

"You're gonna love this crab pie," Mike said, digging into his succulent-looking lunch.

Jane broke off a piece of crust and nibbled on it. She watched her colleague devour his lunch. She broke off a second piece and crumbled it between her fingers. She decided to throw caution to the winds and tell him the rest of her story. Looking down at her lunch, she said, "I know I'm crazy to tell you this, but I went to his house one day and rang the bell. No answer. Then I went around back, looked in windows. Nothing. It was a single-story house, so I could see into all the rooms. Everything was neat and tidy, but there was no one there." She glanced up, and before he could say anything, she added, "I went back a second time and a third. Zilch both times. Please don't chastise me for my lack of professionalism. I know I was wrong. But I did it, okay? And still the question remains—if there is a wife who quit work and hides out in the house, where the hell is she?"

Mike had stopped eating. "You do realize, don't you, that you're breaking the cardinal rule here? You're allowing yourself to get personally involved."

Jane nodded.

Mike laid his fork across his plate. "Where do you *think* she was, Jane?"

Jane cleared her throat. "I think . . . I don't know what I think. If she is in the house, the only place she could possibly be is in the basement," she said, trying not to look at him. "They could have a summer kitchen. I have one in the house where I live now. It's a godsend in July and August. I suppose she could be down there or—he could be keeping her down there against her will. I don't know, Mike. I've never come across anything like this before. Nothing computes. I hope once you meet this guy, you'll understand what I'm talking about. I don't know how to proceed. I'm out of my depth here. Obviously you are, too, since you aren't helping me."

Mike wiped his mouth with his napkin and set it down on the table. She wondered if that was a sign he was interested in her case or that he thought she had a screw loose. She hoped it wasn't the latter.

"This sounds like a plot for a novel. When's his next appointment?"

"This afternoon at four o'clock. He leaves work at three, goes home, cleans up, and he's in my office promptly at four. He owns a trucking company."

"I have appointments all afternoon, but I'll arrange to take a shot at him next Thursday. That'll give you today to pave the way for my sitting in on the session. Just don't be surprised if he balks." Mike glanced at his Rolex and noted the time. "I hate to eat and run, but I have a one-thirty. You should see this guy. He wears some sort of panic button gizmo on his wrist. He sleeps with it, takes showers with it. For all I know he even wears it when he has sex. He carries a pair of spare batteries in his hip pocket and wears a fanny pack holding a dozen more. He reminds me of the Energizer Bunny. With any luck, today is the day I find out what's up with him." Mike pushed his chair back. "Stop worrying. Everything's going to turn out okay. And don't forget, we're on for seven tonight with me bringing Chinese and you supplying the beer, right?"

"Yes," was all Jane could think of to say.

"You're lookin' good, Jane. I like that hat. See ya tonight."

Jane watched as every single female in the restaurant followed Mike's retreating back. He liked her hat. Fancy that.

She finished her lunch, considered dessert, only to wave the waiter away. While her mouth watered for chocolate thunder cake, her hips said no. She laid a couple of bills on the table and left, certain no admiring male glances were following her. She bemoaned the ten extra pounds she'd picked up over the summer. It seemed she would never again see a size eight, just like she'd never again see a size eight shoe.

Inside her tomato red Honda Civic, Jane reached for her cell phone. She dialed the station and waited until she heard Tom Bradley, the station manager's voice. "Tom, it's Jane. I have to cancel dinner this evening. Something's come up. No, it isn't serious, and no, I'm not up for company later." She put her key in the ignition. "Listen, I'll stop by the station tomorrow if I can free up some time, but promise me you won't try to talk me into anything. I'm up to my eyeballs with work as it is. A once-a-week radio show is all I can handle, and besides, why would you want to mess with something that is working perfectly? No, a partner is not out of the question but not Harry Lowell. He's too arrogant, plus he drinks too much. I'll give it some thought, okay?" She pressed the *end* button and tucked the phone into her purse.

Maybe Mike Sorenson would be interested. He seemed impressed with the whole radio-show thing, said it was a coup. Cohosting might work out, especially if he was the co part. It would be one way to see him more often, to get to know him better. Suddenly the idea was immensely appealing. She wished now that she'd worked the conversation around to personal issues, like was he involved with anyone?

She wished she knew someone to call and ask before tonight. She hated the Q & A thing. Maybe she could tell Trixie she needed a rundown on him because she was considering asking him to cohost the show. Trixie knew all the ins and outs and would get off on doing something like that. She'd call her when she got to the office.

Jane slammed through the door to the tiny suite of offices the way she did everything—with gusto. She took off her denim hat with the yellow sunflower and sent it sailing across the room to land neatly on the coat rack. "Bull's-eye!" she chortled, then tossed her briefcase down onto the top of her spindly antique desk. She glanced at the clock. If she called Trixie now, she would use up the eighteen minutes she had left until Brian Ramsey arrived. Maybe it would be better to wait, to use what time she had left to freshen her makeup, go to the bathroom, read over last week's notes, and, most of all, calm down from her meeting with Mike.

Neat stacks of files lined the credenza behind her desk. She really needed to find someone to help out with the office work, until her right hand, Lily Owens, returned from maternity leave. Perhaps a college student or even an office temp. Anyone who could type up her notes, transcribe and catalog the session tapes, set up appointments, run errands, and listen to her bitch and moan. First thing tomorrow morning she would start making calls.

With six minutes to spare, Jane sat down to study the Ramsey file. Her notes were all of two pages long—everything he'd told her about his wife, his feelings regarding her rape, and her refusal to get help; his complaints about the advice

Jane had given to her radio-show callers; her own impressions of him and their sessions. . . . That was it. Not much considering the time she'd spent with him.

She closed the file and took it into the room she used for communicating with her patients. The moment she stepped inside she felt better, calmer. The room was small, cozy, the carpet thick, the two easy chairs deep and comfortable. She'd decorated it herself, using earthy tones that were easy on the eye.

A fifty-gallon fish tank was the room's focal point. She'd opted for large fish versus small ones, and she'd chosen a sunken treasure theme. Even the most uptight patients calmed down and relaxed after a few minutes of staring at the fish.

Her own chair was ergonomic, comfortable but not too comfortable. It helped remind her she was the one in charge.

Jane glanced at her watch as she adjusted a lamp shade. She made a mental note to water the maidenhair fern sitting beneath it. Two minutes until Brian Ramsey walked through the door. Her heart began to race. She gasped when the phone rang.

"Dr. Lewis here." Brian Ramsey's voice came over the line. "No, I don't have a problem with the cancellation, Mr. Ramsey. I'm sorry your wife is under the weather. No, I won't be billing you for the canceled appointment. We normally do bill if a patient doesn't cancel twenty-four hours in advance, but I'll make an exception this time." She remembered what Mike had said about paving the way for him to talk to Brian. "While I have you on the phone," she said, purposely trying to sound upbeat, "I'd like to tell you that next Thursday, Dr. Michael Sorenson will be sitting in on our session. I think you might enjoy having him here. If you have a problem with this, you need to let me know *now.*" She held her breath as she awaited his answer. "Good. Then I'll see you next Thursday. Tell your wife I hope she feels better soon."

Jane hung up and stared across the room at the fish tank.

What was wrong with Mrs. Ramsey? Funny, he'd never mentioned her first name. He always referred to her as *my wife*. A spouse under the weather wasn't enough of a reason to cancel an appointment. Was there something about today that was different from their other appointment days? Only from her standpoint because she'd talked about him to Mike Sorenson. If she hadn't, the cancellation probably would have rolled off her back just like any other cancellation. Mike was right, she was breaking the cardinal rule by getting personally involved. She needed to stop thinking about Brian Ramsey because every time she did, she thought about Connie Bryan.

She had time now to call Trixie. "It's me, Trixie. How's it going?"

"If things get any better, I might have to hire someone to help me enjoy it. In other words, it's *gooder* than grits. Hold on a minute, honey," she said. "Fred," Trixie McGuire called to her husband, "Janie's on the phone. Pick up." Jane smiled as she carried the phone over to the fish tank and checked on her newest additions, a pair of very large angel fish she'd named Gracie and Slick.

Fred came on the phone. "Janie, girl, it's nice to hear your voice. You stoppin' by for a visit?"

"Not today. I might make it out tomorrow, though. Of course that depends on what you're having for supper."

"Whatever Fred picks up," Trixie answered, predictably. What that meant to Jane was, Fred would go to the nearest takeout, probably Roy's, and bring something home. "Spareribs would be real tasty, Fred. Janie likes spareribs, doncha, girl?"

"I sure do. Seven o'clock okay? Tomorrow, not today."

"Okay with me," Fred said.

"Trixie, I know you keep tabs on the comings and goings here in town. What do you know about the Sorensons? I had lunch with Mike today in Lafayette. He didn't say anything about his family. By the same token, I didn't ask."

There was a moment of silence on the other end of the line. "Hmm," Trixie finally said. "As a matter of fact, I do know a thing or two. His parents moved to N'awlins a year or so ago. Rayne was just too quiet for them, and they didn't want to move to Lafayette for fear Michael would think they were trying to keep tabs on him."

"Do you happen to know if he's married or if he's seeing anyone?" Jane ventured, knowing she was probably opening a can of worms.

There was a smile in Trixie's voice when she answered. "No, he isn't married. He was seeing a woman, a young lawyer. Coletta was her name. Vivian, his mother, told me she was cuter than a basketful of puppies but that she was jealous of all the hours Mike put into his practice. So they broke up a couple of months back. Does that help?"

Jane grimaced. Cuter than a basketful of puppies had to mean she was spectacular. "Yes, that helps. Is there anything about anybody you don't know?"

"Umm, let me see," Trixie said as if she was actually considering the question. "No, I don't think so. Why do you want to know about Mike?"

"He's coming over for supper tonight."

"I see," Trixie said, the two words full of innuendo.

"No, you don't see. We met today because I invited him to lunch to discuss a patient I'm having some difficulty with. We got to talking, I mentioned my ghosts, and he said he was interested in the paranormal. There you have it. As much as I'd like to think he could be interested in me, it isn't possible. In high school, he was the kind of guy who always went for the cheerleader type."

"That was then and this is now," Trixie said. "He's a man now, a professional. Trust me, he doesn't want some *hoochie mama,* he wants a real woman. Like you, sweetie." Jane heard the TV in the background. "By the way, what's going on with your station manager? I thought you had a thing going with him, though for the life of me, I can't see what you see in him. The man is uglier than homemade soap."

"Shame on you, Trixie," Fred piped up. "That's not nice. He can't help that he fell out of the ugly tree and hit every branch on the way down. Now, I'm not saying he isn't a nice man, it's just that . . . Janie, you need to think about how your children will look."

Jane shook her head and rolled her eyes. "Not to worry, Fred. I don't plan on marrying him. I'm just using him for sex." She put her hand over her mouth and giggled as she imagined the shocked look on his face. "Besides, the whole thing is winding down. All the surprises are gone. He doesn't have any zip."

Trixie cackled with glee.

"One more thing, Trixie," Jane interrupted. "Do you know a Brian Ramsey? He owns a trucking company outside of town. I was wondering if he's local or if he moved here from somewhere else. I'd like to find out a little about his wife. Don't ask me why I want to know, okay? Don't you have a snoop file or one of those I Spy files or something you use when you're doing your writing and you want to check up on people?"

"I do," Trixie said smartly. "If you have a social, an address, anything that will help in the search, give it to me and I'll see what I can do. You know you can trust me to keep quiet."

"By the way, how's the new book going? What number is this again?"

"One hundred four and going great. Blood and guts everywhere. Fred and I were having a serious discussion when you called. I want the blood to river and he wants it to trickle.

When you slice someone in two with a chain saw, the blood will river, not trickle. Right?"

The visual image made Jane grimace. "I'm not going down that road, Trixie."

"Not to change the subject," Trixie said, "but what are you planning on wearing tonight?"

"Tonight? Why, actually— Absolutely nothing!" Jane teased. "I'll see you both tomorrow and give you a full rundown on what happens tonight." As she was hanging up the phone, she heard Trixie say to Fred, "Did you hear that, Fred, she's wearing *absolutely nothing*!"

"I heard! I heard!" Fred said before the phone went dead.

Jane's face broke into a warm smile when she opened her front door. Olive bounded down the steps. Stepping into the foyer, Jane tossed her gear in the general direction of the antique bench before she hunkered down to tussle with the springer spaniel. "I know you're happy to see me," she said in her baby-talk voice. "I'm happy to see you, too. Did you have a good day? I had a good day and a bad day. Not really bad," she said, letting the dog lick her face. "Hey, guess what? We're having company for supper. *The* guy of my youthful dreams is bringing Chinese. He's got a cat named Noodle, whatya think of that?"

"Woof."

"That's what I thought," Jane said, staring past the dog to her parlor. Thanks to her father, she'd learned to love carpentry and had done most of the wood restoration herself. The fireplace mantel, original to the house, had been one of her biggest challenges, but she'd patched it lovingly and repainted it. At some point in time the former occupants had removed all the crown molding and stored the pieces in the attic. It had taken Jane forever to haul it down, lay it out on the floor, and put it back together. Copies of pictures owned by the local historical society had revealed that there had been bookshelves on either side of the fireplace. Opening up the walls and finding them still there, intact, had been like finding a hidden treasure. Now, the shelves held all one hundred and three T. F. Dingle books, Trixie and Fred's pen name. Their spines were unbroken, the brilliant, grisly covers as shiny as the day she'd arranged them.

A stuffed Taco Bell Chihuahua in her mouth, Olive stood looking at Jane, her eager expression saying she wanted to play.

Feeling guilty that she'd given Olive short shrift, she got down on her hands and knees and took the back side of the stuffed toy between her teeth and played tug-of-war. Jane was winning when the doorbell rang. Thinking it was the paperboy, she called, "Come in," between her teeth.

"Now, this is a Kodak moment if I ever saw one," Mike said from the doorway.

Olive dropped her end of the toy to bark at the intruder, leaving Jane holding the other end. Jane's blood pounded, and she could feel her face growing hot with embarrassment. This was not the way she wanted Mike Sorenson to see her. Annoyed with the picture she knew she was presenting, she yanked the stuffed dog out of her mouth and quickly got to her feet. "We were ah . . . playing," she said.

"I can see that. Who was winning, you or . . . Olive, isn't it?"

"Yes, it's Olive, and I was definitely winning." Jane straightened her shoulders and dusted off her hands. "It can't be seven o'clock yet. I just got home." She glanced down at her watch and saw that it was indeed only six-thirty.

"My last patient canceled. I didn't think you'd mind if I showed up a little early. I was prepared to sit on the porch and wait." He moved past her into the parlor. "You've really done wonders with the place, but—" Jane watched as he made a telescope of his left hand and peered through it. "Who was your carpenter? You need to sue him!"

Olive sniffed Mike's shoes and trouser legs. She was probably smelling his cat.

"Why would I want to sue the carpenter?"

"It looks like the crooked little man's house—everything's crooked, and the corners don't meet. I know a good lawyer." He marched over to the bookshelves. "Good God, do you have the whole set?"

It was a moment before Jane could get far enough past the crooked little man to answer. "Whole set of what?" she asked coolly.

"Dingle. It looks to me like you have the whole set, and they're in mint condition. I only have about sixty in my own library, but I've read every single one of his books, some more than once. I'd kill for these. Did you pick them up at a garage sale or what? I never would have figured you to be the blood-and-guts type," Mike said all in one breath.

"Really. What type books did you think I would read?" Olive's head jerked upright as she listened to her mistress's frosty voice. She slunk closer to Mike, her tail between her legs.

"That sappy romance stuff all women seem to read. These are guy books. You know, murder and mayhem, blood and guts. T. F. Dingle was one of the first authors I read just for myself back in school. The whole set! I can't believe it. I don't suppose you want to sell them, do you?"

"No, I do not want to sell them."

"Over the years I must have written a hundred letters in care of his publisher. He didn't respond to even one of them!"

"He who?"

"T. F. Dingle. The author. I think he must be some kind of recluse. I heard he lives in a shack somewhere and pounds out his novels on an old Underwood. Can you imagine that? Now there's a guy whose head I'd like to get into to know his thoughts. How about you?"

Her annoyance dissolved into smug satisfaction. "No. I can't say that's one of my top priorities," she said, enjoying that she finally had one up on him.

Mike stood back from the bookshelves and did that thing with his hand again. "The whole thing is off a good half inch. How can you showcase T. F. Dingle's books on a crooked bookshelf? Who's Stephen Rhodes and why does he get a shelf all to himself?" he asked, walking over to the shelves to inspect the books. *Velocity of Money, The Money Trail.* "Are they any good?" *Little Women, Gone With the Wind,* the Bobbsey Twins, Nancy Drew? "You do have an interesting list here. Don't you get dizzy when you come in here?"

"Shut up, Mike," she said, surprising herself at her boldness. "I don't want to hear any more. For your information, Stephen Rhodes writes about money. I like reading about money. He's very good. No, you can't borrow them, buy your own. Authors depend on royalties and frown on their books being loaned to other people. He has a shelf to himself because he's going to write a lot of books, and I'm going to buy them all. He might even end up writing more than Dingle. So there. The others are my favorites. Didn't you read the Hardy Boys growing up? Bring the food into the kitchen. If we eat in here, you might get dizzy and throw up."

Jane was aware of him on her heels as she headed into the kitchen. "Sit down," she said, motioning to an oak pressed-back chair. She zipped around the kitchen collecting plates, napkins, silverware, and, finally, two bottles of beer. "*Bon appetit,*" she said, setting it all down in the center of the table.

"I hope I haven't offended you," Mike said, his grin conflicting with his words.

"It takes a lot more than a wiseass psychiatrist to offend me," Jane snapped back as she dug into the carton of fried rice.

"Ow," he said, rubbing his cheek as if she'd slapped him. She ignored him.

"Hey, I like these paper plates—"

"These aren't paper, they're *plastic*. There's a difference. See, these are hard, and the food doesn't soak through."

"Why so testy? I'm for whatever it takes to make life easier. Paper plates. Carryout. Housekeepers. Gardeners. If you can afford it, I say go for it."

"Do you have an opinion on *everything*?"

His composure melted like butter, and for a moment he looked like a shy little boy. "I talk a lot when I'm nervous. I was nervous about coming here. Then, when I saw those books I was off and running." He forked a helping of sweet-and-sour pork onto his plate.

Jane put some white rice and chow mein onto a plate and set it on the floor for Olive. "She's a vegetarian," she explained. "There's no MSG in this food, is there?" *He'd been nervous about coming.* She couldn't decide if she should be flattered or annoyed.

"No MSG."

Jane uncapped the two bottles of Corona and took a swig from hers. When he didn't reach for his, she wondered if he was expecting a glass. A devil perched itself atop her shoulder as she reached behind her for a bright red plastic tumbler.

"The bottle's fine," he said. "How'd your session go this afternoon?"

"It didn't. He canceled two minutes before he was supposed to show up. I explained about you and next week. He's okay with it. How'd it go with your battery guy?"

Mike sighed. "He said he bought stock in Duracell yesterday. A lot of stock. Five thousand shares to be exact. And he found a wholesaler who will deliver batteries to him once a week. Kind of like a home-delivery milkman."

Jane digested the information. "So did you find out why he's so obsessed with batteries?"

"No, not yet. He took a circuitous route around every question I put to him."

Over the years Jane had treated any number of patients with obsessions—hand washing, collections, organization. But never batteries. Was the man worried there would be a loss of power? Or did he think the batteries would *give* him power? "Does he have any health problems?"

Mike finished chewing before answering. "Yeah, a bunion on his left foot. The guy's an ox. He radiates good health."

"What does he do work-wise?"

"He's some big comptroller at a mega chemical company." Mike waved his fork. "Let's not talk about him. It makes me crazy when I think about him lugging all those batteries around everywhere he goes. Tell me about you, Jane. I've seen you at various conferences, and I've heard you on your radio show, but other than that, all I know about you is what I remember from high school. Are you married, divorced, what?"

"Single. Between renovating this house and my practice, I haven't had much time to get involved. That's not to say I don't date occasionally. I do." Carefully, she removed the foil on a piece of paper-wrapped chicken, popped it in her mouth, and savored the delicious taste. Paper-wrapped chicken was her favorite. After that, the dish of choice was moo shoo, which she'd learned to make herself using flour tortillas. "My parents died four years ago, which is why I bought this house—to keep my mind active and positive. I'm close to my godparents and see them regularly. And I have Olive here and a few good friends. How about you?"

"I've been involved a couple of times but never tied the knot. This last time, we found we wanted different things out of life. She moved on, and so did I. Mom and Dad didn't like her, said she thought she was pretty high up on the Christmas tree. I have a brother in Montana and a sister in England. We e-mail. But basically, it's just me and Noodle."

"I had a crush on you back in school," Jane blurted, and immediately wished she hadn't.

Mike put down his beer and cocked his head. "I didn't know that," he said, looking far too deeply into her eyes.

"Of course you didn't," she answered. "You were too busy being Mr. Popularity and running after Ginger and Lonnie and all the cheerleaders."

He threw up his hands in self-defense. "Hey! I admit it. I was a real jerk back then. I thought only of myself, how much fun I could have, and who I could have it with."

"That's a fair assessment," Jane smirked.

"Yeah, but I'm not like that anymore. I've changed. And so have you. You used to be quiet and studious, and you kept to yourself."

"That's because I had low self-esteem. I had a very vain mother, who was pretty and thin and didn't wear glasses. She loved to point out our differences to her friends."

Mike studied her for a moment. "If *I* hurt you in any way, Jane, I apologize."

Jane pushed her plate away. "I'm basically a vegetarian," she confided. The food was good, but she wasn't nearly as hungry as she'd thought. "Would you like to see the rest of the house?"

"You bet, but first I'd like to see the well."

"The well?"

"Yeah, where the guy fell down and the dog died waiting."

"Oh, sure." She shook her head to clear her thoughts. "I don't know what I was thinking."

They left the food sitting on the table and went out the back door and down the steps. A gently curved brick path meandered through the garden, widening and narrowing as it went.

"I've been looking forward to this ever since you mentioned it at lunch," Mike said behind her. "I'm going to sleep like a top tonight. First, I find a complete set of T. F. Dingle, and now I'm going to the site where a ghost might be dwelling. Today was an absolute fluke. I think we should both buy Duracell. My guy might be onto something."

Jane laughed. It was the first good laugh she'd had in a very long while. She led him down the path to the well. She turned when she heard Olive barking. By the time she realized the dog's intentions, Olive already had a hold on Mike's ankle.

"Get her off of me," he yelled.

"Ollie. Let go, Ollie," Jane commanded. But Olive was determined and refused to let go. Jane did the only thing she could think of and struggled to pick up the springer. "I'm sorry," she said, grimacing. "She's become very territorial where the well is concerned."

Mike pulled up his trouser leg. "I think she took a chunk out of my leg." Blood was oozing through his gray sock. "Look, I'm bleeding."

"Oh, it's just a little nip," Jane said, purposely making light of it. For a big man he was certainly acting like a *wuss*. She pulled a tissue out of her pocket, tore off a piece, spit on it, and started toward him. "Here, let me just—"

He dropped his trouser leg. "No! You are not going to stick that on me," he said, backing up a couple of feet.

"It'll stop the bleeding." She continued toward him.

"It'll stop by itself, thank you anyway," he said, holding up his hands to stay her.

Jane repocketed the tissue. "Okay, if that's what you want. But you'd better not sue me."

"I'm not going to sue you, for God's sake. What kind of guy do you think I am?"

"I don't know. I only know the old Mike Sorenson, the one who smoked pot under the bleachers at the homecoming game and who—"

"Never mind," he cut in. "I guess I'll just have to prove to you that I've changed."

"And just how do you intend to do that?"

"I don't know. I'll think on it," he said, hobbling along behind her.

Jane could think of a couple of ways he could show her how he'd changed, but she wasn't about to offer any suggestions. She was still an old-fashioned girl and preferred the man to do the asking. That didn't mean that she couldn't hope. Admittedly, after today's luncheon, she had been hoping that something might spark between them. But as soon as he opened the front door and caught her playing with Olive, her hope died. After that, she figured there was nothing to lose, so she just acted her normal self.

Past experience had shown Jane that her "normal" self wasn't what most men were looking for. But was Mike Sorenson like most men?

Jane grinned as she continued on to the well. If nothing else, she had finally made him notice her where before—in high school—she doubted he'd even known she existed.

That was then, this is now, she thought smugly.

2

The well sat in the corner of the backyard, a good three hundred feet away from Jane's perennial garden. Jane smiled as Mike trudged behind her through the dry twigs and crackly leaves. She wondered how this learned colleague of hers could be so interested in something as nebulous as ghosts.

"Here it is," she said, waving him past her. The well had become the focal point of her backyard, not because of the ghostly legend but because it was so Snow Whitish in design, a real storybook wishing well with a waist-high stone wall and a wooden, V-shaped roof that dripped with ivy.

Mike's expression was eager as he made for the well. She watched him rub his hands together, touch the stone rim, then close his eyes.

Olive howled. Olive *never* howled.

The fine hairs on the back of Jane's neck stood on end at the mournful sound. "Olive, what's the matter with you, girl?" She leaned down and rubbed the dog's neck to soothe her.

"What's all this stuff clogging up the hole?" Mike asked, looking over the edge.

"Rocks. I didn't want history to repeat itself, so I had the guy at the nursery dump a couple of loads of rock into it." Olive inched closer to Jane's leg and howled again. "Honest to God, I don't know what's gotten into her," Jane said, staring down at the spaniel, who was looking up at her as if she was trying to tell her something important.

"Dogs have a sixth sense, you know. She either senses or sees something," Mike said, excitement ringing in his voice.

Jane offered up an indulgent smile. She had never bought into the ghost theory though she'd gone along with it, even encouraged it from time to time when the occasion called for it. All in fun, of course. She glanced down at Olive. A sixth sense? No, she didn't buy into that theory either. More than likely Olive's howl was due to detecting a particularly strong scent—a rabbit or a squirrel, something other than a dog.

Minutes passed during which neither Jane nor Mike spoke. Jane became increasingly aware of the garden's stillness. When she'd first come outside, the birds had been chattering, but now they were silent. The crickets were quiet, too. The only sounds were of her, Mike's, and Olive's breathing. She glanced around at the huge old oaks and realized not a leaf was stirring.

A chill chased itself down her spine. She wished Mike would finish whatever he was doing so they could return to the house. A second later, Olive barked sharply, then took off toward the back of the property at breakneck speed.

"Did you *feel* that ?" Mike asked, rubbing his upper arms.

"Feel what? What are you talking about?"

"It was a—" He slashed the air with his hand "There was a—" His expression begged her to help him out, but she couldn't. She had no idea what he was talking about. "I don't know. But whatever it was, I felt it, and your dog ran after it."

Jane's eyebrows rose to a peak. She was tempted to go into her psychiatrist mode but decided he might think she was making fun of him. It would be better just to act herself and say what was on her mind. "I hate to say one of my peers is nuts, but you are, Sorenson. Certifiably nuts." She leaned toward him, her eyes boring into his. "Read my lips; there is no such thing as a ghost. Olive probably picked up the scent of a rabbit or a squirrel."

Mike shot her a withering look. "Think what you like. It makes no difference to me. I know what I know. There was something here not of this world. So there, Jane."

He was serious. Very serious. And if she ever wanted to see him again, she would be wise not to mock him. "Okay," she said, cautiously backing down off her soapbox. "So maybe you aren't nuts. But if you want me to believe in ghosts, then you'll have to prove their existence to me. Let's start by you telling me exactly what you *felt*," Jane said, stretching her neck to see where Olive had gone.

He thought a moment. "There was a—a presence," he said, squinting as he looked at her. "It was stronger when Olive was here and then . . . there was this flash of cool air. Right after that, Olive took off. I didn't see anything, though. I wish I had." He smiled at her. "Maybe next time."

"Next time?"

"I'd like to come back if you don't mind."

"Why I— No. How about Saturday? We can have a picnic brunch right here next to the well." Picnics were good, she thought, because they were romantic—just the two of them sitting side by side on a blanket eating little sandwiches, nibbling on fruit, and drinking champagne.

"In all the time you've lived here you've never felt or experienced *anything*?" he asked. "Even just something a little out of the ordinary or something you couldn't quite put your finger on?"

Jane gave him an apologetic look. "No, I'm afraid not, but like I said before, every once in a while something spooks

Olive. I've seen her run circles around the well, and the way she took off a minute ago—she's done that before. But she's never howled like that. In fact, she's *never* howled at all."

She could imagine what Trixie would say to all of this. *Play along. If you have to, make something up.* But she couldn't do that. It wasn't her style.

Suddenly, Olive came bounding through the trees and sat down next to her feet. Jane blinked at the way she was panting and shaking—as if she'd seen a—

"I guess I should be going," Mike said, starting back toward the house.

"I thought you wanted to see the rest of the house," Jane grumbled. He'd just gotten there. It was too soon for him to leave. Leaving meant she hadn't passed muster where he was concerned. *Screw it,* she thought as she headed back toward the house.

"I'll see it all Saturday. I really wish I could stay longer, but I need to get home. I've got a couple of cases I need to go over. I enjoyed dinner and our little foray out here. You've really done wonders with the place, Jane."

"Thanks. It's been an experience to say the least."

They walked around to the front of the house, where Jane sat down on the porch step and put her arm around Olive. She loved this time of day, the soft purple shadows of evening, the quietness. She saw a nail protruding from the step she was sitting on. The step had been one of her weekend repair projects. She'd hammered the nail but hadn't driven it home because it had bent. Her father had told her hammering nails was all in the wrists. Obviously, her wrists weren't up to snuff.

"Is it your intention to do a complete restoration?" he asked.

She moved her foot over the nail so Mike wouldn't see it. Suddenly she felt terribly inadequate. Maybe her mother had been right, and she really was a misfit. Plain Jane who couldn't quite cut it according to her beauty-pageant mother.

She thought about Connie Bryan again.

Jane heaved a sigh. "I'm not sure what my intentions are at this point. There are days when I love this old house and days when I hate it because it needs so much more work." She rose to her feet. "I'll see you Saturday." A moment later she was heading up the steps to the porch.

"Jane!"

She glanced over her shoulder.

"How about we take in a movie next week? Say, Thursday, after I sit in on your session. We could grab a bite to eat either before or after, too."

She stared at him, openmouthed, her heart pounding. "You mean a date? Sure." A date with Mike Sorenson. La-di-da. Wait till she told Trixie. A date. Things happened on dates or afterward. Uh-huh.

"Yeah, a date. I come by, ring your doorbell, and say, are you ready? You're on, lady." In two quick strides, he was on the step next to her, taking her face between his hands and kissing her lightly on the lips. "Thanks for inviting me over," he said, gazing deep into her eyes.

"You're welcome," Jane gasped. Her tongue felt like it was glued to her teeth. She wondered if her hair was standing on end with the electricity ricocheting through her body.

"Okay," Mike said, smacking his hands together as he danced from one foot to the other. "See you Saturday mid-morning."

All she could do was nod.

Once he was gone, Jane ran into the house and sat down on the bench in the foyer. He'd kissed her. A light, friendly kiss, but a kiss just the same. To think, in high school he would have gagged at the thought of even touching her. *Funny*, she thought, *how things change. How people change.*

A half hour later, she looked up from her musings to realize the house was completely dark. "You should have said something, Olive, instead of just letting me sit here. Come on, let's put some light on the subject." Jane meandered from room to room, turning on all the lamps and overhead lights so she could see the house through Mike Sorenson's eyes. She did what she'd seen Mike do and made a telescope with her hands. Perhaps the shelves were a hair off, but they certainly weren't *crooked*. Trixie and Fred's books weren't leaning to the side. Stephen Rhodes's books were nestled alongside one another and upright. She uttered an unladylike snort. Just her luck to be attracted to a nit-picking perfectionist.

She turned away from the bookshelves and studied the parlor. It was the only room in the house that had been completely restored to its original grandeur. One day she hoped to replace all the furniture with fine antiques.

Olive barked and ran upstairs. Jane followed her up with the intention of changing into her sweats. She paused on the landing, turned, and looked down past the foyer to the parlor and imagined wide-eyed children standing where she was, gazing at the Christmas tree in front of the bay window.

Her gaze switched back to the foyer when she heard a noise. One of the file folders in her briefcase had fallen out onto the floor. Odd, she thought, frowning. She clearly remembered zipping the compartments closed before leaving the office. She looked down at Olive, who was looking between the stair rails at the fallen file folder. The fur on her back was standing straight up. Jane was about to reach down and pet her when the chandelier tinkled. She looked around and saw the prisms swaying from side to side.

Olive let loose with another ungodly howl, then bounded down the stairs and ran through the foyer to the parlor and beyond. Her barks echoed through the sparsely furnished house.

"Come back here, Olive. What's gotten into you?" Jane kept her eyes on the tinkling chandelier as she crept down the stairs. "Damn you, Mike Sorenson, if you've stirred something up, I'll never forgive you!"

The chandelier had stopped tinkling by the time Jane reached the bottom of the stairs. Nevertheless, she decided to give it a wide berth just in case the nuts and bolts that held it had come loose. She walked over to the bench where she'd tossed her briefcase, picked it up, and saw that *all* the zippers were open—the outside zipper; the inside, change-purse zipper; and the two file zippers. She dropped the briefcase like a hot potato. Her frightened gaze swept to the file folder on the floor. Frightened but curious, she stretched out her right leg and, with the toe of her shoe, pulled the folder toward her until she could see the tab. It was the Ramsey file.

Shivers ran up her arms. Reluctantly, she squatted to pick it up and was knocked off-balance when Olive came from out of nowhere and threw herself onto Jane's lap.

"Olive! What the hell's wrong with you?" she shouted as she tried to get the spaniel off her lap so she could sit up. "Damn it, Olive—" It suddenly dawned on her; Olive was terrified. She was panting heavily, and her entire body was trembling. Overcome with guilt, Jane grabbed the spaniel and held her close. "It's okay, girl," she crooned softly. "There's nothing to be afraid of. It was probably just the house settling," she said, thinking the dog's fear was due to the tinkling chandelier, something she'd never heard before.

Looking over Olive's head, Jane watched in horror as the rest of her paperwork slithered, page by page, out of her briefcase and onto the old pine bench. "Easy, Olive, easy. I'm sure there is a very logical answer to all of this. I don't know what it is yet, but once I analyze everything—" She chuckled. "It's probably just a draft. Yeah, that's what it is. A draft." She twisted her head around to see if any of the windows were open in the parlor. They weren't.

"This is silly. Get up, Ollie." She pushed the dog off her lap and struggled to her feet. "After I pick all this up, I'm going to go—" She stared at the papers in her hand. "What we're going to do is—" They were in order. They weren't that way when she'd jammed them into her briefcase. "We're going to the Ramsey house is what we're going to do!" she said, shoving the folder and all the papers back into the briefcase and zipping all the zippers. She looked around to make sure she hadn't missed anything. With trembling hands, she carefully hung the briefcase by its shoulder strap on the hall tree.

Olive pawed at her leg.

Jane glanced down at her. "You wanna go for a ride?"

Olive stood up on her hind legs and grabbed the leash hanging from one of the hall tree's hooks.

"Okay, okay, calm down," Jane said as she hooked the leash to Olive's collar. The crazy dog loved going for rides even more than she loved pig ears. On occasion Jane had tried to fool her and sneak out of the house without taking her, but Olive always knew and came running, dragging her leash behind her. It was like she had a sixth— She stopped herself from completing the thought. Dogs were "sensitive" to certain weather conditions, earthquakes, and their owners' moods, but they did not have a sixth sense.

With Olive at her side, Jane walked through the house, turning off the lights she'd turned on a little while earlier. "I know this isn't going to make any sense to you, Ollie, but my gut tells me I need to do something about Mr. Ramsey. If that means getting personally involved, then so be it. My patient is my first concern. No, that's not true," she said, bending to pet Olive. "You're my first concern." Olive looked up at her expectantly. The excitement of going for a ride had made her forget her fear. *Wouldn't it be nice,* Jane thought, *if my patients could be cured of their fears so easily?*

Thirty minutes later, Jane pulled into a parking space a

block away and around the corner from the Ramsey house. "I'm going snooping, Olive, and while I'm gone I want you to be a good girl." She turned off the ignition. "I'll leave the windows down for you, but you need to remember the rules, no jumping out like you did at the grocery store last year, no whining to get someone to come over to you, and no barking." She put her right hand under the dog's chin and looked her square in the eyes. "Yes, I know all your tricks. I'll be back in ten minutes, and if you do anything bad, I'll know it."

Jane closed the car door and shook a warning finger at Olive. Confident the dog would be good, she headed toward the Ramsey house. It was raining. Rain was good. People would go indoors if they were outside. She turned the corner and walked down the sidewalk on the opposite side of the Ramsey house to the next corner, then came back on the other side.

Pale yellow light shone through the windows, but no outside lights were on. The streetlights were dim, two of them on the street burned-out. She was soaking wet by the time she tiptoed up the Ramseys' driveway to the back of the house. Sucking in her breath, she waited to see if she had triggered any motion lights. Either Brian Ramsey conserved electricity, or he didn't worry about unwanted visitors. Remembering there was no outside furniture, no outdoor grill, and no hoses to trip over, she found her way easily to the back windows.

As before, the kitchen window gave her a clear view of the entire kitchen, a small hallway, and part of the dining room. Everything was as clean, as tidy, and just as bare as it had been the last time she'd been there. The only difference was that the light over the stove was on, giving an orangey, yellowish glow to the kitchen. She left the kitchen window and moved quickly and quietly, her heart hammering in her chest, to the far side of the house to peer into what she thought was the master-bedroom window. A night-light above the baseboard allowed her to see that the bed was unmade and empty. She continued around to the front of the house, hoping to see someone, something, anything!

Rain dripped down inside the collar of her jacket as Jane stealthily crept up to the narrow stoop to peer into the living-room window. Shivering, she hugged her arms to her chest. A quick glance up and down the street told her no one was in sight. Off in the distance she heard Olive bark. An answering response came from the opposite end of the street.

Jane inched upward to look in the window. Brian Ramsey was sitting in a hunter green leather recliner, a bottle of beer in his hand and a package of cigarettes in the breast pocket of his white T-shirt. He was alone.

Not wanting to jump to any conclusions, Jane looked to every corner of the room and as far beyond it as the view from the window would take her. Nothing. No one.

Where was Mrs. Ramsey?

In the bathroom? But the two opaque windows she'd assumed were bathroom windows had been dark.

Jane gasped when Brian turned his gaze toward the window. She ducked and ran, faster than she'd ever run before, across the lawn, down the sidewalk, her shoes sloshing. When she reached the corner she realized that in her panic, she had gone in the wrong direction. Cursing under her breath, she retraced her steps, taking the long road back to her car. The moment she was safely inside, she locked the door and started the engine, her heart hammering in her chest. For one bad moment she thought she was going to black out. She forced herself to take long, deep breaths, the air hissing from her mouth in a long, unsteady stream. She didn't turn on the car's headlights until she was three blocks away.

"You disobeyed me, Ollie," she scolded once she was on the open road. "I heard you bark." The dog moved closer to the passenger window, pinned her ears flat against her head, and hung her head in shame. "You're a naughty dog, Ollie. No more rides for you this month." It was an idle threat— she knew it and so did Olive.

She'd just risked her professional standing to get a peek at the elusive Mrs. Ramsey. And what had she gotten for all her effort? A look at Brian Ramsey sitting in his chair like a zombie, the same way he did in her office. *If* he had a wife, the woman either spent her life in the summer kitchen or hid out in a darkened bathroom. Because it was a tract house, it was highly unlikely that there was a summer kitchen. That left the dark bathroom. The thought was too ridiculous for words.

All the way home Jane chastised herself. "Stupid, stupid, stupid," she hissed between her teeth. She glanced sideways at Olive. "I think he saw me, Ollie. I swear to God I think he saw me. He looked right at me." Sighing, she returned her gaze to the road. "If I hadn't hightailed it out of there—I can just see him catching me, calling the police, and having me arrested for being a Peeping Tom. Boy, when I do stupid things, I really do stupid things. We aren't ever going to mention this again," she said, tightening her grip on the steering wheel. "Never, do you hear me, Olive? Never!"

Olive inched toward her mistress and lightly pawed her arm.

"Come here," Jane said, putting her arm around the dog and pulling her close. "I'm sorry, too. I didn't mean that about not taking you in the car." Olive snuggled next to Jane's side and licked her face.

Jane's nerves were still twanging when she arrived home. After closing the curtains and checking to make sure the doors were locked, she went into the kitchen and rummaged around until she found the special "brew" she kept on hand for Trixie and Fred. She poured herself two fingers of the finest Kentucky bourbon the state had to offer and tossed it down her throat in one swallow. Coughing and sputtering, her eyes tearing, she collapsed in the chair and waited for the bourbon to do its thing, but after ten minutes, she still didn't feel any better. Maybe a cigarette would help. She wasn't a smoker, but Trixie and Fred were, and Trixie always said there was nothing like a good smoke to calm her down and help her think. As with the bourbon, Jane kept a pack of their favorite brand in her catchall drawer as a precautionary measure in case they ran out while visiting. She lit up, broke into a fit of coughing, and stubbed it out. What satisfaction her godparents got out of smoking was a mystery—one better left unsolved.

Tomorrow morning, when she did her five-mile morning run, something she hadn't done in over a month, she was going to stop by her godparents' house. She needed to talk to someone, someone who would listen, be on her side, and still be objective. Trixie could be painfully objective. Fred, too.

"Enough's enough, Olive. I've had it. Let's go to bed. I'm so tired I can't think straight." She yawned and stretched.

The spaniel waited patiently until Jane turned the lights off before racing up the stairs. When she reached the top, she sat down on her haunches and barked as if to say, c'mon, c'mon, let's go.

Jane went through her bedtime regimen in record time, then grabbed a pair of clean pajamas out of her drawer, her "dream" pajamas she called them because of the fluffy white clouds printed on a sky-blue background. By the time she climbed into the big four-poster rice bed alongside Olive, she was already planning what to dream about—Mike Sorenson.

Jane rolled over and stretched out her hand to cuddle Olive. Just knowing the dog was beside her was comforting.

Instead, her hand encountered the lumpy bedspread. Stirring uneasily, she opened one eye and saw Olive sitting on her haunches in front of the French doors that led out to the balcony. She was wiggling her head the way she did when Jane scratched her ears.

"Hello, Dr. Lewis," a boyish voice said. "*My name is Billy Jensen, and this is my dog, Jeeter. Jeeter likes Olive. They had a wonderful run earlier out by the well, but of course, you already know that.*"

Wearily, Jane propped herself up on her right elbow and stared at the boy and the dog standing by the door. "Who are you? How did you get in here? I locked the doors." That was a stupid question, she told herself. This was a dream and *anything* could happen in a dream. It didn't have to make sense. She yawned. "I'd appreciate it if you'd move on and let me get back to sleep. What time is it anyway?"

"*Time has no meaning to me. Or Jeeter.*"

"Well, it does to me. I have to get up early in the morning. So go away."

"*Jeeter is lonely. And so am I. I thought we might become friends.*"

"Fine, but not tonight, okay? I'm really beat, and I want to dream about someone else."

"*Yes, I know. Your gentleman caller, Dr. Sorenson. He makes you act funny.*"

"Funny? Funny how?"

"*Like this,*" he said, batting his eyes.

"I beg your pardon, but I have never done that to anyone in my life. Dr. Sorenson and I are business associates. Nothing more. Now, please, I don't mean to be rude, but I'd appreciate it if you'd get out of my dream. If I don't get enough sleep, I'm grouchy."

"*I know. I've seen how grouchy you can be.*"

"Go away!" Jane lay down on her back and closed her eyes.

"*I'll leave, but first I want to tell you that I know what you did this evening. You shouldn't do things like that. It's too risky. And what was worse was that you locked Olive in the car. She couldn't have helped you if you'd needed her.*"

"For the record," Jane said with growing impatience, "I didn't lock the car door, and even if I did, Olive knows how to get it open." Something about this dream was very un-dreamlike. She opened her eyes, blinked, and took a good long look at the youth standing by the French door. "Am I supposed to know you? You don't look familiar. But I must have met you somewhere. . . . Dreams are manifestations of what happens in our daily lives. Olive, get over here."

"*You know who I am. I'm a spirit. I'm the one who took the Ramsey file out of your briefcase. You've known about me for a long time, but you've always refused to acknowledge me. You have Dr. Sorenson to thank for opening up our communication wavelengths.*"

Jane snorted. "So . . . Let me see if I get this right. This is not a dream. And I am not asleep. I am, in fact, wide-awake and conversing with a spook."

"*Yes, to everything. But please, I am not a spook. When you call me that, you hurt my feelings.*" The boy laughed, then disappeared.

When he reappeared, he was sitting on the edge of the bed. Jane reared back and pulled the coverlet to her chin. "How'd you do that?" she shrilled.

"*There is a scientific name for it, but I keep forgetting what it is. Let's just say it's a ghostly thing. You know, like walking through walls and stuff like that.*"

Jane could feel her body trembling beneath the covers. "Olive, come over here. Right now, dammit!" Olive and Jeeter jumped up on the bed. Jane grabbed Olive and put her arms around her. "What—What do you want of me?"

The boy shrugged. "*I just want to be your friend. I know*

you're scared of me, but you don't need to be. I won't hurt you."

Jane struggled to relax. This *had* to be a dream. *Had* to be. Didn't it? She stared at the young man sitting on the edge of her bed. He appeared young, fifteen or so, with a million freckles dotting his face, brown eyes, and curly, sandy-colored hair. He wore coveralls and a long-sleeved plaid shirt.

"I don't believe in ghosts, spirits, spooks, or other . . . unearthly things," she said. She rolled over and thumped her pillow. This was one dream she hoped she would remember in the morning. She felt her mattress lift and heard a thump on the floor. Olive was still on the bed.

"Good night, Dr. Lewis."

"Woof."

Oh God! Olive hadn't barked. Her head was plastered against her chest so she would . . . Jane closed her eyes. *That was one hell of a dream,* she thought. *It must have been the bourbon.* She looked at the clock beside her bed: 5:10 A.M. She still had an hour until the alarm went off.

Jane limped up the driveway to her godparents' house. Her legs felt like they were on fire. Why would she be getting shin splints now? Probably because this was the first time she'd gone running in over a month. "Hey, what's for breakfast?" she yelled as she let herself in the back door.

Trixie came out of the pantry, a small bird of a woman with brilliant pinkish red hair, pounds of gold jewelry hanging around her neck, and multicolored half glasses resting on the end of her nose. Gold hoop earrings, big enough for a bird to fly through, dangled from her ears. As always, Jane marveled at the frail body with the stick-thin arms and legs as she hugged her godmother. *Eighty-nine pounds dripping wet,* she thought.

"You're gonna have to drive me home, Trix. I'm outta shape. My run this morning proved it. You cooking breakfast, or are we eating it out of a box?"

"Pop-Tarts," Trixie said. "Strawberry or blueberry? Never mind, I only have blueberry." Trixie laughed as she put the pastries into the toaster oven.

"Nice outfit," Jane said, giggling. "What do you call it?"

Trixie's laughter tinkled around the kitchen. "It's my hanging-out-at-the-police-station outfit. Today is Friday. I always hang out there on Fridays. You never know what you can pick up in a police station. Just a word or an action will trigger something. Then there are the criminals who are innocent. The stories would fill a book. Tell me about last night," Trixie said as she expertly removed the Pop-Tarts from the toaster oven. She tossed one to Jane.

"I still can't believe no one in this town knows you and Fred are T. F. Dingle. That's worthy of a book in itself. Mike Sorenson was terribly impressed that I had a complete set of your books. There's nothing I would have liked better than to tell him that I personally knew his favorite author, but I didn't. Your secret is safe."

"Okay, so you impressed him with our books, then what?" Trixie prompted.

"We ate, we talked, and then I took him out to the well to meet my ghosts. That's why he came in the first place, you know. He has an interest in the paranormal."

"A serious interest, or is he just curious?"

"A serious interest."

"I see. And then . . ." she prompted again.

"He had to go, but he asked if he could come back tomorrow, and he invited me to the movie next Thursday," Jane said all in one breath.

"That's it?" Trixie asked, obviously disappointed.

Jane bit into her Pop-Tart and shrugged. For some strange

reason she didn't want to tell Trixie that Mike kissed her. Her practical self told her it was because the kiss really hadn't been anything more than a peck. And her professional self told her it was because it was special.

Trixie waved an arm. "Phooey. You're no fun at all."

Jane hid a smile behind her Pop-Tart. "Where's Fred?"

"In the bathroom. Where else?" Trixie rolled her eyes and Jane marveled at the half-inch-long false eyelashes her godmother glued on every morning. Once, a few years back, a colleague had said that her eyelashes looked like a herd of tarantulas on the march. It was true. They did. "He takes forever in the morning," Trixie went on. "He spends most of his time grooming his hair, combing his mustache, and blow-drying his beard."

Jane looked around the sterile-looking kitchen. State of the art. The best of the best. Everything was white or black, pretty much the way Trixie viewed everything in her life; it was or it wasn't. Black or white. She supposed it wasn't a bad thing.

"How do you think he'll be in bed, Janie?" Trixie asked without blinking an eye.

Jane laughed. Typical. So typical of her godmother. No mincing of words, not even a warm-up. "I think I have a way to go before that happens. *If* it happens. Let's face it, Trix, the guy can have just about any woman he wants. Why would he want me? I'm overweight. I have curly hair, too curly, and I'm no fashion plate and—"

"Stop that right this minute," Trixie scolded, wagging her finger. "You sound like you're describing a horse at auction. You put too much emphasis on looks. It's what's in here," she said, putting her hand against her heart, "that counts. You're kind, sweet, lovable, and you care about people. Stop putting yourself down. If your beauty-queen mother wasn't already dead, I'd kill her myself for making you think you were a Plain Jane. I never did like that woman. She was a royal pain in the ass. The only one who didn't seem to know or see her for what she was was your father, God rest his soul. There was no finer man in these parts than your father."

Jane licked melted icing off her fingers. "Oh, he knew. We used to have long talks about Mom. He always tried to build me up after Mother ripped me apart. By the way, that old poem isn't true—sticks and stones will break your bones but words will never hurt you. They do hurt." She picked her plate up and took it over to the sink. "I just hate it when I go off on these tangents."

"Like I said," Trixie said to Jane's back, "your mother was a pain in the ass." Reaching behind her, she pulled a pile of stuff off the counter. "Want to see our new book? We just got our author copies yesterday. Fred was going to drop off one for you. And before you ask, yes, we signed it." She held the book. "What do you think? Is the cover gory enough?"

Jane studied the glossy book jacket with a critical eye. The author's name was emblazoned across a black background. The coloring of the lettering matched the blood running off a corpse hanging from a tree. The title, in smaller letters, read *Hang Loose*.

"Ah . . . Trixie, you don't bleed when you're hanged."

"You do if you pump a full round into someone first. We told the art department to hang him up, to make him a red herring. I love it! Fred thinks there's a little too much blood."

"Nah. Your readers would be disappointed without it. Do you have an extra copy I can give Mike? He's a real fan of yours, read every one of your books."

"Sure." Trixie reached for another copy.

"Don't sign it. I don't want him getting suspicious." She stared at the book in her hand. "I couldn't write a book if my life depended on it. My hat's off to you, Trixie. Are you *ever* going to break your silence and come 'out?' "

"Never. They'd run me and Fred out of town on a rail. Anonymity works for us."

"What do the cops think you do? They must be suspicious since you hang with them so much."

"I tell them I write television cop scripts no one wants to buy. They can't wait to share information with me. I guess everyone wants that fifteen minutes of fame. I did promise to dedicate the movie to the entire force if I was ever successful in selling a script."

"You are so devious, Trixie. What are you going to do if someone catches on?"

"If they haven't figured it out in fifty years, I don't think I have too much to worry about. If they do, I'll admit it and 'fess up."

Fred waddled into the kitchen, his shock of white hair tamed for the moment. "Janie, girl, what are you doing up and out at the crack of dawn?"

"Couldn't sleep. I had this really weird dream." She shook her head at the remembered images. "I figured I might as well get up and go for a run. In case you haven't noticed, I'm putting on weight, again." She hugged her affable godparent. "You smell good, Fred."

"I like to smell sweet for Trixie," Fred said, laughing. His whole body shook. Jane had always thought he looked like Santa Claus with his white hair and white fluffy beard. His wire-rimmed glasses were the finishing touch. All he needed was a red suit and a black pair of shiny boots.

"Coffee's hot. Want some breakfast, honey?" Trixie asked.

"I'll take anything but a Pop-Tart. We've had them every day this week," Fred grumbled, snapping his suspenders for emphasis.

"How about some frozen pancakes? I can zap them in the microwave or pop them in the toaster. You can put some of that good jelly on them and roll them up like crepes." Trixie hopped off her chair and scooted for the fridge. "By the way, Fred," she added offhandedly, "you're two chapters behind me. Are you going to catch up today?"

"I will if you don't keep going astray. I thought we had Stuart's character all settled. I don't think he would say 'lick me' to anyone. Where did you hear something like that? I'm taking it out, sugar."

"Don't you sugar me, Fred McGuire. You leave that phrase in there. That's what people say today. I figured I had a choice of 'fuck you' or 'lick me.' I went with 'lick me' because it fit Stuart. If you don't believe me, ask Janie," Trixie said, hands on her hips, her eyes sparking.

Jane put her hands up in front of her. "I don't know anything about fiction writing but whatever is indicative of the character is what you always say, Fred. I think I would go with the 'lick me' as opposed to the other phrase."

"He's getting old, Janie," Trixie said with a wink. "He doesn't know the half of what's going on in the world. When you sit around a police station all day, you hear all kinds of stuff. A writer has to stay up on what's going on." When Fred scowled, she gave him a come-hither look. "C'mere, Freddie, and give Trixie a big kiss," she said, puckering up.

Fred obliged.

Jane had seen them act like this a thousand times before, bantering back and forth. Anyone who didn't know them might think they were fighting, but the truth was they never fought. Never. They loved each other too much.

The minute Fred finished his breakfast, he carried his plate to the sink, washed it, dried it, and put it away. Jane knew that he thought dishwashers were a big waste of time and water.

"I've got to get to work," he said, "or she'll get so far ahead of me I'll never hear the end of it. See you tonight, Janie. Don't spit on any wooden nickels."

Jane smiled. "Trust me, Fred, I won't."

Trixie stopped him before he could get to the door. "This is my day to go to the police station, Fred. So, if you need me, call the station, and they'll page me. I have to drop Janie off at home first. Oh, and be sure to print out a hard copy so I can read it when I get home. And chill some wine, sweetie and we can play house this evening."

Fred waddled out of the kitchen, his girth shaking like the proverbial bowl of jelly.

"I just love that man. We'll be married fifty-five years in two months. And everyone we knew back then said it wouldn't last," Trixie cackled.

3

Trixie shifted into fifth gear as she risked a sideways glance at Jane, who was holding on to the Jesus Christ strap as if her life depended on it. Trixie knew she tended to speed, but so did Jane. Driving fast was just one of the many things they had in common. No, it wasn't her driving that was causing Jane's anxious expression. Something was seriously bothering her beloved godchild. "Wanna talk about it, kiddo?"

Jane shot her a sideways glance. Trixie *always* knew when something was wrong. *Always*. It was positively uncanny. "Not really," she said, her feelings uncertain. "Well, maybe. No, I need to . . ."

"Is it that same *old stuff*? I wish you'd stared it in the face back then and dealt with it," she said, throwing her hands up in a gesture of frustration. A split second later she grabbed the wheel to swerve around a slow-moving pickup truck. "Asshole!" she shouted, one skinny arm shooting out the window to offer up her middle finger in a single-digit salute. "I'm sorry, honey, what were you saying?"

"It was nothing," she said, waving her hand to dismiss the subject. Trixie was assuming that she had been thinking about Connie Bryan. Jane did think about Connie, almost daily, but that wasn't what was on her mind today. It was Brian Ramsey who occupied her thoughts. "I just have a lot going on right now. I feel a little overwhelmed. You know how that goes."

Trixie kept her eyes on the road. "It might be good for you to talk about it. Isn't that what you tell your patients, to talk about what's troubling them?" Once she was out of traffic, she pressed the pedal to the metal and flew through the streets to the edge of town.

"Yes, that's what I tell them," Jane said, relieved to see her house coming into view. "But in this case, I'm governed by patient confidentiality."

Trixie screeched the four-by-four to a stop in front of Jane's house.

"Home sweet home," Jane said, looking out the passenger window at her domain. "Oh, listen." She leaned to the right to listen to the birds. She loved their early-morning litany. One of these days she was going to get a book on how to attract birds to the garden so there would be even more than there already were. "Thanks for bringing me home, Trix." She grabbed the plastic grocery bag with the two T. F. Dingle books in it and opened the car door.

"Oh, wait a minute," Trixie said as she reached into the backpack she carried like a purse. "Here's that disk you wanted. It's one of those bootleg copies, so keep it safe. Trust me when I tell you, you can find out *everything* about *anyone* with this. I have a copy, so don't worry about returning it."

"Great. Thanks. I'll see you tonight." Jane turned to go up the steps.

"Janie?" Trixie called from inside the car. "Do you still have that *paper bag*?"

Jane swiveled around slowly and nodded.

"Janie, you know what? You need to shit or get off the

pot, i.e., do something about it or get rid of it. That's my advice for the day. See you tonight, sweetie." Before Jane could respond, Trixie roared off in a cloud of dust and spurting gravel.

Ignoring Trixie's advice, Jane turned and stared at her house with a clinical eye. The peeling paint and crooked shutters made her wince. She'd had every intention of renovating the outside herself, but it was a monster undertaking, too big for her to tackle with her busy schedule. She made a mental note to add calling carpenters and painters to her "to do" list right after she called about a temporary receptionist.

One of these days the house would look as she'd envisioned it when she bought it. The first thing she would do when it was all finished would be to buy a dozen Boston ferns and hang them on long white chains from the porch rafters. Then she'd buy three or four Charleston rockers and white wicker tables to set tall, frosty glasses of lemonade on, and little pots of English ivy. She would spend every Sunday afternoon on her veranda, rocking, sipping her drink, and reading Fred and Trixie's books. The only sound would be that of the oscillating fans whirring softly overhead.

Olive started barking as soon as Jane started up the steps. It wasn't a typical glad-you're-home bark; it was an agitated bark. Warned that something was wrong, Jane glanced around. Then she saw it. A snake had coiled up next to the banister to sun itself on the warm wooden veranda. "It's okay, Ollie. It's just a king snake, and we both know it won't hurt us. They kill all the rodents you miss." She stepped back nevertheless and contemplated what to do about the snake. Nothing, she decided after considering her options, all of which required her doing something to make it move. "Don't bother me," she said to the snake. "You go ahead and stay right where you are. I'll just go around to the back door."

Thirty minutes later, a coffee mug in hand, Jane slipped

into the fragrant steaming bathwater. She rested her neck against a folded towel, closed her eyes, and did her best to shift into what she called her neutral zone. By definition it meant to give herself up to the pleasures of the moment. It usually worked. But not today.

She hated the way she'd been feeling these last few weeks. It was all because of Brian Ramsey and her inability to get a handle on him. What made things even worse was that she'd felt the need to bring in outside help.

Not for the first time she wondered what she was doing and thought maybe she didn't belong in psychiatry. She'd always known she'd gone into it for the wrong reason— because of Connie Bryan. She'd convinced herself that helping someone else would make up for not being able to help Connie.

Her thoughts went back to *that* night. Her first mistake had been to let Connie bind her to a promise of silence. She should have realized that Connie wasn't herself, that she was in no mental condition to make intelligent decisions. A true friend would have seen to it that Connie went for help or that help was brought to her. Her second mistake was in keeping her promise even after Connie committed suicide. No, it wouldn't have helped Connie, but it might have helped those who loved her understand why she did what she did.

Beached whale.

Miss Piggy.

Fat tub of lard.

Was it her own humiliation that had kept her quiet?

Jane squeezed her eyes shut. She had always been afraid to answer that question. "And I'm not going to answer it now," she said to Olive, who was spread out like a frog on the floor next to the tub. Olive opened one eye to look at Jane. "Go back to sleep. I'm just talking to myself again."

Years after Connie's death, Jane had wondered what kind

of person Todd Prentice was that he would call off his engagement to Connie because she'd been raped. After meeting
Todd at an alumni fund-raiser, she understood Connie's rea-
soning a little better. Todd had been there with his wife, his
"trophy" wife was the way Jane had come to think of her.
Jane remembered her dress—backless, strapless, and halfway
up her ass. A scant quarter yard of material at best. What
was her name? Melody? Melanie? Melanie. Melanie Petitjean of Petitjean Pharmaceuticals, according to the listing for
the Alumni Association's Board of Directors, of which Todd
was a member. Jane knew the company well, even owned
some stock in it.

She scooted farther down into the hot water. It had been
two or three years since the fund-raiser, and she still didn't
know what to make of Todd coming up to her and introduc-
ing himself. They hadn't known each other in college. Never
even met. She lathered her shoulders and neck. "Help me out
with this, Ollie. Talk to me. You woof if I say something that
strikes a chord, okay?"

"Woof!"

"Okay," Jane said, satisfied that Olive was paying attention. "I'm a shrink and a pretty good one so—"

"Woof!"

"Thank you, but you interrupted." The fact that the bathwater wasn't hot anymore was of no consequence. Jane was
thinking, clearly for once. And objectively. There was something about standing beneath a shower or lying back in a
bathtub that freed the mind. Trixie always said her best ideas
came to her in the shower. "Okay now, where was I? Oh,
yeah. I should be able to figure this out." Olive's ears perked.
"I've already ruled out that Todd was just a really friendly
guy because he didn't bother to introduce himself to Rose,
who was standing right next to me. He wasn't interviewing
me for the alumni newsletter. And although he gave me his

business card, he never called me later, so he wasn't trying to sell me anything. And, with a wife who looked like his, he wouldn't have been trying to hit on me." She sighed, thinking she'd covered all this ground before. "What if," she said, using the phrase Trixie and Fred used to come up with plot twists for their books, "he already knew who I was, wanted to meet me, and see if he could establish a rapport because he was looking for a psychiatrist?" Olive cocked her head to the side. "No, huh? What then? You tell me since you're so smart." Olive was silent.

She closed her eyes. "This is making me crazy. I need to come to terms with it. I've been carrying around this guilt for twelve years. It's ruining my life. I wish you could talk, Olive. I need some feedback here."

"Woof woof!"

Jane nodded as if she understood. "You're right. If I was the patient, I would tell myself to call Todd up, make an appointment to see him, ask him why he introduced himself to me, and tell him what happened that night."

Olive bounded to her feet when thunder cracked overhead. Jane hopped out of the tub and pulled the drain plug. She hated and feared thunderstorms as much as Olive did. "Hit the light switch, Olive!" Water gurgled down the drain as Jane wrapped herself in her ratty flannel robe. She ran for the bed, jumped in, and covered both her and Olive's heads.

There hadn't been any signs of a storm when Trixie had dropped her off. Had there? Maybe she just hadn't been paying attention. It didn't matter. The storm was there, right on top of her from the sound of it. She knew she was being silly and even childish, but she'd never been able to control her irrational fear of storms. Maybe if her mother hadn't locked the screen door on her and refused to let her in the house because she was dirty, she wouldn't be going through this now.

Jane knew she would never forget that day. The storm had

come out of nowhere, just like this one. She'd given up bang-
ing on the door and crunched down in the corner of the old
porch and cried. When lightning hit the pillar on the opposite
side of the porch and the roof collapsed, she had screamed
and screamed until she was hoarse. Her father found her
hours later.

Too many bad memories. Too much mental baggage.

A long time later, Jane threw back the covers, her gaze
going to the windows. A steady gray drizzle dripped from the
eaves. It was going to be one of *those* days.

It was eight-forty-five when Jane settled Olive into the passenger seat and buckled her up with the doggy seat belt she'd
ordered over the Internet. She tossed her briefcase, purse,
and flowered hat onto the passenger seat before she buckled
herself up. "Okay girl, we're outta here," she said as she
turned on the radio to get the weather report.

The "uh" brothers down-home voices filled the small car.
So named by Trixie because they couldn't say more than two
words without saying "uh." But when it came to weather, the
brothers were always on the money. Either you loved them or
you hated them as an early-morning start to the day.

Trixie and Fred hated them. In Jane's opinion, KSIG was a
great radio station, the best for Acadia Parish. The moment
the "uh" brothers rattled off the current weather conditions,
she switched to KATC for local news. As always, she felt dis-
loyal because she didn't tune into her own station, KRFG,
but she shrugged off the feeling. Years of habit were hard to
break.

Jane continued down the boulevard to North Adams,
crossed over the railroad tracks, and continued down South
Adams until she came to the small building that housed the
KRFG station. She parked, attached Olive's leash, and headed

for what she called her lair, her briefcase and purse slung over her shoulder.

"Five minutes, Jane!" Tom Bradley shouted from the control room. "Move it!"

Jane adjusted the swivel chair, then slipped on her earphones, all the while keeping her eyes glued to Tom Bradley behind the glass in front of her. The moment his thumb shot upward, Jane knew she was on.

"Good morning. I'm Dr. Jane Lewis and this is *Talk to Me*," she said cheerfully. "I'll be live on the air for the next hour to take your calls. If you've got a problem you can't resolve, pick up your phone and talk to me. I'm hear to listen and to advise you. I have a feeling it's going to be one of *those* days. I've got my first caller on the line. This is Dr. Jane Lewis. How can I help you this morning?"

"First, I want to say that I really enjoy your show," the caller said.

"Thank you. Whom am I talking to? First name only."

"Dewey."

"Okay, Dewey. Talk to me."

"I need you to tell me who is right. My wife says she's with the kids all week long while I work. She thinks I should watch them on the weekend while she goes out to do whatever she wants to do. I say I worked all week long, too, so I should have at least one day to myself. What do you think?"

Jane rolled her eyes as she stared across at Tom Bradley. "What I think is you're both right. You each need a day here and there that's just for you. But you also need to spend some time together without the kids. So compromise and make a plan. You take a day once or twice a month to do what you want to do, and she can do the same. Hire a sitter occasionally and go out somewhere together, even if it's only for a ride. Rides are a great way to enjoy each other's company. How does that sound?"

"There's no money to hire a sitter."

"Okay, how about trading baby-sitting time with some friends of yours. Maybe they'd like to get away, too, or maybe you can trade for services. Where there's a will there's a way, Dewey. It's doable if you're willing to work at it."

"I'll run it by her. You're right, it does sound doable. Thanks."

"Okay, next caller. Stacy, talk to me. What's bothering you on this rainy morning?"

A small, tired voice came over the line. "Life. It's not worth living anymore. I hate my job. I don't have any friends. And my cat just died. I just want to go to sleep and never wake up."

Jane bolted upright in her chair. Her shoulders tensed. "Okay, Stacy, I'm here to listen to your problems and try to help you work them out. Let's start with your cat. I've got my dog right here beside me, and I know how bad I would feel if anything happened to her. It's perfectly natural to grieve over the loss of a beloved pet. It's also healthy. People need to grieve to heal. I suggest you get another cat right away, not to replace the one you lost because nothing will do that but because you need another animal to love. The SPCA has so many animals that desperately need homes. Will you think about it?"

"You don't think I would be betraying her memory to get another cat right away?"

"No. Not at all."

"I'll think about it," she said.

Jane knew by the sound of Stacy's voice that a new cat was in her immediate future. "Now, let's see what we can do about this job you hate so much. Talk to me, tell me exactly what the problem is."

There were several problems, but they all boiled down to

the fact that Stacy hated sitting and staring at a computer all day. After work, she was too frazzled to do anything but go home, eat fast food, and go to bed. And because she never went out, she didn't have any friends.

"Okay, Stacy, you need to find another job, an outdoor job or at least something where you're outdoors part of the time. You also need to join a club, an exercise club or a sport club. We have a softball league here at the station, and we can use some good outfielders. Come by and sign up, today, now. What do you say? Can I count on you coming by in an hour or so?"

"I'll think about it."

"I have another idea. We have a crisis center. How would you like to do some volunteer work? It's just a few hours a week. You can talk to some of our counselors and get on the right track at the same time. I need a commitment here, Stacy. I'll wait for you if you give me your promise to come by."

"Volunteer work? Really?"

Jane saw Tom give her the sign that they were going to break for a commercial. "Really, Stacy," she said, nodding at him. "I'll be expecting you, Stacy. This is Dr. Jane Lewis, and this is *Talk to Me*."

Jane took off her headphones and noted that the *off the air* sign was on. "Did you get her phone number, Tom?" He nodded. "If she shows up, hold her till I go off the air." Tom nodded again.

The hour crawled by, a couple of calls snappy and to the point, one totally off the wall. Tom held up his index finger to indicate another caller was on the line.

"Talk to me, Dennis. Tell me what's bothering you this morning."

"I witnessed a criminal act in which a friend of mine was badly hurt. I wanted to go to the police, but my friend swore me to secrecy. I don't feel good about this. I want the criminals caught, but I swore I would never talk about it. What should I do?"

Jane reared back from the microphone. In all the time she'd been doing the show, she'd never had a caller with a problem even remotely resembling her own. Considering where her mind had been just a couple of hours ago, it seemed more than a little coincidental. But what else could it be?

"Dr. Lewis?" the caller asked.

"I'm here, Dennis. The answer to your question is complicated because there are both legal and moral concerns. I advise you to go to the authorities, report the crime, and get help for your friend whether he or she wants it or not. It could destroy your friendship, but better that than whatever mental pain your friend suffered destroying him or her."

"I was afraid you might say that. I asked a lawyer friend of mine, and he said the same thing you did."

"Well, there you have it, Dennis." Jane almost sighed with relief when she saw Tom's thumb point down. "Our hour is up, but thanks for listening. This is Dr. Jane Lewis. I'll be back next Friday morning at nine o'clock with another hour of *Talk to Me*. Have a great weekend and remember the three R's. Respect for self, respect for others, responsibility for all your actions. If that's too intense for some of you, go with this—don't trust anyone who doesn't close his or her eyes when kissing."

"Good show, Jane," Tom Bradley said, popping his head out of the control room. "Your girl, Stacy, is in the lobby. Listen, would you like to take in dinner and a movie this weekend?"

Jane smiled and shook her head. "Thanks, Tom, but I think our relationship has run its course. I enjoy your company, but I'm afraid I'm never going to feel anything but friendship toward you, so there's no point in continuing to see each other."

"We haven't even been out a half dozen times, Jane. How the hell do you know if you could never feel anything but friendship toward me?"

How many times had she told her patients to stay away from personal involvement with coworkers? Office dating failed more often than it succeeded. This was one of those times she wished she'd followed her own advice. "I just know, Tom. I'm sorry. It's not that I don't like you. You're a good man, but you're not the man for me."

"Is there someone else?"

Was there? Did Mike Sorenson count as someone else? "Not at the moment. I hope my decision doesn't cause problems between us. I love doing the show, and I've been thinking a lot about going to two days a week, but—"

"No, no," he said, shaking his head. "There's no problem."

Jane knew he was agreeing with her for the sake of the show, which was why she'd mentioned it. She wouldn't have even considered the subtle threat had he not been so persistent.

"Where are those softball forms? I want to give one to Stacy."

Tom whipped one out of the basket on his desk. "We could really use a good relief pitcher."

"Thanks for being so understanding," she said with a sincerity she was far from feeling. But to leave him feeling good about himself, a little schmoozing was needed. "See you next week."

"Yeah, next week. Take care of her, Olive."

Trixie McGuire pranced into the police station like she owned the place, and in a way she did. She donated handsomely to any and all fund-raisers in her name and Fred's. Other more costly items, like digital cameras and the latest high-tech equipment were always sent anonymously. Trixie didn't like it when people gushed over her generosity.

"Morning, Miss Trixie, how's it going on this ugly, rainy Friday morning?" Jake Ramos, the on-duty officer asked. "You got any strawberry rhubarb today?" He patted his beer belly with anticipation.

"Two strawberry rhubarbs just for you, Jake," Trixie said, thumping down a box of Krispy Kreme donuts on his desk. "Anything happening?"

"If you call Maude Lassiter swatting Luke and putting him through the wall because he had a snootful at three this morning, then that's what's happening. We got him locked up in the back. Shoulda locked her up, but she skedaddled out the back. She'll come in around noon to bail him out and we'll give her our usual sermon and Luke will be good till next week. What's new with you? Any offers yet?"

"Close, Jake," Trixie lied, straight-faced. "Anything on the wires? What's going on in N'awlins?"

"Quiet, Trixie, real quiet."

"Shoot!" Trixie complained as she bit into her donut. She was nose deep in chocolate cream when the station doors flew open and four men barreled in, simultaneously talking and arguing.

"What are they all arguing about?" she asked, bending close to Jake's ear.

"Bob Henry's been accepted into the FBI, so that means his dog Flash is going up for adoption. Those four all want him. Flash is the best K-9 dog in the state of Louisiana. The department was planning on retiring him next month anyway, but with Bob going off to Quantico, they had to make the decision sooner than expected."

"He must be some dog."

"He's good in the field all right, but he doesn't have many

social skills. Truth to tell, I don't know why anyone would want him. From what I've seen he can be downright vicious."

Trixie gathered her thoughts and analyzed the situation. Chances were those men weren't looking for a pet. More than likely they'd turn him into a guard dog or hunting dog. They'd probably keep him chained outside. "How much?"

Jake looked up in surprise. "How much?"

"What are they selling him for, Jake?"

"He's not for sale, Trixie. We just want him to have a good home."

Trixie pointed a bony finger in the direction of the four very vocal men. "None of those bubbas will give him a good home, and we both know it. But I will. Our last dog died of old age a few years back, and we just never got around to getting another one. Flash is just the kind of dog Fred and I need. How much, Jake? Name your price."

Jake wiped the chocolate off his mouth with the back of his hand. "Trixie, the dog weighs more than you do. You and Fred would never be able to handle him. Flash is not a lap-dog. He's a legitimate police officer with his own badge. He's an expert at tracking criminals and sniffing out drugs and guns. Bob is the only one he listens to."

"Five hundred dollars!" Trixie said smartly.

"Sold!" Jake said, slamming his fist down on his desk. Chocolate cream splattered in every direction.

Trixie burst out laughing. Obviously her offer had excited him so much, he'd forgotten he was holding a cream-filled donut.

Jake stood up, his expression anything but amused as he wiped chocolate cream off his uniform. "You boys can stop your arguing. Flash has been adopted by Trixie here." There was a chorus of grumbling and complaining, which Jake brought to a quick end when he told them Trixie had agreed to pay five hundred dollars for the privilege of adopting Flash.

"The chief will skin me alive if this goes sour, Trixie. What that means is, you take him, he's yours. You can't give him back if it's too much for you."

"He won't be too much for me," she said with more confidence than she felt. He was just a dog, after all. The only thing she was really worried about was what Fred would say when she showed up with a K-9 police dog. Better not to think about that right now. "Where's the dog now?"

"They're bringing him to the station. How about some coffee? I made it myself right before you came in."

Trixie nodded as she contemplated what she was going to say to Fred. She accepted the coffee Jake offered and touched her lips to the rim and sipped.

"Just the way you like it, Trixie, four sugars and a dollop of cream."

She heard Flash before she saw him. And what she heard was enough to make her set her coffee cup down on the desk sergeant's desk, then scurry behind it.

"It's not too late to reconsider, Trixie," Jake said, giving her a sideways look.

"I can handle it, Jake. Let's just see what he does."

"Okay, but there's something I forgot to tell you. He only understands German commands. You might have to get one of those Berlitz tapes and take a crash course."

The door opened. Trixie shrank into herself as she stared at the most magnificent animal she'd ever seen.

"He's a Belgian Malinois," Jake informed her. "Born and bred in Holland before coming to Louisiana. He weighs a hundred and ten pounds."

The dog strained at the leash being held by two patrol officers. A third officer entered the station with two cardboard cartons on a dolly. "This is his gear, Sarge."

"His gear?" Trixie squeaked.

"Yeah, his gear," Jake said. "Bulletproof vest, special leashes, special food, special vitamins, some toys, his toothbrush, hairbrush, nail clippers, eyedrops, his badge, and a bunch of other stuff. He has a bed, blanket, and special towels. You know, Trixie, gear."

The dog started to whine even as he continued to strain at his leash.

Trixie was no dog expert, but Flash did not look like a happy dog. "What's wrong with him? He seems agitated."

"He's been locked up ever since Bob left. I imagine he's feeling abandoned. Bob was the only one Flash bonded with. And he's probably bored. He likes patrol work, loves the siren and all the excitement. I imagine he doesn't know what to think or feel right now."

"I see," Trixie said, studying the dog from a distance.

"By the way, Trixie, Bob said he doesn't like women. Guess I should have told you that straight out, but I forgot until just now."

Trixie's eyebrow peaked. "Are you going to tell me why, Jake?"

"Some whacko broad took a blowtorch to him. Good thing he was wearing his vest. Aside from a little scorched fur, he was fine. You need to start thinking about taking him home, Trixie."

"I'm thinking, I'm thinking," she muttered. She'd never been afraid of anything in her life and she wasn't about to let a dog scare the hell out of her, even if he was a hundred ten pounds and looked like a timber wolf.

Fred had once accused her of being nastier than cat shit. Maybe this was one of those times when being mean and nasty would do more good than harm. With a calm she was far from feeling, she looked at each of the officers. "Let him go."

"This is not by the book, Trixie."

"You got that right, Jake, but that's the way it's got to be. I'm going to sit down here on the bench, and I'm not going to move. Let's just see what happens."

"Let him go," Jake said.

A moment later the huge dog raced around the room, going from person to person, sniffing. Waiting her turn, Trixie bit down on her lower lip. Suddenly the dog's tail settled between his legs and his ears flattened against his head. He charged toward her and skidded to a stop in front of her. Trixie didn't blink. "I don't have a blowtorch, Flash," she said in a low voice. "I don't have anything in my hands." She turned her hands over for him to see. "Yeah, you're almost as big as I am, and you sure as hell weigh more than I do, but I'm not afraid of you," she said, smiling. She watched as the big dog cocked his head, listening. Still, his tail remained between his legs, and his ears stayed flat against his head.

"I need a few minutes alone with him. Everybody take a hike and give me five."

"Are you sure, Trixie?" Jake looked worried.

"Outta here, all of you," she ordered. Once they were gone she looked Flash in the eye. "I'm sorry you lost your handler, but you have to get on with your life. I can give you a wonderful home with a big backyard with lots of trees to lift your leg on and a nice patio to sun yourself on in the summer. Fred and me, we'll take good care of you, and we'll love you the way you deserve to be loved. And you've got my word that I won't give you that food that looks like rabbit poop. But right now you need to know who's the boss. It's me, big boy. Trixie. I'm in charge," she whispered.

The dog inched closer, his fangs bared. She could tell he wasn't buying any of her little speech and that he was probably planning on sinking his teeth into her at the very least. Thinking quickly, she slid off the bench and got down on her hands and knees so she would be eye level with the huge Malinois. She was so close she could smell his breath. Mint. Probably his doggy toothpaste. His head moved imperceptibly, at which point Trixie moved her head and simultaneously clicked her dentures together. "So there!" she said, then worked her dentures back into place with her tongue. "You bite, I bite back. You got that? You wouldn't like me, I'm old and stringy, not good chewing material." The Malinois made a noise that was somewhere between a whine and a whimper. "Now come here, you big *wuss,* and let Trixie give you some loving." She reached out and scratched him behind his ears, which were by then standing at attention. He leaned toward her and licked her face. "Good boy, Flash," she said, letting him lick her again. "What do you say we bug out of this place and head for Burger King? Three Whoppers coming up! Fetch your leash. We can't go out in public without it. You could give someone a heart attack." She stood up. "We're leaving, Jake!"

Jake and several other officers came out of the back. Their worried expressions turned to amazement when they saw Flash sitting in front of Trixie with his leash in his mouth.

Trixie winked and grinned as she fastened the leash onto Flash's collar. "I think he already loves me. How about bringing all his gear out to the truck? I'll send you a check tonight, okay?"

"Sure," Jake said. His eyes narrowed when he looked at Trixie. "One of these days you're going to tell me what you did, aren't you?"

"I didn't do anything but talk to him." She patted Flash's head. "I think this is going to work out just fine. I like this dog. I mean I really like him. I bet you five bucks in two weeks time he'll forget all about Bob Henry."

"That's a sucker bet."

Trixie started for the door. "You guys need to get some air

fresheners for the station. It stinks in there. How many times do I have to tell you that? Some days I hate coming here."

Jake rolled his eyes as he wheeled the dolly out to Trixie's truck. As soon as he'd loaded the boxes up, Flash jumped in and immediately started pawing through his stuff.

"Are you sure I have everything?"

"It's all there. Bob packed it up himself. His new address and phone number are on the booklet. He wants you to call him to let you know how Flash is doing. Will you do that, Trixie?"

"You bet. See ya, Jake."

All the way home, Trixie kept one eye on the road and the other on the big dog in the back. Flash didn't seem to care one way or another when she pulled up to the drive-through window of Burger King. He was much more interested in what was in the boxes than what was going on outside the windows. Even when the clerk handed over the bag of burgers, he made no move to check it out.

"I'll park, and you can eat," Trixie told him as she wheeled the car into a parking space. "I know this is all strange to you, but Fred and I will give you a really good life. I lied when I told Jake that our last dog died of old age. The truth is we never had any animals because we traveled so much. But we've always wanted one. We adore Olive. She's a springer spaniel. I'll bet you'll like her, too." She took the paper off the first burger. "Look, here's a Whopper without all that junk, just good old ground beef." Flash only looked at her. "No, huh?" She shrugged. "Okay, maybe later. Let's go home so you can meet Fred." When he still didn't move, Trixie got out of the car, walked around to the back, opened the tailgate, and climbed in next to him. Tears blurred her eyes as she stroked his massive head. "It's going to be all right, Flash. That's a promise." She continued to croon to the dog, then cupped his snout in her hands and planted a kiss on his nose. "I know just how you feel, big guy. How about I turn on the radio and we listen to Dr. Jane Lewis dispense her invaluable advice?"

Trixie locked the tailgate and stood staring at the dog through the tinted windows. A lump formed in her throat. Had she made a mistake taking on the police dog? Would Fred be upset with her? Yes, but only for a minute. Then he would fall in love with Flash and fret over him the way she was doing now. Together they'd work it out. They always had.

4

Jane groaned as she rolled over and crunched her face into the soft down pillow. Every bone and muscle in her body ached from her run the previous day. She moaned again, knowing she had to wake up. Something exciting was supposed to happen today. What was it? She tried to home in on it as she burrowed deeper into the bedclothes. Whatever it was, it could wait, she thought a moment later. She needed to sleep some more. Besides, it wasn't even light out yet. No one in her right mind got up when it was still dark, especially on a Saturday morning.

She moved her leg sideways under the covers, searching for Olive. There she was, in her usual position, sleeping soundly. One more reason not to get up. Sighing with satisfaction, she rolled onto her side, raised her knees, and heard a yelp followed by a loud thump.

Jane sat bolt upright, thinking she'd pushed Olive off the bed. "Oh, Ollie, I'm—" Olive sat up and looked at her. "I thought—What—?" Her eyebrows arched as she peeked over the side of the bed. Nothing. She threw the covers back, swung her legs over the side, and . . . felt a furry body beneath her feet.

She let out a strangled sound as she hopped across whatever it was.

"What's your hurry, Miss Jane?" an amused voice asked.

Jane whirled around to see the same young boy she'd seen in her last dream sitting in her rocking chair. "I— You— What the hell did I step on?"

"It was Jeeter. You pushed him off the bed."

Jane looked down but didn't see the dog. She rubbed her eyes and yawned. "I hope I didn't hurt him," she said, heading back to bed.

"What are you doing?"

"What's it look like I'm doing? I'm going back to bed. It isn't time to wake up."

The boy jumped out of the chair and blocked her path. *"You can't go back to bed. You've got company coming."*

"Beat it, will you? I'm tired. I've had a rough week, and I need all the sleep I can get. *Dreamless* sleep, if you don't mind."

"This is not a dream. Jeeter and me—we're spirits," the boy said, wrinkling his face into a grimace at the word *spirit.*

"I know, and I'm Madonna. Outta here!" She dodged to the right and went around him.

"If you go back to sleep, you will *dream,"* he warned. *"You'll dream about all the old stuff. It's been bothering you a lot lately. I wish you wouldn't worry so much, Miss Jane."*

She stopped short of the bed and looked over her shoulder. "Who says I'm worried?"

"You worry about everything. You have to stop. You're taking the joy out of living. If you want me to be specific, you worry about Connie Bryan and Todd Prentice. And you worry about Mrs. Ramsey."

Jane raked her hands through her frizzy hair. "How do you know that?" she asked, her voice ringing with a desperation she didn't like.

"I know all kinds of things." He looked toward the door leading to the hall. *"Your doorbell is going to ring in a couple of minutes. You better get dressed."*

Jane sat down on the edge of the bed and covered her face with her hands. These dreams of hers were starting to take a toll on her. Where most people could get along with eight hours of sleep, Jane needed a minimum of nine. Any less and she was a grouchy grump the rest of the day.

The doorbell rang. The opening notes of "Take Me Out to the Ball Game" pealed through the house. Why she'd bought a doorbell that played thirteen different tunes instead of the old-fashioned dingdong was a mystery. She must have been having one of those nuttier days when she ordered it from the one-of-a-kind catalog.

Jane snorted as she pulled on her old bathrobe. Who would be ringing her doorbell at—she glanced at the clock—6:45 on a Saturday morning? She hoped whoever it was had a good excuse, or they would be the recipient of her early-morning wrath. "Come on, Olive." She snatched a flowered headband off the dresser, skinned back her curly hair, and ran downstairs as fast as her still-sore legs would carry her.

The doorbell rang again.

"All right already. I'm coming," she yelled. Didn't the boy in her dream just get through telling her that the doorbell was going to ring?

She skidded across the foyer to the front door and fumbled with the dead bolt. "Whoever's there, you got a helluva lot of nerve coming here at this hour!" She bared her teeth and pulled the door open, ready to do battle with the rude intruder.

"Jane. Did I wake you up? I'm sorry," Mike said, a grin plastered from one ear to the other.

"Mike? Sorenson? It's still dark outside. Aren't you early?"

"You're not a morning person, I take it," he said, a be-mused smile lifting one side of his mouth. He pulled back the screen door and stepped inside.

"No, I'm not a morning person," Jane shot back as she eyed her handsome colleague. He was wearing khaki cargo pants and a pale yellow Polo T-shirt. His clothes had been *ironed*. She could see the creases in his pants and on the sleeves of his shirt. His Docksiders were worn in and comfortable-looking. "What's that smell?" she asked, twitching her nose. "Alpine something, right?"

"Christmas gift from my mother. Look, I brought break-fast." He held up a white bakery bag. "Fresh *beignets*, juice, and coffee."

"I thought we were going to have a picnic brunch around ten or so?"

"We were, but ever since I left here I've thought about nothing except what happened at the well, and I couldn't wait to get back. I hope you don't mind. . . ."

Jane threw her hands up in the air. "No! No problem. C'mon, let's eat," she said, turning and heading for the kitchen. "Since you brought breakfast, you should do the serving. I think you should know I like my juice in a fragile wineglass and my coffee in bone china and my *beignets* on a matching plate. Paper napkins will do nicely. Everything is in the cabinet over the sink."

"Bossy, aren't you?"

Jane grimaced. She didn't bother to respond. "It's not even seven o'clock yet, Mike. You woke me up out of a sound sleep. What do you expect, full makeup and ironed linen?" Miss Congeniality she wasn't. He was seeing her at her ab-solute worst. If he could put up with her until she had her coffee and turned into a human being, it would be a miracle. It would also tell what kind of man he was.

"I really am sorry, Jane. I should have called. For some reason I thought you were an early riser." He followed her into the kitchen and pulled out a chair for her. "You just sit down, and I'll take care of everything."

Jane marveled at how efficient he was, even in a kitchen he didn't know.

Momentarily, he sat down across from her. "I hate eating breakfast alone. How about you?"

Jane shrugged. "I'm not much on breakfast actually. Pop-Tarts on the run most of the time. An apple in the car. That kind of thing. So, what do you want to do today? After I turn into a human being that is," she asked, sipping her coffee.

"I'd like to explore the property and the entire house. Did the Larouxs leave anything behind? People usually do if they consider it junk. When I was here with the realtor, he showed me the attic. I remember there was all kinds of stuff, old clothes, toys, boxes . . ."

"It's all still up there. I've never gone through it, but it's been on my 'to do' list. I guess today is as good a time as any to get it cleaned out. I'll take some trash bags up there with us. Are we going to have time to talk about my patient?"

"Sure," Mike said. "Anytime you want."

"How's your battery guy doing?"

His face split into a wide grin. "He called last night to tell me he's ordering a case of those big D batteries. I asked him why, and he said he liked the curly wire on the top and you can never have enough batteries. By the way, Duracell went up two points. He faxed me a printout."

"It doesn't sound to me like he's unhappy with his life," Jane observed, sipping her coffee from the delicate cup.

"As far as I can tell, he isn't the least bit unhappy. He's just obsessed, and he wants to overcome the obsession. If the rest of my patients were as happy as he is, I'd be delighted."

"And out of a job," she added.

"Well, that's true. But you know, other than him, I don't know anyone who is truly happy. Everyone I know who got married right after college is either already divorced or headed for the divorce court. No one wants to work at marriage anymore. When I was a college student, I decided I wanted to settle into a career before getting married, and I stuck to it. Now I know exactly what kind of woman I want. How about you, Jane?"

"I— How about me?" she stuttered, wondering what kind of woman he was talking about. "I wanted a career first, too." Tomorrow she was going to run ten miles even if she got shin splints all the way up to her neck. "As for the kind of man I want . . . I don't know. I've been so busy I haven't thought about it. I have a very full and rewarding life."

He regarded her with a knowing look. "That's what everyone says when they don't have anyone in their life. I say it, too." His expression lightened. "So, what do you think of my breakfast?" he asked, changing topics.

"For takeout, it ain't bad," Jane said, finishing off the last of her *beignet*.

Mike leaned back against his chair. "Tell you what, I'll clean up here while you shower and dress. Do you wash these cups and glasses by hand or put them in the dishwasher?" He sat forward and rested his arms on the table. "Did you really have a crush on me way back when?"

Jane almost choked on her coffee. "Do you always speak so erratically? It makes it hard to keep up." His eyes flickered with amusement. She put her cup down. "First of all, yes, you need to wash them by hand. Second, no, I do not have a dishwasher. And third, yes, I was joking about having a crush on you. I just said that to flatter your ego." Jane pushed her chair back and got up. On her way out of the kitchen, she said, "By the way, I picked something up for you yesterday. It's T. F. Dingle's new book. It's on the foyer table."

"No kidding! I didn't know the new one was out. Thanks, Jane. I could kiss you for that."

She grabbed on to the doorjamb and looked over her shoulder. "So what's stopping you?"

His coffee cup stopped midway to his mouth. "Huh?"

Jane had meant for her answer to be taken in the same vein as his offer, but she could see by his expression that she'd caught him off guard. All she could do now was brazen it out and hope for the best. "You said you could kiss me for getting you the book. And I said, 'what's stopping you?'"

"You want me to kiss you?"

"Forget I said anything," she said, shooting him a withering look. "The moment is gone, and now you can just kiss my ass, you . . . you shrink!" Jane snarled as she flounced away from him.

Mike stood up and started after her only to have Olive come from out of nowhere and latch on to his pant leg.

"Call her off, Jane!"

"She'll let go when she's sure you don't intend me any harm. I wouldn't move if I were you. I'll be down in an hour or so."

"An hour! C'mon, Jane, give me a break!" Mike bellowed. When there was no response other than Jane's laughter, Mike sat back down in his chair. Olive let go of his pant leg and sat down and stared at him.

"It's good that she's got you for protection, Olive. I'll bet she pisses a lot of people off. Tell me, is she hell on wheels to live with?"

Olive cocked her head to the side and made a noise that was somewhere between a growl and a whine. To Mike it sounded like a definite yes.

"I think I might have ticked her off, but I thought she was joking. Hell, I would love to have kissed her. She even had sugar on her lips. Mighty tasty, I'd say," he said, licking his lips for Olive's benefit. "Maybe I'll give it a try later on." Olive cocked her head to the other side. "You know what I like about her? She's one of those what-you-see-is-what-you-get kind of people. Nothing phony or pretentious about Jane. I wonder if she really did have a crush on me. Stop staring at me for God's sake! I'm not going anywhere."

A half hour later, Jane found Mike still in the kitchen where she'd left him, with Olive at his feet, watching his every move.

"Okay, Olive, good girl. Shake hands and make nice." The dog obediently held out one long-haired paw. Mike reached for it and shook it manfully. "Olive, show Dr. Sorenson there are no hard feelings on your part. Do it like a lady now." She grinned when the spaniel stood up on her hind legs, put her paws on Mike's knees, and lightly licked his chin. "Ah, that's my good girl," Jane crooned. "Now you need to do your part, Mike. She's waiting for you to kiss her."

Mike slowly shook his head. "No. I am not—I repeat—I am *not* kissing the dog."

Jane shrugged. "Okay, fine, but if you don't, she won't let you get up. You can try if you want." Her pigtail swinging, Jane turned to leave the kitchen. "While you're deciding, I'll just mosey up to the attic and start throwing things out." For emphasis, she shook the trash bag she'd gotten out of the hall closet.

Mike rolled his eyes. "Okay, okay, I'll do it. Pucker up, Olive." He bypassed her wet nose and kissed her forehead instead.

"I taught her that," Jane said with pride, as Olive bounded out of the kitchen.

Mike's face was an unflattering shade of red. "You better not plan on telling any of our colleagues what I just did, Jane Lewis."

"It's on the top of my agenda to tell everyone at the psychiatry convention in New York later this year," Jane giggled. "Love is a many-splendored thing, you know. Animals, especially dogs and cats, love unconditionally. It didn't hurt you to do that, and it made Olive feel good. Let's just forget it, okay?" Jane turned and started for the stairs.

"On one condition," Mike said behind her.

Reaching the top step, Jane turned to confront Mike. "I don't think you're in much of a position to lay down conditions, but what is it?"

His gaze was riveted on her face. "That you tell me the truth. Did you or did you not have a crush on me back in high school?"

Jane laughed out loud. "I think I might have been smitten for a day or two. Then again, it was a long time ago, and it could have been Hughey Monroe."

"For a day or two?" His voice rose. "What the hell kind of impression did I make?"

"Actually, you were rather disgusting back then as I recall," she said, enjoying the gentle sparring as much as he did. "That's why it only lasted a day or two."

"Disgusting how?"

"Stuck-up. Full of yourself. I suppose you had good reason. Every single girl in my class would have prostituted herself for a smile from you."

"Except you, right?"

"Except me," Jane lied. She opened the attic door. "Here we are. Are you sure you want to go through all this old junk?"

"Sure I'm sure."

She flicked on the light and led the way up a steep, narrow flight of stairs. "I haven't been up here since just after I moved in." The steps creaked under her weight. "I hope there aren't any mice up here. I don't like mice."

The attic smelled of dust and decay. There were stacks of old books everywhere. A tattered dress form stood off in one corner, looking lost and forlorn. Wooden crates and hump-backed trunks lined the wall beneath the one window—a round, stained-glass window. She looked at the garbage bag in her hand and laughed. One bag wouldn't even make a dent.

Mike reached the top seconds after her. "Wow! This is great. I can't believe you haven't been up here looking through all this stuff."

Jane sighed. "I told you I've been busy." She walked toward the window. "Since I don't know exactly what it is you're looking for, I don't know where you want to start."

"I don't know myself," he said, gravitating toward the trunks. "An old Bible, maybe. In the old days, they used to list the births and deaths in the front of the Bible. You did say the family died off, didn't you?"

"So I've been told."

Jane busied herself going through a trunk of old clothes. They'd been carefully wrapped in an old quilt to keep the dust off them. She found a two-piece dress of a heavy, black material, the bodice decorated with jet beads. She recognized the style as Victorian, around 1885, if she wasn't mistaken. And in mint condition. Not something she should be throwing away. Maybe at some point in time she could donate them to a museum or historical group.

Three hours later, Mike whooped with pleasure. "I found one. Wouldn't you know it would be at the very bottom of the last trunk?"

Jane smiled at his excitement. When was the last time she had whooped with laughter? Probably not since she was a kid, if then. Maybe she should do a little whooping of her own just to show him she wasn't an old fuddy-duddy.

Mike took the Bible to the window. "I think this might be it, but the ink is so faded I can barely make it out. Did you say the boy who fell into the well was fifteen or so?"

"Uh-huh."

"It looks like a capital B for the first name and a capital J for the last name. I guess the writer dipped the quill in the ink for each name, and it came out thick for the first letter."

Jane put the dress back into the trunk, covered it up, then walked over to the window. "Could it be Billy Jensen?" The hairs on her arms stood upright.

"Yeah, yeah, I think that's it," Mike said, peering down at the page. "No, I'm sure that's it. How'd you know?" he asked, looking up at her.

"I've had a couple of dreams . . . At least I thought they were dreams," she said, rubbing her hand across her cheek. "A boy—A boy about fifteen was in both of them. He told me his name was Billy Jensen and that he was a ghost." She waved her hand in dismissal. "That's silly. I think you might have planted the whole ghost idea in my head the other day when you were here."

Mike's left eyebrow rose a fraction. "Maybe. You said there was a dog, too."

Jane stared blankly across the room. "Jeeter," she blurted. "The dog's name was Jeeter. He was a mutt." She glanced at Mike and saw that he had been studying her.

"I'm through here," Mike said a moment later. "Let's take the Bible downstairs. Do you have a magnifying glass?"

Jane nodded.

"I know you don't want to believe it, but I think we

tapped into something. I could just kiss you for allowing me to come up here. This is like Christmas morning when I was a kid. Maybe better."

Jane ignored him and started for the steps.

"Not so fast, Dr. Lewis!" Mike grabbed her, turned her around, and gathered her in his arms.

With cobwebs tickling her face, he kissed her like she'd never been kissed in her life. Long-dormant feelings sprang to life, electrifying her. She felt her knees weaken as his tongue explored her mouth.

"Whoa," Mike said, breaking away to stare into her eyes. "I had no idea."

"No idea of what?" she asked, pulling a deep breath.

"That you would— That you—" He crushed her to him and pressed his mouth to hers.

It was Jane who pulled back the second time, not because she wanted to but because she heard scratching in the corner. "I think we better go downstairs," she said, peeking around Mike's shoulder.

"Not until you answer a question for me. Did you hear bells and whistles?"

"No. But I did hear that." She raised her hand and pointed off to the right, where a little gray mouse was scratching near one of the trunks.

He turned his head to look, then turned back. "No bells and no whistles, huh?"

"Maybe next time." Jane giggled as she made her way down the stairs. "You can wash up in the guest bathroom off the foyer. I'll meet you downstairs. Would you like some sweet tea?"

"I'd love some."

"Good." Jane smiled as she hurried off to her bedroom to collect herself and freshen up. It would take more than splashing cold water on her face to put out the fire Mike had just ignited. She touched her finger to her lips and clung to the memory of his kiss. In all her life, she'd never dreamed a kiss—a simple kiss—could stir such passion. She could hardly wait to tell Trixie about it. Once she got the sound of the bells and whistles out of her ears, that is.

Jane finished fixing the sweet tea just as Mike walked into the kitchen. The moment she saw his face, she knew things had changed between them. The I-don't-care, easy camaraderie was gone now. Mike was looking at her like he'd never seen her before. A slow rush of heat circled around her belly and worked its way upward. She knew her face was rosy pink. God, had she *ever* blushed in her life? Not that she could remember.

"Front porch or back porch? I have some lawn chairs in the garage if you want to get them. They're right next to the door."

"The steps are fine. We can lean against the posts. We can drink our tea and talk about your patient now if you like. Or . . . We could talk about what happened upstairs. I'd like to know more about you. Your adolescence. Your college years. You know, the usual stuff."

"I thought you wanted to have a closer look at the Bible." She pulled a magnifying glass out of the kitchen drawer.

"I'm in no hurry. It's only ten o'clock. We've got all day, don't we?"

All day. Oh, God, she thought. *Will there be more stolen kisses? Will we end up in bed together?* "If I tell you all that stuff, then you'll start analyzing me. I know how that goes."

"I wouldn't think of it." He sipped his tea. "I like sweet tea. Westerners don't know how to make it. In fact, I don't even think they know what it is. They just drink iced tea and put their own sweetener in. This is just right. My mother makes sweet tea like this. Do you hear how I'm babbling? That's because of that kiss. And if you don't stop looking at me like that, I'm going to kiss you again and nothing, not even a herd of scratching mice, will make me let you go."

"There's no such thing as a *herd* of mice," she said, putting the magnifying glass into his pocket. "C'mon, let's go outside where it's cooler."

Once they were comfortably seated on the top step, Jane started to talk. "My childhood wasn't that great. The truth is, it pretty much sucked. My mother wanted a pretty little girl she could dress in ribbons and frills and show off to her friends. Instead she got me and hid me as much as she could. I was a very great disappointment to her. I remember trying to please her until I was around ten or so, then I just gave up. I don't think she even noticed. She was a beauty pageant queen—Miss Louisiana. She was also Miss Rice Queen Festival, Miss Frog Queen Festival, Miss Camellia Queen Festival, and Miss Crawfish Queen Festival. Hell, she was the queen of every festival we have around here, and you know how we love our festivals. She never let anyone forget it either.

"Now my dad, he was wonderful. He did the best he could, but a girl needs a mother. I was fat, homely, mouthy, and wore thick glasses. My dad loved me in spite of it all. So did my godparents, who were my father's best friends. They stepped in. But, you always want what you can't have. And I wanted my mother. She had this incredible ability to make me feel guilty with just a look. Like it was my fault I was so plain, so this or so that. Guilt is a terrible thing, Mike. Believe me, I know from experience. Lots of experience."

"Yes it is," Mike said, taking her hand. "But look at what you've become. I bet if your mother were here now, she'd be so proud of you she'd be chomping at the bit to show you off."

Jane shook her head. "No. The only thing that mattered to her was physical beauty. After her funeral, I had to clear out her things. She had boxes and boxes of makeup and perfume. She had stuff I didn't even know was on the market. I got this old barrel out of the shed, poured in some kerosene, and burned it all up. Then I did the same thing with all her designer clothes and fancy handbags and expensive shoes. I thought if I did all that, I wouldn't feel that awful, gut-wrenching guilt anymore. It didn't work. If anything, I made it worse.

"I remember my mother asking my father once how it was possible for a beauty queen to have an ugly duckling for a daughter, and he said his side of the family was full of ugly ducklings, himself included. She never forgave him for that. When I was nine or so, I overheard Daddy tell my mother that he wanted another child. She said no because she didn't want to take the chance of another child turning out like me. I don't think my parents ever had sex again after that, which explains why my dad had so many affairs."

Mike squeezed her hand. "Sounds like a rough childhood. Is that why you decided to become a psychiatrist?"

A warning bell sounded in Jane's head. If she wasn't careful, she would end up telling him the *real* reason she had become a psychiatrist. She wasn't sure she was ready to do that. They hardly knew each other. But on the other hand, maybe it would help to tell him. The only other people who knew were Trixie and Fred, and while they'd always been sympathetic, they didn't really understand the guilt that continued to plague her. But Mike would.

"My mother might have been one reason, a small one. How about you?" she asked, mentally running away.

"I didn't wake up one morning and say, hey, I want to be a shrink. It just more or less evolved. I think I was meant to do what I do. The mind is just so tricky. I found myself fascinated with why people do what they do and what leads them to make the decisions they make. Like my battery guy. I know he's obsessed, but I don't know why he's obsessed. I'll figure it out one of these days, and hopefully I'll be able to help him get over it. It's there, I'm just not picking up on it. What would be your guess?"

Jane thought a moment. "Obsessions come from so many things. Maybe his parents gave him a battery-operated toy and forgot to give him the batteries. Or maybe the toy made too much noise, and his parents threw away the batteries. I don't know. Did you try hypnosis?"

"Not yet, but I've been thinking about it."

"It'll probably come out under hypnosis."

"Yeah, probably."

"Can I throw out a hypothetical at you, Mike?"

"Shoot," he said with a shrug.

"If you were married or engaged to be married and your wife or fiancée was raped, would you be able to handle it or would you turn away from her?"

He sucked in his lower lip and stared out at the street. "I don't honestly know, Jane. I'd like to think I would be there for her and that I could work through it, but since it's never happened to me, I can't give you a cut-and-dried answer."

Jane steepled her hands and touched her chin. "Okay, let's try a different approach. If the woman you loved was raped, would you feel like she was sullied, dirty?"

"I don't think so. Maybe because of my training. I don't know. I know a lot of relationships end because the man can't deal with it for one reason or another. I remember this one asshole who thought his wife actually encouraged the rape. Mind you, she had been stabbed, too. Like she would really encourage *that*."

"Since you've dealt with it, what's the mind-set, Mike? Try to pin it down for me, will you?" She didn't realize she was digging her nails into his arm until he put his other hand on top of hers.

"Hey, take it easy, Jane, and tell me the truth. Are you talking about your patient or about you?"

"All of the above and before you can ask, no, I was never raped, but a friend of mine was."

"A close friend?" When she shook her head, he went on to the next question. "Married or soon to be married?"

"Soon to be married. She was afraid to tell her fiancé because she was sure he would break off the engagement. I tried to convince her that he wouldn't do that, but now I know I was probably wrong. I don't think most men can deal with rape."

"When and where did it happen?"

"On the campus of LSU, the night before the last finals. There were five guys. Three of them raped her."

"You were there?"

She nodded. The memories of that night had never faded. Each and every detail was crystal-clear—except for their faces. "Yes, I was there. I tried to help her, but they held me down and kept me quiet. They didn't rape me if that was your next question. I was too fat and ugly. Miss Piggy, one of them called me." She paused to get a second wind. It had been a long time since she'd told her story, and yet it hurt her as much now as it had way back then. "I was finally able to get out a scream, and it scared them all away."

"Was your friend badly injured?"

Jane heaved a huge sigh. "No, not that she would admit anyway. I tried to get her to go for help, to the police, the hospital or the crisis center, but she wouldn't do it. She insisted I take her back to the dorm. Once we got there, she said she felt dirty and wanted to take a shower. I saw her ugly bruises. She was battered from head to toe. I could only imagine what she'd been through."

"I'm sure you did all you could. There's only so much you can do. In the end a person has to make up her own mind. You know that."

"I don't know that, Mike," she said, casting her eyes downward. "She was in no mental condition to make rational decisions. I was, so I should have been more persistent and got her the help she needed. Instead, I let her swear me to silence, and I've regretted it every day of my life since. She killed herself two days before graduation."

"Christ." Mike closed his eyes and raked his fingers through his hair. "I'm sorry, Jane."

"I've always wondered if she took my advice and told her fiancé after all. He sure as hell didn't mourn long. He got married a year later, a real trophy wife. They have three kids—the kids Connie had dreamed about having. After I found out what she'd done, I considered telling her parents what happened. I thought they had a right to know. I never did, just like I never took her bag of discarded clothing to the authorities like I swore I would. I thought it would help find the rapists, that the semen would still be on the clothes. A day doesn't go by that I don't think about what I didn't do. Then this jackass patient of mine comes along and starts complaining about his wife being raped. It all came back front and center. The guilt is wearing me down."

"That's a hell of a load of guilt to be packing around all this time. You didn't do anything wrong, Jane. Can't you see that?"

"No, Mike, I should have tried harder. She was such a beautiful girl, so warm and friendly. My mother would have loved having her for a daughter. Connie said her mother was writing out the wedding invitations that very night."

"You have to stop blaming yourself," Mike said, putting his arm around her back and pulling her toward him.

"Easier said than done. I should have gone to Slidell to see her parents. Do you know why I think I didn't go?" Jane said, enunciating each word carefully. "Because I didn't want anyone to know why those boys didn't rape me, too." She looked him straight in the eye. "God, I finally said it out loud." She breathed a sigh of relief. "Maybe you'd better go now. That's enough confessing for one day," Jane said, her voice edgy.

"Go? Go where?"

"Don't you want to leave? I just . . . literally bared my soul. I confessed my horrible, ugly secret so you must be . . . what's the word, *disgusted*?"

He looked at her like she'd just sprouted a second head. "I'm not disgusted, and I do not want to leave. I'd like to help you work through your pain and guilt. I think you should visit your friend's parents like you had always intended to. Give them the bag of clothing and let them decide what to do with it. It's not your decision, Jane. You might even want to talk to the ex-fiancé. I'll go with you if you like. I think it would do you a world of good."

"You know what's funny? He singled me out at an alumni fund-raiser. We had never met before. I only knew him by reputation. He was the star quarterback on the football team. Yet he came over and started up a conversation with me."

"So, why do you suppose he did that?"

"I wish I knew."

Mike upended his glass. "Tea's all gone. Let's change the subject and talk about what happened between us in the attic." His expression dared her to object.

Jane had to admit that she felt better for having told him about Connie. She was far from over it, but now she realized there was hope. She mentally shook herself and put a smile on her face. "Okay. You first."

"You have to admit what we shared was more than just a kiss. It was . . ."

"Spectacular," she supplied for him.

"Right. Spectacular," he agreed.

Was it her imagination, or was the sun suddenly brighter and warmer? She snuggled into the crook of his arm and rested her head on his shoulder. "Are you going to break my heart, Mike Sorenson?"

"Not on your life, lady."

"I should be heading home," Mike said a long time later. They'd spent the rest of the day going through the house room by room and exploring the grounds. "It's a long drive to Lafayette." He looked at the grandfather clock in the parlor.

"So it is. Twelve miles with no stoplights and next to no traffic is an awful lot at this time of night."

"Yeah. Uh-huh."

"Are you hinting that you'd like to stay the night?"

The clock chimed midnight.

"I could sleep on the sofa," he said hopefully.

"The sofa's good. Comfortable, too. I have Frette sheets. Trixie got them for me. Soft as silk. Actually, they're better than silk. I have blankets, too, and extra pillows." She put her index finger to her chin. "But you don't have any clean clothes for the morning, or a toothbrush and shaving gear," Jane said with wicked delight.

"How about you loan me a pair of old sweats and one of those unisex Gap or Old Navy T-shirts? You must have an extra toothbrush, and I know you shave your legs. I could borrow your razor. That would work for me."

"What about underwear?"

"Not a problem," he said with confidence. "I'll do what all us guys did in college, turn them inside out. We did that because none of us were good at washing clothes. We were also lazy. Everything I owned was pale blue because I washed my whites and my blue jeans together."

"Be honest. You don't have any intention of sleeping on my couch, do you?"

"Nope."

"We don't really know one another, Mike. What if we decide tomorrow that it was all a big mistake?"

"What-ifs are not in my vocabulary. That day I saw you in the restaurant with that floppsy-doodle hat I knew I wanted to make love to you. When you smiled at me, I felt this . . . this . . . hell, I don't know what it was, but it was *something*."

"I know. I felt it, too. And I have an admission to make. I did hear bells and whistles." She turned out the light, took his hand, and led him up the stairs.

5

〜

Jane threw her briefcase, purse, tennis shoes, and hat onto the backseat of her car, her nerves twanging with fear. She whistled sharply for Olive, who came on the run. "C'mon, c'mon, girl. Trixie said she needed us on the double. Let's get you buckled up, and we'll hit the road."

As soon as the engine kicked over, Jane slid the car into gear, careened around the corner, and raced down the road, going seventy-five and eighty all the way to the McGuire farm.

What could possibly be wrong? There had been tears in her godmother's voice when she'd called. "Come quick. I need you, Janie, girl," Trixie had blubbered. As far as Jane knew, Trixie didn't know what a teardrop was. She was the happiest, most contented person Jane had ever known. She was also tough as nails and full of spit and vinegar. *Fred. Something must have happened to Fred. Oh, God, please not Fred,* Jane prayed. Tough as Trixie was, she would fall apart without Fred.

Five minutes later, Jane slammed on the brakes and fishtailed to a stop in front of Trixie and Fred's house. "Hurry up, Olive. Good girl." Olive raced up to the front door, Jane right behind her. Jane opened the front door and saw Trixie sitting on the floor, a huge dog half on and half off her lap. Fred was hovering close by, his eyes moist.

"My God, what's wrong?" Jane asked, looking back and forth between them. She was relieved to see that they were both all right. "I got here as fast as I could. Where did that dog come from?"

Olive walked up to the huge Belgian Malinois, lay down in front of him, and looked him in the eye as if to introduce herself.

Tears dripped down Trixie's cheeks. "I never should have taken him," she bleated. "The vet just left. He checked him out and couldn't find anything physically wrong with him, but he won't eat, and he just lies here." She leaned over the dog and hugged him. "We've done everything we can think of to make him happy, but he misses his handler. I think his heart is broken."

Jane moved in for a closer look. "Where did you get him?"

Trixie looked up. There were dark circles under her eyes. "I brought him home from the police station. You should have seen him, Janie. He was one ferocious, kick-ass dog. He's a K-9 cop, with a real badge, a bulletproof vest, and everything. His handler was transferred, and the department needed to retire him, so they put him up for adoption. All those cops down there were salivating over him. I just couldn't let them take him and turn him into a guard dog or a hunting dog. I thought if I took him, Fred and I could give him a good life, a comfortable and easy life. But he's miserable, and I'm afraid if he doesn't snap out of it, he's going to die. I thought you, being a psychiatrist, might have some ideas."

Olive crawled forward and licked the big dog's face. Obviously, she knew something was wrong. She looked back at Jane, and her expression said, do something!

Jane dropped to her knees next to Trixie. "I don't know anything about how a dog's mind works, other than Olive's, and only then because I've raised her from a puppy. Did you call his old handler?"

Trixie nodded. "He said he probably misses working."

"Well, then, you have your answer. You have to get him back on a work schedule." Jane sat down and crossed her legs yoga-style. "Think about it, Trixie. What would you do if suddenly someone took away your computer and all your research books and said you were too old to write anymore? You'd go into a funk, too."

Fred sat down in a chair across from them. "I think she's right, Trixie."

Trixie appeared to give the suggestion some thought. "Okay, so let's say you are right, Janie. How am I going to get him working again? We're writers, not cops."

"Use your writer's imagination! What was he used to? Riding in a cop car with the siren blaring? Wearing his vest? Right? His handler probably wore a uniform and carried a gun. What I've heard about K-9s is that they're used to track down the bad guys and sniff out bombs and drugs. Hey, you have all kinds of acreage here," she said, extending her arms to illustrate. "You could, if you wanted, buy one of those rotating red lights they have at Radio Shack and a musical blow horn and ride over the acreage in hot pursuit of an imaginary something or other. Rent a cop costume. I know you and Fred have all kinds of guns. Strap one on, and you go, girl!"

"Do you think it would work, Janie, I mean really work?" Trixie asked.

"Yeah, Trix, I do. You could even go to the police impound lot and buy an old police car. If you don't take it on the road, I'll bet you could do whatever you wanted with it. I'll tell you what, I'll have my new office girl cancel all my appointments and run you down to the police station right now. Olive can stay here with— What's the dog's name?"

"Flash," Trixie said. "Let's *buy* a police car. He's too smart to fall for anything that isn't real."

"Let's do it then."

Trixie got up off the floor. "Fred, you're in charge. Get his gear out so he can see it and strap on one of your guns. As soon as I get back, we're going to work!"

Flash's head popped up as if sensing something was afoot. Olive barked.

At the police station, it took all of Trixie's persuasive powers to convince the desk sergeant that she meant business. In the end, and with a promise to pay for the entire Christmas and Fourth of July shindigs, Trixie had herself a fully equipped police car and two bags of marijuana that she planned to hide on her farm for Flash to find. Such mundane things as car title and insurance were to be discussed in the days to come. Trixie's promise not to take the police car on the road, once she got it home, clinched the deal. Toby Ellis donated one of his worn uniforms, while Chuck Trask handed over a pair of work boots.

Trixie and Jane walked side by side out of the police station. "What if it doesn't work, Janie?"

"I think it will, Trix, I really do."

"It's been less than two weeks and Fred and I have already fallen in love with that big lug of a dog," Trixie said, getting into the dilapidated police car. "I was afraid of him at first, you know. So was Fred. When he's on his feet, he's one awesome dog." When Jane turned to go to her own car, Trixie called her back. "Wait a sec, Janie, I've got a plan. I'll follow you home and park in the front so he doesn't see the car. Then I'll scoot upstairs and come down in full regalia. While I'm doing that, you go out into the field and bury one of those bags. I'll keep the other one in our safe. It's airtight, so hopefully he won't smell it. What time is it?"

"Two o'clock. Why?"

"Flash worked the three-to-eleven shift. He knows when it's three o'clock. I swear to God he does. We have a whole hour to get this show on the road. Burn rubber, Janie," Trixie said smartly as she turned on the ignition.

At precisely three o'clock, Trixie made her grand entrance into the living room. Fred's eyebrows shot up to his hairline. Jane gasped and Olive let loose with a series of high-pitched, excited yips.

Trixie, resplendent in her black oversize uniform, gun belt secure around her skinny waist, slapped her holster, and shouted, "On your feet, Officer Flash, it's time to go to work!" She minced her way around so Flash could see the shiny boots and black trouser legs. He reared up and barked. "I said, let's go, Officer Flash!"

Jane giggled as Flash, his legs weak and unsteady, made his way to the front door.

"Hold it! Hold it," Trixie shouted. "Full gear. That means the vest. Get over here!"

Fred clapped his hand over his mouth to stop his laughter as Trixie strapped Flash into his bulletproof vest.

"Somebody really needs to take a picture of this," Jane muttered, sotto voce.

Trixie opened the front door. Flash beelined for the police car. Olive stood on the threshold, whining.

Siren blasting, dome light flashing, Trixie pushed the pedal to the metal, careened around the corner, and sped down the dirt road through the open fields that surrounded the house. Twice, Fred and Jane heard the sound of gunshots.

"Dammit, I should have gone along," Fred grumbled. "She's having all the fun."

Jane put her arm around his waist and hugged him. "You can do it next time."

Fred hugged her back. "You're a damn good psychiatrist. I think you should expand your practice to include dogs."

"I don't think so." Jane giggled. On the other hand, if she had to deal with more Brian Ramseys, it was a definite possibility.

"In all the years I've known Trixie," Fred said, thoughtfully, "I never, ever saw her cry. She's been crying every single day since she brought Flash home. She even slept down here in the kitchen with him. She's been cradling that big head of his in her lap and singing to him. She cooked him steak, chicken, liver—everything—to try and tempt him into eating. She would have made a hell of a mother."

Jane looked askance at Fred and saw the love shining in his eyes. What she would give to know that kind of love just once in her life. "I know, Fred. I don't know what I would have done without the two of you. Everyone needs someone to love and have someone love them in return." They held each other a moment. "I think Flash is going to be just fine. I'm sure his problem was nothing more than separation anxiety. First his handler leaves him, then he was retired from the only life he'd ever known. I don't think you're going to need me anymore, and Olive looks like she's getting ready to pitch a fit, so I should head home."

"How's it going with your new fella?" Fred asked as he walked Jane to her car.

"It's going nicely. Actually, it couldn't be better. I really like him, and we have a lot in common: our work, mutual friends, old houses, etc." She flashed him a big smile. "He and Olive didn't get along at first, but they're doing much better now. You know how protective Olive is of me. The other day I asked him if he'd like to cohost the talk show with me, and he said he would, which means the station can expand to two days a week like they've been wanting to do. Mike and I aren't sure if we'll be alternating days or going with companion views like that couple who talk about money matters. It's up to the station manager to decide. I'm leaning toward the two of us on together. I think it would be thought-provoking. And, of course, there's the added advantage that I would get to see him more often. He's going to be sitting in on the show this coming week as my guest expert. I'll field him a couple of questions so the listeners get used to him."

"What about that patient you were telling Trixie and me about?"

"He canceled again last week. Said he had to go out of town. He has an appointment tomorrow, so we'll see. Don't worry about me, Fred. I can handle it."

"Next to Trixie, I love you more than anything on this earth, Janie. I don't want to see you spend even one minute of worry over someone like him."

"I'll let you know how it goes. Give Trixie a kiss for me." She opened the car door, and Olive jumped in. "By the way, how's the new book coming along?"

"I'm doing most of the writing for a change, but I don't mind. Trixie has been so wrapped up with Flash, she couldn't get her mind on murder and mayhem. I know what she would write anyway. Just takes a little more time. If it makes Trixie happy, it's okay with me."

Jane hugged him good-bye. Olive sat in the driver's seat and offered up her paw.

Fred took it and squeezed it. "Take care of her, Olive."

Trixie McGuire knelt in the brush, the Malinois at attention. His huge body quivered, and his nostrils flared with anticipation as he waited for Trixie's signal.

"Go, boy!"

Flash galloped across the field, covering more distance in a single stride than Trixie could cover in five. Then he stopped.

Winded, her gun at the ready, Trixie caught up to him,

dropped to a crouch and fired off a full round into the air. "Now this," she mumbled, "is definitely a Kodak moment."

While Flash sniffed around, she thought about the Bite Suit she would have to purchase and the police-dog training sessions she and Flash would have to participate in to keep up the charade. When in hell was she going to write? "I think I just retired," she mumbled again. She whistled sharply for the big dog, who came on the run.

"Did you find anything?" The dog started back to the car. "Guess not," she said to herself, following him. "We'll try another area. It's out here somewhere, boy."

Back in the car, Flash took his place in the backseat, panting from his exertions. His eyes were bright, and his ears stood tall. He was obviously in his element. Trixie smiled and turned on the siren and the flashing dome light. She drove the car back the way she'd come. Later, when she talked to Fred, she would swear to him that she heard Flash sigh with contentment. Suddenly, she slammed on the brakes and skidded around in a tight circle on two wheels. "I think I saw something, Flash!" As soon as she put the car into park, she pushed the remote control to open the back door, and the dog hit the ground running. Trixie left the siren on and the lights flashing as she rambled after the dog. She shoved a new clip into the gun and as before, fired off the entire round. She repeated the process one more time until she was too tired to continue. "It was dry tonight, baby. Maybe we'll have better luck tomorrow. If I'm still alive," she muttered under her breath. "C'mon, boy. Let's go home and tell Fred you're your old self. Is that goddaughter of mine smart or what?"

It was after midnight when Trixie popped two bottles of Sapparo beer and fired up a cigarette. Flash sat between her and Fred on the sofa, something he hadn't done before. Fred fed him a few pretzels while Trixie expressed her thoughts.

"I've been thinking, Fred. We're getting up in years, and God knows we've got more money than we know what to do with. I think I want to go into semiretirement. I had more fun today than I've had in a long time, and now that I've had a taste, I want more. I want to spend good quality time with Flash and enjoy him."

"Give up writing, Trix? You got to be kidding. It's all you know. All either one of us knows."

Trixie had prepared herself for every possible response. "That's because we haven't taken the time to do anything else. We've let our editor push us into doing one book after another. After we had a couple of best-sellers, and they knew what we were worth monetarily, we should have called some of the shots and set our own deadlines so that we could have had a life. That's it, Fred. We haven't had a life."

Fred looked bewildered. "So what do you propose, darlin'?"

"I don't want to cut off my nose to spite my face, so how about you write the books, and I'll edit them. We'll talk to Frasier and tell him we're cutting back to two books a year, and if he doesn't like it, he can shove it where the sun don't shine."

Fred looked stunned. "I— Well—" he stammered.

"I know it's a bolt out of the blue, but something happened to me when I took on that dog. It was like when we took in Jane. She was so bitter, so hostile, and so miserable she wanted to lie down and die, just like Flash did. We saved her, Fred. You and me. But she doesn't need us anymore and, damn it, Fred, I liked that feeling of being needed. I felt like I counted for something back then with Janie, and I know you felt the same way. I need to be needed even if it's by a dog. We're old, Fred. Whatever time I have left in this world, I want to use doing good for something or someone. Right now that someone is a dog. That's the best I can do as far as an explanation goes. I can edit in the morning and racy it up a bit when you slow down, but that's all I'm willing to do from here on out. What do you think?"

"I think it's about time!" he shouted, grabbing her and hugging her. "I can't wait to call Frasier and give him the news. I wish we had one of those phones where you can see the other person." He pushed back from her. "You're sure you don't just want to quit altogether?"

She shook her head. "No. At least not yet. I think we need to taper off slowly. Going from writing three books a year to two is good for now." She upended her beer. "I know I won't be able to traipse around in those fields shooting off my gun and chasing Flash for more than a year or two. I'm seventy-hmm," she mumbled against the bottle top. She snuggled up against the big dog. "Fred, you should have seen him. He *loves* the siren and those flashing lights. The excitement of it all is what he lives for. I'm going to call Ramos, the desk sergeant, tomorrow and get the phone number of the guy who trains the K-9s. I'll offer him a small fortune to come out here and work with Flash one day a week. For realism, we'll bring Olive over to be trained." She stared straight ahead, her thoughts swirling.

"I'm with you, my little love muffin. One hundred percent. I've become very fond of this dog, and whatever makes him happy makes me happy. It's a good thing our Janie knows her business, or we'd be singing a different tune right now."

They cuddled Flash between them.

Trixie got up. "So who's going to brush Flash's teeth tonight? Me or you?"

"I'll do it," Fred offered. "You go on up to bed. Flash and I will just sit here for a while and watch that old rerun of *Casablanca*."

"You might want to clean off his feet, too. I have a feeling he's going to be sleeping with us now. See you in the morning, Fred." She leaned down to kiss him and found herself kissing Flash's nose instead.

"Hey, Romeo," Fred said. "That's *my* girl!"

Jane stared across the room at the fish tank. Within minutes the tension was leaving her shoulders. Mike should be arriving soon, she thought, her heart taking on an extra beat. She sipped her cup of green tea, her eye on the tiny clock next to her chair. So far Brian Ramsey hadn't canceled his appointment but it was only 3:45. He'd canceled as late as three minutes to four, which meant he could still do it.

The buzzer on her intercom went off. "Dr. Sorenson is here, Dr. Lewis," her new office temp bellowed in a very unprofessional tone. Jane winced.

Jane pressed the button, and said, "Show him in, Wynona, and speak a little softer when announcing people, please."

The door opened, and Mike walked in. "Wow!" he said, glancing behind him. "Leather jumpsuit, spiked hair, green lipstick, and an eyebrow ring." Mike grinned as he flopped down into the chair next to Jane.

"Looks are deceiving. She's actually a scheduling genius and a whiz at filing and bookkeeping. I'm almost all caught up thanks to her." She leaned toward Mike. "I just wish she would dress a little more conservatively. I try not to look at her," she whispered. "It's only until Lily gets back. Would you like some tea or coffee? Wynona makes very good coffee, too."

"Okay, I'll take coffee. What's your feeling, Jane, is he going to be a no-show?"

"My bet is he'll show. I told him if he canceled one more time at the last minute, that I would bill him. He didn't like that." She handed Mike a mug. "Frankly, I think this is a game of some kind with him. He's playing with me. You've read his file. What there is to it. What do you think?"

Mike leaned across the little table that separated their two chairs. "Truthfully?"

"Of course, truthfully. What an odd question," she said, looking at him in bewilderment.

"What I think is you associate this guy with your friend's rape at LSU. I think he said or did something that triggered your memory about that night. I could be wrong. Let's play it out when he gets here and go on from there. Worst-case scenario, we boot his ass out of here or introduce him to my battery guy, who, by the way, just donated tons of the stuff to two different schools. Ask me why, Jane."

"Why, Mike?"

"So he can buy more batteries, of course. Does that make sense to you?"

"Absolutely."

"Good, we're on the same page again." He focused on the fish tank. "I like that you got big fish rather than a bunch of little ones. You named them, didn't you?"

"Sure, that's Gracie, and that long one is Slick." Jane jumped when the buzzer sounded.

"Mr. Ramsey is here," Wynona said in a soft, sexy voice.

Jane rolled her eyes as she pushed the return button. "Thank you. Wynona, please send him in. Oh, and Wynona, get Dr. Sorenson some coffee. Two sugars, no cream. And ask Mr. Ramsey if he would care for coffee or tea."

Moments later the door opened. Jane stood up. "I'm so glad you could make it today, Brian. Please, make yourself comfortable." As soon as he was seated, Jane made the introductions. "As I told you, Dr. Sorenson is going to be sitting in on my sessions for a while, and he'll also be joining me on my talk show. He has familiarized himself with your file and will be handling this session. I will be observing and taking notes."

Mike began the session with casual questions, questions

Jane knew were just warm-ups. As the session progressed, she found herself really impressed with Mike's methods. She didn't like the way Brian Ramsey kept looking over at her. She thought about what Mike had said and wondered if he was right. She could hardly wait for the fifty minutes to be up.

"Correct me if I'm wrong, Mr. Ramsey," Mike said. "You said that there hasn't been any change in your situation? Does that mean you haven't made any effort or that your wife is holding you at arm's length?"

"My wife packed up and went to her mother's."

"Does the mother live close by?"

"New Orleans. Not exactly around the corner. And since I have a business to run—she calls."

"You don't call her?"

"No."

"No? Something isn't computing here. You came to Dr. Lewis for help. Talking is the first step. Putting a plan together is the second step. And trying to work at what you perceive to be the problem is the third step. According to Dr. Lewis's notes, she suggested you follow all three steps. Why did your wife leave?"

Ramsey rearranged himself in his chair. "Because I can't get past what happened to her."

"Have you thought about why?"

"Sure."

"Okay, so why?"

"I'm not so sure she didn't do something to instigate it. You know, with a look or a gesture. Women are always giving guys that come-hither look, teasing them, egging them on. They give you all these go signals, and when you move they stiff-arm you. You're a guy even if you are a shrink, so you know how it plays."

Jane wrote down his responses word for word and wondered why these answers hadn't come out before. She'd asked practically the same questions.

"Come-hither looks are not an invitation to rape. No woman wants to be raped, to be violated like that." Ramsey's expression mocked Mike's statement. "What would you do if someone raped you? Believe it or not, men rape other men all the time."

Ramsey glared at Mike. "That would be the damn day when some guy raped me. It would never happen, Doc. Never," he blustered. "If any guy even looked at me cross-eyed, I'd let him have it."

"What do you weigh? One-eighty? One-ninety? What does your wife weigh?"

"Hell, I don't know. One-forty maybe. She's not fat, but she isn't exactly an Olive Oyl either."

"I assume, then, that you think your wife should have fought her attacker?" At Ramsey's nod, Mike continued. "In all likelihood the rapist outweighed her by forty or fifty pounds. Unless she's taken lessons in self-defense, what chance do you think she would have had against him? And what if by fighting him, she only angered him? He might have done more than rape her, he might have killed her." He paused for a long moment. "Is it possible you wish she had never told you what happened?"

Ramsey eyed the fish tank, then the coffee cup he was holding. He jerked his head around to stare at Mike Sorenson. "No. Yes. Jesus Christ, I don't know. What I do know is I wish to hell it had never happened."

Mike threw his hands in the air. "Why are you here seeking help from a psychiatrist? Your wife should be here. You should be counseled together, then separately. Right now, the way I see it, you're wasting everyone's time and the insurance company's money. Well, Mr. Ramsey?"

Ramsey set his coffee cup down. "My wife didn't report the rape to the police. She wanted to, but I stopped her. We live in a small town. I own a business. That's all people would talk about. How was all that going to look? You know how people gossip. It would have ruined me financially."

"I see. There are monetary considerations. Since you can't seem to get through this, have you thought about divorce?"

"I think we both want out of the marriage," Ramsey said, glancing at Jane.

"Did you have problems before your wife was raped?"

"Minor ones. Nothing serious."

"We'd like to have you bring your wife in to the next session. That way we can level the playing field. If you're not agreeable, then my recommendation to Dr. Lewis will be to cut you loose and let you seek help elsewhere."

"You know what? I think that's a good idea," Ramsey said, standing up. When he reached for his jacket, Jane noticed that his hands were huge and strong. A football player's hands. Now where had that thought come from? she wondered, shivering. She opened the drapes and stood in the warmth coming through the window. "The next time you see Todd Prentice, tell him I said hello," she blurted, surprising herself.

Ramsey stopped in midstride and turned to face Jane, a sly look on his face. "I'll do that," he said, his cold eyes impaling her.

Jane gasped.

There were no handshakes, no good-byes. He was there, and then he was gone.

Jane stared out the window, Ramsey's answer and expression imprinted on her brain. He knew Todd Prentice. *Knew him.* When she'd mentioned his name, she hadn't really thought there would be a connection. What did it mean?

Mike threw his hands in the air. "There's *something* about that guy. . . . Now I know what you meant when you said he made your skin crawl." He got up and walked over to where Jane was standing. "Who is Todd Prentice?"

Jane crossed her arms and hugged herself. She felt like her

body was twitching from head to toe. "The quarterback Connie Bryan was going to marry. The one I told you about. He lives in Crowley." She considered voicing her concern about the connection between Prentice and Ramsey, but decided against it. It was probably just a coincidence, nothing worth thinking about.

Mike nodded. "Right. I think you just told me his first name before." He put his arms around her and pulled her back against his chest. "Ramsey is out of your hair now, so that's one less thing you have to worry about. And don't tell me you weren't worried. You're stiff as a board. Since he was your last patient, what do you say we get a drink and relax?"

"Now that sounds like a plan," Jane said, turning around. "You could take me to dinner, too. Dessert's at my house. You up for a little fun and frolic?"

"Only if it comes with that floppsy-doodle hat and a black garter," Mike whispered in her ear.

Her face beet red, Jane linked her arms in his and turned off the light. "Lock up, Wynona, and don't forget to water the plants, feed the fish, and clean the coffeepot before you leave. I'll see you tomorrow. Have a nice evening."

Once they were outside, Mike pressed her for a commitment. "Well?"

"Well what?" she teased.

"Yes or no?"

She turned to him and looked him straight in the eyes. "Only if you agree to stand buck-ass *naked* in the middle of the bed singing 'Jingle Bells' while everything jiggles. Why should you have all the fun?"

His mouth opened. "Tell me you didn't mean what you just said. Tell me you're joking."

"I never joke, Dr. Sorenson. What's it gonna be?"

"I need to think about it," Mike said, handing her into his low-slung Corvette.

"Nope, you have to decide now, Doctor. My hat's in my car, and we're in your car."

Mike banged his head on the steering wheel. "Get the damn hat!"

"Oh goodie!" Jane said, controlling her giggling until she was out of the car.

Mike banged his head again. He wished he knew what it was about the stupid hat that gave him an instant hard-on.

"You're a beautiful woman, Jane Lewis," Mike said quietly, almost reverently.

Jane felt awkward and flustered. No one had ever called her beautiful before. She wasn't quite sure how she should handle the compliment. She smiled. Maybe when you're in love, you look different to your partner, like in the movie, *The Enchanted Cottage*. There was no doubt in her mind that she was in love with Mike Sorenson. What surprised her was that it had happened so fast. It had only been two weeks!

"I think I want you more than I ever wanted a woman before," Mike said, the admission making him momentarily vulnerable. "I think I love you, Jane Lewis," he whispered in a husky voice.

"I think I love you, too, Mike Sorenson."

Mike met her unflinching gaze. "How'd this happen? We barely know each other, and yet I feel like I've known you all my life. Jesus, you've got me so I can't wait to get here after work."

Jane felt herself blushing. No man had ever told her he loved her. She had been beginning to doubt that there would ever be a man for her. "I don't know how it happened. It just did. And if you want to know, I can't wait for you to get here. If this is just for now, I'll take it. If it goes beyond now, I'll take that, too. I just want to be with you, Mike."

Mike studied her. Jane was a one of a kind. A woman who

made no pretenses. *A rare breed*, he thought. She didn't try to trick him or maneuver him. All the devious things that so many women used to beguile a man were not part of Jane's makeup. She was honest to a fault, plainspoken, even brash. He did love her. He knew it in his gut.

"I was wondering," Jane said, hesitating slightly, "what it would be like to wake up with you next to me in the morning and not have to rush somewhere or do something according to a schedule." She held her breath, waiting for him to give her an odd look. But when he didn't, she continued with confidence. "I was wondering what it would be like to have a baby with you. What kind of father you would make. Would you be stern or permissive? Would you do diapers and bottles? Would you rock the baby to sleep and get up with it in the middle of the night? Would you hold me and say the baby is as beautiful as I am?"

"You've had a lot on your mind, haven't you?"

She smiled and looked down. "Um-hmm."

"Well, it just so happens that I've been doing some thinking of my own," he said, pulling her close. "I've been thinking you're the kind of woman I've been searching for all my life. You're honest, you have integrity, and I like the way you treat your dog and your godparents. I like the slow easy way we make love together. I love it that you don't hold back. I love it that you shared your secrets with me. I wish I had some to share with you."

Tears misted Jane's eyes. "You couldn't have said anything any nicer. I think I will remember it always. Thank you."

Mike gazed into her eyes. Seeing her moist lips part in invitation, he touched his mouth to her lips and tasted their sweetness. As the kiss deepened, searing flames licked his body, and the pulsating beat of his heart thundered in his ears.

Time became eternal for Jane. Deep within her she felt a

desire to stay forever in his embrace, forever in his life. Thick, blond lashes closed over her green eyes and she heard her own breath come in ragged little gasps as she boldly brought her mouth once more to his, offering herself, kissing him deeply, searchingly, searing the moment upon her memory.

In that moment, she knew that this man truly did belong to her, for however brief their time together might be. She had found him, a man who could make her feel like the woman she'd always known she was.

Mike's fingers were gentle as they danced through her hair. He sensed what she was feeling. There were needs of the soul that went beyond the hungers of the body. "I love you."

Jane sought him with her lips, possessed him with her hands, her own passion growing as she realized the pleasure she was giving him. The hardness of his sex was somehow tender and vulnerable beneath her hand as she felt it quiver with excitement and desire for her. His hands never left her body, seeking, exploring, touching. She wanted to lie back and give herself to him, yet at the same time, she wanted to possess him, touch him, commit him to memory, and know him as she had never known another man. Instead of being alien to her, his body was as familiar to her as her own. She felt her body sing with pleasure.

Jane felt ravaged by the hunger he created within her. "Now, Mike, please now," she breathed, feeling as though she would die if he did not, yet hating to put an end to the excruciating pleasure.

They lay together, legs entwined, her head upon his shoulder as he stroked the softness of her arm and the fullness of her breasts. His lips were in her hair, soft, teasing against her brow.

"You're a wonderful lover," he said, his voice still husky with passion.

Jane sighed, happier than she'd ever been in her life. Who

could want more? She did! A devil perched itself on her shoulder. "Up and at 'em, big guy. You promised to sing and dance on this bed. I want to see you . . . jiggle and jingle."

Mike squeezed his eyes shut and looked as if someone had just stuck a knife into his gut. "Jane, have a heart. I won't be able to jiggle."

"If I put on my floppsy-doodle-whatever-you-called-it hat and garter, do you think it will help?" Jane slipped out of bed to get her hat, which was sitting on the dresser. "Ah," Jane said, settling the hat firmly on her curly head. She extended her leg to pull on the black garter.

Mike lifted himself up on his elbow. "I want you to burn that hat, Jane. Swear to me you'll burn that hat tomorrow."

"Okay. Now dance! With gusto!"

6

Jane rolled over, cracked one eyelid to look at the bedside clock, then at the empty side of the bed. She reached out to touch the pillow Mike had slept on before she moved her head to sniff it. One of these days she would have to ask him the name of his cologne. It was so sexy, just like him. There was a smile on her lips when the phone rang. Thinking it was Mike calling to say good morning, she answered with a cheery, "Good morning."

"Dr. Lewis?"

The smile faded. "Speaking," Jane responded to the unfamiliar voice.

"I'm sorry to call so early, Dr. Lewis. This is Emily Quinn, Dr. Sharon Thomas's secretary. Dr. Thomas is in the hospital. Her appendix ruptured, and they performed surgery yesterday. She's fine, but she's concerned about her patients. She wanted me to call and ask if you could take over her free clinic hours for a few weeks. All but one of her patients are routine. If you're agreeable, I could drop off the files at your office on my way to work this morning. Her clinic hours are four to six."

Jane didn't hesitate. "It will take some juggling, but yes, I can do it."

"Thank you, I know she'll be very grateful."

"Is there anything I can do for Sharon?" Jane asked.

"No, but I'll tell her you asked. Oh, and if you decide to send flowers, she's in Room 206, and she's partial to daisies. I'll be by around eight. Again, thank you, Dr. Lewis."

Jane put the phone down and swung her legs over the side of the bed. She eyed her running shoes and sweats on the chair. She could do a two-mile run and still make it to the office by eight. "The hell with it," she muttered as she headed for the shower. She made a mental note to have Wynona order her a treadmill. Maybe she and Mike could take turns running on it. Falling off and making love on the floor would be nice. Real nice. The smile returned to her face as she stepped under the spray.

The thought stayed with her until she parked the Honda in front of Trixie's house. "Okay, Olive, Trixie is doing doggy day care today, so you have a good time with Flash, and I'll pick you up on the way home. Go easy on the big guy, okay?" She tapped the horn and waited until she saw the front door open. Flash ran outside to greet Olive. Jane watched the unlikely pair as they sniffed each other's tails. *True love,* she thought, chuckling. *Maybe humans can learn a thing or two from dogs. I'll have to ask Mike what he thinks.*

Jane arrived at her office at the same time Wynona pulled into the parking lot. They parked side by side and walked together to the office, with Jane explaining the day's switch in scheduling. "Miss Quinn should be arriving shortly. Do the best you can with my own schedule, and if you have to cancel some of my appointments, that's okay. Call Dr. Sorenson and remind him that he has to be at the studio fifteen minutes early. Then call the clinic and tell them I'll be taking over for Dr. Thomas for the next few weeks while she recovers. I'm sure they already know, but do it anyway. I want to see the patient records as soon as Miss Quinn drops them off. Coffee as soon as you can manage it please, Wynona. And before I forget, call Sadie's Flower Shop and have them send a basket of daisies to Dr. Thomas at the hospital, Room 206. Actually, Wynona, have them send two baskets. I'm sure Dr. Sorenson would want to send one also. Just make sure they don't make the same arrangement for both of them. Have them charge it to my account."

"Yes, ma'am. I'll get right on it. Do you want donuts with your coffee?"

"My mouth says yes, but my hips say no. No donuts. No pastries of any kind, thank you. Doesn't that eyebrow ring hurt?"

Wynona raised her hand to touch her right eyebrow. "No," she said, wiggling the gold ring up and down. "I have one in my belly button, too. It doesn't hurt either."

Jane grimaced. She remembered how schizy she'd been when she'd wanted to have her ears pierced. She'd insisted Trixie go with her, just in case something bad happened. "Why, Wynona? Why do you mutilate yourself like that?"

"I don't see it as mutilation. It all goes with being a free spirit. My boyfriend likes it. He has six of them." Wynona took out her keys to open the office door. "Don't you ever do anything impetuous, Dr. Lewis? When I'm old and sitting around in a rocking chair, I want to be able to tell my grandchildren that I experienced all kinds of wild, wonderful things." Wynona held the door open as Jane walked inside.

"I see," Jane said, shaking her head as though to clear away cobwebs. She thought about Lily Owens, who was neat and attractive and who looked like the wholesome girl next door. "Hurry back, Lily," she muttered under her breath as she headed for her own office.

Wynona switched on the overhead lights. "No, you don't see, but that's okay. I'll bring in your coffee as soon as it's ready."

Jane nodded as the door closed behind her. Wynona was easier to take with a good cup of coffee in front of her.

Twenty minutes later, the intercom on Jane's desk buzzed. "Miss Quinn is here, Dr. Lewis."

"Thank you, Wynona. Send her in, please."

Miss Quinn was as wholesome-looking as Lily. Jane walked around her desk to offer her hand to the secretary, who was dressed in a sedate, dove gray suit.

"When I told Dr. Thomas that you had agreed to take over for her, she was so relieved. She said she knows her patients will be in good hands." Miss Quinn smiled at Jane as she set the stack of files on the desk. "As I said on the phone, most of her patients are routine. Only this one, Miss Vance, is a serious concern. She's in a very fragile state, so you will have to be on twenty-four-hour call where she's concerned. Is there anything you want to ask me before I leave?"

"No. I'll read over the files. If I have any questions, I'll call you. If you speak with Dr. Thomas, give her my regards and wish her a speedy recovery."

"I'll do that." Miss Quinn started across the room toward the door. "Oh, by the way," she said over her shoulder, "I like your radio show. I listen whenever I can. My mother thinks you're the greatest. I think she's even called you a time or two about my little brother." She rolled her eyes.

"That's nice to know," Jane replied, a pleased smile curving her lips. "Thank you for telling me."

Wynona arrived with the coffee. Compared to Miss Quinn—there was no comparison. Today Wynona was attired in a dark green jumpsuit with a huge gold emblem on the chest-high pocket. Jane thought she looked like a string bean that was turning yellow from too much watering.

"I wish I had the guts to dress like that," Emily Quinn said as soon as Wynona left.

Jane stared across at the young woman. "You do?"

"You must be a twenty-first-century woman, Dr. Lewis. Dr. Thomas would never hire someone who looked like her. Image is important, she says."

"She's right," Jane said with a nod of agreement. "Wynona is a temp. She's filling in until my regular assistant gets back from maternity leave. I think this whole 'free spirit' thing is fine, but I think it has its place, and a doctor's office isn't that place. But I have to admit, there are times I wish I had the guts to let it all hang out, to dress and wear my hair any way I feel like. I've never once 'broken the rules.' I grew up thinking my full name was Plain Jane."

"That's right up there with what they called me. Prissy Emily." The young woman waved as she closed the door behind her.

"To all the Prissy Emilys and the Plain Janes of the world," Jane said, holding her coffee cup aloft.

Within minutes Jane was so engrossed in Betty Vance's file, a bomb could have gone off outside her window and she wouldn't have noticed. When she finished reading the lengthy reports, she closed the file and leaned back in her chair. Betty Vance was so deeply traumatized she was suicidal. She was also on heavy doses of Valium.

Jane closed her eyes and gave Betty Vance's case serious thought. Should she follow Sharon Thomas's path or strike out on her own? She was no advocate of Valium or any other drug unless it was absolutely necessary. Dealing with a patient in a drug daze served no purpose in her opinion. Maybe she wasn't the right person to treat Betty Vance. Coddling patients wasn't her style. Children, yes. Adults, no. In most cases, six months of once-a-week treatments should have showed some results. But there were always the exceptions. Perhaps Betty needed more time—two or three times a week—and couldn't get it because she was a clinic patient.

Damn, now she was troubled. Betty Vance's profile and record were going to eat at her all day. That meant she was going to have to take extra care on her talk show to put it on her mental shelf. She needed to be sharp and sassy today, with Mike sitting in on the session. She sighed as she reached for her coffee cup.

"Wynona, more coffee!"

Jane's smile was of the megawatt variety when Mike Sorenson walked into the small, cramped studio.

He looked around, his expression a study of confusion.

"You were expecting...what?" Jane asked. *God, he looks good enough to eat.*

"I don't know. Maybe something a little bigger, a little more glamorous. My closet is bigger than this. Doesn't it get to you?"

"Only if the show is going slow. Most times I don't think about my surroundings. I'm too busy talking and listening. It's only an hour. Do you think some air fresheners would help?"

"Are you kidding? Air fresheners just mask odors. We'd be gasping for breath."

Jane pretended to look offended. "Does that mean you aren't impressed?"

He shrugged.

"Better not let Tom know how you feel. He thinks this," she said, moving her arm in a wide arc, "is paradise. He even has a plaque on his desk that reads, SHANGRI-LA. By the way, I took the liberty of sending Sharon Thomas a basket of flowers for you. She's in the hospital. Ruptured appendix. I'm taking over her clinic hours this afternoon, which means I'll be running late tonight."

"I can't make it tonight anyway, Jane," he said, his voice full of regret. "I've got Rotary and a dinner meeting with an old school chum. I haven't seen him in years. I forgot all about it until my secretary reminded me this morning. I can do a hot dog at Roy's if you have time after the show."

"I'd love a hot dog at Roy's after the show. With the

works, of course." Jane smiled as she took her seat. "We're going to be talking about feelings today," she said, putting on her professional hat as she reached for her earphones. "Keep your eyes on Tom. Just relax and everything will fall into place." Jane waited for her cue.

"This is *Talk to Me,* and I'm Dr. Jane Lewis speaking to you from the frog capital of the world. But then you already know Rayne is noted for its frogs. I have with me today Dr. Mike Sorenson, my new cohost. Today we'll be talking about feelings—love, hate, joy, anger. Whatever you're feeling. Give us a call at 1-800-888 TALK. Shelly is on the line. Talk to me, Shelly."

"Yes, Dr. Lewis. I'm worried that I love my dog more than I love my boyfriend, and I don't know what to do about it."

Jane looked at Mike and grinned. "How long have you had your dog, Shelly?"

"Five years. He's seen me through thick and thin. I don't know what I would have done without him when my father died."

"Okay, and how long have you and your boyfriend been together?"

"Six months."

"And has he seen you through thick and thin?"

"No. This last year, my life has been pretty average."

"I wouldn't worry about your feelings for your dog, Shelly. It's perfectly natural to have strong feelings for a beloved pet, especially one who's been there for you when things got tough. My springer spaniel means everything in the world to me. She's my constant companion, my confidante, my confessor. She loves me unconditionally, and she brings me great joy. The longer you and your boyfriend stay together, the better the chance that your feelings for each other will grow. But don't ever try to compare them to what you feel for your dog. That's a unique relationship, and you're entitled to love your dog as much as you want. The only time there's a problem with that is if your significant other becomes jealous. Call me back if that happens, but if it doesn't, feel free to love that dog of yours to your heart's content. The next caller is Dan. Go ahead, Dan."

"Hey, listen," a gruff, masculine voice came over the lines, "is fear a feeling?"

Jane gave Mike a thumbs-up.

"Yes, Dan," Mike said, leaning toward the microphone. "Fear is a very strong feeling. What are you afraid of?"

"Okay, man, I know you're gonna think I'm nuts, but I'm telling you I've seen a ghost, and it's scarin' the hell out of me."

Mike sat up straight, his interest piqued. "I need more information, Dan. First of all, is the ghost male or female, about what age, and where do you see it?"

"You—you believe me, man?"

Mike understood Dan's incredulity. "Sure, I believe you. I've done a lot of research into the paranormal. Now tell me about your ghost."

"It's a woman, a middle-aged woman. She's in my bathroom. I see her in the mirror when I'm shaving but nowhere else. She keeps opening her mouth like she's trying to talk, but I can't hear anything."

"Have you tried talking to her?"

"Hell, no."

"First of all, Dan, let me assure you that there is absolutely nothing to be afraid of. Ghosts cannot hurt you. I repeat. They cannot hurt you. What I want you to do is to talk to her, ask her what she wants? Okay? Can you do that?"

"Yeah, but what *could* she want?"

"For some reason she hasn't been able to cross to the other side. My guess is that when she died, she left something undone or has some unfinished business that won't allow her spirit to rest. She's looking for you to help her, Dan. Call us

back after you've talked to her and tell us what happened."
Mike smiled across at Jane. "Now we've got Georgia on the
line. Talk to me, Georgia."

"Hi," a young girl said. "I like these two guys in my
school, but I can't decide which one to pick."

"How old are you, Georgia?" Mike asked.

"Sixteen."

"You don't have to pick. There's nothing wrong with dating them both."

"But my mom says that I should stick with one or the
other."

"Can you put your mom on the phone, Georgia?" Mike
and Jane listened while Georgia passed the phone to her
mother.

"I'm here," a woman said. "And I don't approve of her
dating two boys at the same time."

"She's only sixteen, Mom," Mike said. "She's much too
young to make any kind of commitment, and dating one boy
and only one *is* making a commitment. Please consider letting her play the field. The time will come all too soon when
that will no longer be an option."

"I don't know," the mother said.

"If she dates one boy for any length of time, she'll be
branded as *his* girl. Once that happens the other boys won't
ask her out, which means she won't get an opportunity to
date other guys."

"This is Dr. Lewis, Mom, and I'd like to add something to
what Dr. Sorenson said. First, I absolutely agree with him. I
think it's important for a girl Georgia's age to date different
guys. It's the act of dating that gives a girl the ability to know
what kind of guy suits her so that later on she can make that
one really important decision—who she's going to marry. Besides that, if she only goes out with one guy, there's a much
greater chance that she'll indulge in premarital sex and—"

"Okay, okay, you win," the mother said with annoyance. They heard the phone being set down.

"Hello, Dr. Lewis? This is Georgia again. Thanks," she said in a *whispery* voice.

"You're welcome, Georgia. Good luck. I'm Dr. Jane Lewis, and my cohost is Dr. Mike Sorenson. You're listening to *Talk to Me*."

The station cut to an insurance commercial, giving both Jane and Mike a breather.

"That was fun," Mike said. "We work well together, but then I knew we would. Everything we do together, we do well." He winked and gave her a sexy look.

"Chili, onions, sauerkraut, mustard. You can barely see the hot dog," Mike grumbled as he bit into his plain mustard dog. "You're the only woman I know who would eat something like that and not worry about it dripping on her clothes and getting it all over her face. I love you, Jane Lewis. For being you. I thought you were pretty much a vegetarian like Olive."

"I am, but when it comes to hot dogs . . . I have absolutely no willpower," Jane said, licking her lips as she stared across the street. A burgundy Chevy half-ton pickup was pulling away from the curb, tires screeching. She got a glimpse of the driver. Brian Ramsey. Or was it? It looked like Brian, but lately she'd thought she'd seen him every time she turned around, which she knew was impossible.

A woman walking a toy poodle bent down with her pooper scooper in front of the telephone pole. That was ordinary. Sam Wallace sweeping the sidewalk in front of his hardware store was pretty ordinary, too. She waved to Sara Titus, her old first-grade teacher.

She looked up and wondered when the sky had turned so gray. There were storm clouds to the west. It would rain before the end of the day and probably through the evening. She hated the idea of spending the evening alone, especially a rainy evening. What in the world had her evenings been like before Mike came into her life? Maybe she could go to the farm and visit with Trixie and Fred. Maybe they would invite her for supper when she stopped to pick up Olive. On the other hand, she could go home and finish reading Trixie and Fred's new book, or she could go on the computer and check out Trixie's snoop file, or go to E-bay and see what was for sale. She looked up at Mike and smiled. "I'm missing you already."

"Me, too. Listen, I have to run or I'll be late. I'll call you tonight."

Jane half expected Mike to kiss her right there on the street. For a second it looked like he was thinking about it until he saw Jasper Dewey watching them.

"Nice-looking young fella," Jasper cackled as Mike walked away. "How's your mama, child?"

"Yes, he is a nice-looking fella, Mr. Dewey, and he's all mine. Mama passed some time ago, but thank you for asking. You have a nice day now," Jane said as she turned to walk in the opposite direction. Everyone knew that sweet, kind Jasper Dewey was senile and couldn't remember anything from one minute to the next. Sooner or later one of the shop owners would take him home and turn him over to his wife, who would profess amazement that he got loose and wandered away. Everyone in town also knew Matilda let it happen so she could have an hour of peace and quiet to watch her soap operas.

Jane used her cell phone to call her office before heading to the clinic and was told things were fine and no, there were no emergencies and her last appointment was at five. She broke the connection and dialed the farm. Trixie picked up on the second ring.

"Is Olive okay, Trixie? She isn't too much for you, is she?"

"Lord, no. She's having a ball with Flash."

"Oh, good."

"Listen, Janie, I need you to do me a favor while you're out. Stop by Radio Shack and pick me up a police scanner and a set of two-way radios."

"Sure. I won't even ask why you want them."

"For Flash, of course, as if you didn't know," Trixie cackled.

"I'm on my way to the clinic now," Jane said. "One of my colleagues is in the hospital, so I'm taking over her patients. I'm running late tonight. Save me some leftovers if you cook."

"Fred's doing the cooking. Flash and I are going to work. I mean W-O-R-K. Flash knows how to spell, Janie. Olive is going along for the ride, literally rather than figuratively. Call me on my cell phone when you get to the farm, and I'll run her on in. Don't forget to stop by Radio Shack."

"I won't forget. Give Olive a hug for me."

"Will do. Over and out."

Jane closed the phone and tucked it into her purse. Over and out. Obviously, the code words were for Flash's benefit. Jane giggled all the way to the clinic at the trouble Trixie was going to for that big lug of a dog. But then, Trixie always did have a big heart.

The clinic was a small red brick building with ivy growing up the front. Six thousand square feet of ten-by-ten rooms and one huge reception area. At best it was spartan. A few prints or watercolors and some green plants would make a world of difference. How could people with mental problems be expected to feel anything but depressed in this gunmetal gray atmosphere? Free clinics had no money for extra trappings, as Trixie put it. She was right, too.

Jane signed in, aware that the waiting room was filled to overflowing with six people standing in the narrow hallway.

She was escorted to a small windowless room with a desk, a swivel chair, a wastebasket, and a patient chair. She opened her briefcase and withdrew Dr. Thomas's file folders. She stacked them neatly in front of her, her pen and yellow legal pad next to them, and waited for her first patient.

For an hour and a half she talked, listened, and made copious notes on each patient's half-hour session. She opened the last file folder, Betty Vance's, and prepared herself to meet her troubled patient.

Jane tried to cover her stunned surprise by turning her head and coughing when Betty Vance entered the room ten minutes late for her appointment. She could have posed for Connie Bryan's double if she'd taken the time to wash and blow out her hair, apply makeup, and dress in something that hadn't been slept in. Everything about her was lifeless and worn-looking. She was also much too thin, and her eyes were dull and lifeless. Her hands played with a wad of tissue.

"I'm Dr. Lewis. I'd like you to call me Jane and do you mind if I call you Betty? I'm taking over for Dr. Thomas because she's in the hospital. They explained that to you at the desk when you came in, didn't they?"

"They called me at home to tell me. Actually, it isn't my home. I'm staying with a friend. My legal name is Elizabeth Marie Vance and, yes, you can call me Betty."

"Did your friend bring you here today?"

"Yes. The medication makes me groggy, and I don't like to drive when I take it."

"Show me what it is you're taking." Jane frowned at the way the young woman's hands twitched as she tried to open her purse.

Betty rummaged in her purse. She handed over three bottles of pills. Jane winced when she looked at them and then at the file on her desk. "You're only supposed to be taking the Valium. Taking these others with the Valium is the reason you're so shaky. This is too much medication. You could do yourself serious harm." Jane put the medications aside. "You're not to take any more medication, Betty. I've read your file, and I think we can do other things to help you."

"Not take my medication? I need them to sleep. Otherwise, all I do is sit and think."

"When was the last time you went for a walk? When was the last time you styled your hair? When was the last time you did anything for yourself? How much weight have you lost? Don't you care if you get well?" Jane asked sharply but not unkindly.

"Of course I care." The young woman appeared stunned by the question, then her expression softened. "Maybe that's not really true. Some days I care, and other days I don't care. Most of the time I wish I was dead. I can't . . . I don't . . . why are you being so hard on me? I'm trying."

Jane leaned forward, her hands on the edge of her desk. "You were trying six months ago, but according to this file you are in exactly the same place you were then. While you're under my care there will be no drugs unless they are absolutely necessary. If that angers you, you can get up and go if you want, but you won't get better. That much I can guarantee. I'd like us to talk. I want you to tell me what happened to you, painful as that may be. I know you told Dr. Thomas, and I know it's all here in the file, but I want to hear you tell me. I can help you if you let me, Betty."

It was Connie Bryan's story all over again. The only difference was, this girl was alive to tell her story. When she finished her painful narrative, Betty stared at Jane, her eyes dull and glazed.

Jane licked at her lips. She had to tread carefully. Did she dare gamble with Sharon's patient? Sharon said she was fragile. *Not as fragile as Connie,* Jane thought. *Betty has hung in, sought professional help. That has to mean she has some guts, some spirit, a will to survive.*

"Why didn't you go to the police?"

"Because the man I was seeing said . . . he said . . . it wouldn't look good for him. We'd just moved in together. It's a small town. People talk in small towns. They point fingers and whisper. I listened to him. I shouldn't have. He turned on me, too. He wouldn't come near me. I could tell that I revolted him. He never said it, but I could see it on his face. So I moved out. But he wouldn't leave me alone. I'm afraid of him. He's older than I am. Not that age makes a difference but—I packed up my stuff and drove to my aunt's in New Orleans, but she has teenagers. I couldn't handle it, and neither could she. I called my friend, and he came and got me. I'm staying at his house. All I do is cry and think. He's going to get disgusted with me, too. I had a good job in Lafayette that I lost because I was such a basket case. My savings are almost gone, and pretty soon my insurance will run out. I don't know what to do. I'm afraid all the time. I can't stand being alone."

Jane watched as the young woman wept into the wad of tissues in her hand. "Do you think it's time to pull up your socks and try to get your life back? You cannot Windex what happened to you. It happened, and you have to deal with it. The first thing you need to do is file a police report. Then you have to talk to the people at the crisis center no matter how agonizing that may be. I realize it is six months later and all the evidence is gone, but your word is good enough. None of this is going to be easy. If you want your life back, then you have to fight for it. I'll help you in any way I can. No more drugs. Can you handle that?"

"I don't know. All I can do is try. What if . . . what if he calls or wants to see me?"

"Are you talking about the man you were living with?" Jane asked, perplexed at the question.

"Yes."

"I don't understand why you're afraid of him. Call him up, tell him you don't want to see him anymore. Tell him it's over. People do that every day of the week. Is he a violent person? You said he didn't want to be near you or to touch you. That tells me it's over. Are you in love with him? You need to help me out here."

Betty leaned back in the chair. She appeared exhausted. Talking seemed an effort.

"Brian was never physical with me. He does have a temper, though. He loses patience really quick when something doesn't go his way. No, I am not in love with him. I don't think I ever was. For a while he . . . dazzled me with gifts, flowers, and fancy dinners. He's incredibly smart. Book smart. He wanted me to marry him, but I wasn't ready. I'm twenty-nine, and I haven't done half the things I said I would do before I settled down. I agreed to move in and try it out. I think I knew it wouldn't work from the beginning. He tried to change me. He didn't like my clothes, didn't like my hair, didn't like the way I drove. I can't really cook, so he picked on that. I throw my clothes around, and he's a neat freak. I like to dance, and he doesn't. He flattered me, flashed his money, and I fell for it. The truth is, we had nothing in common. None of my friends liked him. I don't have those friends anymore, thanks to him. Except Chuck."

Jane sucked in her breath. If she asked Betty now if the Brian they were discussing was Brian Ramsey, she would have to excuse herself somehow. Her mind went totally blank as she tried to remember what the professional rule was. She could feel the tremor in her legs start to work upward. If she didn't get hold of herself, she would fall apart in front of her patient. *Don't ask. Pretend you didn't hear the name,* she told herself. It wasn't the same Brian. Brian Ramsey was married. His problem was his wife. This girl wasn't married. There had to be hundreds of Brians in the three surrounding parishes. *Don't read something into this that isn't there. Move on, Jane.*

"Is there anything else you'd like to tell me, Betty?"

"I think I covered it all."

"Was there anything familiar about your attackers? Anything at all? Think. Was it hot or cold? What did they smell like? Did you feel the material of any of their clothes? Did any of them say anything or gesture in any way that you can remember? Was there anything about their hands that struck you? You don't have to come up with anything right now. But I would like you to think about it. If you're comfortable with your friend, talk about it with him. He's a guy and might be able to offer up some valuable input. You are going to have to relive it. I told you, this isn't going to be easy, but you have to do it. I'm going to give you my card. You can always reach me, day or night. If you need me, I'll be there for you. That's a promise. And, if you like, I can schedule you into my appointment schedule every single day. It might be at the end of the day or it might be the first thing in the morning or during the lunch break. No charge. Will you agree to that?"

"Why are you doing this for me? I'm not even your patient."

Jane almost blurted out Connie's story. Instead she bit down on her tongue. "Because I want to help you. I want to see you get your life back. I want to see you go dancing again. I want to know you wake up with a smile on your face. The bad times are behind you. You have to go forward now. Your life is whatever you're going to make of it. You. Only you. I can help you, the women at the crisis center can help you, but you have to do the work. The fact that you're here tells me you don't like the way you're living. People care. They really do, Betty."

"Tomorrow is Saturday and then it's Sunday. Weekends are bad. I don't know why that is."

"Because families are together. Couples do things together. Everyone seems to be paired up. The weekends are two days of free time. I can open up my office tomorrow and you can come for a session. We can talk some more. How about if I go with you to the police station? I have to stop by Radio Shack and pick up something for my godmother first, but then we can go by the police station. I'll stay with you while you file the report. I can go with you to the crisis center and wait while they register you and assign a counselor to you. Then I can drop you off at home. Here's my card. Remember now, you can call me anytime, day or night."

Betty reached for the card. Jane watched her as she eyed the three pill bottles.

"They're a crutch, Betty. Eventually you would have to throw away a crutch if you wanted to walk again on your own. I'll keep them for you. If you want them back, I'll give them back."

"How long is this going to take?" Betty asked listlessly.

"I don't know, Betty. It's up to you and how hard you're willing to work."

"Okay."

"I have one last question. In your opinion, did Br . . . did the man you lived with love you?"

"I think so. He said I reminded him of someone. Someone he used to know. Is it important?"

Jane thought for one wild, crazy instant that she could feel the blood start to bubble in her veins. "I'm not sure." *Don't ask any more questions, Jane. Don't go down that road.*

"I'll tell Chuck you're going to take me home. Would you like to meet him?"

"Yes. Yes, I would, Betty. He must be a pretty special friend to take care of you like he does."

"He's a good friend. Once I file the report, everyone in town is going to know," Betty said, starting to cry.

"There's a good chance a lot of people will find out. But you have to remember that you didn't do anything wrong, Betty. I have an idea. See what you think about this. How about after the crisis center, we stop at the SPCA and get you a dog. A nice big one who will be grateful to you for taking him out of a cage and giving him a new life. Just the way you're going to get a new life. You know what else? I know just the person who can help you train the dog, but you're going to have to drive there. Every single day. The road to a new life takes many twists and turns. You up for this?"

"I'll give it my best shot. I really will. Promise me you'll stay with me while I make the report."

"Every step of the way. And the crisis center? You can handle it?"

"Yes."

"The dog?"

"That's the easy part. Yes."

"Then let's go."

7

It was ten o'clock when Jane let herself into the house, every nerve in her body twanging and twitching. She bolted for the kitchen and gulped from Trixie's bottle of Kentucky bourbon. Her eyes watered as she coughed and sputtered. Olive whined at her feet. The minute she stopped coughing, she fired up one of Fred's cigarettes and started to cough all over again. Olive pawed her legs in distress. "It's okay, Olive," she choked. "I'm just going through a bad time. I need to unwind and settle down. I'll make some tea and we'll sit in my crooked living room and I'll tell you about my day."

Olive lowered herself to the floor, her brown eyes never leaving Jane as she moved around the kitchen.

The kitchen was Jane's favorite room. It was a big, old-fashioned kitchen with little nooks and crannies that Jane thought were quaint and cozy. Today, however, all the quaint and cozy in the world wouldn't help her feel better.

She wondered if she should throw some logs into the fireplace or just go to bed. It would be nice to sit by the fire in the old rocker Trixie had bought her at a garage sale, sip herbal tea, and watch the flames. The rocker was big enough to hold both her and Olive. They could cuddle up together.

All she had to do was fluff up the bright red cushions, and she would be set. *To do what?* her mind screamed.

To read and reread Betty Vance's file.

Jane got the fire going, fixed her tea, grabbed a crocheted afghan, and sat down. Olive climbed up into the chair and lay halfway across her lap.

Jane was on her third read when she felt a hand lightly on her shoulder. She turned around, thinking it had to be Mike since Olive didn't even bother to glance up.

"You're onto something, aren't you, Miss Jane? I like this kitchen a lot. I sit in the rocker sometimes when you're at work. I wish I could help you."

"Billy! I wish you could help me, too! It was a terrifying day in many respects. I'm starting to question my own judgment. For a person in my profession, that's not good. Listen, assuming I believe you're a ghost, which I don't, can you . . . can you . . . you know, *flit* around, check things out, and report back to me? I've always been told that in dreams you can do anything. Can you do that?"

"Why?" Billy asked, boosting himself up to sit on the kitchen counter. He swung his legs back and forth to a rhythm only he seemed to hear.

Jane closed her eyes. "Because something is going on. At least I think something is going on. I'm nervous that I might miss something or overlook a vital piece of information. I'm just jittery," she said belligerently.

"Your patient isn't married," Billy said.

"Which patient? Betty Vance or Brian Ramsey?"

"Brian Ramsey is not your patient anymore. But he isn't married either."

"How do you know that?"

"I know." It was said with such authority, Jane blinked. *"You're letting it get away from you. You need to be in*

charge. You shouldn't delegate. You lose when you aren't on top of things."

"Do you think I don't know that? I know, trust me."

"I wish you didn't dislike your job so much."

"I don't dislike my job. It's just that sometimes I think I don't belong in this profession. So many people depend on me, and I find it difficult to be there for all of them. Not to mention trying to be in twenty places at the same time. I have too much on my plate. I'm tired, and I need a break."

"What you need to do is pick one thing and see it through to the end. Mark your starting point and work on the problem till you see results. Do you have theories?"

"By the bushel," she said, rolling her eyes. "You're right. I'm going to start with Brian Ramsey. That's where this all started. First thing tomorrow morning."

"What about Dr. Sorenson?"

"What about him?"

"Are you going to enlist his aid?"

"I haven't decided. What time is it?"

"I have no idea. Remember, I told you before that time isn't an issue on this side."

Olive barked and jumped off the chair. Jane woke with a start. She felt herself shrivel into the red cushions as she watched the back door open and Olive walk out. The door closed behind her. Glancing at the clock, she saw that it was fifteen minutes past midnight. How long had she been sleeping? She wasn't exactly sure what time she'd sat down or how long she'd been reading Betty Vance's file, but she guessed two to three hours. Had Mike called? She craned her neck to see the answering machine on the counter. There was no blinking red light.

Going back to sleep is out of the question, Jane thought as she peered through the kitchen window. She wished she could tune out the dreams with the boy named Billy Jensen. She sighed. She might as well make this time count for something. She fixed a pot of coffee, and, while it dripped, she turned on her computer and slid the snoop disk into the slot.

It was 3 A.M. when Jane removed the disk and turned off the computer. In front of her was a stack of printouts. Because she had Brian Ramsey's social security number from his health insurance, she now had a skeleton profile of the man who had been her patient until a few days ago. It was no surprise that he'd attended LSU and had played with the Bengal Tigers. She already guessed that he'd been a football player because of his hands and his build. What was surprising, though, was that though he had attended school on a full-ride football scholarship, he had earned his master's plus thirty.

Next to Ramsey's stack of printouts was Betty Vance's history, also courtesy of the snoop file and the Internet. It was considerably sketchier than Ramsey's but helpful all the same. At least she wouldn't be working totally in the dark now.

As she carried her cup back to the kitchen, visions of Mike flashed before her. Was he sleeping? Of course he was sleeping. It was after three in the morning. Was he dreaming about her? Why hadn't he called? He said he would. It wasn't like him to say he would do something and not do it. She rinsed out the coffeepot, filled it again for the morning, and sat down to smoke a cigarette.

When she saw the headlights arch on the kitchen wall, Jane was on her feet in a second. Mike! She ran to the kitchen door but instead of Mike, she saw Trixie's dilapidated police car squeal to a stop, red-and-blue lights flashing. When Olive came out of nowhere and started barking, Jane realized she'd forgotten to call her back inside.

"We're on night patrol," Trixie bellowed over the screeching siren.

"No kidding!" Jane bellowed back. She walked over to the car and poked her head through the passenger window.

"Yeah. No kidding!" Trixie said above a loud static noise. She picked up the two-way radio. "I'm at Janie's, Fred. Yes, everything is fine. I'll be home in a minute. Over and out."

"My God," Jane said in wonder. "When do you two sleep?"

"We don't. We take naps." She pushed the button to open the back door. "Go, Flash!" The huge dog sprinted off, Olive in hot pursuit.

"I thought you made a promise not to drive on open roads."

"I did. And I didn't."

"Huh?"

Trixie turned off the siren. "I did make a promise. And I didn't drive on open roads. I drove through the fields. So why aren't you in bed sleeping? Do you realize what time it is?"

"Yes, I do. It's just been one of those nights," she told her. "By the way, before I forget, Betty, that young woman I brought by— She found the nicest dog, a yellow Lab named Golda. Her owner died, and there was no one to take her. She took to Betty right away. A little schizy but she'll be okay. So you're going to have another dog for doggie day care to keep Flash company during training sessions."

Trixie looked Jane in the eye. "You think I'm nuts, don't you?" Instead of waiting for an answer, she said, "I guess I don't blame you. But you know what? I don't care. I'm having the time of my life. Flash is so wired up he's amazing. He found the first bag of dope. Fred repackaged it and hid it again. He hid some money, too. While we're here, he's burying different duffel bags and suitcases with a few bucks in each one. Flash is a whiz when it comes to money."

"I don't think you're crazy," Jane said in her own defense.

"A little eccentric, perhaps, but not crazy. I think what you're doing is wonderful! You saved a police officer's life. I've never seen a happier dog, and you tamed him in the bargain. I've never seen you happier either, Trix. That's what it's all about. You're lucky you can afford to do this. You and Fred have my vote," Jane said, reaching inside the car and grabbing Trixie's hand to squeeze it.

"Where's your fella?"

Jane shrugged.

Trixie waved her hand dismissively. "A little mystery is good for a romance."

Jane opened the passenger door, climbed inside the car, and rolled up the window. "I was going to call you first thing in the morning to ask a favor. But since you're here . . . I'd like Betty Vance to spend the weekend on the farm with you and Fred. She's not stable, and I don't want her to be alone. I'd have her stay here except I want to drive up to Baton Rouge and snoop around LSU. I had this dream, and I realized I need to follow all my threads to the end of the spool. That means I have to go back to what I call the scene of the crime. I'll take Olive with me so she won't get in your way with Betty and a strange dog. If either of you need me, call me on my cell phone. I think if she's with you, she'll be okay. I don't want her to think I'm out of reach. She's a little brittle, but she has an inner core of strength I'm hoping she draws on. She needs to know people care about her. You're just what she needs, Trix."

"That's one of the nicest things you've ever said to me, Janie, girl. I am having the time of my life. At my age, this has to constitute some kind of miracle in itself."

They sat together in the police car, waiting for the dogs, listening to the voices coming over the police scanner. Off in the distance they could hear the sound of eighteen-wheelers on the highway.

Jane gathered her thoughts. She had something else she wanted to ask Trixie, but she didn't know how her god-mother would react. There was only one way to find out: ask. "Trixie, what would you say if I told you I want to get out of this business, that I don't want to practice psychiatry anymore?" She held her breath, waiting.

Trixie's eyes searched Jane's, reaching into her thoughts. "Since most shrinks are nuts anyway, I'd probably say what took you so long? Life is short, Janie. In order to be happy, you have to do what you want to do. If you can't whistle on your way to work, you don't belong in that job. That's a Dutch saying," she said smartly. "I guess I would have to wonder why, though."

Jane bent her head and looked down at her hands. "I think I went into it for all the wrong reasons. It wasn't like I had a calling or anything. Now, Mike, he said he just knew he wanted to be a psychiatrist and that it all kind of evolved. I never *knew* anything of the kind. I forced it, out of guilt, I think."

"Guilt for your college friend?" At Jane's nod, Trixie asked, "If you give up your practice, what will you do with yourself?"

Jane sighed. "I don't know. All I know is that a medical ca-reer isn't for me. I should have realized it a long time ago when I couldn't decide on which branch of medicine to go into. First I wanted to be a pediatrician, then a general prac-titioner, then a psychiatrist. I settled on psychiatry because I thought in my own way I would be doing something to help Connie Bryan, but I've failed. I know that now."

"Oh, Janie, girl. What on earth have you been thinking?"

Jane shook her head. "I don't know what profession is for me, but at the moment it doesn't matter. Before I do *any-thing,* make any decisions, I have to keep my promise to myself and do something to help Connie. The fact that she's dead doesn't enter into it. I have to do it the same way you felt you had to do something for Flash. God, look at the lengths you're going to for that animal. I didn't get past square one where Connie was concerned, and she's human. *Was* human." Jane turned her head toward the window to be alone with her thoughts.

"Janie," Trixie said softly, "Fred and I were going to come over here on Sunday to talk to you about something." Jane turned back, her eyes moist. "You know we've made tons of money over the years, and it's all in different trusts that will go to you after we pass on. We were wondering if you would mind if we took some of that money, leased some of your acreage, because it connects with ours, and set up a school for K-9 dogs. A real school that we would fund. We'd hire trainers, buy the dogs ourselves, then donate them to different police departments around the country. When they get to be retirement age like Flash, we take them back and let them spend their remaining days here at the farm."

Tears rolled down Jane's cheeks. "Of course I don't mind. I told you from the beginning I didn't want your money. Dad left me well-off, and I've saved my own money over the years. The truth is, I never *have* to work again. If you're asking for my blessing, you have it. Are you going to breed the dogs, too?"

"The whole ball of wax. Want to come aboard? You know, when and if you ever get out of the business."

Jane didn't stop to think about her answer. "Hell, yes, I do. I would love doing something like that."

"What about your practice and the radio show?"

"I was planning on looking into it all after the first of the year. My contract with the radio show expires January 3. I could sell my practice, and Mike could take over the show. He's a natural. Hey, we could think about doing a show on dogs. Wow! How did this happen in the middle of the night, Trixie?"

"Pure dumb luck! You were up, I came over. I guess the timing was right," Trixie laughed.

"Are you going to give up writing completely?"

"Not just yet. We have two more books under contract. I didn't say anything before because Fred and I weren't sure it would go through, but our agent just sold our last fifteen books in a package deal to a film company in Hollywood. Fred got the call that it's a done deal around six o'clock. Five million bucks, Janie. Course the feds are going to take their cut, plus the state and our agent, but there will be enough left to fund the K-9 project. The trusts will kick in if things go awry or prices go up. Emergency money so to speak."

"Congratulations, Trixie! I am so proud of you, I could just bust. You don't think I'm a quitter, do you?"

"You, a quitter? Never!"

"Do you think Mike will think I'm a quitter when I tell him my plans?"

"If he does, he's not the man for you. Ah, here comes my partner. Time to saddle up and move out," Trixie said, getting out of the car. Jane got out, too.

"Wowee! Look, Janie. Flash did it again! Good boy!" Trixie held up a plastic bag filled with tissue and foreign matter. "Two ten-dollar bills! This dog is a whiz at sniffing out money as well as dope. In the car, Officer Flash! We're done for tonight." Flash barked and jumped in. "This dog is the marvel in marvelous." Olive stood patiently as she waited to be rewarded, too. "Two Oreo cookies coming up. Bob Henry told me he always gave Flash an Oreo when the shift was over. He also used to take him to Burger King on Thursday nights."

"Treats are good. I give them to Olive all the time. She loves veggie burgers." Jane bent down to pet Olive's head.

"It's going to be light out soon. I'm glad you stopped by, Trix. I feel like the weight of the world suddenly left my shoulders. So then it's okay about Betty Vance?"

"Send her over. What time are you going to Baton Rouge?" Trixie belted Flash into the backseat, closed the door, then went around to the driver's side and climbed in behind the wheel.

"As soon as I shower and get ready. I'll call Betty on my way."

"Okay, then. See you. Have a good trip," Trixie said. She switched on the flashing light, turned the key in the ignition, and peeled out across the open field toward her house.

With a smile on her face, Jane watched the flashing lights until the police cruiser was out of sight.

"Olive," she said, looking down, "technically speaking, I just quit my job! I feel so light, I think I could fly if I tried. C'mon, let's get some breakfast. Then we're going to my alma mater to see what we can find out about my ex-patient. We might even go on to Slidell."

"Woof."

Jane parked the car in Visitor Parking. She sat quietly, Olive next to her, as she surveyed the campus spread out before her. "I used to live here, Olive. I spent four long years of my life studying and walking these grounds. I think I was happy right up until that awful night. I don't know, maybe I wasn't and just thought I was. Come on, girl, we're going to walk that same route, then you're going to wait for me while I go to the library."

It was a quiet morning with few students strolling the grounds. Saturdays were for sleeping in after partying all night long. There were a few of the more serious students out and about, students like she'd once been. How young they looked. Had she ever been that young? Of course. Right now she felt vulnerable—so vulnerable she wanted to run back to the car and burrow into the backseat. Her guilt was threatening to choke off her air supply. She took great gulping breaths of air.

Somehow she managed to get herself to the Quad. There, before her, stood the four-story Troy H. Middleton Library. She stared at the bicycles chained to the crepe myrtles. Long ago she'd chained her own bicycle to some of the same crepe myrtles. She continued to stare at them as though seeing the setting for the first time, then turned and started down the path she'd walked that night with Connie Bryan. The only difference between then and now was the time of year. It had been warm that spring night and the azaleas and the sweet olives had been in full bloom. The bubble-gum scent of the sweet olives had been almost overwhelming. She longed to sit down on one of the benches, but there was no time. Maybe later she'd walk over to the parade ground and work her way back to the Quad and sit for a while. From time to time she looked upward to see if the lights were still there and intact. They were. She stopped and looked around to get her bearings. As far as the eye could see were the European red-tile roofs. Those very rooftops were one of the reasons she'd enrolled at LSU. Her ears perked when the clock in the magnificent bell tower chimed. It chimed every fifteen minutes. Jane looked at her watch. To the second.

Keep walking, Jane. Do what you told Betty Vance to do. Relive the experience, she reminded herself. *No matter how painful, relive it. Maybe you'll remember something.*

The first thing she remembered was that she'd felt inadequate compared to Connie—pretty, popular Connie, the Homecoming Queen. She'd asked Jane if she was seeing anyone special.

"No, I'm not seeing anyone special or otherwise," Jane had replied.

"You just haven't found the right guy yet. But you will in time. The moment you look into someone's eyes and know that person is your destiny, it's like no other feeling in the world. Todd and I are going to have such a wonderful life. We have our house all picked out, the furniture, even the kitchen dishes and place mats. We want four children and neither one of us cares if they're boys or girls as long as they're healthy. We even picked out names. I'm going to bake and decorate for the holidays. Todd and I both just love Christmas. We met during Christmas break our first year here at LSU. . . ."

"You're very lucky, Connie. I wish you all the happiness in the world," Jane had told her.

Instinctively, Jane stopped at the exact spot where she and Connie had stopped that night. She felt momentary panic as her mind jumped forward.

"Hey!" a voice shrilled in her head.

Jane sucked in her breath and turned to where she remembered the sound had come from. She could picture them standing there, five dark images right behind her and one standing back away from the group. All of them were tall and broad, like football players. Fear and anger knotted inside her.

"Well, lookee here, boys. We snagged us a real little beauty. The school beauty to be exact."

Jane began to shake as the fearful images of what was coming built in her mind. She could hear Connie ask them what they wanted, then she saw three of the boys pull her away into the bushes.

"Come on, you guys, cut it out," she'd cried. *"This isn't funny—"* She heard a thump and remembered she'd dropped her books.

"It's not supposed to be funny, so shut up. We have plans for Little Miss Homecoming Queen, don't we, guys?"

The memories were so real, Jane could feel one of the boy's arms surround her, hold her so tight she couldn't breathe. She remembered struggling, tugging and pushing at his arms, but he was too strong.

She flinched and took a step backwards as she relived the moment one of them punched her in the stomach. Her legs buckled beneath her, and she sat down on the ground. The dark silhouette of the sixth boy, the odd man out, loomed in front of her now as it did then. He was broader and taller than the others. She remembered his leaving, running, and her thinking that maybe he wasn't one of them, that he was going for help.

Like scenes in a movie, the memories came at her, one on top of another. The three boys who had taken Connie into the bushes came back, slapping each other on the back and congratulating themselves. They'd raped the Homecoming Queen. Yea!

Tears filled Jane's eyes just as they had that awful night. She could feel her anger build. She remembered rising and lunging at the boy closest to her, knocking him down.

"This goddamn beached whale needs a lesson," one of the others had said. *"Which one of you wants Miss Piggy? No takers?"*

A scream rose in her throat, only to be stifled by a beefy hand. Bite him! her mind screamed. Bite him!

Jane took deep breaths, trying to calm herself. *A bite like that was bound to leave a bad scar,* she thought as she gathered Olive close to her. For long minutes she sat staring off into space, thinking, cataloging, and analyzing.

"Back to the car, Olive. I'm going into the library to see who was on the wrestling and football teams that year." Jane opened the car door and got Olive settled with a chewy. "Don't you dare open this car door! I won't be long."

It was noon when Jane returned to the car. Behind her, she heard the tram grind to a stop. She turned to relive another old memory. She'd taken the tram on a daily basis to get from one end of the huge campus to the other. Suddenly it seemed like a lifetime ago.

Olive yipped her pleasure at her mistress's return.

Jane climbed into the car and grabbed the apple she'd snagged off the kitchen counter on her way out the door earlier in the morning.

"No. This is my apple, Olive. I gave you a chewy, remember?

"Shhh, I want to look at all this stuff I printed out." Olive sat quietly, looking out the window. "Look at this, Olive, I don't believe it. Brian Ramsey was a year behind me in school. He was a halfback on the football team. The rest of the first string graduated with me. I've got the profiles on the entire team, but I'm not going to read them until we get home. They were all solid-looking guys, but none of them were as *beefy* as Ramsey. I'll bet none of them had hands like his either. I got all the players' addresses from the alumni book—all the wrestling guys, the first- and second-string football team as well. They all live here in Louisiana. I have my work cut out for me, Olive, but I'm going to follow through. I still have *the bag.* I must have been meant to keep it. Thank God I never threw it away. One quick walk, and then we're off to Slidell."

Olive walked sedately alongside her mistress as Jane made her way to the Student Union and the parade grounds. She walked down the center, her eyes going right and left. There was David Boyd Hall, Charles E. Coates Hall, James W. Nicholson Hall. The fountain across from Thomas W. Atkinson Hall was the same, and still spouting water. How many times she'd sat on the benches, pondering the world. She continued walking, stopping every few feet so Olive could either sniff or squat. There was the red sign saying Disco Tim's was still in business.

She walked toward the Quad to admire the magnificent tree in the middle. She probably had fifty pictures of the tree taken during her four years at LSU. She wondered where they were. Probably packed away in some box in the garage. "See that stuff growing around the tree, Olive? It's called as-pidistra, which means cast-iron plants. You can't kill them. They live on forever and ever. I think we've seen enough. Time to leave."

Mike Sorenson raced up the steps, fished out his key, and let himself into Jane's house. The house was too quiet. Olive should have greeted him by now. "Jane! Where are you?" he singsonged. "I brought some fresh sugar donuts!" When there was no response he ran up to the second floor. He frowned at the neatly made bed. It was a little early in the morning for a made bed. Jane didn't usually make the bed until she was ready to leave for work. He checked the towels in the bathroom. They were damp, the shower still wet. *Damn. She didn't say anything about going out early this morning.*

Mike headed for the kitchen on the first floor. From there he could check the back of the house to see if Jane's car was gone. He saw the note propped up against the cookie jar the moment he entered the kitchen.

> *Mike,*
> *I decided to drive up to Baton Rouge to check on some things. I'm not sure if I'll be back today or not. I may decide to drive on to Slidell. If I do, I won't be back till tomorrow. I thought you were going to call me last night. I missed talking to you.*

I have Olive with me. Leave your cell phone on today. If I get a chance, I'll call you. I made some serious decisions last night. I want to talk to you about them.

Jane

Mike opened the bag of sugar donuts. His mind raced as he munched on the sweets. He could feel himself breaking into a cold sweat. Did those decisions have anything to do with him? Was Jane upset that he hadn't called her last night the way he'd promised? He read the note a second time. It was much too formal, and she hadn't signed it, Love, Jane. If he'd left her a note, he would have signed it, Love, Mike. He wouldn't have started off the note with just her name. He would have written, Dear Jane. Why didn't she write Dear Mike? Sweat dripped into his eyebrows. He swiped at it with the sleeve of his shirt.

At loose ends, he didn't know what to do with himself. Should he go home? Should he wait there? If he wanted to, he could get out the tool kit that was in the garage and fix all the crooked things in the house. Or, he could turn on Jane's computer and do some work. He snorted. What work? He was so on target with his profession there was nothing for him to do except wait for phone calls. Maybe he should call his parents. Maybe he should search out the ghost that supposedly inhabited this house. On the other hand, maybe he should just go home and go to bed and sleep all day. He finally opted for Jane's home office and her computer.

He memorized the condition of Jane's desk before he sat down. If he moved something, he would be able to put it back in its original position. People didn't like to have their things moved. He himself was one of those people. He looked down at the pile of printouts. Today's date. That had to mean Jane worked on the computer after midnight. The snoop disk was half in and half out of the tower. He didn't feel guilty at all as he started to read through the files. When he finished, he leaned back on the swivel chair. On the surface, the files were nothing more than information on Brian Ramsey and Betty Vance. Obviously, Jane read something in the files that made her go to Baton Rouge. A prickle of fear dusted his arms. He stared down at the Betty Vance file. Who the hell was Betty Vance?

"I miss you, Jane Lewis," Mike mumbled as he leaned back in the chair and closed his eyes.

8

Trixie McGuire stared across the kitchen table at her husband, her fingers tight around the handle of her coffee mug. "I don't like the looks of that young woman, Fred. I'm no shrink like Janie, but I've lived a long time and what I see worries me. She's too far over the edge. I don't need a textbook or a case file to tell me this woman is going to be trouble for our Janie. She's not even Jane's patient. Well, she is and she isn't." She picked up her mug and was about to take a sip when she had a thought. "I have a real bad feeling. Something is going to happen and everyone will lawyer up and the dark stuff will hit the fan. What do you think, honey?"

"I think we need to give her a chance, sweetie," Fred said, extending his arm across the table and patting the back of her hand. "That glazed look in her eyes is from all the drugs she's been taking. Six months on strong drugs will do that to you. Jane must see hope for her." He drew his hand back and offered his wife a reassuring smile. "Look, on Janie's recommendation, she got a dog and came here to the farm," he said, pointing outside. "Look at her, sweetie. She's really got a tight hold on that leash. Must be that the dog is new security for her." His gaze returned to his wife. "I'm not saying you're wrong, Trix. What I'm worried about is our Janie, about what she said to you. In the blink of an eye, she's willing to toss in the towel and throw her career away. She's good at what she does. It would be a cryin' shame for her to chuck the whole thing."

Trixie sighed in resignation. "We have to trust Janie's judgment. She's got a good head on her shoulders. She won't take chances with this girl. All that stuff you told me earlier— She's just trying to ease her own guilt or what she perceives to be her guilt over her college friend. If she needs us, we're here.

"Fred, we're *old*. We're both losing it. We sat on our respective asses so long writing books we don't have a clue as to what's going on in the world today. We have senior moments on an hourly basis. We goddamn well *dodder*, Fred. Thank God our minds are still sharp. We need to do something for Janie before our time runs out."

As if in defiance, Fred snapped his flowered suspenders, then adjusted his glasses. "Stop being so morbid, Trixie. I plan on living forever. What we need to do is stay out of Janie's business unless she asks for our help."

"You mean mind my own business, don't you? That isn't going to happen, Fred, so get that thought right out of your mind. You're pissing me off. You don't want to piss me off, Fred." When she slammed her coffee mug down on the table, coffee sloshed all over it. Her eyes sparked angrily.

Fred groaned. "C'mon, Trix. We both know you can't stay mad at me longer than ten minutes. I just don't want to see you get riled up so that you go off half-cocked and hit a brick wall." Fred scooted his chair back. "I have to get to work. By the way, did we ever figure out if a dull ax or a sharp one would make more blood pour out of a wound?"

"Look in my book under *blood*. I think the dull ax will cause more bleeding. I can't think about that now, Fred."

"How about if you think about those three pills left in my Viagra bottle," he said, a sly look on his face.

Trixie's mouth spread into a smile. "You have *three?*"

"Yep. Wear that thing with the sparklers on the shoulder." He winked at her.

"Three! I thought we used them all. See, Fred, this is a senior moment. I must not have been wearing my glasses when I looked at the bottle."

Fred snapped his suspenders a second time as he leered at his wife. "Did we ever decide what would happen if you took one and I took one?"

"Yes we did. One of us would be dead at the end of the night."

"Oh, yeah. Right. I forgot."

"One will do, Fred. Be sure to change the sheets. Put the pink-flowered ones on. It will be like making love in a field of pink roses."

Fred didn't need any additional prompting. He trundled out of the kitchen whistling, his fingers curled around his suspenders.

Trixie made a hissing sound as she waved him away. She walked out to the back porch, where Flash was sitting next to Betty Vance and Golda. "It's pretty out here, isn't it?"

"Yes it is. Who does your gardening? I've never seen so many pretty flowers at this time of year."

"We have a gardener once a week. He takes care of everything. How did you sleep last night, honey, without those pills?"

"Not very well. That's why I was taking sleeping pills and the Valium and that other drug I can't pronounce. And before you ask, no, Dr. Thomas didn't know I was taking the sleeping pills. Dr. Lewis said it will take a while for the drugs to work out of my system. I guess the truth is, I'm afraid to go to sleep. I'm afraid I'll dream about it all over again."

Trixie digested the information. "Dreams can't hurt you, Betty. You have to let go. I don't think you've done that. I don't know, maybe you never will. There are people who thrive on things like this. You know, getting attention, making excuses for not getting on with a life that maybe wasn't all that wonderful. I hope you aren't one of those people," Trixie said bluntly.

Betty looked askance at Trixie. "I'm not one of those people," she spit out. "My life was as good as anyone else's before I was attacked. I had a great job. I had money in the bank, my own car, furniture, an apartment. It's real easy for Dr. Thomas and Dr. Lewis and even you, Ms. McGuire, to be tough and stern and say, c'mon, let's get it together. Life goes on. Until you have a knife held at your throat and one man holding you down while another one rapes you, don't pass judgment."

Trixie nodded. She wasn't the least bit offended. "That little speech took a lot of guts, Betty. You really told me off. That's good," she said, patting the top of her knee. "Jane was right about you. She thinks you have a tough inner core of strength to draw on. I guess the question is, why aren't you doing that? You survived, so that means you are a survivor. You're alive. I could quote you statistics on the ones that didn't survive. From where I'm sitting, I think it's better to be alive than dead. That's just my opinion, Betty."

"I don't know. I guess it's easier to wallow."

"What's going to happen to you when your friend gives up on you? Eventually he will, you know. Where will you go? What will you do?"

"I'm hoping it doesn't come to that, that the sessions at the crisis center help. Dr. Lewis agreed to talk to me on a daily basis. I'm hoping good comes of it."

"Me, too. But you can't depend entirely on others. If you want to get through this, then *you* have to make an all-out effort." Trixie leaned forward and petted Golda. "That's a nice dog you got yourself there. Flash seems to like her, too."

Betty put her arms around the big dog and hugged her. "She slept on my bed last night. I think she's scared. Probably misses her owner."

"Yeah, I know how that is. Flash missed his owner and his work so much that we almost lost him. But as you can see, he's just fine now. Of course, we work hard at keeping him happy, but he gives us plenty of happiness in return." Trixie stood up. "Is there anything I can do for you, Betty? How about some lunch?"

"That would be nice. I'll sit in the sun for a little bit and maybe take Golda for a short walk if that's okay. I see some storm clouds coming in. The weatherman said it was going to rain late this afternoon."

"I think he could be right," Trixie said, looking upward toward the scudding clouds to the east. "I'll call you when lunch is ready. We need to fatten you up. You're almost as scrawny as me." Trixie was hoping for a smile at the very least, or maybe even laughter. Instead, Betty stared out at the garden as she continued to stroke Golda's head.

Trixie's shoulders slumped once she was in the kitchen. *The girl isn't ever going to let it go. She'll go through the motions, but that's as much as she'll do. Janie, girl, you have your work cut out for you where this one is concerned.*

It was close to four o'clock when Jane turned the corner onto a tree-lined street with neat two-story houses set back from the sidewalk. Golf-course green lawns abounded. It was a pretty street. A nice street to grow up on. She wondered if Connie had roller-skated on the sidewalks and ridden her bike to and from school. She wished she knew. Did Connie have friends who lived on the same street or neighboring streets? She made a mental note to ask where the cemetery was. The least she could do was put some flowers on her grave.

From her car window, she scanned the house numbers on the mailboxes. When she found the one she was looking for, she drew a deep breath. Was she doing the right thing coming here? She hoped so. Right or wrong, she had to do it. It was something she should have done a long time ago.

A roll of thunder sounded overhead. Wind whistled through the trees as Jane made her way up the winding walkway flanked on both sides by well-manicured monkey grass. How many times had Connie tripped up this same walkway?

It was a pretty porch, the kind Mike had described to her. Green fiber mats, comfortable white rockers with colorful cushions and little tables with plants on them. She wondered if anyone ever sat there. It all looked new, hardly used. The fans overhead whirled but not from electricity. The wind was stronger, and the long porch was like a wind tunnel. She wondered if the potted plants and hanging ferns would be all right or if they would be blown down.

Jane swallowed as she pressed the doorbell. It chimed inside. Rain began to pour from the dark sky the second an older replica of Connie opened the door. She was a slender woman, petite actually, with blond hair cut in the latest style. She was a nurse if Jane remembered correctly. The father was a teacher. They were probably both retired now or soon to be retired.

"Mrs. Bryan?"

"Yes?"

"I'm Jane Lewis. I was a friend of Connie's," she said, offering the woman her business card.

"Please, come in. My husband is in his workshop. I'm sure he'd like to meet you. I'll fetch him. It will be just a minute. I just made some coffee. Would you like some?"

"Yes, thank you. Coffee would be nice."

Jane looked around the living room. Comfortable was her first thought. She squeezed her eyes shut as she tried to picture Connie lying on the floor, a book open in front of her as she listened to the television. She had probably played the piano on the far side of the room, where pictures of her from babyhood to college graced the top. A huge picture of her in a pale yellow prom gown hung over the mantel. Jane swallowed again. Her parents were probably in the workshop whispering and wondering what she was doing there after so many years. *Please, God, let this be the right thing I'm doing.*

"Dr. Lewis, this is my husband Quentin. My name is Adele. Please sit down. I'll get the coffee."

"Please call me Jane."

"All right, Jane," Quentin Bryan said quietly.

He was short and squat, almost soccer-ball round and totally bald. *He doesn't look friendly at all,* Jane thought. She debated running for the door.

"I don't seem to recall meeting you, Jane. Or is it my bad memory?"

"No, we never met, sir."

"What brings you to Slidell?"

"I drove down here from LSU this afternoon. I've wanted to come here so many times over the years, but I could never get up the courage. I have something to tell you. I should have told you years ago, but I promised your daughter I wouldn't."

A cold congested expression settled on his face. "Young woman, I think you better wait till my wife gets here before you say whatever it is you have to say." There was such a chill in the man's voice, Jane shivered inside her button-down sweater.

"I'm here now, Quentin. What is it you came here to tell us, Dr. Lewis?"

Jane cleared her throat. "Before I tell you, can you tell me why Connie took her own life?"

Tears welled in Adele Bryan's eyes. "We don't know. She took her life during the night. Quentin found her in the morning when she didn't come down to breakfast. There was no reason that we could think of. She was getting married right after graduation, and she was so in love. Todd was so broken up he didn't even go to his own graduation. He didn't know the reason either. It was a shock to all of us."

Jane took a deep breath. "I know why," she said as calmly as she could. "That's why I came here." Jane licked at her dry lips. "The night before Connie's and my last final, we walked home from the library together. Six boys came out of the bushes and frightened us. Three of them grabbed Connie and dragged her into the bushes and then raped her. I tried everything I could to help her, but they kept me from her." In spite of their horror-stricken faces she continued. "Afterward, I begged her to go to the crisis center or to the police to file a report, but she refused. She made me promise not to tell anyone. For some reason she was positive Todd wouldn't want her anymore and would break off their engagement. I kept her in my dorm room with me all night."

Jane watched, her face miserable, as Connie's father put his arm around his weeping wife's shoulders.

"Connie wanted me to throw her clothes away. She didn't want any reminders of what had happened. I put them in a paper bag, thinking she could use them as evidence if she changed her mind about filing a report. I still have the bag, and the DNA would still be as good today as it would have been back then. I would have brought it with me, but I didn't know I was coming here until I got to LSU and made the decision."

"This is preposterous!" Quentin Bryan exploded. "Why are you doing this to us? What possible reason can you have for coming here and stirring all this up again? I don't want to hear this, and neither does my wife. If Connie had been raped, she would have told us. She was a good girl. She didn't keep secrets. Damn it, she would have told us."

Adele Bryan took her husband's hands in hers. "Hush, Quentin," she said, her voice stern. "I *do* want to hear this. I *need* to hear this." She turned to Jane. "Connie wasn't the same when she came back from college, Dr. Lewis. She spoke to us, and she smiled here and there, but all the life seemed to have gone out of her. She lost all interest in her wedding plans, and she said she wasn't going to go to her graduation. She never gave us a reason. We didn't know what to make of it, and neither did Todd. He did everything he could to get her out of what he called her funk. He thought maybe she didn't do well on her finals. Quentin is wrong. She would never have told us something like that. Do . . . do you know the boys' names?"

"No. It was too dark. Some of the campus lights were burned out. That's why we were walking together from the library."

"Why did you feel compelled to come here now and tell us this?" Quentin Bryan demanded coldly.

Jane folded her hands in her lap. "I thought you had a right to know. I didn't want you to think it was something either one of you had done or think that you had failed her somehow. I wish I had come sooner but . . . I didn't. Back then, I doubt if you would have believed me." She leaned forward slightly. "Did you know that Todd Prentice got married? It wasn't even a year later. His wife is extremely wealthy, and they have three children: Joshua, Alice, and Peter."

Adele gasped. "Those are the names Connie wanted to name her children." She turned and clutched at her husband.

Jane frowned as she digested Mrs. Bryan's statement. "I saw him at a fund-raiser a few years ago. I had always known of him, but until then I had never met him personally. For some reason he sought me out. I thought that was very strange at the time, and I still think it's strange."

"What does all that have to do with Connie's death?" Mr. Bryan shouted. "She took her own life. Christ Almighty, can't you let her rest in peace?"

Adele wept into a wad of tissue her husband slapped into her hand. "Hush, Quentin. I want to hear all of this." With shaky hands she reached for her cup of coffee. "For years we've blamed ourselves for Connie's death," she said to Jane. "It's a relief in a way to know that it wasn't something we did. But I'm curious. All this business about Todd marrying, having children, and seeking you out at the fund-raiser. You must think it's important, or you wouldn't have mentioned it. What does it mean, Dr. Lewis?"

Jane took a deep breath. "I don't know, Mrs. Bryan. I'm looking for answers myself. And relief. I've always regretted not taking Connie by the hand and forcing her to get help. All these years I've carried that guilt around with me." She took a sip of her coffee and told herself she needed to say everything she had on her mind. *Everything.* Once she left the Bryan house, she didn't want to have to come back because she'd left out some niggling detail. "I'm a psychiatrist. Not too long ago a man came to me as a patient. He played football at LSU. There was something about him. Something that didn't compute. He *said* he was married. He *said* his wife was raped. He *said* he couldn't bring himself to touch her. He said all the things Connie had said to me in regard to Todd Prentice. Last night I went on the computer and printed out everything I could on the man. Then this morning I went to LSU and got the pictures of the entire football team. I can't prove this, but I think Connie's attackers were football players, and I think my patient was one of them. He is no longer my patient by the way. Another thing, he is not married." She wrung her hands, and flinched when she said, "I bit one of the boys who attacked us. I bit him so hard it went through to the bone. He would carry a scar to this day. That's what I came here to say."

"You should have stayed away. We didn't need to know all this garbage," Mr. Bryan snarled.

"One more word, Quentin, and I swear, I will walk out this door and never come back."

With a huff of indignation, Quentin Bryan left the room. Somewhere in the house a door slammed.

"What are you going to do now, Dr. Lewis?"

"I wish I knew. Coming here was my biggest hurdle. I'm going to go home and think this through. My brain is in over-drive right now. I'm not going to let this matter drop, though. I'm going to see it through to the end, whatever that end might be. I just wanted you to know that."

"How . . . how did you know what Todd named his children?" Adele asked.

"He lives in Crowley. I called his house from LSU this morning and pretended I was doing a survey on popular baby names. The housekeeper rattled them right off."

"Would you like to see Connie's room, Dr. Lewis?"

"Yes."

"I just closed the door that morning. We didn't change or move anything. It's not a shrine or anything like that. I just couldn't bear to . . . to . . ."

"I understand, Mrs. Bryan."

It was the kind of room a girl like Connie would have. Posters on the wall, her own Princess telephone. A coatrack with her cheerleading jacket and pom-poms sticking out of the sleeves. Rollerblades and ice skates hanging from the lower pegs. Stacks and stacks of books. Slippers and robe at the foot of the bed. Piles of *Ms.* and *Cosmo* magazines on the floor by her desk. *A computer with a cover on it.* A busy room, a comfortable room. A safe room.

"Connie and I made the quilt the summer she was ten. She loved to sew and quilt. She was going to take it with her when she moved into her new house with Todd. Quentin and I bought her a sewing machine for a wedding present. It did everything. She never even took it out of the box. Quentin took it up to the attic. Connie said Todd was disappointed in the sewing machine. He was expecting a cash gift."

"I don't much care for Mr. Todd Prentice," Jane said sourly.

"Neither did Quentin or I. But he was Connie's choice, and she was so very happy. She had her life all planned out. I wonder if it would have worked out for the two of them. It didn't take him long to get married. A year isn't very long to mourn."

Jane walked farther into the room. "Did Connie leave a suicide note?"

Adele shook her head.

"Did you check the computer?"

"Good God, no! I told you, we closed the door. I didn't come into this room for years. Four to be exact. Quentin didn't either."

"Would you mind if I took these disks?" Jane said, pointing to a plastic case with a dozen or so colored disks in it. "I'll bring them back. There might be something on them. Then again, maybe not."

"Take them but don't tell Quentin. Put them in your purse. Do you think I should clear out this room?"

"Only if you want to. A first step might be leaving the door open. When you're ready, you'll do what you have to do."

"My husband is a good man, Dr. Lewis. Connie was his

little girl. You know what they say about Daddy's little girl? She was all that and more. He took her fishing, camping, hiking. They washed the car together. He absolutely adored her. He took her death so hard he retired because he couldn't keep his mind on his work. I kept working because work took my mind off my grief. I'll be retiring next spring."

Jane put the computer disks into her purse and turned around. "I should be going. Can you tell me where the cemetery is? I'd like to get some flowers and stop by."

"I can take you there. It isn't far."

Jane shook her head. "Thank you, but this is something I want to do myself. I have some apologies to make to your daughter. I hope she understands."

Adele Bryan nodded. "I think I'll . . . I think I'll just leave this door slightly ajar. For now. Maybe tomorrow, I'll open it a little wider. I appreciate you coming here. It must have been hard for you. Now, here's how you get to the cemetery. . . ."

The stone was square and simple. The chiseled words read, CONSTANCE BRYAN, BELOVED DAUGHTER. There were no dates, no carvings of any kind on the marble. Jane placed the flowers she'd purchased at the grocery store at the base of the stone. She dropped to her knees in the pouring rain. She talked until she ran out of words. "I know you aren't here, Connie. I know your soul, your spirit, is somewhere else, but the part of you I knew so briefly is here. I'll be back. I don't know when, but I'll have answers for you. I owe you that much."

Jane struggled to her feet. She felt cold to her bones. Back in the car, with Olive licking her face, she turned on the heater. She sat shivering in the steamy car, tears streaming down her face. When had she ever felt so inadequate? Wiping her eyes and blowing her nose didn't make her feel one bit better.

The cell phone lying on the console beckoned her. It was time to check in with Trixie and Mike. "How'd it go, Trixie? Is Betty okay? Were there any problems?"

"Everything's fine, Janie. Where are you, honey?"

"Slidell. I drove down from LSU. I'm actually parked in the cemetery. Connie's parents didn't know about the rape. Not a clue, Trixie. I'll tell you about it when I get home. Where's Betty now?"

"Her friend picked her up a little while ago. She spent the morning playing checkers with Fred, then she read the paper and played with the dogs. She ate a good lunch and took Golda for a walk. She came back when it started to rain. She doesn't talk much, and she volunteers nothing. She answers you if you ask a question, but that's it. I left with Flash around three. My battery is low, Jane. I have to hang up so I can charge it."

Jane turned the key in the ignition, shifted gears, then turned on the wipers. She called Mike while she was waiting for the defroster to clear the windows.

"Mike, it's Jane."

"Where the hell are you? Do you have any idea what time it is? I've been waiting all day for you to call. If you ever do something like this again without talking to me first, I'm going to take you over my knee."

"Promises, promises," Jane said lazily. *He cares. He really cares.*

"Where are you?"

"I'm leaving the cemetery in Slidell. I needed to say good-bye. I'm on my way home. It's pouring rain, so it will slow me down. I should be home by nine. A nice warm dinner and a really good bottle of wine would be nice. Pick something up at Roy's, okay?"

"Are you all right, Jane? You sound a little strange."

"Probably not. I relived the whole thing, Mike, and I remembered a couple of things. Afterward, I went to the Bryans' house and told them everything. Adele Bryan let me take Connie's computer disks. I'm hoping there might be something on them." A horn blasted behind Jane. "Listen, there's lots of traffic, and I have to pay attention to the road, so I'm going to hang up. I missed you today. I thought about you a lot."

"I would have gone with you, Jane. You could be meddling in something dangerous here. You're allowing yourself to get personally involved. That's not good."

"It's the only way I know how to do things, Mike. I'll see you soon. I love you," she said shyly.

"If you knew how worried I've been . . . I love you, too. So much my ears are aching with the feeling. I never said that to another woman in my life. What aches on you, Jane?"

Jane laughed as she broke the connection.

She flew into his arms and hugged him until he squealed. "It's been almost two days since I've seen you, Mike." She kissed him until he pinched her to let him go. He pretended to gasp for breath. "That was so you won't forget me while I take a shower and wash my hair. How about if I just put a robe on over my naked body when I'm done? We'll eat and head straight for bed."

"A girl after my own heart."

"What's for dinner?"

"Fried chicken, coleslaw, french fries, and some gravy on the side. That's for me. Sesame-steamed vegetables, grits, and berry cobbler for you."

"Is everything of yours really, really greasy?"

"You bet. Table's already set. I could wash your back if you want me to."

"I haven't had anything greasy in a long time. I might want to pick a little off your plate," she said, looking toward the pots and pans on the stove. She turned away with a sigh. "I don't need you to wash my back, but a back rub later would be nice." She dashed off toward the stairs. "Put the wine in the freezer so it's cold for dinner," she called over her shoulder. "I won't be long."

Jane threw her head back to allow the steamy, pulsating shower to work its magic. She couldn't remember the last time anything felt this good. If she could just crawl into bed and sleep for twenty-four straight, dreamless hours, she might start to feel like a human being again.

Time-wise, she was as good as her promise to Mike when she stepped out of the shower. She toweled off, sprinkled fragrant body powder all over her body, then slipped naked into her old, comfortable flannel robe. A rubber band in her hand, she gathered up the tangled mass of hair and piled it into a big loop on top of her head. She peered into the mirror trying to decide which comic-strip character she resembled. When she couldn't remember, she shrugged and tripped her way down to the kitchen, where Mike was waiting for her.

"Oooo, all that greasy stuff looks awful," Jane said, picking at her steamed vegetables. She snatched a french fry from Mike's plate, then a chicken leg. And devoured both.

"I think you're a vegetarian only when it suits you. Have some more french fries. Tell me about today, Jane."

She grabbed them before he could change his mind. "Not tonight, Mike. I'm whipped. I don't want to think about anything but you and me tonight."

He looked her square in the eye. "You're getting too personally involved, Jane. Nothing good can possibly come of this. I'm starting to worry about you."

"I don't want to talk about this tonight, Mike. You conduct your practice your way and I'll conduct mine my way. I can't turn it off, that's the bottom line. I wish I could be more like you and detach myself, but I can't." That was a lie, she thought. She couldn't imagine detaching herself from her patients. That was the one thing she hated about doctors in general. After a while they all became sort of cold—detached. She'd promised herself she would never do that. "Maybe I should have been a gardener or a carpenter. I probably would have made a good plumber," Jane said, her eyelids drooping.

"I think it's time for bed. I'm going to dump everything in the sink just in case Olive gets adventuresome during the night. Up and at 'em, Jane."

Jane finished eating, then headed up the stairs. She threw back the covers, crawled into bed, and was asleep before Mike finished brushing his teeth.

Olive sat on the floor looking up at him. "It's okay, Olive. I think I'll sit here on the chair and watch over your mistress. You want to come up here and sit with me?" She stood up on her hind legs and put her paws on his knee. "Come on," he said, reaching for her. He settled her into his lap, petting her head. Dogs were great companions. Olive was one in a million.

Mike closed his eyes as he sighed with contentment. They snapped open a moment later when Olive jumped off the chair and raced out of the room, her tail swishing with excitement.

"Hello, Dr. Sorenson. How are you this evening?"

Mike rubbed his eyes. "Who are you?"

"Billy Jensen. Olive just chased my dog, Jeeter, out of the room. They play together every night. It's been a long time since Jeeter had a friend."

"I didn't see a dog," Mike mumbled.

"He stays invisible sometimes. I don't know why. We need to talk, Dr. Sorenson."

"About what? You're the ghost, aren't you?"

"I'm not of your world if that's what you mean."

"Are you sure this isn't a dream?"

"I'm sure."

"What do you want to talk about? I'm all ears."

The boy giggled. *"Then you would have ears all over your head. I only see two."*

Mike couldn't resist. He wiggled his ears the way he'd done when he was a kid. "Talk to me, Billy."

On the adjoining farm, Trixie McGuire snuggled against her husband. "That was nice, Fred. Real nice. And we owe it all to one little pill," she said, eyeing the prescription bottle on the nightstand. Were her eyes playing tricks or were there three pills still in the bottle? "Fred, there are still three pills in this bottle. I don't understand."

"Trixie honey. I can't lie to you." He raised up on his elbow.

"But you said . . . I thought . . . do you mean . . . all those other times you didn't take . . . ?"

He shook his head. "Nope. I didn't need them. I just let you think I took them. Don't ask me why. Maybe because we had that dry spell there for a while. I didn't want you to lose interest in me, Trixie."

"Fred, that would never happen. If I gave you the impression . . ."

"You didn't. It was me. I kept thinking I wasn't the man you married anymore. I want it to be the same as it used to be. We're getting up there in years, but I don't feel old. I don't ever want to feel old. Those pills made me feel old, Trixie."

"I didn't know you felt that way. You should have told me. Fred, it can't be the same. We're in our seventies. All our juices have been drying up. We tried to ignore it, but reality is reality. You never took any of the pills?"

"I washed the others down the drain," he admitted.

Trixie pressed closer. "You're a hunk, Fred McGuire. Those young studs out there have nothing on you. Throw that damn bottle away. When it works, it works. When it doesn't, it doesn't. As long as you're near me and we're together, that's all that counts. Can we go to sleep now?"

"I thought you'd never ask, my little love muffin."

"I love it when you talk like that, Fred."

Flash barked and put his big paws on the side of the bed.

Trixie turned over. "Okay, boy, you can come up here now. We're all through for tonight." She cuddled the dog close to her. "Good boy, yes, we love you, too," she crooned.

9

Jane eyed the kitchen calendar as she stood by the sink drinking her first cup of coffee of the day. One week until Christmas and two weeks until the new year. She closed her eyes for a moment. This was going to be a bad week. A hectic week. A week of decision making. And she still hadn't found a special present for Mike, Trixie, or Fred. Maybe she should go shopping today after the Christmas luncheon her colleagues held every year. Then again, maybe not. She wasn't exactly in the mood to shop. Not for presents and not for the Christmas tree Mike said he wanted them to have.

He wanted to decorate the house, too. A together project, he'd called it. Jane sighed at the thought of all the work. What was the sense in it anyway? They weren't going to be around to enjoy it all. She and Mike were spending Christmas Eve with Trixie and Fred. Then they were going to get up early and drive to New Orleans to spend Christmas Day with Mike's parents. Her heart started to beat faster at the thought. What if they didn't like her? What if she didn't like them?

Jane poured a second cup of coffee, thinking about how much she dreaded today's luncheon because Sharon Thomas was going to be there. The woman had called the office the day before and said they needed to have a talk and could they do it before the luncheon started. Sharon's voice had been frosty and angry-sounding. Jane figured it probably had something to do with Betty Vance's inability to make a decision as to which psychiatrist she wanted to treat her. As far as Jane was concerned, she was Betty Vance's friend, nothing more. She'd turned over her file to Sharon the first day her colleague resumed her practice. Betty still came to the farm with Golda and called Jane to talk about the dog. That, to Jane's mind, didn't constitute patient poaching.

Mike said she should have severed all ties to the young woman so as not to confuse her. But Mike also didn't believe in getting involved with his patients. In Jane's opinion, severing all ties with Betty would be tantamount to abandoning her. Something she could never do. If Sharon Thomas had gotten her panties in a wad over it, she was just going to have to untangle them.

Jane added more coffee to her cup, which was a mistake since it would keep her running to the bathroom all morning. With the office closed for the holidays she had scheduled the morning for a full body massage, a new hairstyle, a manicure, and a pedicure. She'd get home with just enough time to take a warm bath and put on the new dress she'd bought just for the luncheon. Providing she had enough guts to wear the provocative outfit. Trixie had helped her pick out the black silk because of its slimming qualities. "You look like a skinny pencil in it, honey," Trixie had said. The intricate gold belt emphasized her new waistline. She'd dropped eleven pounds since meeting Mike. She'd thought the dress a little too severe, too clingy, until Trixie pointed out the way the dress flirted with her knees and showed off her legs and womanly curves. The diamond frog pin she'd bought to fasten onto the shoulder would complete the outfit. Her strappy, black heels and the small Chanel bag with the gold chain,

Trixie's latest birthday gift, would make Mike do a double take. She crossed her fingers that the new hairstyle would be everything she'd hoped for.

"I have this feeling, Olive, that Mike is going to give me a ring for Christmas. I could be wrong," she said, starting to feel her mood improve, "but I don't think so. You're going to Trixie's today, girl, so get your gear ready. I just want to check my e-mail, and then we're good to go."

Jane turned on the computer and waited for it to boot up. She wondered why she bothered. She'd sent out queries by the dozen over the past two months, to all of Connie Bryan's friends that she'd been able to locate. So far, no one had responded. All her leads, all her ideas were proving to be dead ends. She looked at the plastic container with the disks she'd brought home from Slidell. There was nothing on them of any importance with the exception of one that required a password. A password she didn't have and one Connie's parents weren't aware of. For all she knew, it could be blank. She'd come up dry, too, in regard to Brian Ramsey.

"The one I should probably be checking on is that bastard, Todd Prentice," Jane muttered to Olive, who had gotten her rawhide bone and was patiently waiting for them to go. "Why didn't I put him into this mix? I'm going to do that tomorrow or maybe tonight when I get home. I have an inkling that Joshua, Alice, and Peter's father is in this up to his damn, fat neck." Olive woofed. "Yeah, yeah, I know, I'm getting involved again. Who cares? Not me. I'm going to be packing it in real soon, but first I'm going to get to the bottom of this if it's the last thing I do."

She turned off the computer and closed the plastic square that held Connie's disks. She slid it to the far corner of her desk. At the last second she reached for a green glass frog Beth Goins had given her and set it on top of the Lucite box. Now it didn't look so ominous.

                              *   *   *

Jane gaped at her reflection in the floor-length mirror. Was this svelte, fashionable-looking creature really her? She swirled and twirled as she laughed in delight. The dress really did make her look slim, thinner than she'd ever appeared. The strappy shoes were downright sinful. She did have nice legs, she realized, twisting this way and that to see them from different angles. But it was her new hairstyle that tickled her the most. It was short now, feathering on her forehead and around her ears. The hairdresser had thinned her hair first, then applied a straightening agent to bring her tight curls under control. Jane continued to stare at her reflection. In her entire life she'd never looked this good. The makeup she'd taken an hour to apply looked like she wasn't wearing any at all, which was her intention. A little perfume behind her ears and on her wrists, perfume the salesgirl said would make men melt in their shoes and women drop with envy. Oh, yeah.

Her good mood disappeared the moment she asked herself what her mother would think if she could see her now. "Plain Jane, huh? Up yours, Mother Dearest!" she said, flipping her mother the bird as she pranced out of the room.

For the most part it was your standard Christmas party-slash-luncheon, with the men outnumbering the women and the men letting the women know they were outnumbered in a gentlemanly way. There was the inevitable backslapping, handshaking, and a lot of subdued laughter. The women eyed one another as they calculated the cost of each other's outfits.

Every male eye in the room turned on Jane as she entered. For the first time in her life she knew she was being apprecia-tively stared at. It was a totally new feeling for her and one she liked. What would Mike's reaction be? she wondered.

Where was he? She didn't see him, but she did see Sharon Thomas nibbling from a cheese tray.

"Merry Christmas, Sharon," Jane said, holding out her hand. Sharon's grip was deliberately hurtful. The open hostility on her colleague's face was something Jane didn't understand, but she refused to let Sharon know she'd noticed. "You said you wanted to talk to me about something. Do you want to talk here or outside in the lobby?"

"Let's go to the lobby so I can smoke a cigarette," Sharon said. "I almost didn't recognize you, Jane."

Jane felt her chest puff out. "I lost a little weight and got a new hairstyle. I like your dress, Sharon."

"Is it true you and Mike Sorenson are an item?" Sharon asked, ignoring the compliment.

"Yes." Jane held the door for her colleague. She waited until she lit her cigarette before asking, "What did you want to talk to me about?"

Sharon blew a perfect smoke ring. "My patient, Betty Vance."

Jane repositioned herself so the smoke wouldn't drift into her face. "How is she doing?" she asked even though she already knew the answer.

"She might do a little better if you'd stop horning in. She's torn between the two of us. I wish you hadn't taken her off her Valium."

"As I told you in my report, Sharon, she wasn't just taking the Valium you'd prescribed but at least two other medications as well. She could have easily overdosed. As for *horning in*. She calls me from time to time, but it's always a conversation about her dog. She's not asking for advice, and I'm not giving it. I haven't been face-to-face with her since I turned her back over to you. From the way she talked, I assumed she was doing well."

"I told her I would release her if she wanted to continue

with you, Jane. She said no. This is a bad time of year for our patients, as you know. Betty's on her own now, something you suggested, which I think was unwise. That means she's going to be alone for the holidays, a particularly dangerous time for someone like her."

Jane was determined not to get into it with Sharon, especially in a public place where everyone seemed to have two sets of ears. "My godmother invited Betty for Christmas dinner, so she won't be alone, Sharon. They're good friends now, and Betty visits them often. I wish I could join them, but I'm going to New Orleans with Mike to meet his parents. What is it you want me to do?"

"Leave her alone," Sharon said with icy contempt.

"I can't do that, Sharon. You wouldn't do it either. At least I don't think you would. I'm a friend to Betty Vance, nothing more."

"This isn't going to work, Jane. You telling her one thing, me telling her something else. She's still much too fragile. It will confuse her even more."

"You keep saying she's fragile. I beg to differ with you because that young woman has a lot of inner strength. She's drawing on it without the aid of drugs. When I took over, she was so dopey she couldn't even drive herself to her appointment. She literally could not function. How can that be good? So she had a bad week until the drugs left her system. She survived. She's sleeping, holding down a job again, she has an efficiency apartment, and she's driving again. I'd say that's damn good from where I'm standing. I'll try to talk to her less frequently, but I will not stop being her friend. Let's both make sure we understand that, Sharon," Jane said, looking her colleague straight in the eye.

Sharon crushed out her cigarette, her body rigid with anger.

"Sharon, this probably isn't the time to mention this, but I might not see you again during the holidays. I'm thinking of selling my practice. If you're interested, let me know."

"My, my, my, I guess it is serious with Mike. I'll think about it. I meant it, Jane, leave Betty alone."

Jane stared down at the dirty ashtray and wished she had a cigarette. She wondered how many of the doctors inside the room smoked. She backed up a step when four of her colleagues filed past her and lit up. So much for the Surgeon General's report. She took a seat at the far end of the lobby to wait for Mike. She eyed the elaborate Christmas decorations. How festive it all looked. The tree was fresh, the scent almost overpowering. Packages wrapped in silver foil and tied with huge red-velvet ribbons surrounded the fragrant balsam. She wondered if they were empty or employee gifts. Empty, she decided, her cynicism winning out. The packages were just decorations. This was the new millennium after all, where everything was bogus and phony. Well-meaning psychiatrists included.

Closing her eyes, Jane struggled to remember what the Christmas trees looked like when she was a little girl. They must not have been special because she couldn't remember any of them.

Trixie's trees were always works of art. She hung all her childish trinkets on them: Popsicle sleds, macaroni wreaths, construction-paper ornaments, and a ribbon-framed thumbprint with arms and legs sketched in to resemble a bug. All those keepsake items were worked in with her one-of-a-kind blown-glass ornaments.

Jane clearly remembered making cookie-dough ornaments and painting them when she was at Trixie's house. Afterward, Trixie would hang them in the middle of the tree so everyone could see them. She called them her treasures. Tears burned behind her eyelids at the memory.

"Jane!" a welcome voice called.

She twisted around. "Mike!" She held her breath. This was the moment she'd been waiting for.

His eyes swept over her. "I didn't recognize you at first. My God, you cut your hair!" He looked positively horrified.

Jane's heart fluttered in her chest. "You don't . . . you don't like the way I look?"

"You look . . . totally different."

A cold knot of dread formed in her stomach. "My . . . my hair will grow back," she said apologetically, then wondered why in the hell she was defending herself. "Wait just a damn minute. I happen to like the way it looks, and it's easy to take care of. If you don't, that's your problem! I didn't insult you when you decided to grow a beard." Her gaze boldly met his.

His eyes crinkled at the corners as a smile grew on his face. "Wait a minute yourself and stop making assumptions. I *do* like it. You just took me by surprise, especially because all of a sudden you look like—"

"Like what?" Jane asked coolly.

"Coletta."

"Coletta! Your old girlfriend? Now you are insulting me, Mike." She looked away, her pride and newfound self-confidence wounded.

"Insult you! Coletta is gorgeous. She could have modeled. How can you be insulted by that remark, Jane?"

She turned back, eyeing him narrowly.

"Jane, you should have told me you were getting your hair cut. I loved your hair. I loved all those curls. I wasn't expect-ing—" He suddenly became tongue-tied. "If I wanted an-other Coletta in my life, I would have found one."

Jane gave him her most withering expression. "You should have quit while you were ahead, Mike. Somehow your com-parison just doesn't do it for me."

"I'm sorry, Jane. I didn't mean . . ."

"The hell you didn't. It's time to go inside." Jane flounced her way down the hall to the banquet room. She took her seat on the left side of the room. Mike was sitting on the right side.

Jane made small talk and listened to meaningless chatter as she tried to see over the poinsettia centerpiece. She opened a bright red napkin and settled it on her lap, her eyes sparking angrily as she tried to get her emotions under control. From time to time she risked a glance in Mike's direction as she listened to the boring speeches she wouldn't remember an hour from now. Satisfied that he looked miserable, she relaxed.

She looked better than she'd ever looked in her life and instead of complimenting her, he compared her to Carlotta, or Collette, or whatever the hell her name was.

When dessert arrived, Jane excused herself to go to the ladies' room she had no intention of visiting. In the lobby, she walked toward the exit and out to her car. She put the car in gear and headed for Trixie and Fred's. The two of them were the one constant in her life, her port in any storm or squall. Was this a storm or a squall? By God she would not cry. She simply would not cry.

"I think you better come over here, Fred," Trixie shouted over Flash's and Olive's furious barking. Fred trundled his way from the office to take up a position next to his wife. "Why is Jane sitting in the car like that? How long has she been out there? Is something wrong?"

"She just got here, Fred, and yes, I'd say something is wrong. She's crying. Today was her Christmas luncheon. She was so excited. She got her hair cut this morning. Wait till you see the dress she's wearing. Our Janie turned into a beautiful swan. Okay, she's blowing her nose and wiping her eyes. She's getting ready to come in. Quick, sit down at the table and pretend you weren't watching. I'll make some coffee."

Jane entered the kitchen, a sickly smile on her face. She dropped to her knees to cuddle with the dogs before she sat down at the table. "Make it strong, Trixie, and put three jiggers of something in it!"

"You got it! Wanna talk about it, kiddo?"

"Look at me! Tell me the truth, have you ever seen me look better? No, you have not! I struggled to lose all those pounds. I didn't just struggle, I *battled*. I got sick and tired of wearing those granny dresses and those damn boxy suits. Not to mention those baggy sweat suits. I also got sick and tired of trying to do something with my hair so I don't always have to wear a hat. I can manage this style in minutes. When I walked into that banquet room, every man turned to look at me. Well, maybe not every man, but a lot of them did. That never happened to me before. It felt good."

"So what happened to upset you so?" Trixie asked as she poured a dollop of Kentucky bourbon into the coffee mug.

"I said *three* jiggers, Trixie!"

Trixie continued to pour. She risked a glance at Fred, who was trying to look everywhere but at her and Jane.

"I might have three more, too," Jane said in defiance.

Flash threw back his head and howled. Olive minced her way over to Jane and sat down on her foot. Not to be outdone, she barked.

"You were saying," Trixie prompted.

Jane gulped at the hot coffee until her eyes started to water. She swiped at them with the back of her hand. "I thought for sure Mike's eyes would bug out of his head when he saw me. I guess they did but in the wrong way. He said I looked like Coletta, his old girlfriend. What do you think of that? Then he said if he wanted another Coletta, he would have gone out and found one. And . . . and he said I should have told him I was cutting my hair. Who does he think he is?" She pushed her coffee cup toward Fred and laid her head down on the table between her arms. "I left during dessert," she mumbled. "I paid a hundred bucks for that crappy lunch. I had salmon that was watery, broccoli that was soggy and pukey green, and some kind of potatoes that were cold and tasted like glue." She sat up, a grimace on her face. "I'll have some more of that coffee, Trixie. This is the best coffee you ever made. How about a peanut butter and jelly sandwich to go with it?" She kicked off the strappy shoes and sent them flying across the kitchen.

"I guess what you're saying is the luncheon wasn't up front and personal," Trixie said.

"Not one, warm, fuzzy moment. Thanks, Fred," Jane said, reaching for the sandwich he handed her. "There's more unfortunately. Are you ready for this? Dr. Thomas—the one I took over for while she was recuperating—she had the audacity to tell me to stay away from Betty Vance. She was downright ugly about it. I wanted to smack her face. I hate attitudes, and boy did she have one. I'm so glad I'm getting out of this business. I hate it. I hate all those stuffy doctors. I hate it that they can detach themselves from their patients at the blink of an eye. I hate it, hate it, hate it."

Trixie sat down across from Jane. "Janie, you know how men are. They're forever saying things ass backwards. I don't think Mike meant to insult you. In his own way, I think he was complimenting you. He loves you. I'll bet you anything he was just trying to say that he didn't think there was anything wrong with the way you were before."

"Yeah, right," Jane snorted. "This is the best coffee. What kind is it?"

"It's called one-hundred-proof Kentucky bourbon," Trixie said tartly. "You didn't tell him to kiss your ass, did you? You have a penchant for saying that when you get pissed off."

"No, but I thought about it. There were too many people standing around who would have heard." This time when Jane took a sip of her coffee, she missed her mouth and coffee sloshed down her chin onto the table.

"You're drunk, Janie!" Fred said, grabbing a kitchen towel to clean her and the table up.

"On two cups of coffee! Don't be ridiculous. That's *assurb*!" Jane slurred, her eyes crossing at the bridge of her nose.

Trixie giggled. Jane was always so in control.

"Why don't we put up your Christmas tree? I need to get some Christmas spirit."

Fred glanced at Trixie, a worried look on his face. "It's already up, honey. Eli did it yesterday when he came to hang the outside lights," Fred said, referring to the local handyman who had worked for them for years. "Trixie and I decorated it last night. Wanna see it?"

"No. I think I'll go home. Thanks for taking care of Olive for me. She loves coming here for doggie day care. Is Flash off today?"

"Yes, it's our day off."

"Then how about if I take him home with me so you two can have some time alone. I need the company. Besides, that . . . that . . . *doctor* might come pussyfooting around, and Flash can chase him off. I'm not ready to deal with him. Give me some more of that coffee in one of those *slurpy* cups so I can drink it on the way."

"Coffee, yes. Bourbon, no," Fred said, both his voice and his expression stern.

"You sound like *him*," Jane charged, getting up and heading toward the door in her stocking feet. "You never told me what to do before, Fred, so don't start now. So what if I'm feeling *good*? It's been a long time since I felt good. I'm not hurting anyone. My car's on empty. I need to borrow your cruiser. I'll bring it back in the morning. I'll drive across the field."

"You're drunk, Jane," Fred reminded her.

Jane looked at her coffee cup and saw two of them. "You could be right. But if I am, then that means I'm impaired. So, Flash and Olive can run home and I'll drive myself. Five miles an hour. I promise."

"No!" Fred and Trixie said in unison.

"Yes! Don't go there, you two! I mean it. Now, where's that *slurpy* cup? I'm watching you. You can keep the shoes," Jane said, leaning against the doorjamb.

"Okay, Janie, but this is against my better judgment," Trixie said, winking at Fred.

"What are you up to?" he asked.

"I figure if I can stall her, she'll fall asleep in the car, and I'll drive her home. You follow me and tomorrow she'll think she drove home herself. What do you think?"

"I think it will work." Fred planted a kiss on his wife's cheek. He reached for the keys as Trixie herded Jane out to the police cruiser. "Now, Janie, this vehicle is not as easy to drive as it might look. I want you to sit on the passenger side while I slide in and explain everything. Are you okay with that?"

"Ass-bo-lutely!" Jane said, gulping from the cup.

"See all these gadgets? Here's the switch for the police scanner and here's the thingy to turn on the siren. Now lean back, close your eyes, and see if you can visualize them. When I count to fifteen, you open your eyes and tell me where the siren is and where the ignition key goes."

Ten seconds later, Trixie called, "Okay, she's out!"

Trixie got out of the car to let the dogs in. "In the car, Flash. Olive, hop to it!" Behind her, Fred gunned the Bronco.

A few minutes later, Trixie stopped the cruiser by the front steps of Jane's house. She got out, went around to the passenger door, and pushed Jane into the driver's seat. So what if her godchild had a few bruises on her ass from sliding over the console. "Okay, we're here," she shouted, shaking Jane's shoulder. "What do you think? Doesn't it drive like a tank?"

Jane blinked her eyes open and tried to focus.

Trixie released the back door and the dogs jumped out. "C'mon, Janie. Get out. How about a nice shower and some real coffee? You did real good."

"Get off it, Trixie. You drove me home, and we both know it!" Jane mumbled as she struggled to get out of the car. "What happened to my shoes?"

"You kicked them off, dear. How'd you know I drove you home?"

"Because I wasn't asleep, I was thinking. You can think even when you're three sheets to the wind, you know. You can both go home now. I appreciate your looking after me. I'm okay."

Trixie whistled sharply. Both dogs and her husband came on the run. "We'll be over in the morning. Take it easy, sweetie, it isn't the end of the world, and alcohol isn't the answer. All alcohol does is dull the pain until the next time. Take a nap and when you wake up, call us, okay?"

"Sure. Okay, dogs, let's go!"

Trixie and Fred watched as their unhappy tipsy godchild wobbled up the steps to the front porch. They continued to watch until she opened the door, ushered in the dogs, and stumbled through. When they heard the sound of the lock snicking into place, they looked at one another.

"I can stay, Trixie, if you think it's a good idea. I can hang out on the back porch. The spare key is still under the windowsill, isn't it?"

"No, Fred. We'll go home and come back later. She's going to sleep it off. She must really be hurting to drink like that. I wonder if there's more to this than she said."

"When she sobers up, we'll ask her," Fred said, putting his arm around his wife's shoulders.

"There's nothing I wouldn't do for that girl, Fred."

"I know that, honey, and so does she. She doesn't want us here, so that means we go home and, like you said, come back later."

"All right, Fred."

* * *

Jane wobbled through the rooms, past her office and out to the hall that led to the second floor. The steps looked insurmountable, like a giant mountain she had to climb. Holding on to the railing, she made her way to the top. A wave of dizziness washed over her as she tottered to the bathroom, where she peeled off the designer dress and tossed it in the corner. She was never going to wear it again. Never. Ever.

The shower's needle-sharp spray pummeled her body as she jiggled under the hot water. She turned the hot water off and turned on the cold. She gasped, holding on to the towel bar for support. She felt black-and-blue and cold to the bone when she stepped onto the bathroom rug. Her movements were clumsy as she toweled dry. Goose bumps dotted her arms as she reached for her sweats, hanging on the back of the bathroom door. "Yeah, Jane, this is your speed. This is what ugly ducklings wear. Plain Janes don't deserve anything better than this." She eyed the black dress in the corner. "Screw it!" she mumbled as she ran a brush through her short-cropped hair.

Both dogs sat in the open doorway staring at her with unblinking intensity. "What happened to that old saying, 'be the best that you can be'? Does it just apply to the military and the pretty people of the world? Can't the people who aren't pretty try to look pretty? What's wrong with that? That was just the outside he was looking at, and he made a judgment. I'm the same inside. Why didn't he see that? I waited all my life to look like that. My mother should have named me Cinderella. I'm back to my rags now. Speaking of mothers, I hate you, Mother!" Jane screamed at the top of her lungs. "Do you hear me? I hate you! Look what you did to me! You did this. It's your fault I feel like this. Couldn't you have loved me just a little bit? Did you always have to be so damn critical? Couldn't you have said one nice, kind word to me? Just one nice fucking kind word. I hope you're roasting in hell!"

Jane dropped to the floor, her back against the old claw-footed bathtub, and sobbed. Both dogs flew across the room, each vying for her lap as she continued to cry, her whole body shaking uncontrollably. "Some killer dog you are, Flash," Jane hiccuped, as the Malinois licked at her tears. "I'm just going to curl up here for a minute. Just one little minute."

The dogs looked at one another as Jane curled into the fetal position. When her light breathing told them she was safe and asleep, Flash trotted out to the bedroom and tugged an afghan with a huge bouquet of purple tulips crocheted in the center from the back rest of the rocker. He dragged it to the bathroom. When he whined low in his throat, Olive took one end while he took the other. Together, they tugged, inched and nosed the light coverlet until it covered Jane completely up to her neck. Flash's "officer down" training had just kicked in. One of the first things he'd learned was to cover a body. Both dogs returned to the open doorway and stretched out, their heads on their paws, their eyes wide and alert.

When the room grew dark, Olive got up and with one paw, flicked the light switch. She returned to her position in the doorway next to Flash. Their gaze never wavered until eight o'clock, when Flash's ears went straight up in the air. A deep growl erupted from his belly. Olive turned her head to stare into the darkness of the open hallway. Neither dog made a sound as they raced out of the room and down the steps. The moment headlights arched on the dark living-room wall, Olive ran to the front window and nosed open the plantation shutters. Flash watched her before he, too, raised a paw to press the spring release on the opposite shutter. They waited, their ears flat against their heads, their tails between their legs. The motion light on the peaked roof turned night into day as Mike Sorenson stepped out of his car.

Flash pawed Olive as much as to say, is this the enemy? Uncertain as to what was going on, Olive trembled. The Malinois picked up on Olive's uncertainty. His lips curled back as he snapped and snarled at the paned window. Mike, one foot on the step, the other poised in midair, carefully removed his foot from the step and backed up, his eyes on the snarling dogs at the window.

Flash growled, the hair on his head and neck standing on end. Olive backed away from the window, as did Flash. She used her nose to close the shutters. Flash followed suit. Both dogs ran through the house to the back door. Once again, the motion light over the back porch sprang to life, illuminating Mike advancing up the path leading to the back porch. He stopped in his tracks when he heard a bloodcurdling howl. He backed up slowly, dropping the key in his hand. The dogs waited until the sound of the car's engine sprang to life in the quiet night. The moment the noise from the engine faded into nothingness, both dogs made their way to the second floor.

Jane slept deeply and peacefully on the bathroom floor, her guardians ever watchful.

Mike Sorenson drove his sleek sports car into the crowded parking lot of Snuffy's Bar and Lounge. He sat down at the bar and ordered a scotch on the rocks. Snuffy's had long been a favorite watering hole for many of his colleagues. He looked around now to see if he recognized anyone he could strike up a conversation with. Not that he felt like talking.

What in hell had gotten into Jane? And what was up with the two dogs that were set to eat him alive? Olive acted like she didn't even know him. More to the point, where was Jane and what was she doing? His heart started to flutter when he recalled the conversation they had in the lobby. He'd been stunned at her appearance. So stunned, he babbled the first words that came to his mind. Big mistake, Sorenson. What had he said that had been so awful? Didn't he have a right to act surprised? Damnation, he loved her curly hair, loved having it tickle his face when they made love, loved to run his hands through the springy curls. She could have mentioned it. Mentioning something like cutting your hair wasn't a sin. Shit! He realized more than ever that he knew absolutely nothing about women.

Mike took a healthy pull from the scotch glass as he swiveled around to survey the room. He saw a few people he had a nodding acquaintance with but no one he cared to unload on. He turned back to the bar and reached for a pretzel. He'd finish the drink, go home, and call his mother.

He felt rather than saw someone sit down next to him. Familiar perfume wafted its way to his nostrils. He turned. "Coletta!"

"Mike! I thought it was you. How are you?"

"Fine. You?" He had to get out of there and he had to do it *right then*. The last thing he needed was for Jane to find out he had a drink with his old girlfriend.

"Fine. Why are you drinking by yourself? Holidays getting to you?"

She was beautiful, there was no doubt about it. He narrowed his eyes to see her better. She looked like she'd been *shellacked*. He wondered if her face would crack if she smiled or grimaced. No one had eyebrows like hers. Perfect arches. Once he'd thought he wanted to drown in those dark eyes. Once. Light-years ago. He studied her hair, which was longer now and swept back from her face. There wasn't one hair out of place. Like the rest of her, her hair looked like lacquer had been sprayed on it.

"Actually no. I love the holidays. I was on my way home and was hoping to see Jonesy in here," he said, referring to a mutual friend. "He's not here, though, so I'm going home to work on a couple of case histories. What are you doing here?"

"Meeting a friend, who just happens to be late. I heard you were seeing someone."

"True. Are you seeing anyone?"

"More or less," Coletta said, smiling. "What's her name, do I know her?"

"Jane Lewis. I doubt if you know her. She's a colleague."

"The one with the radio show?" Her expression was incredulous. "My God, Mike, she's positively *dowdy*. I've seen pictures of her in the local paper."

Mike bristled. "What's that supposed to mean? She's not dowdy. Actually, she's quite glamorous," Mike said, remembering their little exchange in the lobby earlier.

"It doesn't mean anything. I wouldn't have thought she was your type. You always went for the flash."

"No I didn't, Coletta. I got your number real quick, didn't I? They don't come any flashier than you," Mike said, sliding off the barstool. He tossed some bills on the counter.

"See you around, Coletta."

In the car with the engine idling, Mike closed his eyes. "I was wrong, Jane. You don't look anything like Coletta. I don't know what made me say that. I don't know what the hell got into me this afternoon. I'd love you if you were bald."

10

The moment Jane stirred, both dogs jumped up and hovered around her as they waited for her eyes to open. When they did, they were all over her, their tails wagging, growling playfully as they nudged her to get up. Clearly it was time to play.

Jane groaned as she struggled to her feet. The Queen Mother of all headaches pounded inside her skull. She reached for the edge of the sink to pull herself upright. Three aspirin found their way to her hand. She stuck her mouth under the faucet and gulped at the water and swallowed the aspirin. "I'll never do that again!" she muttered. Her watch on the edge of the sink told her it was 2:30 A.M.

Holding on to the sink for support, she turned and saw the afghan on the floor and the dogs sitting next to it. She dropped to her knees and cuddled them. "My protectors! You guys are too much," she said, hugging them both. "What do you say we go downstairs and sit on the back porch? Maybe some fresh air will make this headache go away. You can go for a little run while I contemplate the sins of demon alcohol."

In the kitchen, Jane opened the door to let the dogs out.

Coffee and a big glass of tomato juice loaded with Tabasco was definitely called for. She carried the glass with her as she shuffled around the kitchen because picking up her feet and setting them down jarred her shoulders and neck, causing her head to pound even more.

She wanted to die.

In order to check the answering machine to see if there had been any calls, she would have to either turn her head or turn her entire body around to see if the red button was blinking. It seemed like a lot of trouble, so Jane shuffled around in a circle. There was no blinking red light. No one had called. Mike hadn't called.

Jane could feel the tomato juice gurgling in her stomach. "Please, please, stay down," she begged her stomach. "I hate throwing up. I really do." Maybe the coffee would help. Strong, black coffee, Trixie's cure-all for everything. Fred disagreed, saying black rum tea would cure anything, even the warts on a frog.

She inched her way to the door, reaching for the jacket on the hook opposite the door to throw over her shoulders. She used her shoulder to open the old-fashioned screen door, loving the creaking sound it made. Trixie said wooden screen doors were supposed to squeak and creak. The sound was as comforting as seeing the first fireflies of summer or the first gentle rain while the sun was still shining.

Jane looked toward the field and frowned. Headlights. It was probably Trixie coming to check on her. How good and kind she was. How caring. She never would have made it this far in life without Trixie and Fred. She sipped at the coffee in the cup while she waited for her godparents to arrive.

Flash loped up to the porch, the sensor light shining down on something he was holding between his teeth. Jane reached for the shiny key. She stared at it. It looked like her house key. Damn, it *was* her house key. Flash barked. "Thank you, Flash." The big dog's head bobbed up and down—Trixie's version of dog training, teaching Flash manners. Olive should be so talented.

Jane continued to stare at the key. Trixie had one. Mike had one. One was kept hidden under the windowsill with electric tape. Four in all, counting the one on her key chain. Had Mike come by to return his key? Her heart took on a thundering beat inside her chest at the thought.

The police cruiser skidded to a stop. Fred and Trixie got out at the same moment, their faces registering shock at seeing her sitting on the steps. "Are you all right, Janie?" Fred asked, his face and voice full of concern.

"The bad news is I have never felt this bad in my entire life. The good news is I will probably live," Jane said, as Trixie put her arms around her and hugged her. "Trixie, look what Flash found." She handed the key to Trixie. "I think it's Mike's. I must have been out cold because I didn't hear him come by. I'm sure he wouldn't just drop it off and leave without knocking. Still, I think it's pretty shitty, don't you? Damn, I thought he was the one. *The one,* Trixie! Boy, when I screw up, I screw up. Big-time."

"Stop being so hard on yourself, Janie. For starters, you don't know if it is Mike's key. It might not be your house key at all," Trixie said.

"Oh, it's my key all right. There are only four. I had this one made for Mike not too long ago. It's still shiny. You have one, I have one, and there's one under the windowsill. I rest my case."

Trixie sat down on the step next to Jane. "Maybe he dropped it. Maybe it fell off his key ring. There could be a dozen reasons why you're holding it in your hand. Don't jump to conclusions, sweetie."

Jane leaned forward and dropped her head between her

knees. "He didn't call," she said, groaning. "He could have called me and left me a message. He didn't."

"There could be a dozen reasons for that, too," Trixie insisted. "Maybe you didn't hear the phone ring. Sometimes people don't like to leave messages. When it gets light out, things will look differently. Can we do anything for you, honey?"

"Show me how to grow a new head." Jane knew she sounded pitiful, but she couldn't help it. At the moment she was pitiful.

"Hangovers are a bitch," Fred remarked, his sage wisdom coming too late to help Jane.

Jane sat up straight to show them she was fine. "I just came out here to clear my head. You two can go home. I'm okay. I appreciate you checking on me."

"Do you want us to leave Flash with you?"

"No. I think he misses you. You guys are his constant, just like you're mine. He needs you. Olive and I will be just fine. I'm going to go back to bed for a little while. I'll call you in the morning."

"Think about calling Mike," Trixie suggested. "He loves you."

"All right, I'll think about it," she promised as she shoved the key into her pocket.

It was agony to climb the stairs to the second floor, but she made it. She stopped at the top and closed her eyes as she willed the pounding in her head to ease up. When it didn't, she staggered to her bedroom and crawled into bed. She wished Mike was there to hold her close, to kiss her aching head.

Mike.

Maybe she had misinterpreted his reaction to her hair. He'd said she looked totally different. Different didn't necessarily mean bad. It simply meant different. Even she'd thought she'd looked different when she'd gazed at her reflection in the mirror.

"Oh, God," she groaned. "What's the matter with me anyway? Maybe when I wake up it will all be just a bad dream. You're in charge, Olive," she mumbled as she drifted into the arms of Morpheus.

Jane woke with a start. The headache that had threatened to lift her into orbit was now just a dull ache. With more aspirin and a hot cup of tea, it would disappear. She gingerly swung her legs over the side of the bed. When the world stayed in place, she moved into the bathroom, where she showered and brushed her teeth. Afterward, she stared for long minutes at her reflection, particularly her new hairdo, which looked almost as good now as it had at the luncheon. "I like it. I think I have a keeper here," she mumbled as she ran a brush through the soft, feathery curls.

Downstairs she heard her antique clock strike ten. In her entire life she'd never slept past eight o'clock. On the other hand, she'd never been so drunk before either. "Let's see what the world has in store for us today, Olive. With the office closed and Mike in a snit, I'd say we're pretty much on our own. That means we can go Christmas shopping. We can get a Christmas tree if we want or we can sit here and do nothing but watch soap operas. What we are not going to do is feel sorry for ourselves; nor are we going to think about Mike Sorenson."

Jane hung up her soggy towel and left the bathroom, Olive on her heels. She tried not to look at the answering machine but eventually gave in. Her heart felt like it was leapfrogging in her chest when she saw the blinking red light. She put water on to boil, postponing the moment when she would press the PLAY button and hear Mike's voice. When she could no longer stand the suspense, she hit the button and waited.

When Sharon Thomas's voice came over the wire, she said, "Oh shit!"

"Jane, it's Sharon Thomas. I'd like to set up an appointment with your attorney and mine for January 3 if that's agreeable with you. I'm interested in buying your practice. By the way, I saw Mike last night at Snuffy's. Were you putting me on when you said you two were an item? Maybe you should have told him that. He was what I would call being up close and personal with a sculptured-looking model type at the bar. The only way I can describe her is drop-dead gorgeous. Have your attorney get in touch with mine . . . Grover Mandel. Have a great holiday, Jane."

There were no other messages. Jane sat down with a thump and stared at her cup of tea. The shiny house key was lying in the center of the table. She must have taken it out of her pocket last night and put it there. She reached for it and threw it across the room. Olive walked over to it and started to sniff it before she picked it up and brought it back to Jane. "Thank you, Olive," she said, sliding the key into her junk drawer.

Jane upended her teacup and gulped at the contents until it was gone. Then she flew upstairs and changed her clothes. She was going to Crowley later in the week after she called Todd Prentice and invited him to lunch. If she could find his card, that is. She thought she remembered putting it in her desk drawer. Today, she'd do *a late lunch,* she thought, glancing at her watch. After that—Christmas shopping!

When Jane sat down at her desk, she did a double take when she noticed the Lucite container with Connie Bryan's disks on top of the computer monitor. She clearly remembered moving it to the side of the desk and putting the green frog on top. "Who moved . . ." She cut herself off, afraid to voice her question.

She stared at the box of diskettes before she reached for it with shaking hands. Had she moved it and just forgotten? She clearly remembered the day she and Olive had watched her files slide out of her briefcase onto the floor and wondered if there might be something to the whole ghost thing. No. There were no such things as ghosts. Ghosts didn't exist, except in her dreams. Someone had moved the box. Mike maybe. But how? Olive and Flash wouldn't have let anyone in, not even Mike.

Jane let her gaze travel around the room. Nothing seemed out of place. Everything looked the same. An intruder wouldn't just move a box of diskettes and not touch anything else.

Jane rubbed at her temples. "I must have done it myself," she muttered.

Jane reached down to scratch Olive behind the ears. She was wagging her tail so hard her whole body was wiggling. "I'm losing it, girl, really losing it," she said as she opened the box and counted the disks. They were all there, but out of order. The one requiring a password was now in the back. "I know I put it in the front with a rubber band around it." The rubber band was gone, and in its place was a small piece of paper taped to the disk. There was one word printed on the paper: JANE.

Jane's fingers froze in midair. She swallowed and looked down at Olive, who was looking up at her with expectation. Things were getting more interesting all the time. "Whatever is going on here, and something is definitely going on, we're going to take it one step at a time, Olive. Small steps. There's a reason for everything. At least that's what I tell my patients all the time. It's so weird that I'm not afraid. What do you suppose that means? You need to learn how to talk, Olive," Jane groused.

Heart racing, Jane turned on the computer, slipped in the disk, and waited. When the window appeared asking for the password, she typed in her name just the way it was on the piece of paper, in caps. She held her breath, waiting to see if it would say Access Denied. It didn't. Instead it opened up to the file list. There were three files. The first one was a diary of sorts, the second was a daily log, and the third was a letter addressed to her.

A wave of dizziness washed over her, so strong that she had to push herself away from the desk so she could put her head down between her legs to ward it off. It was several moments before she felt confident enough to begin reading.

> *Dear Jane,*
>
> *I meant to write you when I first returned home, but I was in no condition to do much of anything except try to act normal so no one would suspect what happened to me that night. It took such energy it left me drained. All I wanted to do was sleep. I don't know, I may never mail this to you, but then again, who knows what tomorrow will bring. You were such a good friend to me that night. I wish now I had listened to you. Shame, like guilt, is a terrible thing.*
>
> *My parents were so happy when I got home. I playacted for them, but I think my mother suspected something was wrong. I just kept saying it was wedding jitters. So many times I wanted to tell them, but I just couldn't. Even though I knew they would still love me, they would have looked upon me differently, like I was tarnished.*
>
> *Todd changed when I got home. At first I thought it was me, but it was him. He would cut our dates short and make excuses for leaving my house early. We didn't have sex at all. He wasn't interested. I found that strange, but at the same time welcome because I don't honestly know what*

I would have felt. He blamed the change on me and needled me constantly to tell him what was wrong. He kept saying I had a secret and badgered me, wanting to know what it was. I can't explain it, but it was almost like he knew, Jane.

Then my parents went to my grandparents' house for the weekend, and I had the house to myself. I invited Todd over, cooked him a wonderful dinner, wore one of his favorite outfits, and tried to seduce him for no other reason than to prove to myself that I still had feelings for him and he still had feelings for me.

He had every excuse in the book not to get into bed with me. I think that's when I knew for certain that he knew what had happened to me. I suggested we call off the wedding, and he said it would be better just to postpone it temporarily. I agreed.

I was sick to my soul, Jane. I got even sicker as the days went on and I heard he was seeing some girl whose father was sinfully rich. I confronted him, and he said they were just friends. I believed him because I needed to believe him.

I started having really bad dreams then. They were worse than the ones I had when I first returned home. But at least they served a purpose. I remembered two things that might help identify the boys who raped me. One of them wore a thick, heavy ID bracelet and one of the others had a chain on his neck with some kind of medallion on it. It swung like a pendulum over my head while he was raping me. I know I don't have the courage to go to the police with that information now, but maybe I will at some point. I know I should have listened to you that night and at least gone to the crisis center. It was foolish of me to have ignored you, but I was so in love, and I didn't want to do anything that might jeopardize my wedding plans.

Now, in spite of all my efforts, I have no wedding plans. In my heart I know it's over between Todd and me. I don't have the same feelings for him that I once had, and he's made it obvious he doesn't feel the same toward me.

I don't know what I'm going to do, Jane, but I do know that I have to do something. And I have to do it soon. I can't live like this, in fear and secrecy.

I want to thank you for all you did that night and apologize for not saying good-bye before I left. We didn't know each other long, but for that time—you were the best friend I ever had.

I wish you every happiness in the world, Jane.

Connie Bryan

Jane wiped at the tears running down her cheeks. "I guess you decided life wasn't worth living," Jane said, staring at the computer monitor. "Damn it, Connie, you should have mailed me the letter. What can I do now, all these years later?"

Jane continued to skim through the rest of the diskettes but couldn't find anything else that would help her. She made a backup copy of the letter and hid it in one of Trixie's books on the shelf. She didn't know why. It seemed the prudent thing to do at the moment.

As for who had moved the box of disks and written her name on one of them . . . she would take Scarlett O'Hara's cure and think about it tomorrow. Just then she had more important things to be concerned with.

Todd Prentice's business card stared up at her. Her face

grim, Jane dialed the number, got the switchboard, and then Todd's secretary. "I'd like to speak to Mr. Prentice please. Tell him Dr. Jane Lewis is calling." Trixie would tell her to kick some ass and take names later. Well, she was in the right frame of mind for that since she was still smarting over Sharon Thomas's phone message.

"Jane Lewis. Nice to hear from you. To what do I owe the pleasure of this phone call?" Todd boomed over the wire.

"To a mutual friend, Connie Bryan," Jane said coolly. "I'm calling to invite you to lunch. I'll be in Crowley Thursday and Friday," she said, hoping he would choose the former as opposed to the latter.

"Let me check my calendar." There was a short pause. "Thursday is out. I'm up to my eyeballs in appointments, but Friday looks good. You want to reminisce about Connie, is that it? I still think of her often. I never did figure out why she took her life. It was such a shame. She had so much to live for. I thought I knew her, you know? It just goes to show that the ones you think you know best, you don't necessarily know at all."

"That's true, Todd," she replied, thinking of Mike. "You never really know about people or what they are capable of doing. Take Connie for instance. We were really good friends," Jane lied to set the bait. "You would think she would have slipped up and told me what she was planning in the letter she wrote me after she got home, just before she . . . you know."

"You two were good friends? I didn't know that. She never talked about you to me. I wonder why that was."

"You know what, Todd? She never talked about you to me either. Oh, I knew you two were engaged and all that, but that's about it. We talked about other things, the secret stuff girls talk about," Jane said, making things up as she went along.

"I see. Tell me something, Jane. What is this lunch all about?" Did his voice change, or was it her imagination? It sounded chilly all of a sudden.

Jane thought a moment. "I'm doing a paper on drugs for *JAMA*. I thought you might allow me to pick your brain if I give you credit in the article. It's quite prestigious, and a feather in one's cap to be published in such an important publication." She congratulated herself on her quick thinking.

The relief in the man's voice sent shivers up Jane's spine. "Well, sure. Glad to help. Let's say tomorrow, twelve-thirty at Roscoe's."

"Twelve-thirty is great. I'll see you then." *You miserable son of a bitch,* Jane said to herself.

The phone rang the moment she put the receiver down. "Hello?"

"Jane, it's Mike. Where the hell have you been? Are you all right? I came out to the house last night, and those damn dogs wouldn't let me in. By the way, they scared me so bad, I dropped the key in the driveway." He paused as if expecting her to say something. "Look, I'm sorry. You don't look anything like Coletta. You're real and warm and sweet, plus kind and gentle and . . . I love you. I really love you. If I had any doubts before, they're gone now."

"Why is that?" Jane asked, her voice throaty with emotion.

"I stopped at Snuffy's on my way home for a drink and guess who was at the bar? Coletta! She was waiting for her date, and I was just leaving. When I saw her, I realized I must have been deaf, dumb, *and* blind when I was dating her. You're twice the woman she is. No, ten times."

"Only ten times?" she teased him.

"Don't be mad at me anymore, Jane. I can't stand it. I would love you even if you were bald."

"I beg your pardon?" *Was that a compliment or an insult?*

"Even if you had warts, I'd still love you."

"Really, Mike?"

"Even if you were pigeon-toed and knock-kneed, I'd still love you. I want us to grow old together. Have I made my point? Can I stop now?"

Jane giggled.

"Let's go for some of Papa Jo's spaghetti tonight, okay? I'll wear my red T-shirt and you wear your red one so when we drip sauce it won't show. I'll pick you up at seven. I missed you, Jane."

"I missed you, too. And seven is good."

"What are you going to do this afternoon?"

"Christmas shopping. It's now or never. Christmas is only six days away. By the way, I thought you'd like to know, Sharon Thomas is interested in buying my practice. You know what? I wouldn't sell it to her if she was the last person on earth. She's a catty, snotty, mean-spirited woman. I'll close it up first."

"I agree with you about Sharon. She's all that and more. I know someone who might be interested. We'll talk about it tonight. I love you, Jane."

"I love you, too."

Jane sat back. "Did you hear that, Olive? It just goes to show you, you should never make assumptions or jump to conclusions. You should be patient and get the facts. That's what I tell all my patients. I also tell them you need to control your emotions and that when you drink you lose control." She started to giggle. "It's too bad I don't take my own advice. He had an explanation for everything. God, I am so happy, I can't stand it. I'm leaving you behind today so you can sleep while I'm gone. I just have to call Trixie to bring my car over."

Olive reared up and pawed the desk, barking furiously. She backed away, then advanced and finally tugged on the hem of Jane's slacks, her signal to follow her.

"Oh, they already brought my car back. Good girl, Olive. You are so smart. I just love you to pieces. Because you're such a good girl, I'll make you some veggie burgers for dinner. You be good now, okay?"

Jane was back in the house by five-thirty, her arms full of gaily wrapped packages and in her trunk, tied down with rope, was a six-foot Frazier Fir Christmas tree and tree stand. On the backseat, still to be carried into the house, were Christmas ornaments and colored lights.

She'd done her best not to think about Connie Bryan's disk and her conversation with Todd Prentice. She wasn't going to think about it now either. What she was going to do was pop a cola and make a phone call to lock in Mike's special Christmas present. One rainy night while lying in bed after a delicious session of lovemaking, she'd asked him what his most secret desire was and he'd said, catapulting off the USS *Patrick Henry* in a Tomcat. Preferably somewhere in the Adriatic Sea, he'd said. She was going to make that happen via virtual reality and a trip to Baton Rouge, where it was all done in a studio. The gift card along with details would be sent by overnight mail, and she would wrap it up with a big, red, satin bow. Every time she thought about it, she got dizzy with excitement when she imagined the look on his face.

She made a mental note to call Sharon Thomas's office after hours so she could leave a message telling her in no uncertain terms she was not interested in selling her practice to her.

"So there, Olive! I did promise you veggie burgers, didn't I? Two of them coming right up." Before she started mixing and mashing, she withdrew the house key from her junk drawer and placed it in the middle of the table. "You know what, Olive? I don't feel like going out. I'm going to call Mike and tell him to bring the food with him. That way we can spend the evening together and put the tree up. We'll be a family. You know my feelings on family, Olive."

"Woof."

Jane curled up on the sofa next to Mike, Olive nestled in the bend of her knees. They all stared at the beautifully decorated tree. Jane sighed happily. "You were right, Mike, the decorations make this old room come alive. And to think I got it all at Wallace's Hardware."

"I thought you didn't want to do any decorating, but I'm glad you changed your mind. You seemed preoccupied this evening. Want to talk about it? I'm a good listener."

Jane told him about her proposed lunch with Todd Prentice and the disk she'd brought home from Slidell. "Mike, I know where I put that disk container, and I distinctly remember putting Beth Goins's frog on top. I remember it as clearly as I remember my own name. Now, my question to you is this, where did that little piece of paper come from that was taped onto the Lucite box? And . . . how do you explain the password? No one was here last night. You said yourself that the dogs wouldn't let you in. It was the right password. My name was the password." Shivers ran down her spine, and she snuggled closer to him. "Mike, my blood ran cold. I'll show you the letter she wrote me in the morning. It broke my heart and made me cry."

"You're going to try to do something, aren't you, Jane? Do you think you've got enough evidence to charge anyone?"

"Yes, I'm going to try to do something, and no, I don't have enough evidence. Not yet. But I have a feeling I will have that evidence before long. There are some things Connie mentioned in her letter that might help; then there is the bite scar and the DNA evidence off her clothes. I had a lawyer friend of mine check, and it seems that in 1994, they passed a Violence Against Women Law, which made it so there isn't any statute of limitations on aggravated rape. Even if the rape occurred five, ten, or fifteen years ago."

"All this is happening because of that Ramsey guy, isn't it? Jesus, I wish he'd never gone to you. I do not have a good feeling about this, Jane. Another thing, what do you hope to gain by going to lunch with a bastard like Todd Prentice? You said he was a bastard, remember? As to the password, I don't have a clue."

"I don't know, maybe a slip of the tongue. I have Connie's letter to go by now. She thought something was awry, that he seemed to know. Let's not talk about this any more tonight. Tell me, do you really know someone who might be interested in my practice? What'd you get me for Christmas?" Jane said, tickling him under the arm.

He grabbed her hand and held it tightly in his. "I mentioned it to Bill Bennett and Carl Wylie. They just took on two new associates and are looking to expand. I'd say they expressed keen interest. Carl and one of the associates would take over your office and Bill and his associate would stay in Lafayette. Bill said they would be in touch after the first of the year. I can handle it for you until it's all a done deal. Your patients will like them. Are you certain this is what you want to do, Jane?"

"I'm certain. I already feel like a load of bricks is off my shoulders. Now, c'mon, don't avoid the subject, what did you get me for Christmas?"

"You tell me first," Mike twinkled.

"I got you the thing you want most in life. That's all I'm going to tell you. Now, you give me a clue."

"What I want most in life is you, Jane. Anything other than you will just be icing on the cake. I got something for you that is forever. I'm not telling you anything else, either. Don't try weaseling it out of me."

She considered his answer. A ring was forever. A commitment was forever. "Are you sure your parents are going to like me? What if they don't, Mike?"

He nuzzled her temple, her cheek, then her neck. "Trust me, my mother will love you, and my dad will adore you. I know this. I'm their son."

"Tell me what they're like again. I want to feel like I really know them before you introduce me to them."

"My mom is a pretty woman who stands about five-foot-one and has a big heart. She always looks neat as a pin, even when she's cleaning house. She makes the most awesome chocolate cake you've ever tasted. It screams my name. And her gumbo is to die for. Her flower beds have the prettiest flowers on the street, and you won't find a weed anywhere. She knits things, all kinds of things, baby clothes and sweaters and afghans and donates everything to different church bazaars for their raffles."

She laid her head against his chest and he stroked her hair. "My dad is a big man, kind of barrel-chested. He has this booming laugh that makes you join in. He never gets mad. He's sort of laid-back, I guess you'd say. His eyes twinkle and he's really upset because he's losing his hair. He's been using Rogaine for years with no results. He won't give up, though. He has a workshop in the garage, where he builds toys that he donates to bazaars like my mother does. He likes to dance. He has a jukebox in the family room with all the Golden Oldies. He and Mom trip the light fantastic every night after dinner. They both like to go fishing, going to the movies, and doing volunteer work. They really do have busy lives. They call me every Sunday. I call them on Wednesdays."

Jane conjured up a mental picture of his parents sitting side by side on a sofa, his mother in a flowered dress and his father in a golf shirt and tan slacks. "They sound wonderful."

"That's because they are wonderful. They're going to love you. Can we go to bed now? I didn't sleep at all last night."

"Mike, who wrote the password on the disk?"

"I have no idea . . . unless . . ."

"Unless what?"

"It could have been your ghost."

Jane guffawed and sat up. "Really, Mike, that's stretching things just a bit, don't you think?"

"What other explanation could there be?" he asked, his expression sober.

Jane looked him straight in the eye, and said, "There are no such things as ghosts."

11

The air was downright frosty, perfect Christmas weather, Jane thought when she climbed out of her car and handed the keys over to the young man in charge of valet parking. She looked around, thinking the restaurant looked different somehow. Maybe the owners had given the building a face-lift. It had been years since she'd been there, and then it had been at night. The food was exceptional, that much she did remember.

The building was long and narrow, with banquet rooms in the back. At first glance it looked like something the architect had given up on. Gray fieldstone and Tudor windows added to the architectural discord.

Its saving grace was its festive outdoor decor. The restaurant had gone all out on its Christmas decorations. On every door, on every window, in every nook and cranny there were tiny white lights intertwined in the greenery and finished off with red-velvet bows. The interior was dim and fragrant, with the scent of balsam wafting in all directions. Jane sniffed appreciatively. The moment she walked into the foyer she could hear the hum of conversation and the clink of silver and glassware. This was the busiest time of year for restaurant owners. She eyed the tree in the corner, with its expensive gold ornaments. In her opinion, her hardware-store tree looked a thousand times better. Or maybe it was just because she liked things simple rather than glitzy. She sat down in the waiting area and glanced at her watch. She hoped Todd Prentice didn't decide to stand her up.

Five minutes later, he came through the door on a gust of wind. "Jane, I hope I haven't kept you waiting," he said, running his hand over his hair.

"No, as a matter of fact, I just got here myself," she said, discreetly eyeing his cashmere overcoat and pricey shoes. The tie alone probably cost a couple of hundred dollars. She would have had to be blind to miss the monogrammed cuffs of the pristine white shirt that showed at the wrist as he handed over his coat to the hatcheck girl. He deftly switched the manila envelope he was carrying from one hand to the other as he reached for Jane's coat and smiled. He cupped her elbow in his hand to usher her into the dining room, totally ignoring the hostess.

"The firm keeps a table at the back of the room. My father-in-law pays handsomely for the privilege," he confided.

"How nice," she intoned woodenly.

"It *is* nice, believe me. This place really jams, and it's nice to walk in and know you have a table and don't have to wait or tip the hostess. The CFO of the firm holds a percentage of the restaurant, but that's a private matter."

Prentice led the way to the back of the restaurant, stopping momentarily to say hello to other people or just to pat someone's shoulder as he strode by. He was right, it was the best table in the house, Jane thought, as he held the chair for her. She wondered what was in the manila envelope he placed on the table. Probably stuff he thought would help her with the paper she'd said she wanted to write.

"Now, Jane, what would you like to drink?"

"Mineral water with a twist of lime, please. I'm driving." She laid her purse down next to her, then unfolded her napkin and put it on her lap.

"I am, too, but I'm having a double Rob Roy." He raised his index finger and a waiter immediately appeared. He gave the order and shook loose a cigarette.

"You can smoke in here?" Jane asked in surprise.

"I can, yes." His eyes wary, he asked, "Are you set for the holidays?"

"I think so. How about you?"

"My wife handles all that stuff. You know how wives are. They want to be sure everything is perfect and us guys would just foul it up. We go to our condo in Aspen every year for Christmas and stay through the New Year."

A condo in Aspen. The most Connie could have hoped for was a sleigh ride in New Jersey if she had married this dandy.

"I brought some material for you to look over, thinking it would save some time. Why don't you take a look at it while I call the office and check on things. I left a bit of a mess for my secretary."

Jane reached for the envelope. She made a pretense of leafing through the drug periodicals and glossy brochures touting their newest drugs. She raised her gaze once to look around the room and, with the aid of a mirrored wall opposite him, could clearly see Prentice speaking on the lobby phone. If he was talking to his office, she had horns. She had just closed the clasp on the envelope when Todd rejoined her.

"Did any of that help?"

"Perfect. I feel silly now. You could have put all this into the mail to me, and I wouldn't have taken up your time. I appreciate your help."

"When will the article appear in *JAMA*?"

Jane shrugged. "They never tell you. My guess would be

spring. I'll let you know or send you a copy." Enough with the small talk, she told herself. "I'm curious about something, Todd. Why did you come up to me and introduce yourself at the fund-raiser?"

"Well, I—I was just trying to be friendly, that's all. I was on the organizing committee."

She could tell he was lying through his teeth, but that was to be expected. "Oh," she said, laughing. "I thought you might have been looking for a good psychiatrist."

He threw his head back and laughed. "No! I don't need a psychiatrist."

"Don't say it like that. All of us need someone we can dump on from time to time. A psychiatrist is trained to listen, not to judge. You mean to tell me you don't have anything troubling in your life, past or present, that you'd like to talk to someone about?" she asked, setting the stage.

He shook his head. "Nope. 'Fraid not, Doc."

"Tell me, do you ever go back to Slidell?"

"Not if I can help it," he said, gulping at his drink. He signaled the waiter for a refill. "My mother passed away when I was a freshman in college, and my father moved to a retirement home in Coral Gables, Florida, to be closer to his two brothers. There's no reason to go back. Where is it you live again?"

"Rayne. Frog capital of the world. My practice is there. I was in Slidell recently. I stopped to see Connie's parents. I think they're still grieving. I guess you never get over the death of a child. You must have been devastated."

"Oh, I was. I couldn't eat or sleep for months. Connie and I had so many plans for our wedding and our future. I didn't know what to do with myself for months afterward. Like I said before, I don't know why she did it. Her parents didn't know either. She didn't leave a note or anything. It was a terrible time. It finally got too much for me, so I moved to

Crowley." It was all said in a breathless rush as he reached up for his second drink. *Rehearsed* was the word that came to Jane's mind.

Knowing she was about to drop a bomb, Jane picked up her drink and tried to act nonchalant. "Then you didn't hear the news. Connie did leave a note. But no one knew it until just recently. It seems she wrote it on her computer and saved it on a disk. Adele, Connie's mother, finally got up the courage to dismantle her daughter's room and wondered what Connie might have put on her computer. One of the disks had a secret password. She had a computer-savvy friend come over and crack the code for her. That's when they found the note."

Jane heard Prentice's quick intake of breath and looked at him. All the blood had siphoned out of his face. He was white as a ghost.

"Todd, are you all right? Is something wrong with your drink?" she asked with feigned concern. She'd suspected he was in the mix somehow. Now she knew it.

"Yeah, yeah, I'm fine. It's just— Jesus, she left a note?"

"Really more of a letter, from what I understand," Jane said, sipping from her glass. She detested mineral water. It was so blah! "I think the waiter wants to take our order now. I feel positively decadent with the holidays so I think I'll have the shrimp-and-lobster scampi with the pecan tulle for dessert. French dressing on the side, please."

"Sir?"

"I'll have the same," Todd said to the waiter. "You're right, Jane, it sounds decadent." The color was back in his face, and his voice sounded normal.

He's quick to recuperate, Jane thought, wishing his misery had lasted a little longer. But there was more to come. Much more. And she was patient.

"Tell me something, Jane. Why is it you and I never met back in college? I thought I knew all of Connie's friends."

Content with the way things were going, Jane offered him a smile. "I was one of those studious, bookworm types. When I wasn't in class, I think I spent every waking hour in the library. Connie and I shared the same dorm, but we didn't share the same friends. We would meet in my room and talk several times a week. Actually, we spent that night before our last final together in the library, then in my room." She spread butter on her bread. "This French bread is soooo good. How do you stay so trim, Todd, if you eat here so often?"

"Good metabolism," he responded vaguely. "I work out and play racquetball three days a week after work. You literally sweat bullets when you play racquetball."

"I'll have to think about taking up the sport. I don't like to sweat, though," Jane said, reaching for another slice of bread she didn't really want. "By the way, do you know Brian Ramsey?" Jane threw her hands in the air. "Now that was a stupid question. He played football with you, so of course you knew him. He lives and works in Rayne now, you know. I'll bet you miss playing football? You had some really good press back in college as I recall. The media loved the Bengal Tigers." She bit off another bite of bread. "Mmm, this is so good," she said, not wanting to lose her momentum even though her mouth was full. "I wonder if they buy it or make it fresh here. I could sit here and eat it all day long. Do you guys get together and hash over old plays and stuff like that? Jocks always do that in the movies." She shook her head. "Lord, I don't know where half my old debating team is or the girls from the choir. I should make more of an effort to keep in touch, but I'm so busy these days. Isn't life strange, Todd? Whoever would have thought the two of us would be sitting here having lunch one day? Old bookworm Jane and superhero Todd of the awesome Bengal Tigers. So, where *do* you guys go when you get together?" Jane asked again, cutting into a cucumber on her salad plate. She pretended not to see Todd raise his arm for a third drink.

"We try to get together during Mardi Gras in N'awlins. Usually one or two can't make it, but for the most part we all show up and party for a few days."

"That's sweet. All you guys getting together. Bet your wife doesn't like that one bit," Jane said as she popped a cherry tomato in her mouth. She crunched down on it and Todd blinked. "You aren't eating, Todd. This is a wonderful salad. Are you all right?"

"Yes, of course. Why do you ask?"

"You're on your third drink, and you're staring off into space. Am I that boring?"

Todd offered up a sickly smile. "You're not boring at all. I had three *beignets* for breakfast, and all three were loaded with way too much sugar. I rarely eat much at lunchtime. Tell me, how *do* you handle being a shrink? Doesn't listening to other people's problems get to you?"

"Sometimes. But you have to listen to their problems to know how to help them. I often wish I could see them progress a little faster, but everyone has their own pace. Take Mr. and Mrs. Bryan for example. They should have talked to a counselor after Connie's death, but they didn't. I sat talking with them for days," Jane lied. "I think I was a help to them. It was a very rewarding experience. I came away from there feeling much better. What comes to your mind when you think of Connie?" Jane asked, staring up at the waiter holding her luncheon plate.

When the waiter handed Todd his plate, Jane couldn't help but notice that he was looking pale again. "What's wrong, Todd? Isn't the scampi what you expected?"

"No, no, it's fine. It's those *beignets* I had for breakfast. I should have just stuck with the salad."

"But you didn't eat your salad either. I'll have to come here more often. What were we saying, Todd?"

"I don't remember. The waiter came just as you asked me something, but I don't recall . . ." His voice was desperate-sounding.

Fork poised in midair, Jane offered up a winning smile. "I remember now. We were talking about Connie, and I asked you what comes to you when you think about her. Assuming, of course, that you do think of her after all these years."

"Right. Now I remember," Todd said, sticking his fork into a succulent piece of lobster that dripped butter. "College days. Our plans for the future. Getting married and having kids. That kind of thing. What about you?" He said, cleverly throwing the question back at her.

"I guess the way she dressed. She always had the neatest clothes. She liked to sew, I remember that. I can remember so clearly what she was wearing that last night. A pleated, red plaid skirt, a white sweater set, and Keds. She looked so . . . preppy, so collegiate. She left her clothes in my room that night. Do you believe that? I took them home with me when I left the following day. I think they're still in my old trunk. I meant to send them back, but never got around to it. Good intentions, that kind of thing. I guess it boils down to laziness on my part." She pointed her fork at his plate. "I can't tell you what you are missing here, Todd. Shame on you for eating those *beignets* this morning. There's so much garlic in this scampi it's going to ooze out my pores any second." One more bite and she was going to choke. "I think I'm going to pass on the dessert if you don't mind, Todd. Good Lord, would you look at the time. You won't be offended if I eat and run, will you?"

"No. No, not at all," he said, relief flooding his voice. "I need to get back to the office myself. Tomorrow we leave for Aspen."

"Please, Todd, let me pay. I was the one who invited you to lunch."

"We keep a running tab here. Don't worry about the bill. It was so nice to see you again. Let's do it again sometime."

"Thank you. Thanks, too, for all this material," she said, indicating the manila envelope.

"It was nothing, Jane. I was glad to do it."

She put her napkin down and stood up. "I'll be in touch about the article. Will it be all right to call you if I hit a snag?"

"Certainly."

In the lobby, Jane said, "Don't wait for me, Todd. You go ahead. I want to go to the ladies' room. Thanks again for lunch."

"My pleasure." He gave the hatcheck girl a five-dollar bill, then handed Jane her coat.

In the tastefully decorated bathroom, Jane sat down on a velvet-covered chair and gasped for breath. Mike was going to throttle her when she told him what she'd done. Trixie would call it kicking ass. Big-time. "You have a big mouth, Jane Lewis," she said to her mirrored reflection. "Not only do you have a big mouth, you don't know when to keep it shut. Now he knows you know." She started to turn away. "Wait a minute, what do I know?" she said, turning back to the mirror. She knew that one of Connie's rapists had worn a thick wrist bracelet and the other had been wearing some sort of medallion around his neck. She knew Connie suspected that Todd knew about the rape. She knew Connie's parents hadn't liked him and that he'd wanted money rather than useful household wedding gifts. She knew he'd lied when he said he hadn't known what to do with himself for months after Connie's death. If that were true, how could he have gotten to know the woman he married only one year later? And she knew that there was something weird about Brian Ramsey, Todd's former teammate, seeking her out for treatment. There was something she was missing, but at the moment she didn't have a clue as to what it was. "Shit!" she said succinctly.

"That about sums it up," a waitress said over her shoulder as she entered the ladies' room.

"Excuse me. I just had lunch with Todd Prentice. I think he comes here a lot. Do you know him by any chance?" Jane asked, grabbing at straws.

"Are you kidding?" The waitress rolled her eyes. "He's hit on all of us at one time or another. He's a lousy tipper, too. Why?"

"Oh, he just hit on me, too, and I was wondering what kind of guy he is."

"He's the kind of guy that cheats on his wife. Give him a wide berth is my advice."

"Thanks. I will. Have a nice holiday." She tossed the manila envelope into the waste bin.

"You, too."

Jane pulled out onto the highway and accelerated to the speed limit. Every two minutes she checked her rearview mirror to see if anyone was following her. She was so full of anxiety and tension she thought she would explode.

She headed straight for the McGuire farm, to Trixie and Fred. They would calm her down.

Trixie needed a break. Wrapping Christmas presents was a taxing job. She'd been at it for hours. Spools and rolls of gaily colored ribbon were everywhere. Yards and yards of paper covered the long dining-room table, the buffet, and the server. Dozens of presents were lined up against the walls waiting to be delivered to the police department. It was Trixie's way of making good on her promise for the use of the police car. If she ever finished, Fred would deliver the presents in time for the annual Christmas party at seven o'clock. Only seven more to go. Fred was absolutely useless when it came to tying bows and getting Scotch tape on without wrinkles in it. Two left thumbs.

Flash prowled among the presents, sniffing and poking

them with his snout. One moment he was contentedly brows-ing and the next he was running to the kitchen door, barking.

Company.

"Janie, girl! What brings you here in the middle of the af-ternoon? Start wrapping, honey. Fred has to get these to the Christmas party before seven. I know something is wrong, so talk while you wrap. Each present has a name stuck on it, so be extra careful when you fill out the tag."

Jane reached for a roll of paper. "You aren't going to be-lieve what I did, Trixie. God, I don't believe I did it either. You know me and my mouth! Just the other day I convinced myself that Todd Prentice should be added to the mix. You know what, Trix, I was right. I had him so rattled I thought he was going to hop right out of his Jockeys. He had three, that's three, Trix, double Rob Roys. Didn't eat a thing. At the time I thought I was being clever. Now I'm not so sure. I might have gone a little too far."

"Let's take a break. Coffee or tea?"

"Neither. How about some ginger ale?"

Jane sat on the floor rubbing Flash's belly as she recounted her luncheon with Todd Prentice. "I honest to God told him I still had Connie's clothes in my old trunk. Do you have the bag or do I have it? I can't even remember."

"I have it. You were going to take it a couple of times, but you never did. Once you even had it in your hand to take with you and you changed your mind. Unless, of course, you took it and didn't tell me. When we finish wrapping, we can check the garage. Do you want to go to the party with Fred and me tonight?"

"Thanks, but no. Mike is coming over. I still have some of my own Christmas stuff to do. What do you think about all this, Trixie?"

"I think you're bringing it all to a head. But to tell you the truth, I'm not sure if it's good or bad. What's your next move?"

"That's just it, Trixie, I don't know. I suppose I need to get out a magnifying glass and look through my college annual to see who's wearing thick bracelets and medallions. If they're football players, I might be onto something. And I need to go through the rest of Connie's disk. But other than that—I don't know where to go from here. What would you do if you were me?"

"Sit back and wait," Trixie said without a moment's thought. "If Prentice is as you say, in the mix, you put him on alert. Correct me if I'm wrong here. You think he was some-how personally involved with your friend's rape that night?"

"It depends on your definition of personal. He wasn't there, if that's what you mean. Oh God, I forgot to tell you about the disk. Stop what you're doing and pay attention, Trixie."

Trixie's face went from curious to amazement to disbelief as Jane recited the events of finding the disk and reading it. "I'm not even going to ask who you think might have put your name on the disk. Now I see where you're coming from. I don't like this, Janie. If Prentice is involved, and I don't know how he would be, but let's say he is, he's going to alert everyone. I don't even know who everyone is. I should be able to figure this out since it's what I do for a living, but I can't. The boys that harmed your friend that night are now grown men with families and probably good jobs. They won't want anything to disturb their tidy little lives. If any of them find out that you're causing a stir there's no telling what they will do. You could be in danger. Do you think Brian Ramsey was sent to you with a concocted story as a sort of red herring? You know, to see if you knew anything or to get a reaction out of you? I hate clichés, but if that's the case, they should have let sleeping dogs lie."

"That's exactly what I thought, Trixie. But then Betty Vance came along. Was all that planned, or was it a coincidence? Was all that to give me a nudge to see if I'd push the envelope? Maybe it's all one big mind game."

"Sweetie, how would you feel about having Flash stay with you for a while? Two dogs are better than one. He adores you. Fred and I are going to worry ourselves sick over these new developments."

"No. Olive is good. She knows the moment someone turns off the highway. She can literally smell the UPS guy's truck. Mike is with me at night. I think he might be moving in. I'm *hoping* he will. I'm not home during the day, and once my practice is gone, I'll be here working with you. If it will ease your mind, I can have an alarm system put in on the first floor."

"Do that, honey. It will definitely ease my mind."

"I'll call right after Christmas. They aren't going to be able to get to me till after the New Year, though. No one conducts business between Christmas and New Year's." Jane went back to wrapping presents. "So, how's the new book coming?" she asked, changing the subject.

"You mean *Pigskin Bloodbath*?"

"Egads! Is that what you're calling it?"

"What else? It deals with the murder of an entire college football team. This one was Fred's idea. You know how he loves football."

Jane's curiosity was piqued. "Who's the killer?"

"I think it's the guy in charge of the point spread, whatever that is. A fixed championship game or something. I've been so busy with Flash, I just gave Fred his head and let him run with it."

"Oh! Trixie, do you mind if I go into your storage room and fish out some of your older books, the ones Mike doesn't have? I want to give them to him for Christmas. Will you autograph them?"

"Sure, but don't tell him the truth."

"I won't."

"Go get them. Fred will sign them for you."

"I love you, Trixie," Jane said, throwing her arms around the little woman.

It was five o'clock and already dark when Jane parked her car alongside the steps leading to her back porch. The skin on her forearms prickled as she climbed from the car, ever grateful to Fred for insisting on the sensor lights. She bolted up the steps and into the house. Olive welcomed her as though she'd been gone for a month. "Do you want to go for a run, Olive? Around the house a few times then right back in. I'm locking this door so use your doggie door. I'm going to change my clothes. You better be in here when I get back down here. Understood?" The springer looked at her with questioning eyes, her tail swishing back and forth. "It's okay, I'm just spooking myself. Ten minutes." Olive bellied out the doggie door and was gone.

Jane walked through the house to her office, turning on lights as she went along. Her gaze swept the room and settled on her desk. The Lucite container was sitting on top of her computer keyboard, the green frog on top of the monitor. She whirled around. The tremor in her legs forced her to sit down. "Okay, what is it this time?" she demanded, her voice so shaky she hardly recognized it. She answered her own question by opening the Lucite box and removing the disks. She counted them, once then a second time. They were all there. The rubber band was still at the bottom of the box. She knew the hair on the back of her neck was standing on end. She almost jumped out of her skin when she felt a rush of cold air swirl around the room.

Jane whirled about. "Is anyone there?" she asked, peering into the dark corners of the room.

"Just me, Billy," a voice answered. *"I'm over here, next*

to the bookcase. Bad things are happening. You have to be careful."

Jane clenched the armrests of her chair and stared at the apparition. For some reason she wasn't afraid. "All those other times I saw you—I wasn't dreaming, was I?"

"I told you, you weren't, but you wouldn't believe me."

"So . . . what you're saying here is that you're a ghost. A real live ghost."

"Yes. I know you don't believe in ghosts, but we really do exist. And we don't all rattle chains or try to scare people. I prefer the word spirit *opposed to* ghost, *and I definitely do not like being called a spook."*

"Okay, I can accept that. I think. Was it you who moved the box of disks and taped that paper to the disk?"

"Yes. Did it help you?"

"I'm sure you already know the answer to that. Tell me how you knew that letter was on that disk? More to the point, what do you know? Share your thoughts with me, Billy."

"You're too isolated way out here. This is a very old house and easy to break into. I don't want you to worry, though. Jeeter and I will watch out for you. He's playing with Olive in the kitchen. I wish you would call your friend."

"Who? Mike?"

"No. Your lady friend. The one who is troubled."

"If you're referring to Betty, I can't do that. She's the patient of another colleague, and I can't poach. That means it wouldn't be professional."

"I think she needs your help."

"If she needed my help, she would call me. She hasn't called all week. She is having dinner with my godparents on Christmas."

"You could go to visit her the way you visited Mr. Ramsey."

"I can't. Sharon would report me to the Board if I did that.

If she calls me, I can talk to her. Why don't you visit her and plant the suggestion?"

"*I can't leave this house. I'm tied here forever. Mike's turning into your driveway. Be careful, Miss Jane.*"

The apparition faded into nothingness. Jane stared at the bookcases, unconvinced of what she'd just seen. She'd had a stressful day, and she was tired. Either she was hallucinating, or she'd dozed off. She got up to make her way to the second floor when suddenly she turned to see Mike standing in the doorway.

She flew into his arms and held on to him.

He gave her a kiss then pulled back. "Did you see Olive?"

"She was having herself a high old time in the back. She was running in circles and chasing something. She totally ignored me." He started to take off his coat. "The Christmas tree smells really good when you first walk in. I brought a wreath for the front door. There was a hook on it so I hung it up. My mother always said a wreath on the front door made Christmas official. I think she was right. Want to see it?"

"Yeah. Does it have a red bow?"

"Of course and some pinecones and some other doodads." He pulled the door open for her inspection.

The Christmas wreath was almost as big and wide as the old-fashioned door itself. "It's beautiful, Mike. Thanks."

"You're welcome. Are you okay? You look kind of funny." He closed the door and put his arm around her. "You get some wine, I'll build a fire, and we'll sit down and you can tell me what's troubling you."

"I always seem to have a problem of some kind," Jane said.

"Better call Olive in, it's getting nippy out there."

Olive was already in the kitchen, her nose in her food bowl just the way Billy said she was. Jane watched as the springer suddenly moved to the side as though to allow room for someone else to eat from the bowl. Jeeter? "There's no such thing as a ghost," she muttered to herself. Olive walked away from the bowl and Jane did a double take when she saw the food in the dish disappear in front of her eyes. *Don't think about what you just saw. You need glasses, Jane. You know you can't see a thing up close.*

With wine bottle, glasses, and corkscrew in hand, Jane fled the kitchen. She added what just happened in the kitchen to the long list of things she didn't want to think about. "How's that for a fire?" Mike stood to the right of the fireplace, admiring his handiwork.

"Pretty darn nice. I bet you were a great Boy Scout!"

"I have the badges to prove it. Actually, my mother has them. She framed them. Mothers do stuff like that."

"I wouldn't know."

"Jesus, Jane, I'm sorry. I didn't mean . . ."

"I know you didn't. What should we toast? I can't believe Christmas is only three days away. Where did the time go? I say that every year."

Mike raised his glass. "To Christmas! To us! To all our tomorrows, may they all be wonderful!"

"That's a very worthy toast, so I'll drink to it," Jane said, clinking her glass against Mike's.

"Now tell me what's causing that look of worry on your face."

She told him about her luncheon with Todd and how he'd reacted. Then she told him about what had happened in her office. "I was so certain I was wide-awake, but the truth is I must have dozed off. Anyway, I had this weird dream that I should call Betty Vance. Do you think it would be okay to drive by her apartment to drop off a present? For some reason of late, I've been paying attention to my dreams. It would relieve my mind to know she's okay. On the other hand, I could take it with me to Trixie's Sunday evening and leave it there, since she's going to be having dinner with her and Fred."

"I think you should leave well enough alone. I don't like that business with Prentice. I sense trouble, Jane. What in the world possessed you to say those things?"

"He's in this up to his neck. I just don't know how or why."

"You aren't going to leave it alone, are you?"

"No, Mike, I'm not. I'm sick and tired of feeling guilty and ashamed. If there's something I can do now, I'm going to do it. I probably never would have done a thing if Brian Ramsey hadn't come to me. I would have gone through life never shedding this awful guilt. You don't know what it's like. You don't approve of this either, right?" Jane said, moving farther away on the couch.

Mike's arm snaked out to pull her back to his side. "It's not a question of approval, Jane. You're disrupting people's lives. No one takes that sitting down. Eventually someone is going to lash out, strike back, or do something. I don't want to see anything happen to you. Think about it. You're way out here, five miles away from your godparents and no neighbors on the other side of you. You're a mile in off the highway."

"If you're trying to scare me, you're succeeding, Mike."

"That's great. At least you're listening to me for a change."

"Does that mean you won't go with me to Betty's apartment to drop off the Christmas gift?"

"Look, if you're that concerned, call her. Wish her a Merry Christmas and hang up. Sharon Thomas can't find fault with that. Even so, I wish you wouldn't do it. You have to learn when to let go."

"I did let go, damn it. I never call her. She calls me. We talk about her job, her apartment, her dog, her visits to Trixie. The calls last five minutes. Sometimes a friendly voice is all it takes to get a troubled person over a particular hurdle."

"I got a present today from one of my patients," he said, switching topics before an argument started. "Guess who?" he teased.

"From your battery guy?"

"Yep. Battery-operated ski socks, battery-operated ski gloves, a battery-operated ski cap, a battery-operated thermos, and a battery-operated set of Christmas lights, guaranteed to last for six full hours. And a charger!"

Jane burst out laughing. "Guess that means you haven't made any progress."

"Not one bit. He talks and talks and talks, but he doesn't say anything. He is so clueless it's mind-boggling. He told me the other day that sooner or later I would hit on what his problem is. He said he has the utmost faith in my ability. That's the term he used, hit on it."

"I have every faith in you, too, Mike. Sooner or later you will hit on it," Jane giggled.

Mike grimaced. "So, do you want to have sex or do you want to eat?"

"Eat," Jane said smartly.

"Great. You smell terrible. How much garlic did you eat today?"

Jane threw a pillow at his retreating back.

12

"Merry Christmas, Trixie! Merry Christmas, Fred!" Jane said, throwing her arms around both godparents. "Mike's bringing in the presents. Oooh, it smells so good in here! I don't know how you guys do it. You both work all day and yet this house looks like it took weeks to decorate. It looks better than those glossy spreads you see in *Beautiful Homes*. I just love Christmas!"

"Me, too!" Fred said, reaching for the pile of presents as Mike came through the door. "I'll put these under the tree."

"I have two more loads," Mike said, rubbing his arms. "Brrr. I bet the temperature dropped to thirty degrees. It's gumbo weather, as my mother always says."

"I always say that, too," Trixie chimed in, her face aglow with happiness. She was resplendent in an ankle-length, red-velvet skirt trimmed with faux ermine, and a white sweater covered with sparkling beads. She laughed in delight as she plopped a Santa hat on top of her curls. "Flash loves this hat! He grabs it and runs off with it every chance he gets."

Fred rejoined them, smacking his hands together in glee. "This is going to be a wonderful holiday. Dinner won't be ready for at least an hour, so let's sit by the fire and look at that glorious pile of presents. The dogs are curled up toasting on the hearth. Would you like some wine, a drink, or perhaps some of Trixie's famous egg-nog?"

Jane giggled as she stared at Fred's reindeer suspenders. He, too, wore a Santa hat. "Eggnog, of course," she said.

As soon as the door opened, Fred posed the same question to Mike.

"Eggnog, please." He handed the second pile of presents over to Fred and started back for the third and final load. "Who in the world are all these presents for?" he asked, his breathing a little more labored than usual.

"Some are for Trixie and Fred. Some for Flash and Olive. And there might even be one or two in there for you," Jane said as she winked roguishly.

"I do my shopping in the middle of the night by dialing 1-800. I did some on-line shopping this year, too," Trixie chirped.

"Me, too," Jane said, accepting a cup of eggnog from Fred. "I hope you guys don't mind that I had my calls forwarded here. Mike and I were talking about leaving from here for New Orleans. Of course that depends on how much eggnog we drink tonight. I don't think any calls will come in, but you never know. Mike has someone covering for him, so he doesn't have a problem."

"We can handle any calls that come in. What did you decide about the radio show, Jane?" Fred asked.

"My contract is up January 3. If the sponsors are willing, Mike will take it over. I'll guest on it for a little while, so the transition will be smooth. I'm not worried about it. What's for dinner, Trixie?"

"Roast goose, prime rib, plum pudding, shrimp-and-lobster cocktail, crab tart, and all kinds of good things."

"Good lord, Trixie, when did you find time to do all that?" Jane asked in amazement.

Trixie looked at Fred and grinned. "We thought we'd get real creative with dinner this year. When the Neiman Marcus catalog arrived last August, I called them up and ordered two dinners, one for tonight and one for tomorrow night. The deliveryman brought them bright and early this morning. All I have to do is press a button to heat everything. Do you feel cheated that I didn't cook it myself?" Trixie asked, her voice anxious.

"Not at all," Jane said, chuckling. Neiman Marcus! My God! A dinner from them must have cost a fortune, but she wasn't going to ask how much. If she did, she would probably lose her appetite. Leave it up to Trixie.

"It doesn't matter to me either," Mike said, coming in the door with the last load of presents. "I'll eat anything as long as it isn't Froot Loops."

The evening progressed nicely until the eggnog was gone, at which point Fred suggested a sing-along while he played some favorite Christmas songs on the piano. They all sang with gusto, the dogs barking in the background. It was eight o'clock when Trixie called a halt to the festivities and announced dinner.

Jane loved sitting in the old-fashioned dining room. She particularly loved the furniture that had been Trixie's grandmother's. It was old, scarred, and nicked but it had character. Trixie polished it once a week with beeswax and then lemon oil so the wood wouldn't dry out. Jane knew one day it would be hers to polish and preserve.

The tablecloth, another of Trixie's grandmother's heirlooms, was pure linen that had been washed and ironed so many times it had the sheen of satin. The centerpiece was an exquisite, cut-glass bowl with scarlet poinsettias floating in water. Bayberry candles, two inches high on crystal saucers, surrounded the bowl, giving off a heady scent. The arrangement had been chosen so it wouldn't interfere with cross-table conversation. Fred hated it when he had to crane or stretch his neck over a tall centerpiece to talk to someone.

Christmas Eve dinner was a tradition Fred and Trixie had started long ago, when Jane was an unhappy youngster in search of love. Now it would be Mike's tradition as well. Jane glowed with pleasure. She'd never been happier in her life. She reached up to accept a crystal bowl full of ambrosia when Mike winked at her. She got so flustered she almost dropped the bowl.

"It was a great dinner. Now if we all pitch in, we can get the cleanup out of the way and head for the presents. All in favor say aye!" Jane announced.

"Aye!" Four voices shouted simultaneously.

The cleanup was accomplished in under thirty minutes. Fred replenished the fire, handed out treats to the dogs, and sat down next to Trixie. "Janie always hands out the presents. We take turns opening them so we can oooh and aaahh over them. We've been doing it that way for a long time. It does take a bit of time, but everyone spends a lot of time choosing, wrapping, and admiring the gifts, so we want the experience to last as long as possible," Fred said.

"I think I need some help this year, Fred." Jane looked at Mike, who, she noticed, was watching her intently. "My pile goes in front of me, yours in front of you, ditto for Fred and Trixie, and the dogs' pile—I mean presents—go over there by the chaise. The presents wrapped in silver with the bells are opened last. That means they're special presents. Don't screw it up now," she said, shaking a finger at him. She was absolutely giddy. Was tonight the night Mike would ask her to marry him? Would there be a ring? She promised herself that if it didn't happen, she wouldn't be disappointed, but she knew she would be.

"God forbid that I should screw up," Mike grinned, getting into the swing of things.

For two wonderful hours the foursome whooped and hollered over the silly gadget gifts and murmured with pure delight over the more serious, thoughtful ones.

"T. F. Dingle!" Mike shouted. "All the ones I don't have! Jane, where did you get them? My God, I can't wait to read them." He raised his eyes to look at Fred and Trixie. "You must think I'm nuts, but I love this guy. When I was in college, and if a new book came out, and it was a choice between a frat party with three kegs or the new book, the book won. Hands down. I don't know how to thank you, Jane. That must have taken some doing. And they're autographed, too!" he said, slapping his head in amazement. "How'd you do it?"

"Well I . . . what I did was . . ." She looked at her godparents for help.

"She just asked us to sign them," Trixie blurted. "Fred and I are T. F. Dingle. You are the only other person in town besides Jane who knows this. Please keep our secret. We asked Janie not to tell. If you're going to be part of this little family, you have a right to know."

Mike stared at them in disbelief. "You're kidding me. You two are *him?*" he said, looking down at the books in his hand. Fred and Trixie nodded in unison. "My God. I can't believe it. I would never have guessed in a million years. And you're *two* people! I never would have guessed that either." He chuckled and ran a hand through his hair. "Okay, okay, I get it. The T is for Trixie and the F is for Fred. Where did the Dingle come from?" Mike put the books down and walked over to Fred and Trixie. He pumped their hands furiously until Trixie squealed for mercy.

"Fred had a dog named Dingle when he was a boy," Trixie explained, tucking her hand beneath her.

"Well, I'm honored. I'm really honored," Mike said, returning to his seat, a grin the size of Texas on his face.

His excitement was such that he reminded Jane of a little boy getting a much-wanted toy—the toy of his dreams. She smiled at Trixie, silently thanking her for letting Mike in on the secret.

"Your turn, Janie," Fred said.

Jane opened a small box. "Keys! What are these for?"

"A new four-by-four Range Rover," Fred said, sounding just like the announcer on *The Price Is Right*. "You're gonna need it if you and Trixie go into the dog business."

Jane sat staring at them with her mouth open. Tears welled in her eyes as she said, "Thank you. Thank you both so much. You shouldn't have. I was going to trade in my car after the first of the year. What color is it?" Her eyes lit up with devilish delight.

"Dartmouth green, your favorite color. It's in the garage under a tarp," Trixie said.

Jane got up and went over to them, hugging and kissing them each in turn. "I can't thank you two enough. You have to stop being so good to me. You might spoil me."

"Never," Fred said.

"My gift to you is for the both of you," she said with an impish grin that showed her teeth. "If you hadn't told Mike who you were, I was going to wait until tomorrow for you to open it. But since you did, you can open it now."

The gift was huge and leaned against the wall. Trixie and Fred were like two little kids as they ripped at the paper and silver bells. Both of them stood back in awe to see the covers of all their books made into a magnificent collage. Trixie wiped her tears on the sleeve of her sweater. Fred put his arm around her shoulders, his own eyes moist.

"Oh, Janie," Trixie cried. "It's fabulous. However did you think of it? I've never seen anything like it in my life. We can take down that awful painting in the office and put this on the wall instead, right over our desk."

"I saw something similar in a decorator magazine. I'm

glad you like it. Of course I had to steal a hundred and something of your books and take the covers, but I think it was worth it."

"That's an understatement," Fred said, admiring the collage from different angles.

Jane turned to Mike, who seemed almost mesmerized by the collage. "Your turn, Mike. My gift to you," Jane said, her eyes sparkling with anticipation.

They all watched as he carefully tore off the paper and read the printed contents. Even across the room Jane could hear him gasp. "Are you kidding me? Is this for real? It's a joke, right?"

"No joke," Jane assured him. "I couldn't get you the real thing, so I chose this. They said the experience is better than the real thing."

"What is it? Tell us," Trixie demanded.

Mike reluctantly tore his eyes away from the official-looking document. "It says here that I am authorized to catapult off the USS *Patrick Henry* somewhere in the Adriatic Sea in a Tomcat by way of virtual reality in Baton Rouge. All I have to do is set up an appointment." He grabbed Jane and twirled her around until he was dizzy. "Ah, honey, this is so great. I can't believe it. This is a dream come true. In fact this whole evening is a dream come true. First T. F. Dingle and now this. My God, I don't know what to say. Thank you seems inad—" His voice broke off in mid-sentence. "My God, what if I crash and burn?"

"Then they turn on the lights, you take off your glasses, and you're back in the real world. Isn't Christmas wonderful?" Jane chortled.

"It sure is. But guess what, it's going to get even better. At least I hope it will." He dipped into his pocket and pulled out a small red-velvet box. "Here's the last present. It's for you, Jane."

Jane knew this was a moment she would treasure. She

swallowed as she took the box from his hand. Then, holding her breath, she slowly opened the lid. Inside, winking at her, was the most beautiful marquis diamond she'd ever seen. She blinked when Mike got down on one knee and took her hand. "Will you marry me?" he said, taking the ring out of the box and slipping it on her finger.

"Yes and yes and yes," she whispered, then went into his arms. When they broke apart, she asked, "When?"

"June. Is that too soon?"

"No, not at all. June is fine. June is great, isn't it, Trixie?" she said, turning to her godparents.

Trixie was clutching Fred's arm. "June is perfect! Oh, honey, I'm so excited." The phone rang just as she puckered up for Fred's kiss.

"I'll get it," Fred grumbled as he struggled off the sofa. He pointed his finger at Trixie, and said, "Remember where we were, and no senior moments either," he said, heading for the kitchen.

"Who in the world could be calling us on Christmas Eve?" Trixie asked, a puzzled expression on her face. "Oh, I know, it's probably the police station. They called us last year on Christmas Eve, too, to thank us for what we'd done during the year. Be nice, Fred!" Trixie shouted.

"I'm always nice," Fred shouted in return.

"Mike, would you like some coffee?"

"I would, Mrs. McGuire."

"Mrs. McGuire was Fred's mother," Trixie chided him. "Please, call me Trixie. Everyone else does. Jane, do you want coffee?"

"Yes. I can get it, Trixie."

Jane was half out of her chair when Fred shouldered his way past the swinging door leading to the kitchen. "You were right, Trixie, it was the police, but they didn't want to talk to you. They want to talk to you, Janie."

"Me! Why?"

"Betty—" He looked past Jane to his wife as if to say help me, here. Trixie immediately got up and came toward him. Fred put his hand on Jane's shoulder, his expression solemn. "She took her life, Janie. They think it happened yesterday or the day before. The neighbors called the police because the dog wouldn't stop barking. They want someone to take the dog."

"Get our coats, Fred. Are you okay to talk to them, Janie? Do you want me to do it for you?"

Speechless, her body trembling from head to toe, Jane shook her head and made her way to the kitchen. She dropped the phone twice before she was able to get a grip on the receiver. "This is Jane Lewis." She listened, her face draining of all color. When she finally managed to get her tongue to work, she said, "She was under the care of Dr. Sharon Thomas. You should call her. What is it you want me to do?" She waited for the answer. "Yes, I can be there in fifteen minutes." She replaced the phone in the cradle with shaking hands. When she looked up, she saw Mike, Fred, and Trixie waiting for her to say something.

Her throat constricted and tears filled her eyes. "I knew something was wrong. I had this dream about Betty. I should have paid attention. I wanted to go there Friday night. I really did. She considered me her friend. I let her down. God, why did I listen to you, Mike? I should know by now to pay attention to my gut instincts. Every goddamn time I listen to someone else, things go wrong. Now look what happened," Jane cried, wringing her hands.

"Jane . . ."

"Don't talk to me, Mike. Don't say anything because then I'll say something I will regret. I have to go there. Right now."

"I'll go with you," Mike said.

Jane wiped at her tears. "No. I don't need your help. I don't want your help. Are you coming, Trixie?"

"Of course I'm going with you. I'll drive." She turned around. "You two clean up," she said, pointing her index finger at Fred.

In the car, driving at breakneck speed, Trixie said, "You were a little hard on him, weren't you, Janie?"

"I wanted to go over there Friday night. He talked me out of it. I've had a bad feeling about Betty all week. Sharon telling me to keep my hands off her, and then Betty didn't call all week. That wasn't like her. I keep having these crazy dreams. I can't believe this, Trixie. How could I have been so stupid?"

"Just a minute, Jane. This is not your fault. Don't try taking the blame for this girl's death."

"What did I miss, Trixie? Is it my own cowardice that made me knuckle under to Sharon Thomas? The hell with ethics. That girl was more important than some damn ethic Sharon thinks I violated. Then there's Mike and his way of doing things—don't get involved; it's none of your business after office hours; turn it on, turn it off. That's not who I am. Damn it to hell, it is my business! All I have to do is think about Connie Bryan, which I do every day of my life, and I realize it *was* my fault. I could have done something. I didn't try hard enough. I honored a stupid promise, and Connie killed herself. And now this girl is dead. I don't deserve to practice psychiatry. I don't even have the courage of my convictions, and that makes me exactly what my mother said I was, a big *nothing*!"

Trixie slammed on the brakes so hard, the Bronco skidded to the side of the road, jolting both of them forward. She turned to Jane. "Don't you dare say a thing like that again! It's not true! Don't you dare even *think* such a thing! Do you hear me, Jane? I will not tolerate it now or ever. Which apartment is it?"

"The one on the end."

Trixie's angry expression softened a little. "When you say things like that or even think them, it means Fred and I failed you."

Jane was immediately contrite. "Oh, no, Trixie. You didn't fail. I'm sorry. I try not to think like that. I really do, but then someone throws me a curve and sometimes I can't handle it. Come on, let's go inside."

Jane prayed all the way into the building that the coroner would have taken the body away and it would be just the local police she would have to deal with.

The small apartment was crowded. Jane blinked as she looked around. Golda ran to Trixie and threw herself into her outstretched arms.

A young glum-faced man walked toward Jane. "Dr. Lewis, remember me? I'm Betty's friend Chuck. We met briefly that first day when Betty came to see you at the clinic."

"Yes, of course. I'm so terribly sorry. Did they call you?"

"They said they did, but I was at a friend's house. I stopped here on my way home to drop off a gift. The police were already here, and so were these other people," he said, pointing to Sharon Thomas, Brian Ramsey, and two other people Jane didn't recognize. Neighbors maybe. Two police officers stood on each side of the door. Jane fought the sobs in her throat.

"I warned you it might come to this, Jane," Sharon said spitefully, her face furious. "What are you doing here anyway?"

"The police called me to come over. What are you talking about, Sharon? Betty was your patient, not mine. You were the doctor of record. You were the one treating her on a regular basis, not me. Don't try blaming me for this."

"I *do* blame you. I told you to stay away from her."

"I did stay away from her, and this is the result. You need to look to your own motives here. What are *you* doing here, Mr. Ramsey?"

"The police called me. My name was in Betty's address book. I told them everything I know." For such a big man he looked visibly shaken.

"I'd like to go home now," Sharon said. "It *is* Christmas Eve!"

"You go home when I say you go home, Dr. Thomas," one of the police officers said coolly. "I need a written statement from all of you. We can do it here, or down at the station."

"Then let's get on with it," Sharon said. "I'd like to go first so I can get out of here." She walked over to a worn yellow chair. She looked at it for a moment before she perched herself on the arm.

Jane sat down on the matching sofa next to Brian Ramsey. She had a clear view of the kitchen, where she could see Trixie cleaning up Golda's mess. Poor thing. She turned to Ramsey. "Why did you tell me you were married? Why did you think it necessary to lie? What was that all about?"

Ramsey threw his head back against the sofa. "I thought— Oh, shit, I don't know what I was thinking. I did love Betty. In the beginning, anyway. I should have known it wouldn't work. I'm settled, and she was young. I didn't want to party, and she did. I couldn't accept what happened to her, and yet I couldn't let her go. I wanted to. I did try to help her in my own bumbling way, but it was too late. I don't know the why of anything. What I do know is she's dead, and part of it is my fault. I don't know how I'm going to handle that."

Trixie came into the living room. "I'm going to take Golda back to the farm. She'll do better when she sees Flash and Olive. I'll come back, Jane."

Jane nodded.

"You must be Dr. Lewis," a woman said, pulling a chair up next to the sofa. "I'm Inez. I live next door. I knew something was wrong when the dog wouldn't stop barking. Golda is usually so well behaved. Betty loved that dog. I walked her when Betty was at work," the woman said. Jane nodded. "Betty kept this place neat as a pin. I gave her cuttings from some of my plants. Look at them now. They're thriving. I thought she was, too. She told me what happened to her."

"Did she say anything to you that would indicate something had upset her?" Jane asked.

The woman shook her head. "She seemed just fine. She was right in with the Christmas spirit, even bought that little tree over there and decorated it." She nodded toward the window. "She said she was invited out for Christmas dinner, to some farm. She was real excited about going. It doesn't make sense."

"Do you know why they called me?" Jane asked.

"I heard the officers talking. I think it was because she left you a letter. Let me tell you something, Doctor. Betty treasured your friendship. Not like that one over there," the neighbor said, jerking her head in Sharon's direction. "Betty didn't like her at all and was going to stop going to the clinic. She said the people at the crisis center helped her more, and they always called her back when she called them. She said what they told her conflicted with what the doctor told her." She glanced up. "I think it's my turn now." She patted Jane's hand reassuringly before she got up and walked across the room.

Jane watched as Sharon Thomas slipped into her coat. Cashmere. Maybe she should introduce her to Todd Prentice. Everyone in Rayne knew Sharon Thomas had a highly lucrative practice. Jane closed her eyes to think and snapped them open a moment later when she sensed a presence in front of her. Sharon glared down at her. Trixie always said, never let anyone stand over you and talk down to you. Instantly, she was on her feet.

"This isn't the end of it, Jane. I want to see what's in that letter."

"Get out of my face, Sharon, before I do something I'll regret. Just the fact that you're standing here breathing is pissing me off. If Betty left me a letter, and I don't know that she did, it's mine, not yours. I don't have to show you anything. You said you were in a hurry to leave, so leave already."

"Another thing, Jane, don't even think about trying to saddle me with that misfit's funeral."

Something in Jane snapped. She drew her arm back, clenched her fist, and punched Sharon square on the nose. Blood spurted in every direction.

"Jeez, Doc, I didn't know you had that in you!" Ramsey said in awe.

"You saw what she did," Sharon screamed at Ramsey. She held her hand over her nose as she grappled for a tissue in her pocket. "You broke my nose, you bitch!"

"Good," Jane muttered.

"I didn't see anything," Ramsey said.

When Sharon looked at Chuck, he shrugged. "Sorry, I didn't see anything either."

Sharon glared at the three of them. "You think you're all so smart. The cop saw it," Sharon said, turning to the officer, only to find that he had gone. She swung back toward Jane. "You're going to pay for this, you bitch! I'm going to sue your ass off. I'll pick your bones clean."

"You're getting blood all over that nice cashmere coat," Jane said.

"Hey, Ramsey, you're next," the cop said, coming out of the bedroom.

Moments later Trixie returned. "What happened to Dr. What's-her-name? She was bleeding."

"I popped her one," Jane admitted with a smile. "I never enjoyed anything so much in all my life."

"No kidding," Trixie said, looking at Jane with a new kind of respect. "Are you all right, honey?"

"I'm fine. Never been better."

"Mike is just sick over this, Janie."

"He damn well should be sick over this," Jane replied sharply.

Trixie gave Jane a hard look. "Jane, I love you more than life itself, but we both know if you wanted to come over here bad enough, you would have done it regardless of what Mike said. You need to deal with that."

Jane felt well chastised. "I'm trying, Trix. I'm trying. They said she wrote me a letter, but they haven't given it to me yet. I don't think she has any relatives other than an aunt with a bunch of kids. Do you think I should make the funeral arrangements?"

"Do whatever you have to do, Jane."

"This is killing me, Trixie. Is the dog okay?"

"Golda is fine. She's in a good place. This is not your fault."

"Get off it, Trixie. Of course it's my fault. Just like Connie was my fault. You are absolutely right about Friday night. If I'd wanted to come here bad enough, I would have. So you see, that's how I know this is my fault. For the moment it was easier to blame it on Mike. Call him, Trixie, tell him I can't go with him to his parents' house."

"I'm not telling him any such thing. Honey, Betty is gone. You can't bring her back. Nothing is going to get done on Christmas."

"It doesn't matter. I have to be here. I ran out on Connie. I'm not going to do it again. I promised Betty she would be all right if she kept up with the counseling sessions and the therapy. She was making progress, wasn't she, Trixie? You saw her once a week at the training sessions with the dogs. You must have observed some progress."

"I thought she was coming along nicely. She said she was giving serious thought to going to the police academy. Her counselor is the one who said she had the makings of a police officer. She was excited about it. It wasn't till next year, but she was very interested."

"Dr. Lewis," the policeman called.

"This shouldn't take long," Jane said to Trixie.

It was one-thirty when Jane walked out into the night with Trixie. "It's Christmas Day, Trixie. Miracles are supposed to happen on Christmas. What just happened was a tragedy. I don't think I've ever been this tired in my life. My brain is as numb as my body. Let's stop by the church. I don't want to go inside, I just want to sit outside and look at it. The manger should be up because I saw them working on it last week."

"All right, honey."

"What were Fred and Mike doing when you went back to the house?"

"Drinking coffee. Talking. Playing with the dogs. Mike is worried about you, Jane."

"Do you have any cigarettes with you?"

"Since when do you smoke? Cigarettes aren't good for you."

"Since right now. Nothing's good for you. If it tastes good, that means it's bad. If it's white, it's not good for you. Soda pop has too much caffeine. Coffee will give you the crud, tea stains your teeth, fried food clogs your arteries. What's left, Trixie? Nothing, that's what, so give me the damn cigarette. Do you think Sharon will sue me? I heard the bone crunch. She'll end up getting a nose job, then a face-lift to go with it. I did the witch a favor; she's just too dumb to know it."

"Do you care if she sues you?"

"No."

"There were no witnesses. How can she sue you?"

"She'll find a way, but who cares."

Trixie stopped the Bronco alongside the manger. "It's beautiful, isn't it, Janie? Remember how Fred and I always brought you here on Christmas. You'd lift the Baby Jesus out of the cradle and ask where his mother was."

"I remember. Peace on earth, goodwill toward men. I blew that one tonight. Right now I don't have one ounce of good-will in me for my fellow man."

"You're in shock, Jane. Things will look different in the morning."

"That's a crock, Trixie, and you know it. It's all downhill, from here on out. Trust me on that one. We can go home now."

"Good idea," Trixie said, shifting gears.

The brown-and-white spaniel ran to Jane the minute she walked in the kitchen door. She barked a greeting, then ran after Flash and Golda through the open doorway.

It all looked so normal, so Christmas-like, with the fat red candle nestled in a bed of evergreens sitting on the table, a sugar bowl and cream pitcher next to it, coffee cups, spoons, and napkins in front of Fred and Mike. She saw a bourbon bottle on the counter. Fred obviously thought the coffee needed to be fortified.

"Jane, I'm so sorry. Is there anything I can do?" Mike asked, putting his arm around her shoulder.

"Everyone is sorry. No, there's nothing anyone can do. I punched Sharon Thomas and broke her nose. There was blood everywhere. She's going to sue my ass off. That's a di-rect quote," Jane said, sitting down at the table.

"You broke her nose! Would I be out of line if I asked why?" Mike asked, clearly agitated at the news.

"Because she said she wasn't paying for Betty's funeral and said her death was my fault," Jane snarled. "What else do you want to know? Betty's dead. There's a period after dead. That means she is never going to call me to talk about the weather or her dog or to tell me how she's doing. The god-damn period means she's dead. What part of that don't you understand?"

"Whoa, Jane. I'm not the enemy here."

"Like hell you aren't. I'm going home, Trixie. Thanks for

going with me. I'll call you in the morning. Thank you both for all the wonderful presents. Do you want me to take Golda, or are you going to keep her?"

"She's good with Flash. I'll keep her. What time are you going to be leaving in the morning? If you're leaving early, you might as well leave Olive here."

"I'm not going anywhere in the morning. You'll have to go alone, Mike. Whatever Christmas spirit I had is gone. Your family doesn't need someone like me right now. I don't want to argue about it. It's your family, and they're expecting you, so you should go. Don't worry about me. I have things I have to do and things to take care of where Betty . . . details. There are always details to . . . to take care of."

Mike threw his hands in the air. "What can you possibly do on Christmas Day? The answer is nothing. We made these plans a long time ago. My parents are expecting us. Jane, I'm not trying to be unreasonable. Getting away will be good for you. What possible excuse can I give them?"

"How about the truth? Somebody I cared about, somebody I once treated, died. You want me to sit down to eat and open presents? I can't do that. Right now I want to find a safe corner and sit in it and suck my thumb. I need to think, and I need to be alone. If you can't cut me some slack and don't understand, I'm sorry. It's the way it is right now."

Mike looked across the table at Fred and Trixie's blank faces. He wasn't going to get any help from that direction. "I'll drive you home."

"I'll drive myself home." Jane's tear-filled eyes pleaded with her godparents for understanding.

"It's okay, Janie, girl," Fred said, waddling over to her. Jane clutched at his suspenders. "Do what you have to do and don't worry about us. Mike can use one of our cars." Jane burst into tears when Olive pawed her leg. "Get in the car, girl, we're going home."

Trixie's skinny arm snaked out as she reached for Mike's arm. Her nails dug into his wrist. "You need to let her go. I don't want to revise my thinking where you're concerned, young man. This is way more serious than you think. My advice is go to your parents and let Janie do what she has to do. If you don't, you'll be wearing that ring on your pinkie finger. Another thing, that was a pretty selfish display of emotion a while ago. I didn't much care for it. You're a man!" Trixie said, as though that comment alone summed up everything.

Mike sat down. "Do you really expect me to leave her at a time like this?"

"It's not what I expect. It's what Jane expects. Your parents are expecting you, and there's nothing you can do here. Make their day happy."

"She's blaming me," Mike said miserably.

"Yes, she is, but she's blaming herself, too."

"Janie said your bags and presents for the family were in the trunk. I put them in the Bronco. Here are the keys," Fred said.

"My car is at Jane's. I don't want to put you out."

"I wouldn't go there if I were you. Jane said you were having trouble with your brakes and were going to make the trip in her car. Just take the Bronco and head out. Call us when you get there so we don't worry. I'll fix you a thermos of coffee to drink on the way."

"I feel terrible about this. Of all times for something like this to happen. All of a sudden I feel guilty as hell."

"Son, I don't personally give two shits about how you feel right now. I might care tomorrow because you seem like a nice enough fellow, and Janie loves you. Right now all I'm concerned about is Janie and that displaced dog lying over there. Now if that makes me something other than what you think I should be in your eyes, tough shit! Do we understand one another?" Trixie asked bluntly.

Fred blinked. His wife was on a roll.

"Yes, ma'am, I understand perfectly. Thanks for the coffee, Fred. I'll call when I get there."

"Don't call Jane. You call us here at the farm. Fred, write the number down for him. Remember what I said about wearing that ring."

Mike nodded. He shuddered from head to toe as he walked toward the door. "Merry Christmas," he said hoarsely. He wasn't surprised when no response followed him out to the car. The sound of the door closing was terminal-sounding. He shivered again. Maybe things would look better when it got light out.

Christmas Day.

13

Jane's mind was in a turmoil as she drove home. She drove slowly, not because of the speed limit or road conditions, but because her eyes were too blurry with tears to see well enough to drive any faster.

Olive sat beside her, whimpering as if to say she understood.

At length, Jane pulled onto the shoulder and brought the car to a stop. When she turned to look out the window, she saw St. Andrew's. She stared at the manger scene she'd had Trixie drive past earlier. She had no conscious recollection of driving here and yet, here she was. Maybe she was supposed to come here. Maybe . . . The driver door seemed to open of its own volition. Jane climbed out. How quiet it was. Midnight mass was over. Father John was probably sound asleep.

Olive next to her, Jane walked around the front of the car to the sidewalk leading to the manger scene. It was so beautiful up close. Did they keep the lights on all night? She dropped to her knees beside the manger and reached for the wooden statue of the Baby Jesus. "I was just here a little while ago with Trixie. I wanted to come back. No that's not true, I *needed* to come back." She hugged the statue to her breast and cried silently. Olive continued to whimper at her side.

A long time later, Jane sensed a presence. She looked up and gasped in surprise. "Father John! What— Did someone see me and think I was—"

"No one saw you, Jane," he interrupted. "For some reason I can never sleep on Christmas Eve. It's been that way for as long as I can remember. I was going to turn the big light off and turn on the smaller one when I saw you sitting here. Can I help, Jane?"

"No, Father, but thank you. I guess I should put Him back." She struggled to a better position to return the small statue to the manger, her eyes never leaving those of the priest at her side.

"Only if you want to," he said, putting a comforting hand on her shoulder. "Does He give you comfort?"

"I was hoping He would. But to tell you the truth, Father, I really don't feel any better now than when I first got here. When I was a child and rode my bike here after everyone was asleep, it was so wonderful. I always went home feeling like I could take on the world. I don't remember if I prayed, though. I think I did. I didn't pray tonight. It doesn't seem fair that I should dump my problems in God's hands. I spent long years going to school to learn how to deal with problems, my own and everybody else's. But now— Now, it's as if I didn't learn anything at all. I feel like an imposter. Oh, Father, I have so much emotional baggage. I don't know what to do anymore. Sometimes I'm afraid I might lose my mind."

"When I don't know what to do about something, I find the best course of action is to do nothing. It works for me." He sat down on the ground next to her.

Olive wiggled and squirmed until she was between them.

"I'm a good listener, Jane."

"If I unburden my soul to you, do you think you could just

listen and not say anything? Then when I'm finished, I'll go home and we'll never talk about it again. Can we do that? Can we pretend it's a confession of sorts?"

"If that's what you want, Jane."

"Did Trixie or Fred call you?"

"Trixie called earlier. She said she had a feeling you might come here. I've been watching and more or less waiting for you. I wouldn't have said anything if you hadn't brought it up. I can stay here until it's time to get ready for six o'clock Mass."

Jane opened her coat, pressed the small statue against her chest, and started to talk. From time to time she looked up to see the priest's reaction. All she could see was love and compassion. When her words finally trickled to a conclusion, she removed the statue from inside her coat and replaced it in the manger. She squeezed Father John's hand before she got to her feet. "I might need a character witness if she sues me and takes me to court," she called over her shoulder as she was walking away.

"I'll be in the front row, child. Are you coming to Mass this morning?"

"Probably not, Father." She wanted to say Merry Christmas, but she couldn't get the words past her lips.

Jane felt a hundred years old when she walked up the steps to her front porch. She was colder than she'd ever been in her life. She sniffed at the evergreen wreath on the door, Mike's Christmas contribution. She hung up her coat, and then put it back on. She'd forgotten that she'd turned the thermostat down to fifty when she left with Mike earlier in the evening. She turned it up now and built a fire. The moment the room warmed, she removed her coat and plugged in the tree lights. A trip to the bathroom and one to the kitchen for a bottle of wine completed her chores. With the bottle between her knees she applied a corkscrew. The moment it popped she took a swig. "This isn't your regulation-size bottle of wine, Olive. This is one of the *big boys*! In other words, a *half gallon*. I'd give you some, but wine isn't good for dogs. It probably isn't good for me either. But you know what, I don't give a good rat's ass if it is or isn't."

Outside Jane's house, in the quiet, frosty night, Trixie McGuire looked at her husband. "Slurping from a wine bottle is better than her driving around aimlessly. She'll fall asleep when she's had enough. I think it's safe to say she's okay for the rest of the night and into tomorrow morning. That girl is in so much pain I can feel it, Fred. There must be something we can do."

"She has to find her own way, Trixie. I want to believe she'll come to realize and live with the knowledge that her character is her destiny. My money is on our Janie. This is just another one of those rough patches we all hit from time to time."

"Damn it, Fred, that girl has had nothing but rough patches and potholes from the day she was born. When in the hell are they going to pave her road? I'm not sitting still for this. We have to do something," she said, defiance lighting her eyes. She blew on her bony hands to warm them.

"Get in the car, Trixie, I'm taking you home. We'll talk about this over some hot chocolate." Trixie didn't argue and allowed herself to be led to the car.

"Is this where you tell me two heads are better than one?" Trixie groused as she buckled her seat belt. "I don't want to hear any fortune-cookie wisdom tonight...I mean this morning, or whatever the hell time it is."

"It will be sunup in about twenty minutes," Fred said.

Jane knew if she closed her eyes, one of her dumb dreams would take over. She fought valiantly to keep her eyes open but she was too tired. Much too tired.

"Okay, Billy, tell me again, why you can't leave here?" Jane asked.

"This is where I was born and where I died. My soul didn't pass naturally. I can't go where the others are until I'm released."

"Who does the releasing? Do you have to qualify or something? You know my position on spooks."

Billy gave her a narrow look. *"I'm going to overlook that comment, Miss Jane."*

"Ask me if I care. I have more important things on my mind. Tell me something, please. Do you know where my mother and father are?"

"Your father was pure of heart so he passed to the other side but your mother—she's on this side, also waiting to be released."

Jane laughed, an eerie sound. "Who in their right mind would release my mother?"

"You!"

Jane laughed until the tears came. "That's a good one, Billy. Guess she's destined to stay on your side for all eternity because I'm not the one. She can burn— Oh, never mind."

"Then why did you ask me?"

"Conversation. I'm trying to get a handle on this dream stuff. I'm a lousy shrink, but who knows, I might become a *dreamologist.* Someone who interprets people's dreams. But before I can become an expert, I need to interpret my own dreams. So where does my mother hang out?"

"In your old house. She can't leave there just like I can't leave here."

"A prisoner in her own house. Imagine that! Okay, here's another question for you. Obviously you know everything that goes on here at this house so that means you heard Mike and me talking about his battery guy. What's the answer?"

"Energy." Billy smiled.

"Energy?"

"*Yes. When he was a small boy, he was sickly and his parents coddled him. Day after day, he did nothing but sit on the porch and watch the other children play. Even after he regained his health, he had little energy to do physical things. He got the idea that carrying batteries around with him would give him energy. He doesn't remember his early childhood because it is too painful. The mind is a curious thing, Miss Jane, as you well know.*"

"Batteries equal energy," Jane said to herself, shaking her head. "I knew it was something simple." She looked askance at Billy. "The question is how do you know about him? You just told me you can't leave here."

"*I read Dr. Sorenson's file on the man. He brings his briefcase here when he comes to visit you.*"

"Let's get back to my mother. Why didn't she pass over? Not that I care. I'm just curious. My mother the spook. I can't wait to tell Trixie."

"*You shouldn't speak disrespectfully of the dead, Miss Jane,*" he scolded.

Jane bristled. "Oh, but it was okay for her to speak to me, a child, with disrespect. Life and death, what's the difference? If I go to that old house, will I be able to see her, talk to her?"

"*I don't know. But I do know this, you're the only one who can release her and put her at peace. Do you want to do that?*"

"Hell, no, I don't," she shouted. "It gives me a lot of pleasure to know she's flopping around out there somewhere. It gives me even more pleasure to know I'm the one who's in charge of her staying or leaving." She hooted with delight. "That's what I call divine retribution, Billy. Absolutely divine!"

"*It's sad that you feel that way, Miss Jane. Very sad.*"

"Is anyone living in the house where she is? Wait a minute,

let me rephrase that. Is any live person residing in the house where she is?"

"No. *She drives everyone out. The fifth owner just moved. The house is for rent now.*"

"You know this . . . how?"

"*I just know.*"

"Yeah, well guess what? I'm going to wake up now so you can go away."

"*I wish you well, Miss Jane.*"

"And on that note, Billy, I will now leave you." She grappled with a line she used on her radio show. "Remember now, learn the rules so you know how to break them properly."

"*Yes, ma'am. It sounds like you're saying good-bye to your listeners on your radio show.*"

Jane rolled over on the sofa and opened her eyes a fraction. She brought her arm up to look at her watch. Noon! Noon on Christmas Day. The fire she'd lit when she came home was nothing more than smoldering ashes. The tree lights twinkled.

Olive licked her face.

"I love you, too, Olive, but I'm too tired to get up just yet. Those dreams of mine wear me out. I'm just going to catch a few more winks." She rolled back over and closed her eyes. When she woke later, it was starting to get dark outside. Maybe she should take a shower. A shower always made her feel better. Brushing her teeth always made her feel better, too. Too bad there weren't more things that would make her feel better.

She looked at the ring on her finger, the beautiful ring Mike had given her. Where did it fit into things now? Nowhere. She removed it and stuck it in the toe of one of her socks in her sock drawer.

The long night loomed ahead of her.

* * *

Trixie poured two glasses of wine and took them to the kitchen table. "I think this was the worst Christmas ever," she mumbled as she sat down. She knew she must look like hell. God knows she felt like hell. Neither she nor Fred had had more than a few hours' consecutive sleep since they'd gotten the telephone call from the police department on Christmas Eve. They were getting too old for this kind of thing. But what could they do? Their Janie was in trouble and they needed to keep an eye on her.

"You said you had an idea, Fred. Share it with me. I need something to make me feel good. If I have to make one more trip over to Janie's house, I'm going to collapse. She slept the day away, and now she's in bed again and it's only seven o'clock. She didn't eat either. Mike's called six times. I'm about ready to pull the phone out of the wall. So, what's the idea, sweetie?"

Fred looked up from the piece of paper he'd been doodling on. "How would you feel about endowing LSU?" His eyes clung to hers, analyzing her reaction.

Trixie's eyes flashed with impatience. "Forget it, Fred. I want to use our money for the K-9s."

"I know, doll, but I have a plan. I've been thinking about it all day. Tell me what you think. Janie told us that she bit one of the boys who raped her friend. Bit him clear to the bone is what she said. I think we all agree that a bite like that would leave a pretty nasty scar, agreed?"

"Yes," she said, eyeing him suspiciously.

"Okay, so now here's the deal. Our new book is called *Pigskin Bloodbath*. The whole football team gets wiped out. Pigskin, Trixie, you know, a football. I see the cover art as a pair of strong, bloody hands holding that pigskin high in the air, getting ready to toss a pass." To demonstrate, he grabbed the cantaloupe out of the fruit bowl and raised it over his head as if he were going to throw it. "We hold a contest to find a pair of hands to put on the cover of our new book. A football player's hands, big, strong, and . . . scarred. We limit the contest to LSU football players, past and present. We would know what year they played by the form they would have to fill out. We give a hundred grand to the university and fifty thousand to the football player whose hands we choose. We'll do it through our attorney so we can stay anonymous." His excitement increased as the words began to flow. "Because we'll be opening the contest to all the years, it'll look legit. Hell, it will be legit. But it will also give us a chance to find the guy Janie sank her teeth into. I think it will work, Trixie, I really do. Who's going to turn down fifty grand? The school won't turn it down, that's for sure. It will be wonderful publicity for them and us as well. We can afford to do this." He dropped the cantaloupe back in the bowl. "What do you think?"

"I think it's a wonderful idea, but Janie isn't one hundred percent positive it was a football player. She said she just had a strong sense that it was because they were all big, tall, and strong. It could just as easily be a wrestler or maybe even a track athlete. I hope you're right about it being a football player."

Fred took her hand and squeezed it. "Janie always had good intuition, and if she said she had a sense of it being a football player, that's good enough for me. We have to go back to the beginning and the beginning is that awful night. That will lead us to now and Betty Vance. Janie is convinced it's all tied together, and I think she's right." He tilted his head and looked into his wife's eyes. "I'd like to put the wheels in motion the first of the year if that's okay with you, honey. If you're okay with this, we can contact our attorney tomorrow so he can start putting it all together."

Wise to his sweet talk and hand-squeezing, Trixie drew her

hand away so she could think. "What you're saying is if we find a pair of hands with a scar, the guy is one of the bunch that did that awful thing. That's a bit of a stretch, even for us, Fred. But I'll go along with it. I'll do anything if it can get our old Janie back."

"Shazam!" Fred said, hitting his hand flat against the table.

"Not so fast, Freddie. So we get lucky and the guy that Janie bit enters the contest and we identify him by the scar. Then what?"

"Then Janie has to take the ball. Are you with me all the way on this, Trix?"

"There's nothing I wouldn't do for our Janie." Trixie turned to the sound of growling. "Would you look at those two!" she said, motioning to Flash and Golda tussling near the back door. "I can't wait for the first of the year and our first batch of dogs. The trainer is coming January 4. The inside of the barn will be finished tomorrow. Fred, do you think we'll live long enough to see the results?" Trixie asked anxiously. "This is such a good thing we're doing. Are you sure you don't want to retire, Fred?"

"No, I'm not ready. I thought I was, but I'm not. I think I have a few more stories in me. You might get another wild idea that will cost money. Reserves are real nice and handy. And, of course, we're going to live to see the results. You know the *D* word is not in our vocabulary. Don't ever bring that up again."

"I think about it, Fred. It's a fact of life. We're *old*. When you get old, you die. Our senior moments are going platinum in case you haven't noticed. Honey, we have more than enough money. Don't you want to go fishing and crabbing? Don't you want to take days off and do nothing?"

"Nope."

"Okay," she sighed. "Why is it I can never say no to you?"

"Because you love me." He gave her an irresistible grin.

She could only laugh. "Yes, I love you. Forever and ever and even then, remember? That's what we promised each other all those years ago." She raised up out of her chair, stretched across the table, and kissed him. "We should have gone to church today. This is the first Christmas we've missed in forty-five years."

"We'll go twice next week, Saturday night and Sunday morning. How's that?"

"That's good, Fred. Now what are we going to do? The night is still young. And it's Christmas!"

"Well, we could . . ." His eyes said it all.

"Hmm, yes, we could."

Jane opened her eyes.

Olive stirred and watched her mistress as she tried to decide if she was going to get up or lie back down. The moment the light went on, Olive hopped off the bed and waited patiently for Jane to lead the way downstairs.

"I'm turning into a vampire, Olive. I sleep by day and prowl by night." Jane washed her face, brushed her teeth, and ran a brush through her hair. "I have to get busy. I have a funeral to plan, and I need to do some heavy-duty thinking. I also have to wash some clothes because I don't have any more clean underwear. That's as bad as running out of toothpaste or toilet paper. We could both probably do with a little breakfast, too. You go outside and do your thing and meet me in the kitchen in ten minutes."

Twenty minutes later the eggs on Jane's plate stared up at her like two angry eyes. She pushed the plate away and concentrated on the coffee in her cup and the notepad in front of her. She was going to write something, make notes, fill up the page. She pushed it away, too. She stared at Olive who stared back. "We'll do a simple funeral. We can't ask Father John to do it since Betty can't be buried in the Catholic cemetery, so I have to make arrangements at Acadia Resthaven Cemetery. Did I ever tell you, Olive, that St. John's cemetery is all wrong? The person who designed it was supposed to lay it out so it was east to west. You know, sunup, sundown. But it's north and south. I wonder if that makes a difference to dead people. St. John's is consecrated ground, and since Betty took her own life, she can't be buried there." If she remembered correctly, she had told someone to send the body to Duhon's Funeral Home. She would wait until eight o'clock before trying to call them. She hadn't read Betty's letter, and she didn't know why. Part of her wanted to know what was in the letter and part of her didn't.

Jane took a deep breath, got up, and walked into the foyer, where she'd tossed her purse and coat. It wasn't a letter per se but more like a Christmas card envelope, completely square. She carried it back to the kitchen and dropped it on the table. She stared at it for a long time before picking it up and slitting the envelope. Her eyes filled with tears as she read Betty Vance's last words.

> *Dear Dr. Lewis,*
>
> *I'm sorry I disappointed you. I tried doing things your way. I tried doing things Dr. Thomas's way, and I tried doing things Corinda's way. I thought I was making progress. Corinda said I was. I even managed to get through a visit with Brian. We had a long talk, and I fixed lunch for us. I was okay with all of it. Trixie and Fred helped a lot. Dr. Thomas said I was a weak person.*
>
> *I went to the drugstore for shampoo and razors and a refill on my Thorazine prescription this morning, and I heard this man talking to his friend in the shaving cream aisle. I recognized his voice as*

*being one of them. I couldn't believe it. They saw
me staring at them, and they recognized me, too. I
couldn't move, Dr. Lewis. They walked over to
me, and one of them touched me. I think I
screamed. I don't remember. Then one of them
said, "We know where to find you so keep your
mouth shut." I was so hysterical, the salesclerk
called the manager, and they drove me home. I
locked the door and hid in the bathroom with
Golda for hours and hours. I wanted to call you
and Corinda, but I called Dr. Thomas instead. I
called her four times, but she never called me back.
I did deep-breathing exercises and jumping jacks
till I thought I would faint. I couldn't stop shaking. It was hard to breathe. I can't go through that
again. I just can't. Please don't think too harshly of
me. Thank you for being my friend, Dr. Lewis.
Please take care of my dog.*

Betty Vance

Jane sobbed her misery, her clenched fists beating at the
table. The springer spaniel leapt onto her lap. Jane clung to
the quivering animal as she continued to sob, her entire body
shaking and twitching. A long time later, when there were no
more tears to shed, Jane eased Olive to the floor. "We're
going for a ride, Olive."

Jane drove up and down the streets of Rayne, past Sadie's
Flower Shop, past Depot Square, and then on to the boulevard, postponing the moment when she would turn onto the
street where she once lived. She sensed rather than saw the
police station. It was all so long ago. A lifetime ago. An eternity ago. What the hell was she doing here anyway? She was
here because of a cockamamie dream. Always return to the
scene of the crime, Trixie said. She also always said follow

the money, whatever the hell that meant. Trixie said a lot of things. Most times they made sense. This was the crime scene of her childhood. She had a right to be here. She wasn't doing anything wrong. She doused the lights of the car and opened the door. "Shh, Olive, no barking. Not a sound now. We're going to go around the back and go in through the root cellar. You wait here for me, and I'll open the back door for you. I know how to get into this house."

Jane was as good as her word. Ten minutes later she opened the dead bolt on the back door and let Olive into the kitchen. With the help of a full moon shining in through the curtainless windows, she easily made her way from room to room, remembering how miserable she'd been when she lived here. She walked upstairs, Olive behind her, whining deep in her throat. "I used to live here, Olive." She opened the door at the end of the hall. "This was my room. It's not much bigger than a cubbyhole. I should have had a bigger room. There's carpet in here now. Oh look, there's a balloon light switch. That must mean another child had this room."

Jane closed the door behind her and walked to the opposite end of the hall, to her parents' room. It was carpeted, too. She walked to the center of the room and shouted, "I'm here, Mommy Dearest! Come out, come out, wherever you are!" When nothing happened, Jane shrugged. She sat down Indian fashion, her back against the wall, Olive's head in her lap. "We'll wait a little while. Maybe she needs to plug in or something. I don't know how this spook business works, so we'll go with the flow. She was a beauty queen, Olive. Excuse me, beauty *pageant* queen. Miss Louisiana." Jane yawned. "She wasn't good enough to be Miss America, though. She wore tons of makeup. I finally figured it out when I was around fourteen. It was to cover up how ugly she really was. I burned it all. Every single pot of eye shadow and every tube of lipstick . . ." She twiddled her thumbs as she sat staring out the window at the tree beyond. If she was smart, she would go home. There was nothing to be gained sitting there staring at a tree on the front lawn. She yawned again and closed her eyes, thinking she would rest while she waited.

"I knew this was going to be a big bust. You'd think I'd know better. Let's try this. Here she comes, Misssss Americaaaa. . . ."

"Stop that this instant! You always were a wicked child."

"I thought that would get you!" She held up Olive's chin. "This is Mommy Dearest, Olive. So you do hang out here, Mother. Imagine that! You look haggard. I'm sorry to say this, but death doesn't become you." She eyed the vision of her mother with disgust. "All this time, I thought you were somewhere in the great beyond. Couldn't cut that either, huh? You're just another *hoochie mama*. Just tell me one thing. Is it true that I'm the only one who can, you know, boot your ass to the other side?"

"Unfortunately, yes."

Jane laughed until she gasped for breath. Olive growled as she pawed at Jane's chest. "That's the funniest thing I've ever heard in my life." She rocketed into peals of laughter again. "Not in this lifetime," she finally managed to gasp. "Of course I'm speaking of *my* lifetime. I think I'm going to buy this house just to make sure you stay put. I'll come by from time to time to check up on you. Always go back to the scene of the crime, Trixie said. This is the scene of the crime—the crime you committed against me! I'm going to figure it all out. I don't know when or how, but I'm going to do it. What do you have to say for yourself, Mother?"

Olive licked at Jane's face until she opened her eyes.

"We can go home now, Olive. Jeez, I fell asleep and had this dream that I was going to buy this house. You know what, it's not such a bad idea. I'm going to think about it. That dream was a doozie. If anyone finds out we broke in here, we'll not only be guilty of breaking and entering, but they'll send the guys in the white coats with the nets. Shh, we have to be quiet when we leave. Not a sound now."

Jane stopped at Frog City and bought a pack of cigarettes, a loaf of bread, cream for her coffee, and a beef jerky for Olive. She was back home just as the sun crept over the horizon.

At eight o'clock, Jane was on the phone to Duhon's Funeral Home. She scheduled a service for three o'clock and the interment for four o'clock. She called Trixie, Fred, Betty's friend Chuck, and Brian Ramsey. All promised to attend the service. She debated a long minute before calling Sharon Thomas, knowing she'd get her service, which she did. She left a short message and hung up.

"I don't know what to do, Olive," Jane cried, wringing her hands.

Olive was all over her a second later. "What would I do without you, girl?" Jane sobbed.

It was Flash who alerted Fred to the fact that a car had stopped in front of the house. "Trixie, there's a strange man walking up to our front porch. You better get out here before Flash goes through the window."

Trixie came on the run, her jewelry clanking, her hair standing on end. "Easy, boy, easy," she said, grabbing hold of Flash's collar. "It's okay for people to come to the door. Sit like a gentleman." She opened the door a crack, Flash's snout pressed against her leg.

"Mrs. McGuire, I'm Bob Henry. I came back for the holidays and wanted to stop to see Flash. Is it okay for me to come in?"

Trixie wanted to scream, no, it isn't all right. Flash is my dog now. Go away. Instead, she said, "Yes, of course, come in." She leaned into Fred, her heart pounding in her chest. "You can't have him back. He's mine!" she blurted.

"I know that, Mrs. McGuire. I just wanted to see him. We were partners for a long time. The guys at the station told me what you did for him and your plans for the future. I wanted to see you and tell you how wonderful that is."

Bob Henry bent down to the dog. "Hey, buddy, it's me, Bob! Shake hands."

Trixie let her breath out in a loud whoosh when the big dog remained at her side, his big paws firmly planted on the floor. His body quivered.

"It's okay, Flash," she said, patting his head. "Go shake hands with Mr. Henry. Be nice now. Give Mr. Henry a kiss."

Henry reared back, almost falling over. "A kiss! He gives kisses! You took a killer dog and taught him to kiss people! I don't believe it."

"Believe it," Trixie snapped. "Flash is retired, so that means it's okay for him to do whatever I teach him. He's just being social. This dog almost died on me, Mr. Henry. I did what I had to do to save him. We have a good thing going here, so don't go screwing it up on me."

"Please, don't get me wrong," he said, holding up his hand. "I just meant I didn't think it could be done. For one thing he hated women. You're a woman. It's wonderful what you've been able to do. I did some heavy-duty worrying about him, but Jake kept assuring me you were taking good care of him."

Henry cupped the big dog's head in his hands. "You're one lucky guy, so make sure you behave yourself. Okay, okay, one kiss."

Flash licked him once, then inched closer to Trixie and Golda. His tail swished furiously as he watched Henry straighten up. He pawed the carpet and snorted.

"That's my signal to leave," Henry grinned. "He's viewing this visit as me stepping onto *his* turf. It's his way of telling all of us the old days are gone, and he likes what's going on now. See ya around, Officer Flash!"

"Woof."

"Yeah, woof," Trixie said, shutting the door. "Did you see that, Fred? I had nightmares about this happening. I knew the day would come when he'd show up. I thought Flash would want to go with him. I really did," Trixie said in a choked voice.

"That dog loves you heart and soul, Trixie. He isn't about to abandon you. Not now, not ever. He's yours just the way Golda is yours now."

Trixie dropped to her knees. Both dogs were on her and she squealed with laughter as they rolled around on the carpet. "Killer dog, my ass." Trixie grinned. "This is one hundred and ten pounds of pure love. Right Flash? You, too, Golda. Come on now, give Trixie some loving."

"I gotta get back to work. What are you going to do, honey?"

"I've got some stuff to do in the barn for the dogs when they get here. John Murray is coming by later today to show me how he's going to do the training. I want to be in on everything. He's doing it on his off time, so I have to be available. Right now he's on a temporary leave. I'm hoping I can entice him to a permanent deal. Did you call the attorney?"

"I called him a half hour ago. He said he'd get right on it. By that he means he's going to write the letters and follow up with a phone call right after New Year's. If he has to, he'll go up to LSU to speed things up. He thinks it's a good idea. Did you call Janie?"

"Yes, but she didn't answer. I didn't think she would. She needs this time for herself. We'll talk at the funeral home this afternoon. Wear your blue suit, Fred. You look distinguished in your blue suit. Janie might want you to say a few words."

"Okay, honey."

A light rain was falling when Fred brought the car to a stop behind the funeral hearse. Three other cars stopped behind him: Betty's friend Chuck, Brian Ramsey, and, in the last car, four of Betty's neighbors. Jane looked around to see if Sharon Thomas was anywhere to be seen. She wasn't.

The service was pitifully short, with everyone huddled under umbrellas. Jane stared at the casket, with its blanket of daisies. She wondered if she should have done more. Paying for the funeral and flowers hardly seemed enough.

"Ashes to ashes . . ."

Tears misted Jane's lashes as she stepped forward. She was supposed to say something, but what could she say that would bring some meaning to Betty's death? She cleared her throat. Out of the corner of her eye she saw a car approach. "We all take different paths in life, but no matter where we go, we take a little of each other with us. Amen."

Jane's heart fluttered when she raised her eyes to see Mike standing next to Fred, who was stepping forward, a single white rose in his hand. He, too, cleared his throat before speaking. "We only knew Betty for a short while, but we grew to care for her and she for us. My definition of a friend is someone who knows the song in your heart and can sing it back to you when you have forgotten the words. Betty was that kind of friend. She's in another place now, and I can only hope she's singing."

Jane dabbed at her eyes as she followed the others to file past the casket. Why did it always rain at funerals? It had rained the day her father was buried and the day her mother was laid to rest. She felt Mike cup her elbow in his hand and was grateful for the support.

Back at the car she shook hands with Chuck, the neighbors, and Brian Ramsey, who looked visibly shaken. He looked as if he hadn't slept in a long time.

"I want to thank you for what you did for Betty. And for trying to help me, too," Brian said.

Chuck stepped forward. "I called Betty's aunt. She said she couldn't come for the funeral. She said as soon as she had a

free moment, she would come to pick up Betty's car and personal possessions," he said, disgust written all over his face.
He hugged Jane before he climbed into his pickup truck.

The neighbors shook hands politely, then left without saying anything. In the end, what was there to say? A young
woman lived, then she died. A beginning and an ending. Life
would go on.

Jane rubbed at her temples. She could feel the beginnings
of a headache. All she wanted was to go home and go to
sleep.

"I'll ride with Mike, Trixie. Thanks for everything. How's
Golda doing?"

"She whimpers once in a while, but she's fine. Flash is with
her. Are you okay, honey?"

"No, I'm not okay. That will change, though. Sharon
didn't come, Trixie. How could she not come to her patient's
funeral? I don't understand. Do you understand?"

"No, Janie, I don't understand. She has to live with this.
You did everything you could. Put it behind you now. Tomorrow is a new day."

Back at the house, Jane tossed her coat and purse on the
foyer table. "How was your holiday, Mike?" she asked, her
voice dull and lifeless as she headed for the sofa where she
curled up next to Olive.

Mike frowned. No kiss, no hug, no real greeting. "Where's
your ring, Jane?"

"Upstairs. I've been thinking, Mike. I think I need more
time."

"You're blaming me, aren't you?"

"At first I did. Not now, though. I blame myself. I should
have been more alert, more involved regardless of Sharon's
demands. What did I miss? How could I have missed it whatever it was? My relationship with you colored everything. I
should have tried harder, done more. When she didn't call

earlier in the week, I should have called her. I keep asking myself why I didn't do that. The only answer I can come up with was I didn't want to disturb my life where you were concerned. I put you first."

"How could you know, Jane? We aren't mind readers. You did exactly what you were supposed to do. I don't want you trying to take the blame for something that isn't your fault. Going there the other night wouldn't have solved a thing. Betty was already dead."

"I need to be alone, Mike. I have a lot of thinking to do. Let's leave it that I'll call you."

"That . . . that sounds . . . final."

"Lock the door when you leave, okay?"

Mike stared helplessly at the woman on the sofa. "If that's what you want. Will you promise to call me?"

"At some point. I don't know when that will be, though." A minute later she was sound asleep.

Mike wanted to kiss her good-bye but he knew the springer would rip out his throat if he made a move in Jane's direction. "Take care of her, Olive," he whispered.

Olive whimpered as she licked at Jane's face. When she heard the sound of the lock turning over, Olive laid her big head on Jane's shoulder, her eyes on the front door. Eventually she, too, slept.

14

Trixie McGuire stood on her back porch with Flash and Golda at her side. She watched as an eighteen-wheeler pulled alongside her newly renovated barn that would be the home for the K-9s scheduled for training. Somewhere, some-place, something had gone wrong. Instead of six dogs, there were eight, which required many hours of last-minute rescheduling and reshifting of the dogs' quarters.

Fred watched his wife from his office window. He could feel his heart swell with happiness at her excitement. Trixie had finally found what she said was her niche in life. He smiled when he thought about the dedicated hours Trixie spent with Flash, she in her police uniform and Flash in his bulletproof vest. At one point, he wondered if she had the stamina or the endurance to continue, but she had. He was so proud of her he wanted to shout it from the rooftops. He was considering doing just that when the phone rang.

"Fred, this is Daniel Warner," the lawyer said. "I wanted to let you know everything is a go."

"No kidding," Fred said. He could hardly wait to tell Trixie the good news.

"No kidding. In fact, I'm looking at our approval letter as

we speak. Okay, have I got this straight? You want me to send out all the contest notices FedEx overnight with a one-week response deadline, right?"

Fred closed his eyes as he pictured Jane the last time he'd seen her. She'd been wan and listless. "Yes. Time is of the essence, Daniel. We need to wrap this up ASAP."

"I thought you would say that, so one of the secretaries is on it right now. The letters will go out this afternoon for a 10 A.M. delivery tomorrow. Some of the players could have moved, relocated for job purposes, etc. The Alumni Association said the records are up-to-date, but that doesn't really mean anything. You might not get a good response rate because of the short deadline. On the other hand, the money may bring them in on time and in record numbers. The dean wants to see your check. Since I have it here, I'm going to overnight it to him along with all the other things he requested. You might actually pull this off, Fred."

A cacophony of barking, yipping dogs made it difficult for Fred to hear. "I hope so. Listen, Daniel, I have to go now. Things are happening here, and I need to step in."

"I'll be in touch."

Fred ran to the kitchen and met Trixie as she was coming inside. "What the hell is going on?"

"Not now, Fred. Can't you hear I have my hands full!"

Fred stared out the window at what Trixie called the compound, where eight monster-sized dogs were chasing one another as they snapped and snarled in their frenzy to understand these new circumstances. They'd traveled all the way from Holland, had a brief respite of an hour, and were then put back onto a plane and flown to New Orleans where they'd been picked up by the trucking company and delivered to the McGuire farm.

"You have no control, Trixie!" Fred shouted above the clatter.

"No shit, Fred! Call Janie and tell her to get over here. Tell her I don't care if she is wallowing in self-pity. Tell her I said she's been moaning and groaning for three full weeks now and my patience is at an end. And, tell her she committed to this little enterprise, and her help would be much appreciated." Trixie grabbed her cigarettes off the kitchen table and went back outside, Fred right behind her. "On second thought, never mind all that. Just tell her to get her ass over here and help me. Then get inside before one of these dogs jumps out and chews your ass off," Trixie shouted over the barking dogs.

Fred scurried inside to follow his wife's instructions, leaving her to deal with her new business.

Trixie lit up a much-needed cigarette and inhaled deeply. "Okay, okay, that's it!" she yelled in her drill-sergeant voice. "Flash, round them up. Golda, don't take any crap off any of them. You two have seniority. Strong measures are called for here," she said, pulling her gun free of the holster. She held the gun, barrel pointed up, and fired off a shot. When the commotion continued, she fired off a second then a third. Finally, in desperation, she pointed the gun at the ground and emptied the clip. The dogs immediately stopped barking, at which point Trixie sat down on the ground and rubbed her ears.

Flash and Golda ran over to her.

"No, no, you guys. I am not officer down. It's okay," she said, reassuring them. "I'm just taking a break." As soon as Flash and Golda calmed down, Trixie turned to see what the others were doing. One by one they crept closer to the fence, sniffing, whining and growling. Flash reared up to his full majestic height and balanced himself on his two hind legs. He let loose with a murderous bark that made the hair on Trixie's arms quiver.

Trixie looked from Flash to the other dogs. "Listen up!

He's letting you guys know he's top dog around here," she said in a firm voice. "This one," she said, pointing to Golda, "is Top Dog Two, and Top Dog Three is on her way over here. I hope." She stood up and waved them all back. "Okay, you've had your romp. You've peed and pooped. Now it's time to get a bath because you all stink from the kennels. You aren't going to be caged again, so don't look at me like that." She reached inside her shirt and brought out a Ziploc bag full of weenies. "These are just for now, so you know I'm the good guy. Later you get that rabbit-poop food that is supposed to be good for you. Come on now, come get your weenie."

"My God, Trixie," Fred said from the back porch, "you're going to spoil them all rotten. By the way, Janie said she's coming right over."

"I need more weenies, Fred," Trixie called over her shoulder. "Look, they're just little pussy cats. Ahh, they're scared is what they are. Flash knew that. So did Golda. What's holding you up, Fred?"

Moments later, Fred trundled to the middle of the yard and handed Trixie two packages of hot dogs.

"Stand here next to me, Fred. I want them to get to know you. Be gentle with them. Talk softly and stroke them carefully. This is what they're going to remember. Kindness and food. Once they accept that, authority kicks in."

Fred looked at Trixie in utter amazement. "How do you know all this, Trixie?"

"I read a book, Fred. You know, the one sitting on the kitchen table that I asked you to read two weeks ago."

"Oh, *that* book," he said sheepishly.

"How did Janie sound when you talked to her?" Trixie finished passing out the weenies and rubbed her hands on her jeans.

"The same, unfortunately. Like she was in a deep hole somewhere." He sent Trixie a worried look, then brightened.

"Daniel called. The university approved our little project. Letters are going out today, FedEx overnight. I hope a week is enough time, not that we have any choice what with Janie and all. Speaking of Janie, when are we going to tell her?"

"Today might be good, providing she gets here. If she doesn't show up in the next half hour, I want you to go over there and drag her here by the scruff of the neck. I mean it, Fred. If she goes on like this much longer, she's going to slip into that dark hole, and we might not be able to get her out of it. She needs to settle things with Mike, too. I feel like shooting him just to put him out of his misery."

Fred put his hand down for one of the dogs to smell. "Do you know their names, Trixie?"

"Yes, but I don't know who is who yet. Their names are on their collars, but I haven't wanted to touch them yet. We have four girls and four boys. They're in tip-top shape and perfect health. It's our job, Janie's and mine, to keep them that way. Aren't they beautiful, Fred? See, they're quiet now. They were just scared. This is a good thing we're doing, Fred. A real good thing. We're going to do something here we can really be proud of."

"I'm already proud . . . of you," he said. He turned his head to the right. "I hear a car. It must be Janie. Do you want me to stay here or go inside?"

"It depends on whether or not you want to hear me read her the riot act. We can play good guy, bad guy. She'll run to you when I'm done with her. It's the only way, Fred. She's losing it. I can't and won't stand still for that." Her determination was like a hard knot inside of her. She would not let Janie drift away into depression.

"Whatever you decide to do is okay with me, sweetums. I'll go inside and get back to work. If you need me, whistle."

Trixie did a double take when Jane walked through the gate. Who *was* this person walking toward her? Three weeks couldn't make that much difference in a person's appearance. But obviously it had. "Shh," she whispered to the dogs, trying to quiet them down.

"I'm here," Jane said in a flat voice. Her face was devoid of makeup, and her hair looked like it hadn't been washed in a week. The gray sweats she was wearing were way too big for her and the front of her sweatshirt was food-stained.

"I can see that," Trixie said, looking her over from head to toe, "but the question is, are you here in body *and* mind? You can't skate on this, Janie. As you can see," she said, gesturing to the compound full of dogs, "the first batch of trainees arrived this morning. If you had been here on their arrival, it would have made things a lot easier on me. But, no, you chose to sit home sucking your thumb and feeling sorry for yourself. You wouldn't be here now if Fred hadn't called you. We had a deal, Jane. I expect you to uphold your end of it. I don't want an attitude either." Her stern expression brooked no back talk. "You want to know about misery, then let me tell you about misery. Look at these poor creatures. They've been cooped up in kennels on airplanes for two days. They stink from poop and pee because they had to use their kennels to go in. They were hungry and scared out of their wits. This is new, so new, they don't know what to make of it. Right now they're grateful because I gave them water and food. I hope you're getting my point here before I'm forced to bring out the big guns."

"Look, Trixie, I'm sorry. I—" Her voice broke miserably.

"I don't want to hear it, Jane. The past is prologue. You can't go back. You can't undo anything. What you have is today and today is where it's at. When was the last time you looked in the mirror?"

"A mirror? What's a mirror got to do with anything?"

"A lot from where I'm standing." Trixie put her hands on Jane's shoulders. "You have bags under your eyes, not to mention dark circles. You're gaunt and haggard-looking. You look like you lost about fifteen pounds, which means you aren't eating. Your hair's a mess, and you smell almost as bad as these dogs. That tells me you've been drinking. A lot. Then you sleep, wake up, don't shower because it's too much trouble, and then you smoke, drink some more, and then you sleep. You wake up and do it all over again."

Jane flinched at the tone of Trixie's voice. She had enough on her plate right now. She didn't need Trixie laying another kind of guilt trip on her. "Maybe agreeing to do this was a mistake. Why are you acting like this? I've never done anything but love you. Can't you cut me some slack?"

"Slack?" Trixie removed her hands and dropped them to her sides. "If Fred and I cut you any more slack than we already have, you'll drown in self-pity. You're at the edge of the dark hole right now, Janie. We're going to ride you until you come out of this. Do you hear me? We're doing this because we love you, and we want you to be happy." She paused a moment, cocked her head, and scrutinized her god-daughter. "Unless, of course, you don't want to be happy. Maybe you want to be miserable and make everyone around you miserable." She raised an eyebrow. "It never occurred to me before, but I suppose we could have been wrong about you all these years and you really are just like your mother."

Jane's eyes flashed with anger. "How could you say such a thing to me? I am *nothing* like her. Nothing!"

Trixie felt an adrenaline rush. "I'm not so sure anymore. I remember a time, no a couple of times, when your mother played 'poor me' to get attention. We finally got wise and learned to ignore her. And speaking of ignoring. . . . How long do you think Mike's patience will last? He's been down-right saintly through all of this. I think you should give him back his ring so he can get on with his life. You can't keep jerking people around like you've been doing. By the way, where's Olive? I hope to God you've been feeding her."

"She's with Fred. She saw all the dogs and got scared. Of course I fed her. What do you think I am?" she asked sharply.

Trixie reached out and framed Jane's face with her hands. "I think, Jane, you are a wonderful, caring, loving person who stepped off the path. That's understandable and acceptable to a point. But we're past that point now. You know what Fred says, fish or cut bait. What's it going to be, Jane?"

"It's been hard, Trixie," she said in a low, tormented voice. "I need a little more time."

"No, Jane," Trixie said, shaking her head. "Time ran out early this morning. The dogs are here. If I can't depend on you, then you're outta here, girl. Permanently. Fred feels the same way. We'll take Olive, though."

"Oh no, Olive is my dog," Jane said, her temper flaring again. She was beginning to feel like a yo-yo. "Olive stays with me. I can't believe you said that. Okay, okay, you made your point. I'll take a shower since you say I smell, then I'll be out here to do whatever it is you want me to do." When she turned to go, Trixie put a hand on her arm and turned it back.

"It doesn't work that way, Jane. It's got to be what you want to do, not what I want you to do. I told you, I don't want an attitude. If your ass isn't out here in this compound in fifteen minutes, our deal is off. You have clothes in the top dresser drawer in the spare room."

Trixie watched as Jane shuffled her way to the house. "No shuffling. Pick up your feet. Better yet, *RUN!*" She grinned when Jane sprinted for the house. *Sometimes,* she thought, *age works in one's favor. That definitely was* not *a Hallmark moment.*

The moment Olive pranced into the fray, the dogs were on their feet. Flash strutted alongside the springer. It was almost as if the others recognized Olive as Top Dog Three.

The day went off without a hitch as all the dogs were washed, dried, and clipped. They broke once for lunch when

Fred brought down BLTs and a sack of dog food. Trixie watched as Jane choked down the food. She showed her god-child no mercy. "You've been drinking so long you forgot how to chew. I want you to stay here with us for a few days so I can watch over you. Fred will go over to your house and get your things."

"No, I am not staying here, Trixie," Jane said adamantly.

"Oh yes you are," Fred said, agreeing with his wife.

Jane shrugged. She knew she was overruled. "All right, I'll stay."

"Good. Fred and I have something we want to talk to you about over supper. Wipe that look of panic off your face, sweetie. It's a good thing. We did real good today. Real good."

"Could it wait? I'm really tired, Trixie."

"Stop whining, Jane. I'm just as tired as you are, and I'm older. Lots older. We took on this responsibility, and we can't shirk it because *you're* tired. You need to take vitamins and you need to call Mike when we finish up. Another shower, fresh clothes, and you'll be ready for dinner."

Jane winced. "Sharon Thomas is suing me. I was served papers this morning."

"Don't tell me you're worried about a little thing like that," Trixie scoffed. "You need to play hardball where that witch is concerned. Trust me when I tell you we can make it all go away in the blink of an eye."

"For God's sake, Trixie, I broke her nose. I'm responsible. She could take me for everything I have."

"What's that you always say on your radio show? Follow the *three* R's: respect for self, respect for others, responsibility for all your actions. I rest my case."

Jane smiled in spite of herself. Trixie was right again.

"John Murray and his trainers will be here all day tomorrow, but I think we can squeeze in time to visit Dr. Thomas.

Aren't they beautiful animals, Jane?" she asked, flitting from one topic to the other without a hitch.

"Yes, they are. They're magnificent. The big question is, are you going to be able to give them up?"

"Not easily, I can tell you that right now. But I have the right mind-set. I know their leaving and going into service will be for the greater good. Lives will be saved because of them." She looked down at Olive. "Olive is doing well with them. Dogs have this innate sense where other animals are concerned. It's not just people. They know we're taking care of them. I think they're over the worst of their fear. Tonight is going to be tough on them." She stared at them and sighed. Then she turned to Jane. "So, are you going to call Mike or not? He's been calling and stopping by so often I want to shoot him to put him out of his misery. You aren't being fair to him. Why aren't you wearing his ring? He's doing what you wanted him to do, staying away from you. How would you feel if he looked up that plastic doll he used to date? What's her name?"

"Coletta. I don't think I'd like it."

"Damn straight you wouldn't like it. That's what's going to happen. You mark my words unless you do something. You know I'm always right, Janie."

"Trixie, lay off, okay?" Jane mumbled. "I'll call him. I haven't been in a good place these past weeks. Yes, I drank too much. It was the only way I could sleep."

"You're no boozer, honey. Drinking isn't a sleeping pill. Facing up to your problems is your pill. Fred and I will help you. But first you have to want to help yourself. Today is a good start. C'mon, let's get back to work."

"I'm sorry I let you down," Jane said, needing to get back into Trixie's good graces. Trixie and Fred were the two most important people in her life, and she didn't want them to be upset with her.

"I really thought you were tougher than that," Trixie said.

"Nah. I'm all mush."

"Mush hardens if you let it sit long enough," Trixie shot back.

"*Touché,* Trixie."

"What do you think, Fred?" Trixie whispered.

"I assume you're referring to that little stroll Janie and Mike are taking? I think it's looking good, but our girl isn't out of the woods yet. I'm glad you convinced her to stay here. How'd you do that?"

"You don't want to know." Trixie poured herself and Fred coffee. "I actually saw a spark in her eyes when you told her about the hands contest. She even asked questions. That's a good sign. We're going to work on the rest of it." She handed Fred his cup and sat down. "Tomorrow we're going to see her colleague so I can flatten her out. Don't say it, Fred. I know what I'm doing. Then, as long as I have Janie in the car, I'm taking her to the lawyer's office so she can sign the release forms for Mike to take over the radio show. She seems to be having a problem signing off on things." When Flash snuggled at her feet, she pushed off her shoes and buried her toes into his fur. "I saw the letter Betty Vance wrote Janie. It's sad, Fred. So sad."

Fred sat back and sipped his coffee. "I can't imagine things getting so bad that I would end up taking my own life."

"Me either," Trixie agreed, rolling her eyes. "Did I tell you that Janie wants to buy her parents' old house? I asked her why and she said—you won't believe this, Fred—for sentimental reasons. Sentimental my ass. She's done a lot of weird things lately. I'm beginning to think it has something to do with all those dreams she's been having." Trixie took a deep breath and leaned back in her chair. "We have a couple of cans of worms here, and they're wiggling in all directions."

"You'll handle it, honey. You always do. Would you mind scratching my back just a little?" Fred turned around and presented Trixie with his back. "Aaahhh, that's good. A little lower. Perfect."

"Mike's gone," Trixie said. "I just heard him start up his car. Guess it's safe to leave the kitchen now."

"Guess so," Fred said, yawning elaborately. "Let's go to bed."

Trixie yawned, too. "I'm so tired I don't know if I can go to sleep." She took Fred's hand and let him lead her to their bedroom.

Flash lay down on the braided rug in the bedroom. The moment Fred and Trixie's breathing evened out in sleep, he was on his feet. He waited for Golda to crawl out from under the bed before making his way down the steps to the first floor where the two of them waited for Olive to join them. Flash waited like the gentleman he was until both Golda and Olive bellied out the doggie door. Because his size prohibited him from following suit, he lifted his paw, pushed the lock, and, with his snout turned the knob. Once he was out, the three of them sprinted to the barn, where it was Olive's turn to open the door.

The eight new arrivals sat up expectantly, unsure what the game plan was. With Olive and Golda flanking him, Flash danced and pranced until the others realized they were to follow the three top dogs. Outside in the clear, crisp night they all stared at their leader, awaiting his instructions. Flash, with Olive's help, herded the newcomers into a line with Golda bringing up the rear. He looked back once. Satisfied with what he saw, he walked toward the house and into the kitchen. The other dogs followed him, curious but quiet. They waited while Olive nosed the door shut and snicked the lock back into place.

Eleven dogs paraded single file through the kitchen, dining

room, living room, and into the foyer where they sat at the bottom of the stairs awaiting further instructions. Flash led the way. When he reached the top of the stairs, he looked around as though doing a body count before starting down the hall to Trixie and Fred's bedroom. He herded the dogs into the bedroom, silently ordered them to sit. He waited a full minute before he reached his paw up to flip the light switch.

Trixie blinked and sat up in bed. When she saw the dogs, she gasped, then shook Fred. "Wake up, Fred! You aren't going to believe this. Damn it, Fred, wake up!"

Fred looked from left to right. "What's wrong? Is the house on fire? Are you sick?" Then he saw the dogs. "Oh, sweet Jesus! Flash, what have you done?"

Flash leaped on the bed and nuzzled Trixie under the chin before he sat down to wait for praise. "Fred, we can't scold him. He thinks he did a good thing. Good boy, Flash," Trixie said, gurgling with laughter as first one dog then another jumped up and down off the bed. Thinking the trip to the main house was some kind of game, the mini herd started to bark. And bark.

Jane poked her head in the door and collapsed in laughter. "How'd they get in here?" she said, gasping for breath.

"I think it's safe to say Olive taught Flash how to open the door and the three of them decided . . . whatever they decided. We have eleven dogs here!" Trixie said, hugging one of the new dogs. A male shepherd sat between Fred's legs, licking his beard.

"Now what?" Jane asked.

"I think they're here to stay, for tonight anyway," Trixie laughed.

"That's what you get for teaching Flash about a family." Jane crossed her arms and leaned against the doorframe. "He's more human than you know. When you think about it, what he did is quite wonderful. As you so aptly pointed out to me today, what's more important than family? That attitude and that kind of thinking are what makes you such a success in life, and it's working now with the animals."

"We have to take them back outside. I'm not sleeping in a kennel," Fred grumbled.

"C'mon, Fred, just until they get over their fears. A few days at the most. What can it hurt? If you nix this, then you'll force me to take this bed into the barn and you can sleep on the couch. You know how you like to cuddle."

"All right, all right! Now, can we go to sleep?"

"You can try, honey. Anything is possible," Trixie said, curling next to a shepherd named Picco.

"Something smells wonderful," Jane said, sitting down at the table. "I just love to smell frying bacon and coffee. I love it even more when I'm not the one doing the cooking. You're up early, Fred."

"I didn't sleep much. I don't know if I can handle this, Jane. What are you doing up so early?"

"I didn't sleep at all. I sat up in bed and did a lot of thinking. I even made notes. Trixie was right yesterday when she said I lost my way. But I think I've got all my ducks together now. They might not be in a tidy row, but I have them. Why is she always right, Fred?"

"I wish I knew," he said, shaking his head.

"What *are* you cooking over there? And where is Trixie?"

Fred grinned. "I'm making banana-macadamia nut pancakes with banana syrup and melted butter. Trixie is in the barn with John Murray. She said she'll be up by eight because the two of you are going to town. How many pancakes, Jane?"

"Four," Jane said smartly. "And four slices of bacon."

He made a show of flipping a pancake into the air. "How did things go with Mike last night?"

"Pretty good. He's trying not to be angry with me, but he

is. I understand what he's feeling. He doesn't understand what I'm feeling, though. He says he does, but he doesn't. Mike likes things to be black or white. The biggest sticking point right now is that I didn't go to his parents with him for Christmas. He's taking it personally. When I have to explain myself to the person who is supposed to love me, then there's something wrong. It seems to me that he of all people should understand where my emotions were and why. He is a psychiatrist, for God's sake. He's also upset that I'm not wearing his ring. But I'm not going to put it back on until our playing field is level. What would be the point? We'll see what happens. I do love him."

"Then it will all work out. Just be patient."

Jane jumped up from the chair. "See! See! You're doing it, too. I don't want to be patient," she shouted. "You men are all alike. I say love me, love my faults. Accept me as I am. Don't try to change me. Don't tell me your way is better. I cannot change the way I feel, and even if I could, I don't know that I'd want to. I want to be able to feel pain and guilt and love and anger. They're all honest emotions." She stomped across the kitchen to look out the window. "Mike has a shutoff valve that he turns on and off. He calls it being professional. I can't do that, Fred. That's not who I am. People bleed, they cry and hurt when something doesn't work out. If what Mike and I have doesn't work out, it will be for the right reasons. Now, can I have some of those pancakes?" She grabbed a plate and held it close to the griddle.

She regretted pouncing on him the way she had, but she was tired of people, even her beloved godfather, thinking patience was the cure for everything. "I'm sorry, Fred. I haven't been myself lately. Forgive me?"

"It's okay, Janie, girl. It takes a lot more than a little temper tantrum to upset me."

Jane sat down at the table and slathered her pancakes with

butter. "How's the book coming? It must be kind of weird doing all the writing yourself after working hand in hand with Trixie all these years."

"I'm almost afraid for Trixie to read it. She hates all contact sports and football in particular. I'm hoping she'll gloss over it and won't be too critical."

"Fred, these pancakes are delicious." Jane downed the four in no time and was ready for more.

Fred plopped a fresh stack onto her plate. "You better eat up, it's quarter past seven, and Trixie said she wanted to leave at eight."

Jane wolfed down the pancakes in record time and got up. On her way out of the kitchen, she walked around behind Fred's chair and put her arms around his shoulders. "I'm sorry for the past few weeks, Fred. I needed to wallow, cry, moan, and groan. Trixie made me realize without actually saying the words, that I was copping out and doing the same thing Connie and Betty did. She was right. I'm sorry for the bad moments I gave you both."

Fred's head bobbed up and down. "You're back on the path now. Where you go on that path is strictly up to you."

"Fred, there's something I want to tell you, and you have to promise that you won't think I've gone off the deep end."

"I promise," Fred said, crossing his heart.

Jane took a deep breath. "I broke into my parents' old house and encountered what I think was my mother's ghost, upstairs in her and Daddy's bedroom. For a while, I thought it was another one of those funny dreams I've been having. But now . . . Do you believe in ghosts?"

"Ghosts are a little out of my realm, Janie."

"At first, I tried to tell myself that I'd dozed off, but I know I didn't. I couldn't have. I mean, I was involved in a full-blown conversation with her. I said hateful, ugly things to her. Spiteful things." She rested her chin on his shoulder. "I don't know if Trixie told you or not, but I'm seriously thinking about buying the house. Not for good reasons, though."

"Then why?" he asked.

"To keep her there, in limbo, for eternity. It seems the only way she can get to the other side is if I release her. Me! Is that funny or what?"

Fred grabbed Jane's arm and pulled her around so he could look at her. "You have to let it go, Janie. It's in the past. You aren't that wounded little girl anymore. Let it go. When you do, the dreams will go away, you'll feel the peace you deserve. You're the only one who can do that."

"You're saying I have to forgive my mother for hating me, for making my young life a hell on earth? You want me to forgive her for all the ugly things she said and did to me? You want me to forgive the hateful expressions I used to see on her face when she looked at me, and you want me to forgive her leaving me on the back porch in the rain? No. Not in this lifetime," Jane said, bitterness ringing in her voice.

"You need to practice what you preach, Janie," Fred said, getting up and carrying their dishes to the sink.

"I can't," Jane muttered, as she made her way to the guest bedroom.

The building was old but beautiful, teeming with character. Astronomical rents and a waiting list two years into the future made it all the more desirable to ambitious professionals who knew a prestigious address was almost a guarantee to wealth and success. Jane wondered how Sharon Thomas had lucked into the building.

Trixie looked over the rim of her glasses at the imposing facade, then at Jane. "How'd she get here?"

Jane shrugged. Age and the elements had weathered the brick to a pale pink. Ivy grew up the building and curled around the diamond-shaped windowpanes. The entire front of the four-story building was covered with the ivy working its way around to the sides. Double teakwood doors varnished to a high sheen, complete with brass kickplates, greeted visitors. A brass plaque, equally shiny, stated that the building was named the Brousard. There was no number, no street address. It simply wasn't needed. Everyone for miles around knew about the Brousard on Tulip Street.

Tulip Street was a skinny little one-way street with a cobblestone sidewalk. Leafy branches on magnificent oak trees created a canopy over the quaint, narrow street like a row of golf umbrellas. At the base of each tree were clumps of winter pansies and monkey grass in colorful clay pots that matched the striped awnings on the Brousard building. It was obvious the premises were meticulously cared for. Trixie sniffed as she opened the heavy door.

"I wonder if they serve high tea or scotch on the rocks to their tenants," Trixie whispered, as they walked inside. Beautiful old paneling, royal blue carpets and drapes, and the smell of leather greeted them. Small groupings of chairs and little tables dotted the spacious lobby. "This is a business building, but it looks like a cocktail lounge. Why do they need a lobby like this?" But it was the atrium that drew the eye, along with huge colorful wall murals of Mardi Gras on all the walls. "Look, there's no elevator. How can that be? Old is old, but no elevator! What are old people supposed to do if they can't climb the stairs?"

"I guess whoever you're coming to see would come down here to the lobby to discuss business. I agree, four flights is a lot of steps to climb. We're in luck, though. Sharon's office is on the first floor."

"Before we go in there, it might help me to know why this woman hates your guts. Is it just because of Betty Vance, or is it something else? She must have thought highly of you to ask you to take over her patients when she was hospitalized."

"I was probably her last choice. She was dating Tom Bradley from the station around the time I started the radio show. However, I didn't know that at the time. When Tom asked me out, I said yes. We saw her at dinner one night, and she said some unpleasant things. A lot of people heard it. Tom was embarrassed. I tried to cover for him by saying it was a business dinner, but she didn't buy it."

"Do you have the copy of Betty's letter in your purse?"

"Yes. Why?"

"Give it to me and let me do the talking. Let's get this over with."

Jane didn't know what she was expecting, but Sharon's office fell short of the mark. She blinked at the chrome-and-glass interior, at the impressionist paintings on the wall, and the deep pile carpeting. The skinny wooden blinds seemed out of place, as did the pink-and-purple silk plants.

Sharon's secretary, Emily Quinn, recognized Jane immediately. "Dr. Lewis, how nice to see you again. Oh dear, do you have an appointment? If you do, it isn't in the book. That's okay, Dr. Thomas is alone. Go right on in. I'm sure she won't mind. By the way, thank you for taking such wonderful notes. I didn't have one bit of trouble transcribing them."

Jane knocked on the door at the same moment she opened it. She quickly closed it behind her so Emily wouldn't hear Sharon's outraged voice.

"Sharon, this is my godmother, Trixie McGuire. Trixie, this is Dr. Thomas."

Trixie took charge. "Jane received the papers you had served on her. What will it take to make this all go away, Dr. Thomas?"

Sharon didn't appear to give the question even a moment's thought. "She broke my nose, for God's sake. We'll just see how many of those witnesses with their selective memory are willing to lie for her under oath."

"Jane is not denying she slugged you. Personally, I think you had it coming. What kind of person are you that you didn't even go to Betty's funeral? You were treating her. You owed her that much. And while I'm on the subject, why in the name of all that's holy would you prescribe Thorazine for her? Spit me out a number, and let's end this right now."

Sharon stood up behind her desk. "You made a fool out of me." She pointed to Jane. "And besides that, you poached," she said, raising her voice.

"I poached. As in Tom Bradley? I'm sorry, Sharon, but I had no idea you were seeing him."

"Enough already," Trixie warned. "This is far more important." She waved her ace in the hole under Sharon's nose. "This is a copy—I repeat, copy—of Betty Vance's letter to Jane. In it, she says she called you four times, and that you didn't return even one of those calls. She says some other pretty telling things, too." Trixie dropped the letter in the center of Sharon's desk. "We're thinking about going public with this, to disclose what kind of psychiatrist you really are. Or is it just your clinic patients that you treat so shabbily? I'd advise you to think how this is going to look, Dr. Thomas. Are you sure you want to go down that road? Now, why not be reasonable? Call your attorney now, while we're here, and drop the suit. In return, Jane will pay for the nose job you're going to need. Just have the surgeon send her the bill. Deal?"

"You're a real bitch, Jane," Sharon said between her teeth, "and so is that person standing next to you." She picked up the phone and pressed the automatic dial.

"It takes one to know one," Trixie retaliated, her voice dripping venom.

Back downstairs in the lobby, Trixie looked at Jane, her eyes sparkling. "How'd I do, Janie?"

"Great. I don't know why I even bothered to come with you."

"You came because you got your guts back. That's a good thing. Personally, I think you got off cheap."

"You're right." Jane started to laugh. "Did you see her nose? I'll never forget the way my fist connected with it. I probably did her a favor. She'll be a ravishing beauty when the surgeon is done with her. Thanks for taking her on. Okay, the next stop is the police station, then the lawyer's office."

"Why the police station?" Trixie queried.

"Betty's letter."

"Okay. You're on a roll, Janie."

"It feels real good. I'd go nuts if I had to work in this building."

Trixie laughed. "It just goes to show, what you see isn't necessarily what you get, nor is it always the best."

15

While Trixie socialized with the desk sergeant, Jane made her way to the rear of the building to talk with Detective Dave Mitchelson. She'd gone through high school with Dave and knew him well. He invited her to sit down. They made small talk about Dave's family, the weather, and Trixie's new profession before Jane got down to business.

"I should have come sooner, but Betty Vance's death hit me pretty hard. I couldn't seem to get a handle on anything for a while." She opened her purse and pulled out the original of Betty's letter. "One of your officers gave this to me after he questioned me." She handed him the letter and waited while he read it. As soon as he looked up, she said, "I treated her for a short time while her regular doctor was recovering from an emergency appendectomy, so I know her case history. Betty Vance was raped by *two* men. She was so ashamed she didn't report it. Afterward, she couldn't deal with what happened and went into a deep depression. A few months ago, I talked her into going to the crisis center. Her counselor's name there is Corinda. You can check all this out with her if you want." She could see by Dave's blank look that he didn't know what she was getting at. Maybe he had just skimmed the letter, she thought, giving him the benefit of the doubt. "The point is, that letter may be the key to finding out who the two men were. Frankly, I'm surprised the officer gave it to me. I would think he would have kept it for evidence."

"I'm sorry, Jane, I'm not following you," Dave said.

Jane could only stare at him, remembering how back in high school Dave hadn't exactly been the sharpest point on the pencil. She stood up and walked around to the side of the desk where she leaned over and put her finger on the second sentence of the second paragraph. *"I recognized his voice as being one of them,"* Jane read. "She's referring to the rapists, Dave," she said, determined to make him see the connection. Then she pointed to another sentence and read it. *". . . the salesclerk called the manager, and they drove me home.* So it seems to me if you go to the drugstore and speak to the salesclerk and the manager, they could verify Betty's condition the day she took her life. Also, I think that drugstore has surveillance cameras. Maybe the two guys Betty was afraid of will show up on the film, in which case you might be able to identify them and bring them in for questioning. Betty, as I recall, had clear recollections of her rapists. Corinda has it in her file. What do you think?" She walked back to the front of the desk and sat down.

"I'll look into it, Jane, but don't get your hopes up. You're right, the drugstore does have a camera, but still, a conversation in a drugstore, even if it is on tape, doesn't prove anything. A smart lawyer would drag in your friend's mental state. You're right about something else, too, even though the case was an open-and-shut suicide, this letter should have been kept as evidence. I'm glad you brought it in."

Jane resisted shaking her head. "Dave, I don't think you understand. Betty recognized one of the men as being her rapist. That's why she was so afraid, why she had to have someone drive her home."

PLAIN JANE   291

"Like I said before, I'll look into it. Thanks again for bringing the letter to my attention. Maybe something will come out of it. We'll let you know." He stood up and started toward the door. "I heard you were giving up the radio show. Wendy loves listening to you," Dave said, referring to his wife. "She said you're a pistol."

"Tell her I said thanks. Tell her, too, that I'm still going to guest on it until Mike Sorenson gets the hang of it. I think it's going to work out. Say hello to Wendy for me. Let's get together one of these days."

"Sure thing. I'll let you know how things progress."

"I'd appreciate it, Dave."

In the lobby, Jane waited until Trixie finished her conversation with the desk sergeant before she walked to the door.

"How'd it go?"

"Hopefully okay," she said, trying to sound optimistic. "I gave Dave Mitchelson Betty Vance's letter and pointed out the possible clue to Betty's rapists. He didn't seem to get the connection at first, but I think he understands now. He said he'll get right on it. He may be a little dense in some areas, but he's a good cop, and I like his wife. Even if the rapists can be identified from the videotape, I don't know if there would be enough to take them to court unless they scare the hell out of them or one rolls over on the other. They cut deals all the time, but I'm not counting on anything. I did what I could."

"If memory serves me right, Fred and I more or less played out a scenario like this in one of our earlier books. I'll look it up when I get home. A smart lawyer could probably get them off, but then again, Betty's letter is like a dying confession. A prosecutor smarter than a defense lawyer might be able to nail it down. You did what you had to do, Jane. It's in the proper hands now. That's two of your ducks down now. Lawyer's office next?"

"No. Tyson Realty. I'm going to make an offer on our old house."

"Sweetie, have you thought this through? Fred told me the real reason you want to buy the house. I think you're making a huge mistake. You're reacting to a dream. A very realistic dream, but a dream nonetheless. Don't rush into anything is what I'm trying to say."

Jane climbed into her new Range Rover, the ghostly vision of her mother still fresh in her mind. "Thanks for the advice, Trixie, but I'm doing it provided the price is right. Whatever I saw that night, it brought everything all back front and center. All my old hatred just bubbled up and exploded." Jane's cell phone rang. She flipped the antenna up and said, "Hello."

"Jane, it's Mike. Do you have a minute?"

Jane mouthed the words, it's Mike, to Trixie. "Sure, I have a lot of minutes. I'm in the truck with Trixie. Is something wrong?"

"It's my battery guy. His physician just called me because they found my card in his pocket. Seems someone broke into his house, robbed him, and beat the hell out of him. He's in Intensive Care. It happened sometime yesterday, but they just got around to calling me."

"Is he going to be all right?"

"The doctor doesn't know yet." Mike paused as if to gather his thoughts. "You know what the thief stole, Jane? Batteries. Nothing but my guy's batteries. Every damn one of them, right down to the triple A's. Can you believe that? My theory, for whatever it's worth, is someone's been stalking him. Maybe someone thought he was onto something with all his talk about batteries and his stockpile of the damn things. He didn't try to keep it a secret. The police are involved in this. What do you think?"

"I think the thief is on a par with someone who would steal a bottle from a baby," she said.

"No, I don't mean that. I mean about my patient."

Jane's eyebrows furrowed in confusion. "I don't know

what to think about your patient, Mike, since I only know what you told me. Maybe we can talk later when we meet up at the lawyer's to sign the papers."

"You must have some thoughts about this," he insisted. "I could use a little help here. I don't know what's going to happen when the guy wakes up and realizes all his batteries have been stolen." His voice sounded so desperate, Jane found herself wincing.

"No, Mike, I don't have any thoughts on it. At the moment, I've got all I can do just thinking about myself, trying to get back on the path, so to speak, and get all my ducks in a nice straight row. You sound a little overwrought. Surely, you aren't getting *personally involved,* are you?"

"Stop being a smart-ass. I'm not personally involved. I'm his doctor. I'm concerned about my patient's welfare. I'm having a bad time trying to figure this one out, and I thought you might be someone to brainstorm with. Obviously, I caught you at a bad time. I'm sorry I bothered you."

"Not a problem. Call me anytime. That's what I'm here for," Jane snarled before she pressed the END button. She glanced sideways at Trixie. "Guess you heard, huh?"

"I guess I did. You really can be a hard-ass when you want to be. You got that from me, didn't you? It's not really a bad thing. You getting traits like that from me is what I mean. Seems to me, though, you're going from one extreme to the other."

"Uh-huh," Jane agreed. "I hate being dumped on. What is it with you, Trixie? First you want me out of my funk, and when I come out of it and do what you want, you tell me I'm a hard-ass."

"All things in moderation, Janie. You must have an opinion on the battery guy. You always have opinions, and most times you can't keep them to yourself."

Jane felt impaled by Trixie's words. "What's that supposed

to mean?" she asked, pulling the truck into an extra wide space behind the Tyson Realty office.

Trixie sat up straight and gave Jane a hard look. "Don't play dumb with me. I *know* you. You're still blaming Mike for Betty. As I see it, that means you haven't got all your ducks in a row. You need to get a handle on it. If Mike needs your help, why would you turn your back on him? I thought you loved the man and wanted to spend the rest of your life with him."

Tears filled Jane's eyes. Trixie was right as always. "I do love him," she said, her heart heavy. "But I don't know anything about his battery guy. I haven't even read his case file, and I don't know his name."

"But from what you've heard, you must have formed some sort of an opinion," Trixie persisted. "Hell, I even have an opinion. I think the guy is a nut."

Jane chuckled in spite of herself. If Trixie was anything, she was opinionated. "There are all kinds of nuts, but that kind of opinion isn't what Mike is looking for." She sat staring out the window, wondering if she should tell Trixie about one of her other dreams. What could it hurt? "Okay, I'll tell you this. I had this dream, and the kid in my dream told me that the guy thought the batteries gave him energy."

"Energy. No kidding. I can see that," Trixie said. "You need to tell Mike."

Jane shook her head. "Why would one dream make sense and another not make sense? I am, of course, referring to the dream about my mother. Do you really think Mike would appreciate my dispensing advice based on what a kid in a dream told me? Get real, Trixie."

"You're thinking about buying a house based on a dream. Explain the logic in that," Trixie snapped.

Unable to control herself, Jane burst into tears. "I feel like I'm in the tall grass again and I can't see through it or over it.

This is a test where Mike is concerned. It's important to me to know and believe that he . . . I want him to care enough about his patient to go to the hospital. I want him to worry about him. I don't want to see him turn it off and go play tennis and not think about it again until something comes up that he has to deal with it. Mike's patient is real. Flesh and blood. Just the way Betty was. Somebody has to care enough to *want* to get personally involved. Fifty minutes one day a week doesn't cut it. At the moment, he's pissed at me. That's okay, because now he has to think. At least I think that's what he's going to do. It's all mixed up in my head, Trixie."

Trixie's facial expression softened. "You'll figure it out, Janie. You always do. Take some time. Think things through, then make decisions. Are we going to sit here all morning or are you going to go in and make an offer on the house?"

"I'm going in. I know you don't understand, but this is something I need to do, Trixie. Not want to do, *need* to do."

"Then do it already!"

16

The legal offices of Lewellen, Chakis and Dwight were so shabby and dingy Jane didn't want to sit down. From the expression on Trixie's face, she felt the same way. Mike, oblivious to his surroundings, was busy talking to Tom Bradley, who seemed animated about something. She wondered if he knew she was dating Mike. Probably not. She looked around at the tiny, sparsely furnished waiting room—two chairs, a worn carpet and a round piecrust table. Magazines with tattered covers, dating back several months, were in a plastic box nailed to the wall. Everything looked dusty, even the wooden shutters on the window and the olive green swag draperies with a cobweb in the middle. She had the feeling that if she sneezed, the room would fly apart. How old were the firm's attorneys? Ancient by the look of things. Obviously, they weren't worried about billable hours.

Tom Bradley walked over to her. She politely introduced him to Trixie, who held out her hand, and said, "Charmed to meet you, Mr. Bradley. Jane has spoken about you so often. Is there a delay or is something wrong?"

"Neither, actually. I already looked over the contracts, and one of the secretaries is typing in some changes." He turned to Jane. "I had to acquiesce to the wishes of the sponsors by telling them you would cohost twice a month instead of once. Just for the first four months. After that it's once a month for six months. From there on in, if Dr. Sorenson does well, it will be his show. You can guest anytime you want. There's still pending interest in you doing a television show in New Orleans. If you change your mind, call me."

"I will, Tom. Thank you."

"Dr. Sorenson said he's okay with everything in the contract. All we have to do is sign on the dotted lines, and it's a done deal. You didn't change your mind or anything, did you?" Bradley asked anxiously.

"Everything is fine, Tom," Jane assured him. She moved a little to the right to be closer to Mike. "As you can see, you aren't going to get rich doing this, but it's wonderful exposure. And . . . you help people at the same time." She playfully nudged her shoulder against his. "If you want, I can share my zingers and some of my one-liners with you."

When Mike smiled at her, she took it as a signal that he wasn't quite as angry at her now as he had been earlier on the phone. "Have you heard how your battery guy is doing?"

Mike compressed his lips and stared at a distant object. "They don't know if he's going to make it. It was a senseless, brutal beating."

"What are you going to do?" Jane asked quietly.

"When I leave here, I thought I'd stop by the hospital. I . . . canceled all my appointments until after lunch." He turned toward her. "Do you want to come along?" he asked, looking hopeful.

Jane stared into Mike's eyes and knew he was miserable. "And risk becoming personally involved with your patient? I-don't-think-so."

"All right, Jane. You were right, and I was wrong. Do you want me to grovel? Jesus, you have no idea how bad I feel." He looked completely deflated.

He's finally getting it, she thought. *Somehow I've gotten through to him.* "Actually, Mike, I do know how you feel. I'd love to go with you." She turned around and looked at Trixie. "Will you drive my truck home?" At Trixie's nod, she took Mike's hand and squeezed it.

He breathed a sigh of relief. "Thanks, honey. I hate hospitals. People *die* in hospitals. Everyone says that. As soon as you tell people someone is in the hospital, that's what they say. People die in hospitals. People also get well, but we never say that. I wonder why that is. I don't want this guy to die, Jane. I need to help him. I've got everybody in the world trying to figure out what his problem is."

She couldn't stand to see the man she loved so miserable, but she wasn't yet ready to tell him what she thought was wrong with his patient. "It looks like the contracts are ready. Let's sign off and be on our way. By the way, I made an offer on my parents' old house today. The realtor said the owner is looking for a quick sale and thinks he'll take it."

"Nice going. Are you going to rent it out? Did you do it for investment purposes?"

"Nah. I'm gonna burn it down with whatever is inside."

Trixie gasped, and Mike laughed.

"I guess that makes some kind of sense depending on where you're standing," Mike said, still laughing. "You aren't going to do stuff like that after we're married, are you?"

Jane squinted her eyes. "I am a woman of many mysteries. You'll just have to wait and see."

It was like all hospitals, a place of hope and a place of despair. She'd only been there twice in her life. Once when her father died and a second time when her mother passed on. With her father, she'd been full of hope, but with her mother, she'd experienced nothing but despair. Afterward, she'd cried for weeks on end. Even now, if she closed her eyes, she could remember the lobby, the waiting room, the smells, the generic pictures on the wall, the small chapel, the gift shop, and food counter where all you could smell was licorice, coffee, and egg salad.

She sat down on a blue plastic chair to wait while Mike talked to the volunteer behind the desk. The chairs used to be a muddy brown color. A few of them, the ones on the end, had been orange. Evidently plastic chairs didn't last forever. Nothing lasted forever.

Jane went into the gift shop and looked around. When she didn't see what she was looking for, she asked the clerk, "Do you have any batteries?"

"Sure. What kind?"

"C's, D's, whatever."

The clerk pointed to a small rack at the end of the counter. Jane spun the rack around. Which ones should she get? Which ones would give off the biggest charge? The D's, of course. She bought two packs of D's and a pack of triple AAA's. She opened them the minute she paid for them and slipped them into her purse. By the time she returned to the hard, blue plastic chair, Mike was walking toward her.

"They're going to let us see him. His family isn't here yet, so they said we could visit once I explained we, as in you and I, were his doctors."

"Bending the rules, eh? Do you think that's from hanging around me, or are you finally realizing you don't always have to go by the book?" She was pushing it, she knew, but better to push it now so it hit home rather than later when he could shrug it off.

"Both. His doctor is Jim Yahner, and he's on the floor. Maybe he'll talk to us."

They rode the elevator in silence to the third floor. Mike headed for the nurse's station where two doctors were discussing a chart one of them was holding. They both looked up, recognized Mike, and offered their hands.

Jane waited on the side while they talked. She heard snatches of the conversation. The patient they were talking about was William Winslet. If it was the same William Winslet, she had gone to school with him up to the seventh grade.

Mike reached for her hand. "We can go in, but only for ten minutes."

"Wait a minute, Mike. Is your patient's name Willie Winslet?"

"Yeah, how did you know?" he asked, looking perplexed.

"I heard one of the doctors say his name. I went to grade school with Willie. His parents took him out in the seventh grade and had him tutored at home. He was very frail and sickly. I don't remember what was wrong with him, though. What did the doctor say?"

"He said Willie suffered multiple broken ribs, a concussion, a broken shoulder, and a ruptured spleen. They taped his ribs, set the shoulder, and removed the spleen. It will take time, but physically he should be fine. Mentally is another story. Jim said he's not responding. He can't understand why."

They entered the room and stood looking down at the frail-looking man in the bed.

"I know why, Mike. I'm no magician, so don't go thinking I am. But watch this," Jane said, taking two of the D batteries out of her purse. She walked over to the bed and put one in each of Willie's hands. She put the Triple AAA's behind his neck on the pillow.

Mike grabbed her and pulled her back. "What the hell are you doing? Those aren't sterile. Jesus, this is Intensive Care. You can't do stuff like that in Intensive Care," he hissed.

Jane ignored him and kept her eyes on Willie. "Look, Mike!"

Slowly, Willie opened his eyes and blinked. "Doc! What

are you doing here?" he asked in a raspy voice. He lifted his hand to look at the battery. "Hey, man, thanks. That son of a bitch took all my batteries. Every last one of them. How'd you know I was here?"

Mike let go of Jane's hand and stepped forward. "The police found my card in your pocket and called me. The doctor said you're going to be okay. Whoever attacked you really did a number on you. Can you tell me what happened?"

"This real bad-ass jerk broke into my house and started whacking me around. He wanted the batteries. I guess I blacked out, and the next thing I knew I was here. Who's this with you?" Willie gestured toward Jane.

"Willie, it's Jane Lewis," she said. "You used to sit behind me in homeroom. Do you remember me?"

"Yeah. You had so much hair I couldn't see over your head. I've called into your show a couple of times. You sounded like you really cared. Remember that time you said don't trust anyone who keeps their eyes open when kissing? I dumped the chick I was seeing right then and there."

Jane laughed as she discreetly slipped two more D batteries into Mike's hands.

Mike opened his hands and showed them to Willie. "Here's a couple of spares in case you need them," he said, setting them on the bedside table.

His voice was so choked up, Jane had to turn away to wipe at the tears misting her eyes.

"Hey, thanks for coming and . . . thanks for caring," Willie said, smiling weakly. "You psychiatrists aren't cold fish at all. You get a bum rap from what I hear."

"We'll leave you alone now, Willie. They said we could only stay a few minutes. If you need me, have one of the nurses call me, okay?"

Jane wrapped her arm around Mike's waist and hugged him. "He's asleep, Mike. Look how peaceful he looks."

"Yeah, he does, doesn't he?"

Before leaving the hospital, Mike tracked down Willie's doctor and told him that under no circumstances was he to take Willie's batteries away.

Once they were in his car, he turned to her, and confronted her. "Spit it out, Jane."

She took a deep breath. She'd been dreading this moment. "I had this dream, Mike, and when I woke up, I knew." That wasn't quite the way it happened, but better to let him think she just woke up with the idea than to tell him the boy in her dream gave her the answer. She watched his facial expressions to determine what he was thinking. So far, he was buying her story. "Now that I know your patient is Willie Winslet, it makes sense. When he was in school he had no energy, no stamina. He was pale and listless all the time. He couldn't do anything but sit. I don't know if he grew out of whatever his problem was or what. Anyway, something must have triggered an alarm somewhere along the way, and he started buying batteries, thinking they would give him energy. You said he was healthy and robust when he first came to you. I think he experienced some kind of trauma before he started seeing you. If you stop to think about it, it does make sense in a weird kind of way. The elder Winslets still live in town. You could talk to them. But I want to caution you. If you do, you'll be getting even more personally involved. If it was me, I'd do it. If Willie was my patient, I'd suggest hypnosis. The flip side is you can let him walk around with his batteries for the rest of his life."

Mike leaned toward her and kissed her. "I have to admit, you're one smart lady, ya know that?"

"How about buying me some lunch? I'm starved. Maybe you can help me figure out what to do with Todd Prentice and Brian Ramsey. You aren't going to believe what Trixie and Fred are doing. I'm not sure I believe it myself," Jane said, smiling at him. "An expensive lunch, Sorenson, because I'm worth every penny of it."

It was one o'clock on the dot when Mike dropped Jane off at the farm. "I wish I could stay, Jane, but I have to get back. I'll see you around seven, give or take a few minutes, okay?"

"I'll be waiting. There isn't a whole lot to do here right now with Murray working with the new dogs. Loads of paperwork, though. I need to get on that. Are you bringing dinner or am I cooking?"

"We haven't had Chef Roy cook for us in a while. How about some crawfish gumbo for you and some shrimp en brochette for me. Salad with fig vinaigrette and potato salad on the side."

Jane licked her lips in anticipation. "Perfect. Get Olive the steamed vegetable platter and make sure they season it."

Mike put his arms around her and pulled her close. "I love you, Jane. I didn't realize just how much until . . . until I had to think about what I would do without you." He touched his lips to her forehead, then looked down at her. "Are you really going to burn down your old house?"

"Maybe not burn. I might implode it. I have some people to talk to about the best way to do it. But the answer to your question is that one way or another I'm going to destroy it."

"I'll see you tonight."

Jane watched the fancy sports car until it was out of sight. She felt lost until Olive and Golda came up behind her to nuzzle her legs. "He's coming back. I'm going to change my clothes and get to work, but I need to talk to Trixie first." Jane held the screen door for the dogs to enter. She called to Trixie.

"I'm in the kitchen, Janie. How was the hospital?"

"Mike and I are finally playing on a level field, if you know what I mean. I was wondering if nothing is going on that isn't too terribly pressing, if I could bail? I want to drive over to Brian Ramsey's trucking company and talk with him. It's time. I saw a side of him that night at Betty's that I would like to explore."

"Better now than later," Trixie said. "Next week the officers we're assigning the dogs to will be here, at which point it will get hairy. John is putting them through their paces. Flash is a tremendous help. You just wouldn't believe how smart that dog is. In my opinion that dog is one hair away from being human. Olive is getting the hang of it, too. Golda is a natural."

"Okay, then, I'll see you bright and early in the morning. By the way, Trixie, Mike did real good with his battery guy. I was so proud of him. He finally let his hair down. Like all of us, he has a vulnerable button. Today he let it show. Everything is going to be okay. I think I just erased my last worry where he's concerned. See ya."

Jane parked the Rover next to a Chevy Blazer and looked around. She nodded approvingly. It was obvious Ramsey Trucking was a profitable enterprise.

The offices were small, but clean and neat. The receptionist was middle-aged with a warm welcoming smile. Jane smiled in return.

"You must have a green thumb," Jane said, waving her arm about.

"No, Mr. Ramsey has a green thumb. He takes care of all the plants. He has a small greenhouse in back. You should see his African violets. He wick waters them with old, cut up panty hose. What can I do for you?"

"I'd like to see Brian. Will you tell him Jane Lewis is here?"

"Sure thing. Brian, there's someone here to see you," she called over her shoulder.

He dwarfed the doorway. The shock on his face at her

presence surprised Jane. "Brian, I hope I haven't come at a bad time. Can we go outside? I'd like to see your greenhouse."

"Louise, hold all my calls. I won't be long."

"Sure thing."

"I didn't tell her I was a doctor, Brian. Your personal business is your own. Besides, I'm not here on a professional call. I do need to talk to you, though. First, I want to show you a copy of the letter Betty left for me. I gave the original to the police. If you don't want to read it, it's okay. I understand."

"No. I'd like to read it. I took some flowers out to the cemetery the other day. I felt just as bad then as I feel now. I wanted to help her. I swear to Christ I did. I went about it all wrong. I blame myself for a lot of what happened to her. She was so young. For her sake, I wish I had never met her." Jane watched as he blinked away tears when he folded the letter and handed it back.

"I want you to tell me every single thing you know about what happened. I want your side of it. Don't worry if you come off as not being what you would have liked to be. I'll sift through it. If this isn't a good time, we could arrange a more convenient time. I'm tied up until next Wednesday. How about Thursday? There's something else, Brian. Something just as serious but somehow more evil." She watched the ruddy color in Brian's cheeks leave his face. She ushered him to a stack of crates filled with lettuce outside the terminal building. She perched on the edge of one crate. He did the same.

He shook his head. "I have to go up to LSU next Thursday. They're doing some sort of contest for all the football players. The sponsors are giving a hefty donation of $100,000 to the university. I'm on the Alumni Committee, so I have to be there. There's a chance for one entrant to pick up fifty grand if he wins. Could we do it when I get back?"

Jane sucked in her breath. "Sure," she said, trying to keep her expression normal. "How about the next Friday?"

"Make it around this time. I'll clear the decks and we can talk as long as you like."

She stood up, preparing to go. "You were a year behind me at LSU, weren't you? I wasn't into sports much, but I remember your name. You jocks all hung out together, didn't you?"

Brian stiffened. "Not all of the time, but yeah, we did. We all belonged to the same frat house."

"Let's see," Jane said, putting her hand beneath her chin, "there was you, Todd Prentice, and who were the others?"

"Why do you want to know, Doc?"

Jane smiled innocently. "You know us shrinks, Brian. We like details. You know what they say, the devil is in those details." She stood directly in front of him, eye to eye. "So, who were the others? I know you didn't forget them."

He was starting to sweat. "The guys I hung out with were Marcus Appleton, Tony Larsen, Todd, Mitch Iverson, Pete Zachary, and Ben Nolan. They all graduated a year ahead of me, with you. Like I said, we all belonged to the same frat house."

"Brothers, huh?"

Brian mopped at his brow with his sleeve. "You could say that although I never quite belonged. I was there to get an education and to play football. I came out with a 4.0, and they were lucky if they had a 2.2. I went on to get my master's plus thirty. If you want my honest opinion, they weren't worth spitting on. I played their game, I had to. I was on a football scholarship. That didn't mean I had to like it."

"Are those guys going to enter the contest at LSU?"

"Yeah, but for the fifty thousand the winner gets. Not for their alma mater's sake. They don't give a hoot if the university gets the endowment or not. Therein lies the difference. I happen to care. Look, Doc, I didn't just fall off the watermelon truck. I think I see where this is going. You got the wrong guy here."

"I know that," Jane said, crossing her arms. "Just tell me one thing. How are you in the guts department?"

"No better or no worse than the next guy," Ramsey said, jamming his hands into his pockets.

"Wrong answer, Brian. This isn't going to go away. You need to know that. Wouldn't you finally like to be at peace with yourself? Wouldn't you like to find a nice woman and raise a family without all those old ghosts from the past rearing their ugly heads? Do you have any idea how wonderful, how cleansing life would be for you if you had, let's say, a bushel and a half of guts and weren't afraid to use them? I'll call you next Friday. You still okay with that?"

He nodded.

"See you then."

"Doc?"

Jane turned around. "Yes, Brian."

"How public are those guts going to go?"

"Whatever it takes. It always helps to put your side out first, you know, first one out of the gate. That kind of thing. It usually works best before everyone starts scrambling. Did you ever stop to think there might have been a witness?" Jane wouldn't have thought it humanly possible to see a human being shrivel in front of her very eyes. But Brian Ramsey did just that.

Jane took every shortcut and back alley she knew so she could get to Trixie's house faster and report the afternoon's events. When she burst into the kitchen, she was breathless. "It's next Thursday, Trix. Brian Ramsey is going up to LSU, and so are all the others. A week from today is the day! He's scared witless. I gave him a lot to think about. He's going to do one of two things. Either he's going to tell the others, or he's going to keep quiet and when they get to him, he's going to roll over. If it wasn't for all this baggage, he'd probably be a nice guy. He told me he took some flowers out to Betty's grave. His eyes filled up. That has to say something for the man. On the way home, I was comparing him to myself. If, and it's a big *if,* he was the sixth guy, he didn't do anything. I know he was off to the side and kind of arguing with one of them, but I was so scared I couldn't hear, and they were hissing at each other in low angry voices. I honest to God don't believe he knew I was the one there that night with Connie Bryan. I could see him putting it together in his mind. Graduating with a 4.0 doesn't make for stupid in my book. Plus the guy went back for his master's plus thirty. I wish . . . God, Trixie, I wish so many things."

"One day at a time, Janie. I think you're on the home stretch now."

"It took me long enough. It's the right thing, isn't it, Trixie? I know lives are going to change, families will be torn apart. Do I have the right to do that?"

"Honey, all you have to do is ask yourself if Connie Bryan had the right to live. Or if other people had the right to violate her. You did what you thought was right at the time; you honored a promise. You know my philosophy on life. Kick ass and take names later."

"I'm going home to think, Trixie." She turned to leave.

"Wait a minute. I almost forgot. Tyson Realty called. The owners of your parents' house accepted your offer. That was pretty quick if you want my opinion. You better think on that while you're in your think mode."

"I will, Trixie," Jane said grimly.

17

Jane rolled over and was instantly aware that Mike was gone. She fumbled for the bedside clock: 5:45 A.M. She had an hour and fifteen minutes until it was time to drive across the fields to Trixie's house. She snuggled deep into the covers as she willed her mind to go back into the dream she'd been having before she'd awakened. Olive snuggled beside her and licked her face.

"I didn't think you were ever going to wake up, Miss Jane."

"Go away. You're not in the dream. You're in a different dream. I appreciate all your help, but you make me nervous. I'm beginning to wonder if you aren't actually a spook and not a dream."

Billy stood at the end of the bed and laughed. *"It's about time!"* he said. The smile left his face as suddenly as it had appeared. *"I want to tell you something, Miss Jane. It isn't necessary to burn down that house or implode it. All you have to do is tell your mother you forgive her, and she'll pass over to the other side."*

Jane grimaced. "You need to mind your own business where my mother is concerned," she chided. "It will be a cold day in hell before I forgive her for the things she did to me. I hope she flops around over there until the end of time. There's no room for discussion where she's concerned. But you can tell me how to free you, and I'll do it. You didn't jump into the well, did you?"

"*No. My brother and I were playing and things got too rough. He pushed me and I fell in. Then he was afraid to tell. It was hours before they found me and by then it was too late. I drowned. If you really want to help me, you'll have to do away with the well. There's a boulder in there that is preventing my spirit from leaving. If you could do that for me I would be forever grateful.*"

"In a heartbeat. Are you sure about this? What about Jeeter?"

"*I'll hold on to him, and he'll pass over with me.*"

"Okay, kid, pack your duds and I'll get on it today. People around here already think I'm nuts, so don't be surprised if they don't hustle their fannies to get out here to do this. I'll give it my best shot, though."

"*What can I do for you in return, Miss Jane? Turnabout is fair play.*"

"Nothing, Billy. I just want to see you happy. I'm trying to clear up all the old baggage in my life. If I marry Mike, I don't want any of that old stuff cluttering up our lives. I'm going to live here on this property until I die, and I don't want you scaring my kids. Or me. I like you, but you don't belong here."

"*I can tell your mother what a nice person you are.*"

"It ain't gonna happen so shut up about that or I'll change my mind where you're concerned, Billy."

"*Why are you so angry? You haven't even gotten out of bed yet.*"

"Why don't you mind your own business?"

"*You are my business, Miss Jane.*"

"Then forget that part of it. Please."

"*I wanted to tell you, Jeeter is learning a lot at those training classes.*"

"Huh?"

"*He can do everything the other dogs do. He can go over there to your godmother's house because he passed naturally. I'm so proud of him.*"

"If you go to the other side, will you ever be able to come back? You know, just to check on things."

"*I think so, but only if you really need me. First you have to believe, and you have to stop calling me a spook.*"

"Okay, you're a spirit and my mother is a spook. Howzat?"

"*Your English is terrible, Miss Jane. It's how is that.*" He leaned forward, his hands on the footrail. "*In spite of what you think, your mother did love you. She cries a lot because she's sorry for the way she treated you.*"

"My ass! There isn't a remorseful bone in her body. And the crying is a trick. She used to do that with my father to get her way. There were never any real tears. If there had been, all that junk on her face would have made her look like a ghoul. Did she put you up to this?"

"*No. You have to stop being so suspicious. What I said is true. She loved you, and she's sorry. She's over at the old house waiting for you. If you want happiness in your life, you have to set her free. Burning down the house isn't the answer you're looking for. What will you tell your children about their grandmother?*"

"The truth—that she was a raving bitch, as hateful as hateful could be."

"*If you do that, they'll see and hear all the hatred you have in you. You have to let it go. I know you're a smart lady. Can't you figure it out?*"

"Listen, kid, I'm going to wake up now, and you better be gone. Don't give me any more advice even if I ask for it."

"What you just said sounds really dumb."

"About as dumb as you being a spook!"

Jane bolted out of bed when Olive started barking. "I'm up. I'm up! What? You want me to follow you? Okay, okay," Jane said, slipping into her robe and slippers.

Jane shuffled her way through the house, out to the back porch, then onto the driveway, where Olive raced to the old well. It was just light enough for her to see a small speckled dog. "Jeeter?"

The dog barked in answer.

Jane pinched herself to make sure she was awake. She was. And there was Jeeter, or rather the ghostly specter of Jeeter, sort of foggy and see-through. "Okay. Okay, girl," she said, patting Olive. "You go ahead and play with him. I'm going to get dressed, then I have some phone calls to make." She shook her head to clear her thoughts. Spirits, ghosts, spooks. Was she turning into a believer? Why wasn't she running and screaming the way most people would do at just the mention of the word *ghost*? She shook her head again. "Seeing is believing," she muttered.

If she was going to send Jeeter and Billy home, wherever that was—heaven, the great beyond, outer space, whatever— she needed to get a move on.

It was noon before John Murray called a halt to the morning's K-9 training session.

Jane walked out into the sunshine and did some stretching exercises to ease her aching back. Dog training required a lot of bending and stooping. "I'm going to skip lunch, Trixie. I have an errand to run. Did anyone from LSU call?"

"Not yet. I think it's going to rain. Looks like a storm's brewing. You better do what you have to do before it comes. Isn't today your meeting with Mr. Ramsey?"

"Yes. I'm caught up on the paperwork. I did it all last

night. Twelve new dogs are due next week." She looked
across the yard at the prefab building the contractors had put
up over the weekend. "I think we can handle it. Okay, I'll see
you later. I'll pick Olive up on my way back."

Jane drove across town with one eye on the road and the
other on the approaching storm clouds. A fine mist started to
settle on the windshield. She could feel the trembling start in
her legs. Before long she'd be consumed with fear, the way
she always was when a storm came. The moment she saw the
sign for Rosemont Street, her breath escaped in a loud hiss.
This time she wouldn't have to crawl in through the root cellar. This time she had a key to the front door, compliments of
Tyson Realty.

*"Burning down the house isn't the answer you're looking
for."* Billy's words echoed in Jane's ears as she turned the key
in the lock. Then what was the answer? She wondered. Before she could give it another thought, the door opened.

She scurried indoors just as the skies opened up. She stood
for a moment, her arms crossed against her chest in fright as
she stared out the front window. Lightning zigzagged across
the sky as thunder rumbled and rolled overhead. Where
could she go? The rooms were open and empty, the windows
bare. There was no safe place to hide. Suddenly, she was a
petrified child again, running from room to room.

"Come with me, Jane. I know a safe place."

"Mama?"

"Hurry, Jane. Take my hand." Her hand felt so soft, so
warm, so safe. *"There's a little cubbyhole under the stairs."*
She led Jane downstairs and opened a small door at the end
of the foyer, beneath the stairs. *"We used to keep your father's tools in here. There's just enough room for both of us.
Don't be afraid. I'm with you."*

Jane crawled inside on her hands and knees. It was dark,
but she wasn't afraid. "I like it here. It's cozy."

"This was your special place. Don't you remember?"

"I remember. I hid here after I burned all your stuff. Were you watching me?"

"Yes. And I know why you did it, too." She put her arms around Jane and held her. *"I'm sorry, Jane. I wasn't a good wife, and I was a worse mother."*

"Why were you so mean, so hateful?"

"Because I didn't know how to love other people. The only person I loved was myself. I loved my body, my beauty. All I thought about was my hair, my clothes, and how I looked. I am so sorry I couldn't be the kind of mother you wanted. You won't be like me when you have children, will you?"

"No. I'm going to love my children. I will always make time for them no matter how busy I am. I'm going to teach them to be good people who care about others. I want them to grow up strong and independent and loving. Mike is going to help me with that. I'm never going to be like you. I don't want my children to hate me."

"Do you really hate me, Jane?"

Jane pulled away from her mother's arms. "Yes. I try not to, but I can't get rid of the feeling. What am I going to tell my children when they ask me about their grandmother? Should I say you didn't love me, but in spite of you I grew up and got a life of my own? Should I tell them you were so obsessed with yourself that you had no time for anyone else? Should I bring them here to this house so they can see you do all your spook tricks? I don't think so. Goddamn it, I can't even say you died and went to heaven because it would be a lie. You know something else? You aren't beautiful at all. It was all that stuff you plastered on your face that made you look beautiful. Without all that junk you're almost ugly."

"Careful, Jane, you're beginning to sound just like me," her mother warned.

"Tell me something, Mother Dearest. If by some chance you could make it to the other side or wherever Dad is, would you be the same as you are here? You know, ugly and mean and hateful?"

"I think everything changes when you get there. I guess you don't much believe in second chances and forgiveness, do you, Jane?"

"Only with you, Mother. Only with you."

"Believe it or not, Jane, I loved you. I used to go into your room when you were little and watch you sleep. I always covered you and turned on your music box even if you were sound asleep. Sometimes I would even sing to you. I didn't have a very good voice though, so most times I just hummed the tune. I read you stories, too. I'd make all these promises to myself that tomorrow I would do better, that I would take you to the zoo, the movies, for an ice-cream cone, but I never did."

"I don't believe you. You never tucked me in, or read or sang to me. I'd remember if you did."

"You were asleep. How could you possibly remember? You need to sleep now, Jane. And when you wake up the storm will be over. I'll lie here next to you."

"I'm not falling for any of your tricks. You just want me to forgive you so I'll release you."

"Whether you release me or not, the only thing that matters is that you are happy and at peace. Hush now, I'll sing you a song like I used to do. Are you warm enough? Come closer, I'll hold you. Hush little baby . . ."

When Jane woke, she was so befuddled she started to scream and pound at the floor. Was she losing her mind? Maybe she already lost it and was too stupid to know it. She crawled out from the little room on her hands and knees and looked around. The worst of the storm was over, but it was still raining. She stood up and brushed off her clothes, then turned and looked back into the little cubbyhole. A lightbulb dangled from a long chain. She hadn't turned it on, yet the light was burning. She reached in to pull the chain. The instant darkness made her shiver.

"Mama," she whispered.

"I'm here, Jane. It's safe for you to leave now. Be careful, the roads are slick. It's all right, Jane. You didn't promise me anything."

"Mama," she whispered again. Jane felt something brush her cheek, something soft, feather-light, and warm. Had her mother kissed her? She reached up to touch her cheek. It felt moist to her hand.

"Come back and visit, Jane. I get lonely."

Jane ran from the house, jumped in the car, and sped away. She was halfway to Ramsey Trucking before she remembered she hadn't locked the door. She wished she'd brought Olive with her.

The moment Jane parked her truck in the Visitor Parking area, Brian Ramsey walked over to her. For a big man he looked incredibly put-together: Khaki trousers, white shirt, open at the neck, sleeves rolled up, and Docksiders. He was wearing sunglasses. She wondered why since it was such a dismal, gray day. She found out the reason a moment later when they entered the greenhouse and he removed the glasses. He sported a magnificent shiner. She winced. "Does it hurt?"

"Yeah, it hurts like hell. It was worse yesterday. Today I can at least crack my eye open a little. Sit down and let's talk, Doc." He pointed to a redwood bench.

Jane sat down and crossed her legs. In spite of what had happened earlier, she felt pretty good. Almost peaceful. Maybe the word was contented. She fixed her gaze on Brian Ramsey and waited.

"Clarify something for me, please," he began. "We were talking about the Connie Bryan mugging, weren't we?"

"Mugging?" Jane echoed. "You call gang rape a mugging! Not from where I'm standing. There was a witness, remember?"

Brian's face registered pure shock. "Whoa, Doc. Whoa, whoa, whoa. I don't think we are talking about the same thing here." He shook his head, his eyes wild.

"Yes we are, Brian. I'm talking about the night before the last finals. About ten o'clock. Six guys. Big guys. Football players. Three of them raped Connie. Don't even think about telling me you didn't know those guys raped her. You aren't stupid. Or are you?"

"You're wrong. All they did was rough her up," he insisted. "There was another girl with her, probably the witness you were referring to. Find her, ask her. She'll tell you there wasn't any rape."

Jane stood up, furious. "I don't have to ask her, Brian. I *am* that other girl, and I witnessed the whole thing," she said, pointing her finger at herself. "Maybe I looked a lot different back then, but I'm telling you, I was there. I know what happened. It wasn't a mugging. It was rape. Gang rape." She took a moment to regain control of herself. "Afterward, you all ran away like the cowards you were. I helped Connie back to our dorm and tried to comfort her. But she couldn't be comforted. She was beside herself with fear and grief and despair. She told me to throw away her clothes, that she didn't want to be reminded of what happened to her. But I didn't throw them away, Brian. I put them in a paper bag and kept them. A bag full of DNA. Proof. I even kept the pictures I took of her bruises. Polaroids." She looked past him at a row of dark purple African violets. Her mind scampered around as she took in their beauty. Every African violet she'd ever bought had died in a couple of months. "Connie made me promise not to tell what happened to her, and all these years I kept that promise. But I'm through keeping it. It's time justice is served." She looked down, her eyes meeting his. "When you came to see me that first time, everything that happened that night came back, and it's been haunting me ever since. A while ago I decided that I couldn't live with myself anymore until I told what happened." She took a deep breath and sat back down. "Do you want to tell me how you got that black eye?"

Brian's expression was grim, his massive shoulders slumped. "I went a couple of rounds with Ben Nolan. He claims to have absolutely no memory of that night. I think he remembers now, though." His hands clenched into fists. "Don't get the idea I condone brute force. It was called for, just the way it was called for when you socked Betty's psychiatrist. To my knowledge no one ever talked about what happened that night. I was only a third-year man then. The others all graduated, but I saw them over the years, and no one ever said a word." He picked a dead flower off one of his African violets and rolled it between his fingers. "I see Todd Prentice on alumni business all the time. Most of the time all I get is a curt nod. He looks right through me." He turned sideways on the bench. "I didn't know Connie died for almost a year. I didn't find out she took her own life for something like four or five years. I never asked questions. She was out of my league, like the rest of those guys. I swear to God, I did not know. It sure as hell makes sense now, and you're right about me needing a lawyer. Look, Tony and Mitch knew I left that night. They were busy holding down the other girl . . . you. I met up with them at the library. Marcus is the one who said we had to do one of our brothers a little favor. Son of a bitch!"

"The favor was . . . what?"

"Rough up Connie. Todd was trying to break off the relationship because he'd met this rich girl, but his wedding was like six weeks away. I think the invitations were in the mail or something like that. It was his way of picking a fight with Connie so he would have an excuse to break off the engagement and cancel the wedding. I thought that's the way it happened since he married Miss Rich Bitch!"

"Maybe that's what they told you, but that wasn't what Todd Prentice intended. I went to see Connie's parents because I was carrying around all this guilt. They gave me some computer disks of Connie's. Some of them read like a diary. She detailed Todd's visits, his conversations, his accusations. She said it was like he knew what had happened to her. All those things you said about Betty when you came to me that first time—those were the very things Connie said. She was afraid Todd wouldn't want her once he knew she'd been raped. She was a victim, just the way Betty was a victim. Now they're both dead."

Brian dropped his head into his hands. "What are you going to do, Doc?"

"I'm going to take my evidence to Baton Rouge and turn it over to the police. Then I'm going to call Connie's parents. I'll be a witness when it goes to trial. Mr. and Mrs. Bryan aren't going to sit still for this. Nor should they. Connie was their only daughter, their only child. They had every right in the world to want and expect her life to be happy and to see grandchildren. If I were you, Brian, I'd get your two friends, the two you said didn't do anything, and make a full confession. Stat. And I'd think about selling your business before the dark stuff hits the fan. There's going to be a lot of media coverage. A lot of lives are going to be uprooted by what you all did. When you think about it, the only one who benefited from what you all did was Todd Prentice. He got rid of Connie, married a rich wife, and got a position in her daddy's firm." Jane's throat was tight with the emotions she was holding back. Sitting beside her was one of the people who was responsible for Connie's death and her own years of torment. She should feel nothing but hate for him. Hate and loathing. Ironically, she felt sort of sorry for him. Because his years of torment were just beginning.

"Tell me what to do, Doc."

"You took the first step by admitting your part in it. Go to the others, tell them the situation, and all of you lawyer up. You need to get there first, Brian, or you're going to hang by your thumbs. I can testify for you to a point. You are the one who was on the sidelines, right? I didn't see your face, but I sensed when you left. I didn't see the faces of the others either. But I bit one of you, clear through to the bone. He should have a dandy little scar on his hand."

"Oh, Jesus! Is that what that contest was about?"

''Uh-huh."

"I'm scared, Doc."

"Fear is a healthy emotion. All you have to do is tell the truth. I have to go, Brian. Do whatever you have to do."

Brian nodded. "Here, take this," he said, handing her a beautiful African violet. "It's called Wisteria, because of the color. I gave one to Betty that last day. She loved flowers and green plants."

Jane accepted the gift and got up to leave. "Yes, she did. Thanks."

"I don't mean to scare you, Doc, but if I tell those guys that you're going to blow the whistle on them, you could be in danger."

Jane shrugged. "By the time you tell them, my attorney will already have their names and my evidence: the computer disks, the bag of clothes, the pictures, everything. They'd be wise not to get themselves in any deeper than they already are. Get right on it, Brian. Don't waste time. This is going down as we speak." Jane took a deep breath and walked outside.

"I don't understand why you're giving me an edge. It's true that I left, but I knew they were planning on roughing Connie up. I was a real prick when I first came to you. I lied to you. I didn't even show you the respect you deserve. Why?" His broad shoulders were heaving as he breathed.

She walked a few steps ahead of him, thinking. She turned around. "Because you made me take a long, hard look at myself, something I hadn't been able to do before. I've wanted to make this right for a long time. Odd as this may sound, you gave me the guts to do it, and now that tremendous weight I've been carrying on my shoulders for so long is starting to ease up. If you were on the sidelines, that gives you a bit of an edge. It's a wonderful feeling, Brian, to have the burden eased."

Jane looked at the kitchen clock: 7:45 P.M. It was going to be a long night. Trixie had said she was coming down with a cold and was going to turn in early. Mike was attending a seminar that would go on all evening, so she wouldn't be seeing him. She looked down at her dinner. Since meeting Mike she'd developed a distaste for eating alone. Olive had gobbled her food and was asleep under the kitchen table. She could go into her office and pay bills, read through Connie's files again, or she could watch the tube.

Maybe what she really needed to do was sit and think; work out a plan of action. There were at least a hundred phone calls she needed to make. Maybe she should square that away before she did anything else. If Trixie was under the weather tomorrow, too, that would mean she would have to do double duty.

Jane pushed her salad plate to the center of the table. The cup of tomato soup followed. Coffee cup in hand, she headed for her office and the computer. The Bad Dog screen saver popped up. As always, it made her smile. She typed in her password and opened her files. She brought up her "to do" list and typed furiously. Thirty minutes later she scanned her progress. Well diggers would arrive early in the morning. Pending: Connie Bryan . . . all evidence and computer disks to be delivered to police in Baton Rouge by way of her attorney tomorrow. Pending: Mike . . . wedding. Pending: Mother/ rethink destroying house. Pending: Brian. Settled: Todd Prentice. Pending: Other Rapists. Pending: Betty . . . in hands of police.

Jane was about to close the file when the phone rang.

"Dr. Lewis, it's Brian Ramsey. Tony Larsen and Mitch Iverson stopped by. They want to know if they can talk to you. We can come to you or you can come to my house. I think you know where I live. Yeah, I saw you peeking through my window that night. It isn't too late, is it? They lawyered up this afternoon."

Jane hesitated before answering. What would it be like to have three out of the six who had been there that night in her own house? Mike would tell her she was crazy even to talk to them and that she would be insane to let them come over. But she wasn't Mike. "You can come by, but I can't do anything. Make sure you tell them that."

"I did. They still want to talk to you."

Jane waited.

When she opened the door, she cringed. They looked just the way she thought they would look. Both men had put on a few extra pounds and both had receding hairlines. Both wore the same panicked expressions. Brian made the introductions.

She invited them into the living room, offered coffee, which they all declined, and sat down on the chair closest to the fireplace. She'd built a fire just after Brian called. A good blaze always gave her comfort.

Olive circled the chairs, her tail between her legs, her eyes alert and wary.

The three of them sat down on the couch. "I just want you to know I didn't do anything," Tony Larsen blurted. "Neither did Brian or Mitch. Marcus said Todd wanted Connie roughed up and scared so he could pick a fight with her and get the wedding canceled. That's what he told *us,* anyway. I didn't rape Connie, so you won't find my DNA on anything. Brian split first. Mitch and I right afterward." He steepled his hands as if praying. "Look, this is going to ruin my family if it gets out. It was a stupid, dumb-ass thing that happened. Connie wasn't supposed to get hurt. At the time it seemed like we were helping a buddy. Even that was wrong. We should have had more sense. I'm not taking the fall for Marcus, Ben, or Pete, and Todd can go straight to hell. All of us will testify the whole thing was his idea from the git-go."

"What do you think that's going to get you? Todd Prentice has a real rich daddy-in-law. He's going to get the best of the best when it comes to lawyers. His DNA isn't going to be found. He was probably miles away with sixty witnesses who can testify to that very fact. Guess you know where that leaves you guys."

"What about the disks you said Connie made? Don't they make him a suspect?" Mitch asked.

"A smart lawyer would cover that right away," Jane said. "He'd say Todd broke the engagement, Connie was despondent, girls keep diaries, and sometimes they're fanciful. Your buddy, Todd, is going to skate. Isn't that the term they use on those crime shows?" She felt no pity where these two were concerned. But neither did she feel glad that she'd finally brought them to their knees.

"Won't you help us?" Mitch Iverson pleaded.

"There's nothing I can do. As I told Brian, it's out of my hands. I've turned all the evidence over to my attorney, who turned it over to the police in Baton Rouge. And don't even think about asking me to lie. Connie Bryan's parents lost their only child, Connie is dead, and I've spent the best years of my life plagued with guilt because I felt like I didn't do enough to help her. Like it or not, gentlemen, you all were part of it, and now it's time to fess up." She sat opposite them, clutching a small pillow. "I don't know anything about the law, but I can tell you that Louisiana is still under the Napoleonic Code as opposed to all the other states, that go by case law. That could be bad for you. I suggest you all get together, talk things out, and see what you can do so you can help yourselves. You know, character witnesses. Job records. That sort of thing. Don't forget your buddy, Todd, is involved. You might want to put him on notice, too."

"Listen, Doc, how would you feel about hosting a meeting with all seven of us?" Brian asked.

"To what end, Brian?"

"The rest of them need to hear it all from you. Will you do it, Doc?"

Once a fool, always a fool. "Sure. How about tomorrow night, eight o'clock?"

Three heads nodded. "Okay, I'll see you all here at that time. Call me if the others don't agree. Don't take up my time with just one. It's all or nothing, and that means Todd, too."

Jane heaved a sigh of relief when the taillights of Brian's car faded into the night. It wouldn't happen. She was almost sure of it. But if it did, she was going to need a plan.

18

The bulldozer and the well diggers' equipment stood idle as the men stared in dumbfounded amazement at the skeleton resting at the bottom of the well.

"I guess those stories were true after all," the foreman said. "Tuben, fetch Ms. Lewis. Henry, get me my cell phone so I can call the police."

Jane wiped her hands on the dish towel as she followed Danny Tuben out to the site of the old well. Tears burned her eyes when she saw the skeleton—Billy Jensen. All she could do was stare while Olive wiggled her way in between her legs, whimpering softly.

"What do you think we should do, ma'am?" the foreman asked. "This is your property. I called the police, but I think they'll leave the decision up to you. You certainly have enough acreage here to bury the boy's remains."

Jane found her voice. "We can't . . . we can't just . . . I'll call . . . what I'll do is call the funeral home and have them bring out a . . . a coffin and we'll give him a proper burial in the flower garden if the police say it's okay. You have the machinery to do that, don't you?"

"Yes, ma'am, we can do that. You pick the spot." He

turned to his men. "Don't disturb anything, guys. The police and the coroner need to do their thing first."

Jane pointed to the far side of the flower garden. "Right in there, someplace. Did you find a boulder in the well?"

"Sure did, ma'am," he said, pointing to the back hoe. "It was bigger than a bushel basket. My guess is it's what killed the boy if it fell on him. Then, of course, he could have drowned."

"Please, I don't want to talk about it," Jane said as she eyed the boulder. "I want you to take it away or smash it up but don't leave it here. If I have to pay extra, I will. Just do it." She ran to the house, Olive at her side.

Jane dialed the funeral home first, then Father John. She heard the police siren and wondered what the emergency was. The boy had been dead for over a hundred years. What was the hurry now? She felt like crying.

Every emotion she'd ever felt in her life seemed to attack her at once. She ran through the house calling Billy's name. After searching the second floor and still not finding him, she gave up. "I think he's gone, Olive. He's already crossed to the other side, and we didn't get to say good-bye. I didn't think it would happen so quick. I thought there would be time . . ."

Olive dropped to her belly and whimpered.

Jane sat down on the bed and sobbed her misery. What seemed like a long time later, she wiped at her red eyes, then, with Olive at her side, she walked downstairs to open the front door.

Father John was coming up the porch steps. "Don't you worry, Jane, I'll take care of everything. The police said it was okay to move the . . . remains, so I'll lay out the skeleton in the casket and seal it up. Then I'll say a prayer and we'll lower it into the ground."

"His name . . . his name was Billy Jensen," Jane said, then

pressed her hand against her mouth to stop the strangled sounds that were about to erupt.

It was five-thirty when Jane walked away from the flower garden. She felt like she'd lost one of her best friends. The urge to cry was so strong she had to bite down on her lip as she made her way to the old well. The boulder was gone and the hole filled in. The workers were grading the soil as she watched. Piles and piles of rock and brick waited to be carried away. In another hour, the ground would be level and no one would ever know there had once been a well on the spot. Maybe in the spring she'd lay some sod and perhaps plant a shade tree and some flowers around the base. Maybe she could make it look like the old trees on Tulip Street. Billy would like that if he ever came back. He could sit under the tree and watch Jeeter dig up the flowers. When the tears she'd been trying to hold in check burst from her eyes, she ran into the house.

It was late, and she had to get her act together. Since she hadn't heard from Brian, she assumed the meeting was going to come off on schedule. That meant she had to call Trixie and put her plan into action. If she had anything to be grateful for, it was that Mike had gone to his parents for the weekend to bring his father home from the hospital. The elder Sorenson had undergone knee-replacement surgery, and Mike wanted to be on hand to make sure his father did what the doctor ordered. Mike definitely would not approve of this little meeting tonight. She was grateful also that Trixie had somehow blown off her head cold by drinking eight ounces of Kentucky bourbon and was back on the job. Without Trixie, there would be no way to carry out her plan.

"Let's go upstairs, Olive. Come on, girl. It's not the end of the world even though it seems like it at the moment. I have to get ready for this evening. Just a quick shower and a change of clothes, then I'll fix us some supper." Olive sat looking up at her, her tail still against the floor. "Please, Olive, you're making me feel bad. God, if you could only talk." When the springer wouldn't budge, Jane sat down on the floor and cuddled with the dog. "Billy and Jeeter didn't belong here, Olive. They sort of went home. It wasn't fair to keep them here when I had the ... power ... for want of a better word, to ... to make things right. Look, I don't know if this is real or not. Whatever it is, we have to live with it. Don't make me carry you, Olive. Get up!" she said in her most authoritative voice. Olive whimpered but obeyed the command, followed Jane upstairs, and headed for her bed in the corner. She never slept in the bed, but she did keep all her toys and treasures along with a bunch of dog bones in it.

Jane was on her way into the bathroom when Olive started barking. It was such a loud, joyous bark that Jane turned around to see what was going on. Olive was nosing her sheepskin bed. Jane walked over for a closer look. On top of a pile of stuffed animals was a tattered burlap ball tied together with a vine. Jane watched as the springer gently nosed the ball from the pile of toys and bones. When it toppled onto the floor, she rolled it toward Jane.

"It's Jeeter's isn't it, Olive?" She smothered a sob. "He left you his ball. See, I told you it was okay." She watched as Olive flopped down and worked the ball until it was under her chin. Once she had it secure, she sighed with contentment and closed her eyes.

"Thanks, Billy," Jane said. She waited to see if there would be a response. When nothing happened, she wiped her eyes on her sleeve and once more headed for the shower.

Jane watched their arrival from the small window on the first-floor stair landing. Brian must have used some extraordinary force or else he was more verbal than she had previously given him credit for. They were all there, even Todd Prentice. But they were in two groups—the good guys, as she more or less thought of them: Brian, Tony, and Mitch. And the bad guys: Marcus, Ben, and Pete. Todd Prentice brought up the rear. The pariah. Even a blind fool could see the others were distancing themselves from Todd.

Long years of hatred bubbled in Jane as she stared with narrowed eyes at the men responsible for Connie Bryan's death. She wished she had the guts to shoot them dead on the spot. She mumbled a prayer that she wouldn't do something she would regret later on. The bastards were actually there, in her house. She closed her eyes for a moment to ward off a wave of dizziness. She thought she could feel strong hands pinning her arms to her side, thought she could smell her own fear and Connie's as well.

When the doorbell rang, Jane almost jumped out of her skin. She made her way to the door taking deep breaths as she went along.

"Gentlemen, come in. Let's go into the living room. I can offer you coffee or beer." There were no takers. *Why in hell am I acting so civilized? Because I am, and they aren't,* she answered herself.

Jane's furniture was arranged in a *U* to take advantage of the beautiful fireplace. Four of the seven ex-football players squeezed together on the couch behind the coffee table. Two others sat in overstuffed chairs at each end of the coffee table, and Todd sat in one of the two straight-backed chairs flanking the fireplace.

Marcus pulled a pack of Marlboros out of his pocket. "Mind if I smoke?"

"No. Go right ahead." She opened the end-table drawer and took out two large ashtrays and set them down on the coffee table. Three of them lit up. Before long the room would be filled with smoke, and she'd have to air out the house.

Brian opened the discussion. "I told everyone what you told me, Doc. Pete, Ben, and Marcus don't seem to want to believe me. They say they didn't do anything but rough Connie up. I told them about your evidence. Maybe you should clarify it for them. They don't believe you were the other girl that night either," Brian said, looking directly at her.

Jane hated being in the spotlight. They looked so big, so . . . menacing. Just the way they'd all looked on that dark night so long ago. She must have been out of her mind when she concocted this plan but now . . . Now it was too late. Displaying a confidence she didn't feel, she sat down and crossed her legs. "What Brian told you *is* the truth. I was the other girl, the one you didn't take into the bushes. If you still doubt me I have pictures . . . pictures of the bruises, cuts, and abrasions you inflicted on Connie. I also have, *had* rather, all the clothing she wore that night. The police have it now," she lied, straight-faced. "Your DNA, gentlemen, has been preserved. While I can't show you the actual physical evidence, I can show you the pictures. What that means to all of you is you do not have one iota of wiggle room here." She turned toward Todd. "The only one here tonight who wasn't physically at the scene is, you, Todd," she said, retaining her affability even as her eyes narrowed in revulsion. She swung her gaze back to the others. "If you want him to walk away from this and continue to enjoy his good life while all of your lives go down the drain, then by all means keep lying for him."

Jane got up and walked over to the cherrywood secretary, opened the drawer, and withdrew a large envelope of computer-generated pictures, scanned from the Polaroid originals. She handed them to Brian to pass around.

"As you can see, the first three pictures are of Connie and the other pictures are her clothes, the ones that are full of your DNA. It only takes a drop, gentlemen, one tiny little drop, and bingo, a match! If you look carefully at the pictures, you will see her name label on the garments." Perverse though it might be, she was enjoying their looks of fear. "Your legal fees are going to be astronomical. Your families are going to be sick over this. Your wives might even divorce you. And your kids will be tormented in school. No matter how you look at it, your lives are never going to be the same. Just the way my life was never the same after that awful night. We all know what happened to Connie."

Jane walked behind the sofa where Marcus, Pete, and Ben were handing the pictures to one another. The moment she saw the scar on Marcus Appleton's hand something in her snapped. "You stick out in my mind most of all, you sick son of a bitch! I'm surprised you don't remember me. I'm the one who bit your hand and left you with that dandy little scar. You called me a beached whale and a tub of lard, remember? You're one of the reasons Connie Bryan is dead."

Marcus leapt up off the couch and turned toward her. "I'm not listening to this. So what if I have a scar on my hand? Millions of people have scars on their hands. I don't even know who the hell you are. Ramsey here said you were going to go to our families and tell them some wild story. The only reason I'm here is to see for myself what kind of nutcase you are. Come on, guys, I'm leaving." He took a step around the coffee table.

"Sit down, Mr. Appleton," Jane said, pointing her finger at him. "You leave when I say you leave. Not one minute before." She might have been holding a gun for the way he stopped midstride and stood statue-still. "What do the rest of you have to say for yourselves?"

"It was Todd's idea," Pete blurted. "He had this plan. He said he'd get us all good jobs with his wife's family business. Back then, he used the word *girlfriend.*"

"This is bullshit!" Todd yelled as he stood up, his hands clenched into fists.

Before he could say another word, Ben Nolan was in his face. "Don't try weaseling out, Prentice. If I go to jail for this, so are you. We go down, you go down."

"I'm not going anywhere," Brian injected. "Mitch, Tony, and I had nothing to do with Connie's rape. The worst thing Tony and Mitch did was hold the doctor down. I was there, but I left before things got out of hand. Tony and Mitch can verify that. We'll take whatever punishment the courts want to inflict on us for that part of it, but that's it. The rest of you are on your own."

"Don't try pushing this on me," Prentice blustered. "You all acted independently. I didn't tell you to do anything, and you can't prove I did. I'm outta here."

"Sit down, Todd," Jane shouted, stopping him short. "Trixie, this might be a good time to bring in our big guns."

Wearing his bulletproof vest and his badge, Flash, followed by Kimba, a soon-to-be K-9 graduate, trotted into the room, each coming around the *U* of furniture to stand next to the two fireplace chairs.

Jane was rewarded with instant silence and a rapid scramble for seats. Confident that she'd made her point, she sat down opposite Todd and crossed her legs, affecting a casual pose. "Flash, Kimba, *seitz,*" she said, her voice quiet but firm. The dogs obeyed instantly. The sitting dogs reminded her of the stone lions guarding the New York Public Library. "You were saying something, Todd? I couldn't quite hear what it was," Jane said coldly.

"What the hell is going on here?"

"Not much from where I'm standing." She strived for an innocent look. "Oh, you mean the dogs. Are they bothering you? I know they're big and ferocious-looking, but I assure you they're very well trained. They'll do *anything* I ask." Todd's look of smug confidence was gone. "Now where was I? Oh, yes. In one of Connie's letters . . ." She slapped her face and clicked her tongue. "Oh, jeez, I forgot. You don't know about her letters, do you?" She waved her hand. "Let me get you guys up to speed here. I visited Connie's parents and they gave me her old computer disks. I recovered her letters off of them." She looked directly at Todd. "Anyway, she said that after you two were married you were going to get a dog and a cat. You do like dogs, don't you? Listen, if you want to leave, go ahead." She moved her gaze around the room. "You can all leave if you want to." *If you dare to,* she thought and almost laughed. "Trixie, do we have any refreshments? Cocoa with those little marshmallows and some of those gingersnaps would be real good about now."

"You're using those dogs to hold us here against our will. That's illegal," Ben Nolan blustered.

Jane pretended to look shocked. "Surely you jest, Mr. Nolan," she said, giving him a sideways look. "If you want to leave, then by all means leave. *I* wouldn't think of stopping you."

"Yeah, right. The second one of us heads for that door, those dogs will be on us like stink on shit."

"Shit? Hmm. What an interesting way of putting it," she said. "Tsk, tsk, gentlemen," Jane said, clucking her tongue. "Flash and Kimba are highly trained K-9s. They would never attack unless they were given a direct order to go after a bad guy. You know, a robber, a mugger, or a rapist."

"Screw this. You're trying to intimidate us with those dogs," Pete Zachary sputtered. He was so deep into the cushions of the chair, Jane thought he was going to push through to the other side. "You can't do this. This is illegal. You're threatening us and holding us here against our will, hoping we'll confess to what you want to hear."

Jane clucked her tongue again. "Let's see if I have this right. You think I'm threatening you and using these dogs to hold you here against your will." She placed her index finger on the side of her nose, pretending to give the matter some thought. "Correct me if I'm wrong, but didn't you all threaten Connie and me? Didn't you hold us against our will? Don't you think we were afraid of what you would do to us?" Her voice dropped an octave. "How does it feel, you miserable, stinking bastards?"

"I don't have anything to say to you," Marcus said, his face ugly with fear. "You'll hear from my lawyer. I'll sue your ass off."

Jane bristled. "Lawyers and lawsuits don't frighten me. And you don't frighten me. Not anymore. Let's cut to the chase here and spit it all out, shall we?" She reached over and petted Flash's head. "Now what's it going to be?"

"Fuck you," Marcus spit.

Kimba, a sleek ninety-pound, black-and-gold shepherd growled at his tone.

"It's okay, girl. You didn't mean that, did you, Marcus? You have to be careful what you say around these K-9s. These dogs are easily agitated, and they pick up on emotion and tone."

Trixie entered the room carrying a tray with two cups and a plate with four cookies on it.

"Ohhh, this is good. It really hits the spot." Jane turned her back on the men in the room and winked at Trixie. "So listen, Trix, I need some advice," she said just loud enough for the others to hear. "What do you think I should wear next week when I go to meet Mike's parents? I could wear that burnt orange dress I bought before Christmas or maybe that frilly thing with the lace at the throat. What do you think?"

"I like that cranberry-colored dress with the slit up the side. Wear your Vera Wang scarf with it. Chunky gold earrings. That will make a nice impression."

"What are they doing?" Jane whispered.

Trixie lifted her eyebrows and looked askance at the seven men. "I think they're dead. Not a one of them is moving, not even twitching," Trixie hissed.

"Let's smoke a cigarette. They're all smokers, and they must be dying for one about now. Make sure you blow the smoke in their direction."

Jane had never enjoyed a cigarette so much. When she was through, she crushed the cigarette out in the ashtray, grabbed two dog treats off the tray, then returned to her chair between Flash and Kimba. One of the treats she handed to Flash and the other she tossed to Kimba, whose jaws snapped shut on the morsel of food like a sprung trap.

"You three," she said, pointing to Mitch, Tony, and Brian, "can go. If you want to file charges against me, get in line. I'm never going to forget or forgive you for what you did that night. I want you to know that. I also want you to know that I won't shed one tear when you're all sentenced. And you *will* be sentenced. That's a given."

The three left the *U* of furniture, walking slowly, cautiously, past Flash and Kimba.

"I don't think any of us are going to be filing any charges, Doc," Brian said.

"I waited a lot of years to see this," Tony Larsen said. "You know what? I'm glad it's coming to a head. I'll do whatever it takes to put it behind me."

"That goes for me, too," Mitch Iverson added.

"I'll walk you to the door." Jane motioned them ahead of her. "I want you to know that I didn't see anybody's face that night, so other than my gut instinct, I don't know who did what."

"I told you the truth. We aren't the ones who raped Connie," Brian said. "The DNA will be our safety net. Our proof."

Jane nodded. "I believe you. How long do you think they'll hold out?" she asked, glancing behind her.

"It's anybody's guess," Brian said grimly. "Todd is never going to give it up. He has too much to lose. You might have to call his father-in-law."

She let them out and watched the three men walk away, then made her way to the kitchen, where Trixie was brewing a pot of coffee, Olive and Golda at her feet.

"I don't know what you've got planned, Janie," Trixie said. "Where is this going? How long do you think you can keep this up?"

"I've come this far. I can wait until they're ready to confess. They can't hold out forever. You know what, Trixie? If I'd thought of this sooner, you and Fred wouldn't have had to do that thing with the contest at LSU. I think this is going to wrap it up."

"It doesn't matter, honey. Endowing a university is never a waste of money. I'm glad we did it. Like Fred said, a pair of hands on the book cover with the football will make it a great jacket. We'd do it all over again."

Jane smiled wanly. "All the hatred, all the misery, it's gone, Trixie. I feel like I've been reborn. When they first walked into the room, I knew I was capable of killing. If I'd had a gun, I would have fired it. I never felt such blind rage in all my life. One second it was there, and the next second it was gone."

Trixie wrapped her skinny arms around Jane's shoulders. "That's a good thing. I bet if I wanted to, I could work a whole series of books around this one event. What we're doing here is definitely illegal," Trixie said, her voice cheerfully at odds with the situation.

"I know. Even if they confess and we get it on tape, will it hold up in court? I can only hope so. Hell, Trixie, I have my doubts it will ever even *get* to court. I don't know what to do now."

"What do you want to do?"

"An hour ago I would have said I'd like to cut off their balls, but now, I don't know. I'm way out of my league here and we both know it."

"Let's give them an hour or so, then you can tease them a bit with the telephone. You have the computer line in the office. I can go in there and turn down the ringer and you can call that number and pretend you're calling whomever. You have all their info from the alumni, right?"

"Do you really think they'll fall for the telephone thing?"

"Right now, I think they'll believe anything. They all look a little green to me, but then maybe it's your lighting. Are Flash and Kimba priceless or what?" Trixie trilled.

"You're really getting off on this, aren't you?" Jane snapped.

The only sound coming from the living room was that of panting dogs guarding their captives. The room was exactly as she'd left it . . . the ashtrays dirty and the two cocoa cups on the table. It seemed to Jane that something should have changed.

She sat down and crossed her legs. "Doesn't anyone want to say anything?" She looked from one to the other. "No, huh? Okay, how about this? One minute from now, unless somebody starts talking to me and telling me what I want to hear, I'm going to call your families, then the police, then the news hot line. So, I'm asking you nicely, do any of you have anything to say?"

"You're crazy," Todd said, eyeing Flash, then Kimba. "If those three raped Connie, they did it on their own. I did tell everybody I was trying to break it off with her, and I asked them for advice. But that's all. I didn't want to hurt her. I was young and stupid. I should have had the guts to just come out and tell her, but I didn't. How the hell do you tell someone you've been sleeping with and who was as nice as Connie that you're in love with someone else?"

"You liar," Marcus Appleton shouted. "You set it up. You had a goddamn diagram showing us where to do it and how messy you wanted it to be. You were so specific I wanted to puke. You know what else, I kept the fucking diagram in case something ever went down like it's going down right now. It's all in your handwriting." He turned to Jane and laughed. "And here's the best part. I couldn't get it up that night, so you aren't going to find any of my DNA on Connie's clothes. If you stop and think about it, Miss Shrink, I was the one who punched you in the gut. I did that while the rape was going on. If you think hard enough, you'll remember. Ben and Pete did it. And yeah, I'm the one you bit. That's it as far as building a case against me, Doc."

"What's your feeling on writing all that down?" Jane asked, her head whirling with the information Appleton had just given up. A diagram. Todd Prentice had actually made a diagram. Like Marcus, she wanted to puke.

"Swear to me that dog won't attack me, and I'll write it in capital letters for you."

"And . . ." Jane prompted.

"And this never happened. I'm giving a statement of my own free will. Get that other lady to witness it. You don't get the diagram, my lawyer gets it."

Trixie, her face blank, handed over a legal yellow pad and pen. "That's fair. You best get yourself a good lawyer, son," she said quietly.

Both women watched as Appleton scribbled furiously.

The room still hadn't changed. Why weren't things different? Everybody seemed to be breathing the same way, taking little gasping puffs of air for fear of aggravating the dogs. A sliver of moonlight could be seen on one of the end tables. *That* was different. It hadn't been there a little while ago. Did that count as a change? There was a second little difference, Appleton's scratching pen.

Jane waited patiently for Marcus to finish writing. Four down and three to go. *I'm doing my best, Connie,* she thought. *My methods might be a tad unorthodox, but if I get the job done, who cares? I'll try to find a way so that your parents don't have to see that diagram. I don't think they can handle that.*

"You better read it, because you aren't getting another crack at me," Appleton said, his voice tight.

Jane read the paper carefully, amazed at how graphic, how explicit, and how detailed the account was. She handed it to Trixie.

"Okay, sign it, date it, and we'll both witness it. You can leave after that."

Trixie escorted the ex-football player to the door. The sound of screeching tires rang in Jane's ears.

"Okay, who wants to go next?" Jane dangled the portable phone by the antenna.

"I want a lawyer," Pete Zachary said.

"I do, too," Ben Nolan agreed.

"Do you hear that, Trixie? These guys want lawyers. Guess we have to let them go. Soon as a suspect says *lawyer,* you gotta back down. Flash! Show these guys the door."

Jane looked around. The room was still the same. Damn, why was that? She'd actually done something momentous, and nothing changed. She was finally going to get some justice for Connie Bryan.

"Guess you're the only one left, Prentice. I want to tell you that I think you are the scum of the earth. It's all over. You really thought you were going to get away with it, didn't you? A diagram? You made a *diagram*? Mister, you are one sick, sorry, son of a bitch. I hope you realize there's no way out of this for you. When Pete and Ben get done with you, they'll have you at the scene of the crime. They'll probably say you were lurking in the bushes shouting instructions. For your information, Article 571.1 says there is no time limit on aggravated rape or aggravated sexual battery. Your lawyer will know the article numbers. Go on, get your sorry ass out of here before I boot it all the way to Baton Rouge."

"There goes a piss-poor excuse for a man," Trixie said, popping a bottle of Corona. She handed it to Jane. She took a long pull from her own bottle before she said, "You did it, Janie. You pulled it off. I have to admit I had a few bad moments there for a while. The man actually made a diagram. That's the sickest thing I've ever heard in my life."

"I had a lot of bad moments," Jane said. "I feel like I've been to war and back. I thought I was going to feel good, but for some reason, I don't. I don't know what I feel. At the very least, I should be feeling relief that I finally, finally, had the guts to bring this all to a head. Maybe tomorrow will be different. What do you think the outcome will be, Trixie?"

"It will go to court. Everyone will cut deals. It will make the papers no matter how they try to keep it quiet. As far as punishment goes, I don't know, Janie. If this was a book and I was writing this particular ending, I'd have Todd Prentice cash in whatever he had in his name and split. Don't be surprised if that happens. I just don't know, Jane. For you, it's over. I think your friend Connie can rest in peace now."

"I hope so."

"If you help me load up my dogs, I think I'll head home. My fella is waiting to hear the outcome of this little party we had. Sleep tight, baby."

"I'm too wired to sleep. I think I'll sit here and do nothing.

PLAIN JANE   341

Just me and Olive. Mike might call later. I miss him. You
don't think any of them will come back here, do you?"

Trixie laughed. "You are the last person on this earth that
they ever want to see again. Trust me on that one."

"Thanks, Trixie," Jane said, herding the dogs into the van.
"See you tomorrow."

Trixie waved, sounded the horn, then roared off across the
field.

19

Spring came to Rayne, Louisiana, the same way it did every year. The lion had roared briefly, but the gentle lamb had somehow managed to win out by sheer perseverance. Gentle rains had fallen for days on end, followed by long, lazy days of warm, golden sunshine. The perfect mix of rain and sun were just what the earth needed to bring it back to life.

This year the flowers appeared more lush, more plentiful, and incredibly fragrant. The perennial flower beds were alive with color and growth, a perfect background for the fifty-gallon magnolia tree Jane had planted over Billy Jensen's grave. Jane stared now at the magnificence of the tree, at the huge, emerald, waxy leaves that already created a shady resting place for the young boy's remains.

Spring is always a time of new beginnings, Jane thought. When the rains started to fall, she'd spent hours on the back porch thinking and planning. In the end, she came to the conclusion that the rains had a cleansing effect not only on the land and gardens but on her heart as well. Billy was right. You have to let it go, he'd said. That meant letting go of all her old hatred and insecurities where her mother was concerned.

Let it go. Let it go. Let it go.

How many times had she said those very same words to her patients? Hundreds. And when they'd asked how, she'd answered "forgive them."

Jane sipped from her coffee cup, her third so far this morning. She liked watching the sun come up and loved sitting in her nightgown on the back steps with Olive. This was her favorite time of day, when things weren't yet under way. A time when she could still make a decision and know she could either carry it through or cancel it out. A precious time. A private time.

She leaned back against one of the pillars that supported the roof and closed her eyes. *Let it all go, Jane. Forgive and forget. You're starting a new life soon. Don't carry even an ounce of your old baggage into your marriage with Mike. Just open your heart and let it all go.*

Jane stared out across the garden. It was the second day of April, over two months since she'd hosted the meeting with Connie Bryan's attackers. Two long months since she'd turned over the pictures, the computer disks, and the paper bag containing Connie's belongings to her lawyer, who in turn handed them over to the police.

After the initial flurry of newspaper articles and the daily five-minute segments on the local news, things had died down. They reared up again when indictments came down. Things had heated up even more the day Connie's parents came to town and gave interviews to anyone interested in hearing their story. They'd even stopped by her house and thanked her by giving her a needlepoint pillow Connie had made the summer before she died.

It was over. She'd handed over the evidence, given her deposition, and as far as she was concerned, she'd done all she could do. She had even come to terms with the fact that she'd broken her promise to Connie. Sometimes the end did justify the means. Just yesterday Trixie had asked her if she knew what was happening with Brian and Pete and the rest of them. Other than knowing they were all out on bail, Jane didn't know anything else; nor did she care to know. It was out of her hands, and her life was going to go on no matter what happened to them.

Her coffee cup was empty. That meant it was time to go indoors and get ready for work. After today there would be a thirty-day period of doing nothing but paperwork until the next wave of dogs arrived. She was going to use those same thirty days to prepare for her wedding at the end of June.

She looked down at Olive. Ever-loyal, ever-faithful Olive. "I bet if we really try, we can be ready and at work in forty-five minutes, give or take the eight minutes it takes to get to Trixie's house. You up for a little hustle and bustle, Olive old girl?"

"Woof."

Jane was about to set her replenished coffee cup down on the night table, only to realize there was no space. Next to the lamp, nestled between the digital clock and a picture of her and Mike, was a lavender, double blossom azalea bloom. Beside it was Jeeter's ball. Jane whirled around. "Billy! Jeeter!" She searched the room but didn't see them. "Olive, are they here?"

Olive pawed at the burlap ball until it fell on the floor. She picked it up and carried it over to her bed.

Jane picked up the delicate bloom. It was perfect in every detail and incredibly fresh. Why didn't azaleas have a scent? Something so gorgeous should have a heady, intoxicating fragrance. "I think Billy likes what we did, and this is his way of thanking us," Jane said. Olive cocked her head to the side as if to say, "so you finally believe." "I know, I know. I was a doubting Thomas, but I'm a believer now. I just wish I hadn't called him a spook."

Jane headed for the bathroom, the azalea bloom still in her

hand. She rinsed out the glass she used to gargle with, filled it with water, and carried it back to the bedroom, where she set it down next to the picture of her and Mike standing by the newly planted magnolia tree. "Thanks, Billy," she whispered.

A short while later Jane stopped the car at the gates to the McGuire farm. "Told you, Olive, fifty-one minutes flat. I should have been an accountant since I'm so good with numbers. Bean counters are boring, though. It just means I'm punctual. Let's see what Trixie has on deck for us today." Jane held the car door open for Olive.

A cigarette dangling from the corner of her mouth, coffee cup in hand, feet propped on a chair, Trixie beckoned for Jane to sit down. Today she was attired in her favorite going-to-the-police-station outfit, a leopard print jumpsuit.

"You look like you're going somewhere, Trixie."

"I'm taking Flash and Golda down to the station to see the guys. We've been working round the clock, and they need a day off. Olive is welcome to come. We're going to Burger King for lunch. I miss John and the dogs already, and they only left yesterday," she went on. "I hope we made wise decisions where their handlers are concerned."

"Trixie, you gave them the third degree, you had them investigated out the kazoo, and you threatened them with castration. You told them in gory detail how bloody they would be if one of those dogs got so much as a scratch. I don't think you have to worry about the dogs."

Trixie's feet slapped down on the kitchen floor. She looked around at the messy kitchen. "Why do you suppose I never got a housekeeper, Janie?"

"You didn't want anyone underfoot, and you were afraid if you did get one that she might ferret out your secret."

"Tell Fred it's his turn to clean up. Don't do it for him. He's getting lazy where his chores are concerned. I mean it, Janie."

"Okay, okay. When I finish entering everything into the

computer, do you mind if I take the rest of the morning off? I want to look for a wedding dress. Time is flying by, and I haven't done much yet."

"Take as much time as you want. The only thing that's imperative is the paperwork for the dogs' shields."

"I'll finish it up this morning and take everything to the post office on my way. Have a good day, Trixie."

"You, too, sweetie. Let's haul ass, gang!" Trixie shouted as she opened the screen door. Jane laughed the whole time she was cleaning up the kitchen.

Jane sat in her car in front of her parents' old house and stared at it. She wondered where she'd gotten the idea that destroying it would give her the peace she longed for. Obviously, she hadn't been thinking rationally at the time. A house was just a house: wood, drywall, and shingles.

She'd signed the escrow papers two weeks ago, done her walk-through with the realtor, and hadn't come back since. She stared at the house, trying to block out all the bad memories. The past was gone, and she'd promised herself she was going to let it go. Now was the time to keep her promise and now was the time to make peace with her mother.

First, though, she needed to call Mike. When she heard his voice, the tension left her shoulders. She leaned back and relaxed. "Hey, it's me. Whatcha doing?"

"I was sitting here thinking about you as I eat my lunch, which, by the way, is three hours late. Before you can ask, it's an apple and a yogurt. Where are you?"

"Sitting in my car in front of my parents' house. You'll be pleased to know I found a wedding dress this morning, so it's okay for us to get married now. It's not fancy or anything, but I like it. It just goes to my ankles, kind of *cocktailish* if you know what I mean. And a veil and shoes. I'm good to go."

"That's great. See? You were dithering over nothing. I

knew you'd find just what you wanted. Hell, you could wear burlap and that funky hat, and it would be okay with me. I miss you, Jane. We haven't seen each other for three days."

"Whose fault is that?"

"Mine. This is what happens when you allow yourself to get personally involved. Your time is no longer your own. It really is a great feeling, though. By the way, Willie is only packing one D cell battery these days. The hypnosis is working. He says he carries it now for good luck only. I'm okay with that, and so is he. I figure I can cut him loose after a few more sessions. You wouldn't believe the change in him. He sent a fruit basket to the office."

Jane watched a group of children playing stickball in the middle of the road. "That's great, Mike. I'm glad it all worked out. What was the trauma?"

"He was watching television one night and there was a kid in a wheelchair who lost control and rolled down a hill and into a pond. In the movie the child died. That's it in a nutshell."

"That'll do it. Mike, a strange thing happened this morning. Tell me what you think." Jane rattled off the early-morning episode with the azalea bloom.

"I get goose bumps just hearing about it," Mike said. "Does this make you a believer now?"

"More or less. I was thinking about Billy while I was drinking my coffee on the steps. Then when I went upstairs . . . A flower is a tangible thing. You can touch it, feel it, smell it. Well, you can't exactly smell azaleas, but you know what I mean."

"Accept it or reject it, Jane. The choice is yours. Listen, I have to go. My next appointment is due any second. By the way, what did you think of the show this morning? Was I hot or what?"

Jane didn't have the heart to tell him she hadn't tuned in.

"You were hot, Mike," she fibbed. Little white lies were acceptable if they made another person feel good.

"I think the audience is starting to accept me," he said, sounding excited. "You were right, I had to loosen up and go with the flow. Willie called in, and that was good. Gotta run. See you around nine, okay? Love you."

"Love you, too," Jane said, pressing the END button.

Jane got out of the car and walked up the driveway to the house she'd grown up in. She turned to survey the neighborhood. She could barely remember it. What she could see told her the neighbors took pride in their lawns and shrubbery. Her parents' house, with its overgrown lawn and unpruned bushes, was the sloppiest one on the street. She really and truly hated this place, and that's what it was, a place. It's now or never, she thought grimly as she unlocked the kitchen door. While the temperature outside was seventy degrees, the inside of the house felt like it was fifty. She shivered as she walked through the rooms.

"I'm here, Mother! Come out, come out, wherever you are," she singsonged. "This is going to be the best day you've had for a long time. Where are you? Come on, I don't have all day. Let's get to it," she said as she opened the little cubbyhole under the staircase. She yanked at the string attached to the light socket, but nothing happened.

"I'm here, Jane, behind you."

Jane whirled around.

"I know why you're here, Jane. It's wrong. Please, I don't want to hear the words."

"How could you possibly know why I'm here? I didn't know myself that I was coming here until a little while ago. I came to . . ." A featherlike touch to her lips stopped her short of speaking.

"Don't say it. Once you say the words it will be too late. Please, sit down here on the window seat and listen to me. I

don't want you to forgive me, Jane. I don't want you to send me to the other side. Please, let me stay here. Let me try to atone for all my past wrongs. I told you when you were here the last time that I get lonely. If you let me stay, you can visit me from time to time. When you have children, you can bring them here so I can see them. Please, I don't want to leave," she begged.

Jane leaned back against the wall and rubbed her temples. She could feel the beginnings of a headache forming behind her eyes. "Let me get this straight. You don't want me to forgive you. You want to stay here in this empty house and flip-flop around for all eternity. Then you expect me to come here and visit you and bring my kids if I'm fortunate enough to have any. This will make you feel better about being such a lousy mother?"

"Yes."

"I should agree to this . . . why?"

"Because despite everything I did wrong, you turned into a beautiful human being. I want to prove to you that I love you, that I care about you. Staying here instead of going to the other side is the only way I know how to do that."

"One of us is crazy, and it isn't me," Jane mumbled. "Trixie always said you were nuts. She hates your guts . . . did hate your guts. Fred never liked you either. Did anyone ever like you? Did you have any friends? Of course you didn't. You loved yourself, and that was all you needed. I get so tired listening to you." She drew her knees toward her chest and looked out the front window. "I'm getting married in June," she said for no reason she could think of. "I picked out my dress today and my veil and my shoes. Fred's going to give me away, and Trixie is going to be my matron of honor. Don't say what you're thinking, Mother. Trixie is going to make a wonderful matron of honor."

"Yes, she will. I'm sorry I won't be able to attend."

Jane was incredulous. "Would you want to?"

"*Of course.*"

Taken aback by her mother's words, Jane could only nod.

Jane thought a moment. "I *could* have the wedding here, then you could . . . you know, circle around, do your thing. Mike might agree to that. Trixie and Fred won't like it, but if it's what I want, they'll go along with it. I'll think about it."

"*Your headache is getting worse. You should sleep now, Jane. It will help relieve it. So you agree to let me stay here?*"

"If that's what you want, you can stay."

"*Shhh, sleep now. Hush little baby . . .*"

It was dark when Jane woke. The lightbulb dangling from the living-room ceiling shone directly into her eyes. She stretched and looked around. How long had she been sleeping? Her watch was in the car. She shook her head. "I'm not even going to try and figure this one out," she mumbled.

She had her hand on the kitchen doorknob when she turned around to peer into the darkness. "Good night, Mom."

"*Good night, Jane. Will you come back?*"

"Yes, I'll come back. Do you think you could give me a hug, Mom?"

"*I thought you would never ask.*"

It wasn't one of Fred's bone-crushing hugs or one of Trixie's skinny-armed hugs nor was it one of Mike's intimate hugs. It was ethereal, warm and peaceful, almost like warm water and filmy veils caressing her body. She felt like singing when she left the house. She looked back once and thought she saw her mother waving from the front window. She stood still and wiggled her fingers and laughed. This feeling had to be right up there with winning an Oscar on Academy Awards night.

Mike's eyes lit up, a silly smile spreading beneath his sexy new mustache. Jane ran straight into his arms. She buried her face in the crook of his neck, wrapping her arms around him, wanting to dissolve inside him. She began kissing him, soft little kisses at first, then longer, more seductive caresses with her lips and tongue contrived to evoke his passions and responses.

Mike seemed overwhelmed by Jane's sudden display of emotion, but primal need kicked in, and he lifted her into his arms, carried her up the steps, and took her to the bedroom.

Jane's fingers were frantic as they worked the buttons of his shirt loose and the fastenings of his belt. She murmured breathless, desperate words of need. Her hands touched his bare chest, caressing the smooth expanse of his skin. Then she explored the skin she touched with her mouth. Impatient with the confining fabric of their clothing, Jane practically ripped the garments from her body, then turned back to hurry Mike with his.

Feeling him against her, his skin melding with hers, their hearts beating the same beat, Jane stretched out beneath him and gave herself to the moment, to the desire she felt for him.

"Take me now, Mike!" she implored, thrashing wildly under his weight. "Take me now!" she pleaded.

The desperate edge in her voice was disguised by the passion in her words. He covered her, rocked against her. She trapped him in the grip of her thighs and the clutch of her arms. She knew that his love for her was compelling him to satisfy her desires.

Jane tried to lose herself in the arms of the man she loved. She tried to hide in him, to make herself safe from those nebulous spirits who had invaded her life. Mike pulled back, the expression on his face telling her he knew something was wrong.

"Do you want to talk about it, Jane?"

She told him about her decision not to destroy the house and her desire to make peace with her mother. "I saw her ghost, Mike. I saw her just as plain as I'm seeing you right now. We talked, and she told me she knew why I was there and that she didn't want me to forgive her, that she wanted to try to atone for all her past wrongs. She begged me to let her stay in the house and to visit her from time to time." Jane glanced out the window. "I told her I was getting married, and she said she was sorry she wouldn't be able to attend." She looked at Mike. "She *could* attend, Mike . . . *if* we had our wedding there, at the house. Do you think I'm crazy?" she dithered.

Mike put his arm around her and pulled her close. "No, of course not. I think it's a great idea. You've been trying for years and years to deal with all the things that went wrong with your life and your mother. Having the wedding there . . . that's the perfect reconciliation."

"Then you . . . you believe me. About her ghost, I mean."

"Hell yes. I haven't forgotten that one encounter with what's his name, Billy. To this day I don't know if it was a dream or if I really saw a ghost. It was damn real in my opinion. There are some things in life, Jane, that defy explanation. And ghosts are one of them. Whatever you want to do is okay with me. The one thing that will not be okay is if you shut me out. Let's make sure we understand each other on that point."

She sat up and inched over to the edge of the bed. "I will never shut you out again. Hey! I have a yen for a hot dog. How about you?"

"Why not? Does that mean you're eating meat again?"

"No. Sometimes I just want certain things." She pulled her robe off the hook behind the door. "Mike, when she hugged me? It was real. I think it was the best hug I've ever had."

He bussed her lightly on the cheek. "God, I almost forgot, how'd the closing go?" Mike asked, referring to the sale of her practice.

"They canceled. It's tomorrow at three o'clock. I feel sad about it," Jane said, tying the belt of her robe. "So many chapters of my life have come to a close lately. Pretty soon I won't have anything to worry about." She looked him straight in the eyes. "I want to get pregnant right away," she blurted.

Mike's eyebrows shot upward. "You do! That's great! God, I can't wait to be a father. I bet you turn out to be the best mother in the world."

"That's probably the nicest thing you've ever said to me," Jane said, linking her arm with his. "You do the chopped onions, sauerkraut, and I have some canned chili. I'll do the dogs and buns."

"If we eat all that, we won't be able to sleep."

"I know," Jane drawled. She offered up a wicked grin. Mike chased her all the way to the kitchen.

Jane stood patiently in the doorway of Tramway's Furniture Store waiting for the owner to park his car and open the store. It was two minutes to nine.

Inside, she was like a whirlwind as she walked up and down the aisles, saying, "This one, this one, and that one." At five minutes past ten she walked out of the store. The furniture of her choice, taken right off the showroom floor, would arrive at her parents' house by twelve-thirty.

She was feeling especially good as she walked down the street to Rich's Department Store. Once inside, she headed straight for the cosmetic counter, where she bought two of everything from just about every brand the store offered, including six different bottles of perfume. When she left the cosmetic counter, she headed for the designer racks, where she rifled through the clothes, picking things she knew her mother would have approved of if she were alive. From there it was off to the lingerie department, and again, she picked up two of everything, the frillier, the lacier the better. With twenty minutes to spare, she literally ran to the shoe and handbag department and told the clerk, "Those, this, these and that. Follow me with the packages to my car."

She would have made Trixie proud the way she drove to the house—like a demon on wheels. No sooner had she pulled into the driveway than the Tramway delivery truck rounded the opposite corner. She was Trixie personified, pointing and shouting, "Put that over there, this goes over here and I want that in the corner." The moment the truck pulled away, Jane made one trip after another from the car to the house where she dumped all her purchases in the middle of the living-room floor. The moment she finished, she left to go to the drapery shop and nursery. Money talks, Trixie always said. It not only talked, it shouted, Jane thought as she wrote out check after check. By the time she'd finished, she'd made arrangements for the drapery people to come out and take measurements and the nursery people to plant all the flower beds around the house.

She raced home, changed her clothes, applied makeup, and tore down the road to the lawyer's office, where she signed her name in a half dozen different places, grabbed the check, and ran from the office without even looking at it. It was ten minutes past four when she again let herself into the house she'd lived in as a little girl.

"Okay, so I'm stupid. I might even be crazy, or maybe I have some kind of shopping disease," she muttered as she set about emptying the bags and boxes. At five-thirty, with the last box and bag carried out to a battered trash can the previous owners had left behind, Jane collapsed. "Shit!" She'd forgotten the dishes. She got back in the car and drove to Wholesale Appliance & Kitchen Wares, where she bought dishes, pots, pans, silverware. By six-thirty everything was washed and put away.

At ten minutes to seven she walked into her own house, to see Mike sitting at the kitchen table.

"How'd it go?" he asked.

"Mike, it was the most exhilarating day I've ever had. I didn't stop for two minutes. Believe it or not, this is the first chance I've had to sit down. I can't begin to tell you what a satisfying day it was. I don't know, maybe it was *electrifying*. Whatever, it was damn wonderful."

"Jeez, I thought selling your practice would be a downer."

"Selling my practice! Oh that! Yeah, it went off without a hitch. That's not what I'm talking about."

"Then what?"

Jane told him what she'd accomplished. "Dammit, I forgot the sheets and blankets." She sighed. "Oh, well, I can do that tomorrow. Why are you looking at me like that? Do you think I'm nuts?"

"Do you really think your mother . . ."

"No, no, no. I just want the stuff there so she can see it. I burned all her other stuff. It was only right I should replace it. It's more like if you and I ever have a fight, and don't say we won't because we will, or when the kids get too much for us, we can go there to cool off. Look at it as a separate residence. I am truly at peace with it all now. It is such a wonderful, contented feeling. I know there must be better words to describe it, but I don't know them. Right now I have to believe she's real. I know as time goes on that feeling will fade, at which time I'll be able to send her to the other side, if she wants to go. Let's not talk about this again, okay?"

"Okay. C'mere."

Jane sat down on his lap. "I love you, Mike Sorenson."

"I love you more, Jane Lewis. God, Jane, did you hear the news today? I knew there was something I wanted to tell you. They indicted those two guys who attacked Betty Vance. It was the craziest thing. They were in the clear because the drugstore video just showed them talking to Betty in the aisle, but one of them owed money to some other jerk, and he rolled over on both of them. Said they bragged about it and bragged about scaring her in the drugstore. It was all over the news today."

"My cup runneth over," Jane said. "The only thing left to think about or worry about is you. You know what? I wouldn't have it any other way. You spending the night, or just taking up space in my kitchen?"

"I thought I'd stay. I'm in the mood for a long, lazy shower. How about you?"

"That, Mr. Sorenson, is the best offer I've had all day."

20

The small backyard garden was secluded and literally soundproof with an eight-foot privet covering the ugly, wooden fence. It was picture-perfect for the intimate wedding of Jane Lewis and Michael Sorenson. Aside from the minister, the bride, and the groom, the only guests were immediate family.

It was an ideal day for a wedding, sunny and warm, but not so warm as to wilt the rainbow flower borders. Brilliant Shasta daisies, beds of impatiens, and greenhouse irises lined one entire side of the yard. Opposite them, periwinkle petunias, geraniums, and larkspur grew in such density they brought to mind a Marty Bell painting. The center of the fence, a perfect backdrop for the white wicker arch, was alive with blooming crepe myrtle, long-legged poppies, and sunflowers. Emerald green ivy, Queen Anne's Lace and white-satin ribbons covered the arch, all compliments of Brian Ramsey's greenhouse. A white satin runner ran from the back porch steps to the arch, completing the outdoor wedding decorations.

Through the bedroom window, Jane watched Father John test the spiky grass with the toe of his shoe. It was sod, the joint seams still visible. He looked around, his face a study of bewilderment. Jane smiled. She just knew the cleric was thinking this was the strangest wedding he had ever presided over. Trixie had called him and asked that he perform the ceremony here in the garden first, then, an hour later, in the church. He hadn't asked any questions, evidently assuming that the garden ceremony was sentimental. "At least you aren't getting married in one of those drive-through chapels in Las Vegas like some of my parishioners," he'd said earlier. She'd giggled at the remark even though he'd been serious.

She continued to watch the priest as he looked down at his wrist to check the time. Was he nervous? What was he thinking? Jane's own gaze went to the small travel clock she'd brought with her and placed on the dresser. Ten minutes and counting. She'd been here over an hour and there was still no sign of her mother. Had she imagined seeing and talking to her or was she staying out of the way due to shyness? Jane laughed. Her mother had *never* had a shy moment in her entire life.

Trixie adjusted Jane's veil. "Honey, I've never seen you look more beautiful. I cannot tell you how happy Fred and I are for you. "Is *she* here, Janie? We only have ten minutes until it's time for the ceremony. Fred, Mike, and his parents are in the kitchen. Maybe you should, you know, whistle or whatever it is you do to get her to appear. I don't feel anything. Shouldn't there be a breeze or something?" Trixie's gaze darted around the room.

"No, she's not here. I called her several times. I don't understand . . . unless . . . she never was here and it was all just my imagination. I'm starting to worry, Trixie. This whole garden wedding was . . . is . . . you know, for *her*. By the way, Trixie, thanks for not saying anything about the furnishings. I guess you think it's all pretty silly. Maybe *stupid* is a better word. But it was something I needed to do."

"Don't go putting words into my mouth, Janie. I don't think furnishing this place was the least bit silly. I think . . . I think what you've done is wonderful. It shows you've grown as a person and as a woman."

"You always know the right thing to say, Trixie. That's just one of the reasons I love you so much." Jane kissed her on her rouged cheek. "Damn, where is she? Wait here for me while I freshen my lipstick. Back in a minute."

Trixie sat down on the edge of her bed. She closed her eyes and tried to picture Jane's mother. "Margaret Lewis, you better show me your beauty-queen ass on the double, or you'll be sorry. That girl has gone to a lot of trouble so you could be at her wedding, and we both know you don't deserve it." Trixie looked from one side of the room to the other. "I never made any bones about hating your guts when you were alive. But I think I hate you more now because of the insidious way you've intruded into Jane's life. We only have a few minutes. If you don't show yourself, Janie will never come back here. You need to know that, Margaret."

"Trixie, Trixie, you haven't changed at all. I'm here and I have every intention of attending my daughter's wedding. And by the way, I never liked you either. Especially after you stole Janie away from me. I'll never forgive you for that."

"Don't go down that road, Margaret. You threw that child away. Fred and I thank God every day of our lives that we were there to catch her. Oh, and in case you weren't listening, no one cried at your funeral," Trixie said, unable to help herself. "Jane wanted to, but she didn't. She'd already used up all her tears. And afterward, she burned all your things. It was terribly sad. I just want to know why you aren't burning in hell for what you did to her!"

"This is my hell, Trixie. Cut me a little slack, will you? I'm trying my best to make amends. I can't do it overnight, but I think I can do it eventually, if everyone cooperates. Maybe I

can even make amends with you. I really didn't mean what I said to you. You just have a way of getting under my skin."

Trixie laughed. "I'm no hypocrite, Margaret. I meant every damn word I said, and a few I didn't say." Trixie shook her head to clear her thoughts. She must be getting old. She was nodding off in the middle of the day.

Jane was blotting her lipstick when she saw her mother's reflection in the mirror.

"You look beautiful, Jane, more beautiful than I ever looked. I think it's because you're beautiful on the inside as well as the outside. I never was, so I'm able to recognize it in you."

"Mom," Jane said, breathing a sigh of relief. "I was beginning to wonder if you were going to come."

Margaret smiled. *"I know you still have your doubts about me, but believe me when I tell you I wouldn't have missed your wedding day for anything."* She leaned forward and kissed Jane's cheek. *"Thank you for making it possible for me to be with you today. I can't begin to tell you how much it means to me."*

Jane smiled. Now her day was perfect. She touched her cheek with the tip of her finger. Her skin felt warm to the touch. She was all smiles when she poked her head into the bedroom. "She's here, so we can get started."

"I now pronounce you man and wife. You may kiss the bride."

Mike lifted Jane's veil and smiled. "This is the second time I get to kiss the bride in one day. Pucker up."

Jane giggled. It was a kiss that promised a lifetime of sweet tomorrows.

The church organist struck the opening chords to "Here Comes the Bride." Dr. and Mrs. Michael Sorenson started down the aisle, their faces wreathed in smiles.

Outside in the warm sunshine, the bride and groom giggled and laughed as the guests blew bubbles and let loose one hundred monarch butterflies from their triangular envelopes.

"Are you as happy as you look, kiddo?" Trixie whispered.

"Trixie, there are no words to tell you how happy I am. I had two weddings today and got married twice to the same wonderful man. I feel like I have it all and then some. It's all because of you and Fred. I wouldn't be who I am today if it wasn't for you two. I'm sorry if I don't tell you often enough how much I love you. I promise to do better in the future." She hugged Trixie, then Fred. "I didn't expect so many people to come to the church. I think most of them are Mike's colleagues."

"Janie, I think I saw . . ."

Jane placed a finger against Trixie's lips. "Shhh, I know. Mom told me. She also told me to tell you that green is not your color. She likes you better in that leopard outfit." Jane grinned.

Trixie's eyes almost popped from their sockets. "Fred-dddd!"

"They're leaving, they're leaving!" Trixie shouted to the assembled guests. "She's going to throw the bouquet. All the girls over here," she said, pointing to a circle in the court-yard. Jane obediently turned around and tossed her bridal bouquet of lilies of the valley into the air.

Sharon Thomas squealed her pleasure as she held up the beribboned bouquet. Jane laughed as she walked toward her old colleague. Tom Bradley, Sharon's escort, grinned from ear to ear.

"Guess you're next, Sharon." Jane leaned closer, and whispered, "I like your new nose. The eye job ain't bad either. Do I see a chin tuck?"

"Yes, to all of the above. Tom didn't even notice. Listen, Jane . . ."

"I was wrong, but so were you," Jane stopped her. "Let's

leave it at that. Invite us to your wedding and we'll call it square." She turned to walk away.

"Jane!" Sharon called, stopping her.

"What?"

Sharon smiled. "You make a beautiful bride. Be happy, okay?"

"I will, Sharon. You, too." Jane smiled back.

"Come on, Mrs. Sorenson," Mike said, waving Jane over to the car. "We don't want to miss our flight. Just think about it, thirty whole days in sunny Hawaii!" Mike held the door open for his new wife. He leaned over and whispered, "Let's make a baby right away."

Jane threw her arms around his neck. "Oh, Mike. Are you sure?"

"I'm sure. I want a bunch of little Janes running around our house."

"What if we end up with a bunch of little Mikes instead?"

"We'll take them. God, I love you, Jane," he said, looking longingly into her eyes.

"I love you more." She tweaked his nose. "We aren't going to fight over this are we?"

"Nope. Did you bring that floppsy-doodle hat?"

"First thing I packed," Jane giggled. Funny how he loved that hat.

Mike leaned on the horn as he headed out to the main road, the guests clapping and whistling until the car was out of sight.

Thirty minutes later, the caterers arrived just as the last guest drove off. While they worked at cleaning up the party remains, Trixie sat down on the porch steps next to Fred. "It was such a nice wedding and reception. Those kids have some nice friends. Even Janie's archrival was nice. I want to ask you something, Fred. I'm an old woman, creeping up on eighty. How is it possible that my heart and mind feel like they're only twenty years old? My memories are so wonderful. When the music was playing, I was young again. When I watched all the young people dance, I was dancing in my mind. My feelings for you haven't changed one bit. I don't understand it, Fred. I'm old. You're old. We look old. Sometimes we act old. More often than not, we feel old. At least I do when I look in the mirror. Lately, I don't look anymore. I need an answer, Fred."

Fred put his arm around his wife. "I guess you feel young because you think young." He lifted her chin and looked into her eyes. "And because we're still in love. Love keeps people young, Trixie. And ours is the truest kind of love. We never faltered. We stayed the course. You respected me, and I respected you. Our memories are golden. If you want something better, you're going to have to get a book on the subject or better yet, write a book." He kissed her lightly on the mouth. "I think we should go upstairs and get our dogs. They've been cooped up long enough."

"All you have to do is whistle, Fred. Flash knows how to open the door." Fred whistled and the dogs came on the run, the magnificent Malinois and the yellow Lab. Olive lingered behind, then crept closer to Trixie. Trixie moved so there was room on the step for all of them. She leaned her head against Flash, who nuzzled her neck while Golda did the same with Fred. Olive wiggled onto her lap. "We have a nice little family here, don't we, Fred?"

"Trixie, my love, it doesn't get any better than this."

"Woof."

"Woof."

"Woof."

Epilogue

～

Louisiana State University
Baton Rouge, Louisiana

The turnout was nothing short of spectacular. Jane sucked in her breath as she looked around at the media trucks, the throngs of people, the representatives from the various police departments, and, of course, the K-9 Corps from Louisiana, Kentucky, and Alabama.

It was all to honor Trixie and Fred for their unselfish generosity and devotion to the K-9 Corp they founded. Even the weather had cooperated, with warm breezes and bright sunshine. A picture-perfect day for such a momentous honor. The only problem was, where were the guests of honor?

Jane craned her neck to look around. A squeal of babyish delight brought her back just in time to see her six-month-old daughter smile and gurgle at the yellow butterfly perched on the side of the two-seat stroller. Mickey, the baby's two-year-old brother, tried to catch the elusive creature with chubby fingers. He laughed happily when it took wing and circled overhead.

"How late am I, Janie?" Trixie asked breathlessly as she came up behind her goddaughter. "I got hung up with one of the police commissioners. He said we have a discrepancy

where the dogs' shields are concerned. Do you know anything about it?"

Jane kept a straight face. Of course she did, but she
wasn't going to admit to it. "What kind of discrepancy?"

"One too many badges. I told him it was nothing to get
excited about. He started to get a little pissy, and Flash let
him know we didn't much care for his attitude. He backed
right down and said he was sure it would be resolved, that it
was probably some sort of computer-input error."

Jane nodded. "Yeah, that's probably what it was. I don't
think it's anything to worry about." She glanced to her right.
"Have you seen Mike?"

"He's headed this way with Fred." Trixie bent over the
stroller. "And how are my two little darlings today?" She
tweaked the children's cheeks and kissed them. "Ooh, you're
both just too cute." She straightened and looked around.
"My God, Jane, there are so many people."

"Uh-huh. Are you nervous?"

Trixie made a hissing sound.

"You're supposed to wait until the LSU Golden Band
winds down. John Murray is going to escort you, Fred, and
Flash to the parade ground, where you'll review your
troops." Jane took Trixie's arm and squeezed it. "All one
hundred thirty-seven dogs are here with their handlers. I
think the whole state has turned out to see you and Fred re-
ceive this honor."

"Do you think any of the dogs will remember me?" Trixie
asked, her voice anxious.

"Every damn one of those dogs is going to remember you,
Trixie," Jane said in no uncertain terms. "You wait and see!
Oh! Here comes the band. Straighten up, lady, this is your fif-
teen minutes of fame. Enjoy it."

Trixie grimaced. "I feel like a cat on a hot griddle."

"You're whining. Stop it right now," Jane scolded.

The Golden Band from Tigerland as they liked to be referred to, marched onto the parade ground. John Murray appeared to take Trixie's arm.

"I don't know if I can do this," Trixie bleated as she stared around at the enormous crowd.

Jane leaned toward her and whispered, "You have to do it. You bought that ass-kicking outfit just for this occasion. And Flash wants to see all his old buddies. I'm so proud of you I could just bust." Jane grabbed her and hugged her, then turned her around and pointed her in the right direction. "Get moving, lady!"

"You should be over there with me," Trixie said over her shoulder. "You did as much as I did."

"Go!" Jane commanded.

"Okay, okay, I'm going."

As soon as Trixie moved into the crowd, Jane turned to her husband. "Mike, will you watch the kids for a minute? I have to do something. I'll be right back."

"Don't be long, or you'll miss the introduction," Mike called after her.

Jane sprinted toward the Student Union. Breathless, she leaned against the tree and opened her clenched fist. A shiny police shield winked up at her. Police Officer Jeeter, Shield number 138. She closed her fist again. "Billy, it's me, Jane. You said if I ever needed you to call. I'm calling. Hurry. Billy, can you hear me? Please, Billy, hurry."

"*I'm here, Miss Jane. Turn around,*" a distant voice said.

Jane turned to see him standing at the top of the steps, looking just as she remembered him. Still a boy. Forever a boy. Her breath exploded in a loud sigh. She lifted her hand, and said, "Catch!" She tossed the official police shield through the air and smiled when he caught it. "Hurry, Billy. You need to put it on Jeeter!" She watched Billy tie a bright blue bandanna around the speckled dog's neck and then pin the shield on it.

"Go, Jeeter!"

The speckled dog raced to the parade ground and came to a halt next to Flash, who stopped his parade strut long enough to acknowledge his ghostly friend. He continued on, his tail swishing furiously.

Jane clapped her hands in delight as tears dripped down her cheeks. She motioned Billy over to her. "Come with me and meet my family, Billy. You'll be able to see Jeeter better."

Mike held out his arm to his wife. "It's about time. What took you so long?"

"I had something I had to do, honey. It's awesome, isn't it?" she said, gazing lovingly at the parade of K-9s, dogs she and Trixie had trained and loved.

"Why are they playing the 'Marine Corps Hymn'?" Mike queried as he tapped his foot to the rousing music.

"That was one of the conditions Trixie imposed. We play it all the time to psych up the dogs. They love it. They're prancing now. See? They remember. Oh, God, look at Flash!" They watched as the big Malinois used his nose to inch two of the K-9s into a straighter line, the speckled dog at his side.

"I must need glasses," Mike said, blinking his eyes. "For a minute I thought I saw a brown-and-white-speckled dog next to Flash."

The inspection over, Trixie pulled her whistle out of the pocket of her dress. She brought it to her lips and let loose with three sharp blasts. "Drill's over! Stand down, troops! Come on now, give Trixie some loving! One at a time. I have all day!" Trixie shouted at the top of her lungs.

"Jesus, I've seen everything now!" Mike whooped as all 137 dogs dragged their handlers toward Trixie. "It looks like she's holding something on her lap. Does it look like that to you, Jane?"

"Yeah. It's Jeeter, Mike. See, he has his shield just like the rest of them. The first command those dogs learned was, give

Trixie some loving! And she was afraid they wouldn't remember her. Can you see him, Mike? Can you *really* see
Jeeter?"

"I—Yes, now I can. That has to mean Billy is here. Is he,
Jane?"

"Over there." Jane pointed to the smiling boy.

"So that's what the extra shield that police commissioner
was in a tizzy over was all about."

"Uh-huh."

Mike pulled Jane into his arms and hugged her. "God, I
love you."

"Him loves you, Mommy," two-year-old Mickey giggled.

Jane patted his little head. "I know, Mickey. I love him, too."

"Forever and ever," Mike said.

"Forever and ever. And then some," Jane said.

Keep reading for a sneak peek at
the next gripping novel from
Fern Michaels
NO WAY OUT,
available soon
from
Kensington Books

1

Ellie Bowman knew that there were murmurs from the neighbors and cruel jokes from the kids on the next block, but it didn't matter. It had been two years since the thirty-four year old had moved into the cottage at the end of Birchwood Lane. She was happy that it was located where it was—as far away from the rest of the houses on the block as possible. With each house sitting on a full acre, there was a comfortable distance between them. The homes were modest ranch-style houses built in the fifties.

Thank goodness for Hector, her gardener, assistant, and friend. Without him, she would not have been able to look outside her window and see beautiful flowers. Without him, she wouldn't have groceries, either. He knew the rules and respected her wishes. The only access he had to the house was to the rear porch, where he would deliver her packages and pick up her trash.

The other thing she was grateful for was his willingness to clean up after Buddy, the black Labrador retriever she had rescued from the local shelter when she had moved to Hibbing.

The fenced-in yard made it easy for Ellie to let him go out

through his doggie doors to do his business and chase the squirrels around. Percy, her cat, couldn't care less about going outdoors, which was a good thing. Ellie wouldn't have let him out even if he wanted to go. Her seclusion was a comfort. It was better than the alternative.

Colleen Haywood lived down the street from Ellie with her eight-year-old son, Jackson. She was excited when she learned another woman was moving onto their street but was disappointed never to have met her. It had been two years, and the woman appeared to be a hermit. A total recluse.

She had tried numerous times to get Ellie to come over for tea. She didn't have Ellie's phone number, so she would leave notes in her mailbox. In turn, Colleen would get a note back in her mailbox politely declining, saying she had a headache or was on a deadline.

One afternoon, Colleen thought a personal invitation might do the trick, so she walked over to Ellie's and rang the doorbell. Colleen was about to leave when she caught a glimpse of Ellie's face as she moved across the living room. From the brief peek, Colleen saw that Ellie was pretty, with big eyes and blond hair in a short, blunt cut. She couldn't tell how tall the woman was, but she looked like she was in pretty good shape for someone who never left the house. At least, no one had ever seen her leave the house.

Colleen was about to give up. Obviously, the woman didn't want to be bothered. Then Colleen jumped as Ellie's disembodied voice came through the speaker on the intercom. They had a brief exchange, but Ellie once again politely declined Colleen's invitation.

Colleen made another attempt, but when Ellie had made another excuse, Colleen gave up trying to be sociable. It was too bad. They were around the same age, and Colleen could use a friend.

Colleen finally accepted the idea that Ellie was very shy and probably a shut-in. It was odd for someone so young to have agoraphobia, but she could not think of any other reason for her behavior. But if she really was agoraphobic, then how did Ellie's notes of regret get into her mailbox? *Maybe she's a vampire and only comes out at night.* Colleen laughed to herself. Even in witness protection, people who assume new identities live a somewhat normal life.

The only interaction between Colleen's household and Ellie's was that Colleen's eight-year-old son, Jackson, would visit Buddy, Ellie's Lab, every afternoon while the dog was in the yard.

Ellie didn't mind Jackson's leaning against the fence across the front yard and talking to Buddy. Jackson was just tall enough that his head was barely above the top of the fence. As long as she didn't have to go outside, it was all right; she figured Buddy could use the company.

Ellie had a job that preserved her anonymity. She was a tech geek in the world of IT. She worked from home, answering questions from frustrated people who could not set up their computers or whose computers had crashed. She also worked with a number of tech companies, testing new software programs. Being a techno whiz, she had no problem hiding her real identity from others, including those who were as savvy as she was with technology. That was the reason she was able to live a quiet, solitary life. It also enabled her to communicate with her mother and best friend, Kara.

Before moving to the small town of Hibbing, Ellie had purchased dozens of burner phones to use to make calls. She also changed her Internet service provider address every couple of days. She didn't want anyone to be able to trace her location. If anyone asked, which was usually only her mother and her friend Kara, she would tell them she was working on a government contract and being sent to various parts of the world and would not be able to return until all the aspects of the project were complete. It was all "very top secret." So far, she had been able to pull off the deception for two years. As much as she missed the two of them, she had no other option.

Ellie also didn't use any of the video-calling technology. No FaceTime, Zoom, Skype, or anything where they could see she had cut her bangs, chopped off her hair, and bleached it blond. That was another thing Ellie missed: going to a salon and getting her hair and nails done professionally. She had learned how to do both by watching YouTube videos. She remained isolated from any direct human contact. *For the moment, there was no way out.*

2

Colleen was a second-grade schoolteacher at the local grammar school. Colleen had recently separated from her abusive husband, Mitchel. She and Jackson spent their weekdays at the same school. They would walk to school together until the last few blocks. Jackson didn't want the kids to make fun of him for "walking with his mommy." The routine reversed going home. They would meet up at the same corner every day. Once they got home, Jackson would do his homework, then go outside to play. He was particularly interested in the dog down the street, the one who lived with the strange lady who never went outside. Colleen tried to explain to Jackson that the lady was nice, but she wasn't well. She didn't go into any detail about what the word "well" meant because she didn't really know, but it seemed to satisfy her son's curiosity. And Colleen was grateful that Jackson had a new way of spending his time, playing fetch with Buddy. That was, at least, one thing she got out of her brief conversation with Ellie through the intercom. Colleen recalled the encounter.

"Hello, Ellie. How are you today?"

"I'm OK. How are you?"

"Very well, thank you. Listen, I wanted to see if you'd like to come over for tea?"

"Uh, thank you, but I'm on a deadline," Ellie answered.

"OK. Perhaps another time?" Colleen offered.

"Maybe," Ellie lied.

"I hope you don't mind my son, Jackson, stopping by to say hello to your dog."

"No. Not at all. Buddy can use the company since I'm so busy." Ellie was calm and collected.

"Well, thank you for indulging him. He's been through a rough patch lately. His father and I recently separated, and he's having a bit of a hard time adjusting." Colleen could have stayed there and chatted for an hour, but Ellie cut the conversation short.

"I have to get back to work, but thank you again for your offer. And tell Jackson he can stop by anytime Buddy's in the yard." She smiled and pulled the curtain back in place.

Colleen turned her thoughts back to the job at hand—grading papers—while Jackson finished his homework.

"Mom? Can I go visit Buddy now?"

"Of course. But remember, don't bother Ms. Bowman. She is terribly busy with work."

"Mom?"

"Yes, honey?"

"Why do you think she never comes outside? I mean, like never."

"Honey, I'm not really sure, but I think she may have some health issues and can't go out. But let's not dwell on that, OK? She's totally fine with your tossing the ball over the fence to Buddy."

"Goodie! I really like Buddy. He's one smart dog!" Jackson grabbed his baseball glove and a ball he set aside for playing with Buddy. He pulled on his cap and headed out the door. "Bye, Mom! See ya later, alligator!"

"After a while, crocodile!" Colleen said in return, chuckling.

Once Colleen finished grading the papers, she went into her bedroom to finish sorting out Mitchel's clothes. She had a court date to get the temporary restraining order made permanent. The custody battle was just beginning, and she was anticipating that it would be brutal.

As it stood, Mitchel's visits with Jackson had to be supervised. He could see Jackson one weekend day each week. Had Mitchel not tried to punch her in the face, which had resulted in his fist going through the wall, or had he not trashed the kitchen, perhaps things would have gone differently for him. But the police report told of bruises on her arms and a hole in the Sheetrock. She shivered at the memory of that particular night and recalled the days preceding it. In retrospect, what had happened was inevitable.

Things with Colleen and Mitchel had been escalating, along with his drinking. With each argument, she thought he would strike her, but she had always managed to defuse the situation by agreeing with him or taking the blame for something she didn't do, something he imagined she had done. It was when he grabbed her by the throat and pushed her up against the wall that she knew the end was in sight. But she didn't want it to be the end of her. Just the end of their marriage. She couldn't count the number of times she cried herself to sleep, waiting for him to stumble home. She had tried to shelter Jackson from Mitchel's hostility, but Jackson was a smart kid. He knew when his dad was acting mean.

At first, Jackson thought his dad was mad at him. But then he overheard his father screaming at his mom, using some awfully bad words. Jackson had pulled the pillow over his head to muffle the shouting. The next morning, Jackson noticed that his mom's eyes were really puffy and her nose really red. He knew she had been crying, but she smiled anyway and made breakfast.

Jackson was fiddling with his cereal. "Mom?"

"Yes, honey."

"What were you and Dad fighting about last night?" He looked up sheepishly.

"Oh, just grown-up stuff. You know. Mommy and Daddy stuff." Colleen was trying to smooth over Jackson's fears.

"But I heard Daddy call you some very bad names."

Colleen put her coffee cup down on the table and pulled up a chair. "Daddy and I are trying to work out some problems. You know, like the ones they give you in school?"

"Like a puzzle?"

"Sort of. But I don't want you to worry about any of it, OK?" She took his chin in her hand.

Jackson grimaced. "Well . . . OK. But it scared me."

She gave him a big hug. "I don't want you to ever be afraid because of us." She looked him straight in the eye. She knew that if Mitchel ever tried to do anything to her son, she would kill him. Literally.

"No, I mean I'm scared you and Daddy will break up. Like Judy's mom and dad." Jackson started to sniffle.

"Sweetie, we'll figure it out. Now, let's get ready to go to school, OK?"

He hopped off his chair and got his jacket and backpack. "Ready when you are!" He dashed out the front door. He wanted to be out of the house before his father got out of bed. His dad was often in a nasty mood in the morning, especially if he and his mom had been fighting, which seemed like almost every night. And Jackson especially didn't like the way his father smelled in the morning. It was a stinky beer odor, and his face was scratchy from not shaving for days at a time. Jackson wondered why things had changed. And when. He was deep in thought when his father came roaring out the front door.

"Hey! Jackson!" Mitchel shouted as he stood on the front porch in a stained T-shirt and boxer shorts. "Don't you want to say good morning to your old man?"

Jackson looked around to see if there was anyone watching. This was the first time his father had put on such an embarrassing display outside the house.

"I said, 'Say good morning!'" Mitchel's eyes were wide with fury. Jackson didn't know what to do and was frozen in place. A minute later, Colleen was out on the front porch.

"Mitchel, please get back in the house," she said in a very mild-mannered voice.

"Don't tell me what to do!" Spittle was coming out of his mouth.

"Mitchel, please. You're making a scene."

"Making a scene?" His voice got louder.

Colleen knew there was no way she was going to convince Mitchel to go back into the house, so she pushed past him, grabbed Jackson's hand, and hurried down the street.

"Yeah! Go ahead! Run, you stupid wretch!" he screamed at the top of his lungs. "And Jackson, you spoiled little creep . . . I'll remember how you treated your daddy."

By the time he choked out the last sentence, Colleen and Jackson were no longer within the sound of his maniacal voice.

Colleen knew Jackson would have a lot of questions and also a lot of anxiety. After they crossed the next block, she stopped.

"Are you OK?"

Jackson tried to remain calm, but the tears were streaming down his face. Colleen pulled out a tissue and handed it to him.

He was starting to stutter, something he hadn't done since he was five. "MMM . . . Mom . . . I . . . I . . . I'm rr . . . really sccc . . . scared. DD . . . Daddy nnnn . . . never did th . . . that . . . bbb . . . be . . . fffore."

"I know. But listen to me. It's not your fault. Daddy was in a very bad mood this morning."

Jackson had calmed down a bit. "Because of the fight?"

"That's part of it."

"And why is he so stinky in the morning?" Jackson had a lot of questions that Colleen knew she couldn't answer at the time. How do you tell your child that his father has become a raging alcoholic? Perhaps that was a question for Al-Anon. Going for help was something she had been reluctant to do, but clearly it was time for some intervention. If not for Mitchel, then for herself. She had a child to protect.

"I want you to listen to me." Leaning over, she looked him straight in the eye again. "None of this is your fault. Daddy is going through something right now that I can't explain. I just want you to try to do the best you can today. Try not to think about his bad behavior. Remember, the only person who should feel bad is him. Not you. Got it?"

Jackson wiped his nose with the tissue and saluted. "Got it."

"Great. Now, you go catch up with your friends, and I'll see you in a bit. OK?"

"OK!" Jackson gave her his best smile and headed down the street.

Colleen was certain that would not be the last of Mitchel's outbursts. That very evening, he stumbled in around midnight, reeking from booze and cheap perfume. There was the clichéd lipstick on his collar, too. But she didn't care. She suspected he had been having sex with someone, probably another drunk. The trick was to figure out how to extricate herself and her son from this whirlpool of horror. She just didn't think it would be that day.

As he staggered into the bedroom, he blew up at her for the morning's clash on the front porch. "How dare you take my son when I'm trying to talk to him?" He pushed her onto the bed.

"Mitchel, please. I was not trying to take your son anywhere except to school." Colleen was desperately struggling to defuse the situation.

He caught her wrists, held her down, and pushed his face into hers. She could almost taste the foulness of his breath. "You don't ever try to keep me from my son." He loosened his grip, and she rolled out from under him. He grabbed her shoulder and aimed his fist at her face, but she was quick enough to dodge the punch, causing him to put his hand through the wall. Colleen ran from the bedroom into Jackson's room, locking the door behind her. She pushed his dresser against the door.

Jackson awoke with a start. "Shhhh . . ." She put her finger up to her lips as Mitchel made his way down the hall and into the kitchen.

He began clearing the counters with his arms flailing, breaking dishes and glasses along the way. Thankfully, she had had the presence of mind to grab her cell phone as Mitchel cursed and freed his bleeding hand from the wall. Praying she had service, she dialed 911.

"Nine-one-one. What's your emergency?"

"Domestic dispute at Thirty-two Birchwood Lane. My name is Colleen Haywood. My husband is on a rampage."

"Where are you right now?"

"My son and I are locked in his bedroom. Please hurry."

"Yes, please stay on the line with me."

"OK." Colleen made her way to the window, just in case

she and Jackson had to climb out. She could hear Mitchel's manic behavior and cursing through the walls. The dispatcher continued to talk to her.

"Are you and your son all right? Do we need to send an ambulance?"

"We're fine right now." Colleen kept the panic out of her voice, clutching Jackson in her arms. She whispered in his ear, "You're being very brave," and kissed him on the top of his head.

Jackson whispered back. "Why is Daddy so mad?"

Colleen gave him the finger-to-her-lips signal again.

"We have a patrol car a block from your house. Please continue to stay on the line."

"Yes. Of course. We're next to the window, and we can climb out, if necessary."

"OK, Colleen. What's your son's name?"

"His name is Jackson."

"How is he doing?"

"He's a bit scared, like me." She winked at him, trying to keep him calm.

After what seemed like an eternity, Colleen finally heard the siren of a police car and could see the flashing lights. A moment later, there was a loud bang on the front door.

"Police! Open up!"

"Go to hell!" Mitchel screamed back.

"Mr. Haywood, if you don't open the door, we are going to have to break it down."

"Screw you!" Mitchel shouted.

Colleen and Jackson heard the rumbling of the front door being bashed open. "Mitchel Haywood?"

"Who wants to know?" he said in a surly manner.

"Officer Pedone. Hibbing Police Department. Put your hands behind your back, sir."

"Put your hands behind *your* back, sir," Mitchel replied mockingly.

"Mr. Haywood, you are under arrest for assault."

"Like hell I am," he slurred back. "I didn't assault anyone."

"Then can you tell me how your hand got so bloody? And how your kitchen got trashed."

There was a knock on the closed bedroom door. "Mrs. Haywood? This is the police. I'm Officer Davis, with Officer Pedone. Are you all right?"

Colleen spoke to the dispatcher and told her that the police had arrived. She pushed the small dresser away from the door and unlocked it. She almost crumbled in relief. "We have your husband in custody now. It's safe for you to come out."

She peered down the hall and saw Mitchel slouched over on the sofa. "Can you take him outside so my son doesn't have to witness this?"

"Certainly. As long as you are both all right. Do either of you need medical attention?"

"We're OK." She hugged Jackson tightly against her. "No need for an ambulance," she said, reiterating what she had told the dispatcher.

"Wait right here, please," Davis instructed her.

Mitchel was still protesting as Pedone escorted him to the patrol car, guided his head into the vehicle, and locked him in the back seat.

"Jackson, honey, I want you to stay in your room for a little while, OK?" Colleen pulled the words out as soothingly as she could muster. "You can even play with your tablet."

"But, Mommy, what about Daddy? And the policeman?"

"I'll tell you all about it in a little while. First, I have to talk to these nice policemen. Then you and I will have some ice cream."

Jackson wasn't sure how to react to any of this, but he listened as Officer Davis squatted down to talk to him. "It's going to be OK, son. Do as your mom asks, then ice cream. You got any questions for me?"

Jackson was immediately distracted by the interest the police officer had shown. "Did you ever shoot anybody?"

Davis chuckled. "Do you know how many times people ask me that question?"

Jackson smiled. "A bazillion?"

"Yep. And, no, thankfully I never had to shoot anyone." He tousled Jackson's hair.

"So what's going to happen to my dad? Is he going to jail?" Jackson sat down on his bed, trying to hold back tears.

"That's going to depend on your mom. Like I said, we have to clear up a few things. Now, go do what your mom said. We'll be right down the hall."

"OK." Jackson seemed to be a bit more relieved. And safe.

Colleen's eyes swept across the kitchen. It looked as if someone had thrown a hand grenade. "Do you mind if I pour myself a drink?" She began to shake. It's common knowledge that during times of extreme stress, our fight-or-flight instincts take over. She had fought back, and now what had just happened began to sink in.

"Let me get that for you," Pedone offered. Colleen pointed to the liquor cabinet above the refrigerator. "Scotch, please." She rarely drank any hard liquor, but it seemed like a good idea at the moment. He looked around for something to pour it in.

"There are glasses in the dining-room cabinet," Colleen said.

A few minutes later, Pedone returned with her drink. Her hands were trembling so badly she needed to use both of them to hold the glass.

"Can you tell me what happened this evening?" Pedone pulled out his notebook and began to write as Colleen recalled the events of the evening. It took about a half hour for her to explain everything, starting with Mitchel's behavior that morning.

"Do you want to press charges?" Pedone asked.

Colleen gave it some thought. She knew it was going to be a nightmare going forward, but she also knew that the marriage was over, and she could be putting herself and Jackson in further jeopardy by pretending it hadn't happened. Besides, she just didn't care anymore. Not about Mitchel. Not about the marriage. The only thing she cared about was raising her son in a loving environment. And this certainly wasn't it.

"Yes. What do I have to do?"

"You'll have to come down to the station to file a formal complaint. Is there anyone who can look after your son?"

"I'll call my mother. She lives about fifteen minutes away."

She dialed her mother's phone number, knowing the woman would panic at her phone ringing in the middle of the night.

"Yes! Colleen! Is everything OK?" She could barely catch her breath.

"I'm OK. Jackson is OK." Colleen took in a big inhale. "We have a situation here, and I need you to come by and sit with Jackson for the rest of the night."

"What on earth is going on?" Judith Griffin demanded.

"Mom, I'll explain everything later. Can you come over now? Please?" Colleen knew her mother had never approved of Mitchel, and she wasn't in any sort of mood to be lectured.

"Yes. Of course. I'll be there as soon as I can." She sounded a bit exasperated rather than inconvenienced.

Colleen thought to herself, *If she hadn't been so controlling, maybe I wouldn't have rebelled and married that creep.*

"Thank you. And don't freak out when you see the police car." Colleen cringed, waiting for the interrogation.

"What police car? What are you talking about?" Judith was incredulous.

"Mother, please. Just come over. I will tell you everything later. Please!"

Connect with  U s

Visit us online at
KensingtonBooks.com
to read more from your favorite authors, see books
by series, view reading group guides, and more.

Join us on social media
for sneak peeks, chances to win books and prize packs,
and to share your thoughts with other readers.

facebook.com/kensingtonpublishing
twitter.com/kensingtonbooks

Tell us what you think!

To share your thoughts, submit a review,
or sign up for our eNewsletters, please visit:
KensingtonBooks.com/TellUs.